hILL OF BONES

A Historical Mystery
By
The Medieval Murderers

Susanna Gregory
Bernard Knight
Karen Maitland
Ian Morson
Philip Gooden

Medieval
Murderers

SIMON &
SCHUSTER

London · New York · Sydney · Toronto

A CBS COMPANY

First published in Great Britain by Simon & Schuster UK Ltd, 2011
A CBS COMPANY

1 3 5 7 9 10 8 6 4 2

Simon & Schuster UK Ltd
1st Floor
222 Gray's Inn Road
London WC1X 8HB

www.simonandschuster.co.uk

Simon & Schuster Australia
Sydney

A CIP catalogue record for this book
is available from the British Library

Hardback ISBN: 978-0-85720-425-7
Trade Paperback ISBN: 978-0-85720-426-4

Typeset by M Rules
Printed in the UK by CPI Mackays, Chatham ME5 8TD

The Medieval Murderers dedicate this book to our agent, Dot Lumley, who has steered us through seven books now. She has done it with patience as we talk and correspond endlessly with each other in order to settle storylines. She has done it with attention to detail, pointing out our errors and omissions. Moreover she has done it with a kindness and enthusiasm that has been difficult to imagine anyone else emulating. Thank you from all of us. We are Philip Gooden, Susanna Gregory, Michael Jecks, Bernard Knight, Karen Maitland, Ian Morson, and C J Sansom.

The Medieval Murderers

A small group of historical mystery writers, all members of the Crime Writers' Association, who promote their work by giving informal talks and discussions at libraries, bookshops and literary festivals.

Bernard Knight is a former Home Office pathologist and professor of forensic medicine who has been publishing novels, non-fiction, radio and television drama and documentaries for more than forty years. He writes the highly regarded Crowner John series of historical mysteries, based on the first coroner for Devon in the twelfth century.

Ian Morson is the author of an acclaimed series of historical mysteries featuring the thirteenth-century Oxford-based detective, William Falconer, and a brand-new series featuring Venetian crime solver, Nick Zuliani.

Philip Gooden is the author of the Nick Revill series, a sequence of historical mysteries set in Elizabethan and Jacobean London, during the time of Shakespeare's Globe Theatre. The latest titles are *Sleep of Death* and *Death of Kings*. He also writes 19th century mysteries, most recently *The*

Durham Deception, as well as non-fiction books on language. Philip was chairman of the Crime Writers' Association in 2007–8.

Susanna Gregory is the author of the Matthew Bartholomew series of mystery novels, set in fourteenth-century Cambridge. In addition, she writes a series set in Restoration London, featuring Thomas Chaloner; the most recent book is *A Murder on London Bridge.* She also writes historical mysteries under the name of 'Simon Beaufort'.

Karen Maitland's novel *Company of Liars,* a dark mystery thriller set at the time of the Black Death, was shortlisted for a Shirley Jackson Award 2010. Her latest medieval thriller is *The Gallows Curse,* a tale of treachery and sin during the brutal reign of King John.

the programme

Prologue – In which Philip Gooden relates how two young brothers from Somerset travel to join King Arthur's forces in a final battle against the Saxon invaders.

Act One – In which Susanna Gregory describes how Sir Symon Cole and his wife Gwenllian are ordered by King John to investigate the suspicious death of Bath Abbey's unpopular prior.

Act Two – In which Bernard Knight records how treasures from Bath Abbey are stolen and a how a cat-catcher and a royal steward help a luckless lay-brother to avoid a hanging.

Act Three – In which Karen Maitland tells how the mysterious survivor of a shipwreck flees to Solsbury Hill to escape his nemesis, only to find himself unwittingly embroiled in a plot of treachery and treason.

Act Four – In which Philip Gooden recounts how Nick Revill arrives in Bath with the touring players and swiftly finds himself persuaded to impersonate a dying man's son and comes into possession of a dangerous secret.

Act Five – In which Ian Morson describes how Joe Malinferno and his companion, Doll Pocket, find themselves in Bath escaping Joe's dalliance with the Cato Street Conspirators. Unfortunately, the threads of Radical agitation follow them, and they are faced with solving a murder which casts a shadow over a very senior member of the royal family.

Epilogue – In which Bernard Knight reveals an unexpected ending when police and archaeologists investigate the top of Solsbury Hill.

PROLOGUE

I

Geraint watched the lizard basking in the sun on the tiled floor. Its head was canted towards where Geraint sat a few feet away on the grassy slope. The creature was so still it might have been carved out of stone apart from the tiny pulse that throbbed on the underside of its silver-grey neck.

The lizard, about the length of a man's hand, was crouching above a fish with a great mouth and with water spouting from the top of its head. The lizard was directly over the gaping mouth. Geraint amused himself with the idea of the lizard's surprise if the fish were to come to sudden life and swallow it down in a single gulp. Geraint knew the fish could not come to life, of course, since it was made up of countless little tiles that were coloured red and blue and green and silver.

Shifting his gaze without moving his head, Geraint looked across the rest of the ornamented floor, beyond the lizard and the great fish. It lay bare to the sky but was edged with random blocks of stone, the remains of the walls to the chamber. Beyond were the outlines of other rooms and even fragments of columns. The house had been built on a ledge of land on a hillside. It looked out on a circle of hills and a town below in the valley basin. Geraint wondered how the inhabitants of the villa had defended themselves, isolated, far from other habitations. Perhaps they had not needed to.

He returned his attention to the tiled floor, which showed a picture of the sea and its inhabitants but quite unlike any that Geraint had ever seen. There were creatures with swollen heads and many arms, and others whose foreparts were similar to birds, with beaks and claws, but whose hindquarters were those of fish. Among these monsters sailed small ships containing smaller men holding nets and spears.

Closer to Geraint and riding out of the sea was a great bare-chested man or god, twenty times the size of the men in boats. He was in a chariot drawn by horses with scaly fins for tails. The face of the man-god – wise and vigorous – reminded Geraint of their leader, Arthur. He had seen Arthur astride a horse holding the reins in the same easy fashion as the man-god in the chariot. Arthur had even spoken to Geraint as he rode by. He had scarcely been able to look at him nor had he heard the leader's words, his ears were buzzing so. But he knew the words were firm and, in their way, kindly. Kinder than he was used to hearing from Caradoc, for example.

A rustling in the grass behind him did not cause him to look round – he already knew who it must be – but, instead, to flick his gaze back towards the lizard. But the lizard had gone. For an instant, Geraint wondered whether the creature had been swallowed up by the great spouting fish. But that could not be, because the fish's jaws were still gaping with hunger. And because, although the lizard was real, the fish was no more than an image.

Someone clumped down the slope and clouted Geraint across the back of his head. He sighed and clambered to his feet. He turned to look at his brother, Caradoc, standing on the higher ground above. The sun was behind him so Geraint couldn't see his brother's expression but he sensed it was showing the usual mixture of irritation and impatience.

'What are you doing?' said Caradoc. 'We must be on our way. There's no time to waste.'

As if to show that his own time had not been wasted, Caradoc held up a cony by the hind legs.

'Tribute,' he said. 'A contribution to supper. When we get there.'

The dead animal swayed in the evening air, its white front speckled with blood. Further up the slope sat Caradoc's dog, Cynric. It stared fixedly at the rabbit, but gave no sign of anger at being deprived of its prey.

Geraint did not move. He thought of the much more valuable tribute he was bringing and his hand closed about the pouch that was attached to his belt. Then, as if to distract Caradoc from the gesture, he swept his arm over the mosaic sea-scene.

'What happened to them?' he said.

'What are you talking about?'

'The ones who lived here. The Roman people who made these pictures.'

'Who knows?' said Caradoc in a tone that meant, 'Who cares?'.

'They left long before the time of our father's father but their traces are all around us,' said Geraint. He was thinking of other villas, in better condition, that they had passed on their journey up from the south. Not just villas, either, but terraces of land with strangled vines and neglected orchard plots. Now Geraint looked in the direction of the old town tucked into the fold of the river below. He knew this was Aquae Sulis. The upper parts of the buildings glowed in the evening sun but even while the brothers watched, the light

dimmed and died as if an invisible hand were wiping it away.
In reality it was only the sun slipping down behind a neighbouring hill but Geraint shivered.

'Dreamer,' said Caradoc. 'And trust you to miss the only
thing of value here.'

He bent down and picked up a battered coin from the
edge of the mosaic floor. It was true, Geraint had been so
intent on the sea picture that he had overlooked the little
tarnished disc. Then Caradoc swung away in a downhill
direction, still holding the dead rabbit and skirting the
remains of the villa, with its exposed floors and weather-
beaten columns. Cynric leaped from a sitting position and
bounded after him.

Geraint paused for a moment longer. Perhaps it was the
image of the sea on the floor that made him think of waves
of people, waves of men, flowing across this land. Men who
were of a different race from him. Men such as the ones
who had built this villa on the outskirts of the town in the
valley and then, in a time before his father's father, abandoned it and withdrawn like the tide. Or perhaps they had
not withdrawn at all but simply died out. Which came to
the same thing.

And now there were different waves of men from the east
and north, fresh and fierce, Saxon barbarians, threatening
this land with fire and slaughter. For years, they had
advanced like the incoming tide but now there had come a
chance to stem the tide, even to turn it back. The only
chance perhaps, but a fair one under their leader, Arthur.

He stood up and gazed across the valley towards the hills
to the north-east. One hill stood slightly separate from the
others and was distinguished by a flattened top. In the clear
light of evening Geraint was able to see that the lines of the
hill top looked too straight to be completely natural. There

were few trees growing on the lower slopes and none at all on the upper, which meant that any approaching group would be easily seen. It reminded him of the great hill town in the south, near the village that he and Caradoc had come from. The town called Cadwy's Fort, which Arthur used as his headquarters when he was in the region. The size of Cadwy's, with its towering grassy flanks and deep defensive ditches surmounted by walls of pale stone, made Geraint think of the work of gods rather than mere men.

The hill opposite where he stood was less imposing than Cadwy's, but that it was occupied by men was not in doubt, for he now saw a thick column of black smoke rising from a point near the centre of the flattened top. Then other spirals of smoke sprang up, and carried on the breeze there came cries and screams, the scrape of metal on metal, the thud of blows. Geraint had never been in battle, never been close to the scene of battle, but he recognised this for what it was. Had he and Caradoc arrived too late? Was the decisive encounter already taking place?

He felt confused and dizzy and almost sank down on the ground. When he looked again at the flattened hill, its top was placid and the pillars of smoke had vanished. In his ears there rang no sound except birdsong. Geraint was familiar with these moments, which overcame him occasionally. He had told no one of them, except one person.

Geraint blinked and followed his brother downhill towards the town in the valley. It was an open evening on the edge of midsummer. Threads of innocent white smoke wavered from the encampments set around the town of Aquae Sulis. The distance and the fading light made it impossible to judge numbers. You would scarcely know that there was an army camped about the town. You would not know that there was another army on the march in this direction.

Caradoc and Geraint crossed the lower-lying meadows, where the ground was soft underfoot and the breeze rippled through willows and rows of poplars. Geraint said nothing of the battle-scene he had witnessed on the opposite hill top. Either it had happened in the past, in which case there was nothing to be done about it, or – and this was more likely – it was still to come. The question was, would the battle take place in Geraint's presence? Was he one of the fighters? Was his own voice among the screams and cries he had heard? Or Caradoc's?

As they drew nearer to the encampments, with Caradoc still in the lead and the dog off to one side on some mission of its own, they could smell distant wood smoke and roasting meat, could hear a whinnying horse. It seemed to Geraint that his brother knew exactly where he was going, he walked with such confidence. Then Caradoc halted. He was standing on the edge of a marshy, reed-fringed stretch of water. They might have been able to wade through it, but beyond the reeds was a faster-flowing current, which caught up all the light remaining in the sky. Geraint realised that this must be the Abona. From their vantage point up in the hills the course of the river down here had been concealed. Now it was going to require a detour before they could reach the encampments or the town.

'There must be a crossing point further along,' said Caradoc, gesturing towards the west. 'There must be a ford.'

How much further along? thought Geraint. He saw the pair of them blundering about in the gathering dark, their nostrils tickled by the smells from the other side of the river and their eyes distracted by the twinkle of fires. He suddenly felt hungry. Caradoc whistled for Cynric and the black shape came crashing through the long grass.

Distracted by the return of the dog, neither brother

noticed the small boat sliding noiselessly out of the reeds. When they did, Caradoc dropped the dead rabbit and his hand jumped to his sword hilt. Geraint tensed and Cynric growled. The occupant of the boat had seen them before they were aware of him. He was a lean and wrinkled man – quite old, to Geraint's eyes – and he was crouching in the centre of the boat, which was about half as broad as it was long. He was pushing himself towards the bank with one hand but there was a paddle resting across his knees.

'I had my eye on you as you came across the meadows,' said the boatman.

'Where is the crossing place?' said Caradoc.

The boatman did not answer until, with a final flick of his wrist, he caused his craft to crunch softly into the mud and reeds a few feet from where Caradoc and Geraint were standing.

'Over there, but you will not reach it this side of night,' he said, jerking his head in the direction of the now vanished sun.

'We are here to join Arthur's host,' said Caradoc.

The boatman cleared his throat and spat into the water. Evidently he was not impressed. 'Is Arthur here?' he said.

'Yes,' said Caradoc with a confidence that was based more on belief than knowledge.

The boatman cast his eyes up and down the length of the brothers as if assessing their fitness as warriors. Geraint was conscious that he cut a boyish figure but his brother now, Caradoc, he had more bone and sinew on him.

'You will carry us over,' said Caradoc.

'And you will pay what?'

'We are here to fight our common enemy,' said Geraint, speaking for the first time. 'The Saxon horde.'

'Oh, that enemy,' said the boatman. He flexed his arms

and the oval boat rocked in the water. 'What are your names?'

'I am Caradoc and this is my brother, Geraint.'

'And I am Brennus,' said the boatman. He had a high-pitched voice, disagreeable. Geraint was reminded of an ungreased axle on a cart. 'Talking of enemies, mine are the cold in winter and the hunger and thirst all the time. You've got something to drink?'

'The dregs of some water only,' said Caradoc, 'warm and stale from being carried all day.'

The boatman laughed, an odd sound like the squeak of some water bird.

'You must surely be carrying something of value,' he said. Instinctively, Geraint's hand tightened on the pouch, which was fixed to his belt across from his sword. Despite the growing gloom, he could have sworn that Brennus the boatman observed this slight gesture.

Caradoc retrieved the coin he'd picked up from the villa floor. He held it towards the boatman.

'This will more than do,' he said. 'It's a coin from the old days and it is silver. You can have it if you ferry us both across. And the dog.'

'The dog will swim behind us. You can't have a dog in a small boat like this on account of the balance,' said Brennus, stretching out a sinewy arm and waggling his hand to illustrate his point. He gathered a coil of rope from the bottom of the boat. 'Here. Tie a stick to this and throw it out when we are afloat. The dog will seize hold of the stick.'

Caradoc found a fallen branch along the bank and, using his knife, sawed off a section. He secured one end of the boatman's rope to the piece of wood. Cynric sat and stared with his head on one side, baffled by his master's actions. The boatman watched with almost as much interest, stroking his chin with one hand and grasping the long paddle on his knees with the other. At one point his gaze wandered casually towards Geraint, then flicked away again – too quickly, Geraint thought. Clouds of midges hovered in the half-light.

Brennus was suddenly struck with a fresh idea. 'Come to think of it, my little craft will not carry three at once. I will take one of you over and come back for the other. Out of goodness of heart, and seeing as you are to join the fight against the Saxon horde – our common enemy – I will do two journeys for the price of one, and in any order you please.'

Geraint was about to protest at their separation but stopped himself. It would sound feeble and unmanly. This Brennus was quite old and withered, for all his sinewy arms. The brothers were young and strong.

If Caradoc had any doubts he did not show them. He nodded. 'Very well. But you will not be paid until we are both standing on the far bank.'

'Step in,' said the boatman, 'but carefully now.'

Geraint nodded at his brother as if to say, you go first. Brennus shuffled backwards as Caradoc, holding the coiled rope, stepped into the boat and sat down at the near end. Cynric quivered on the edge of the reedy bank, uncertain of the next stage in this game. The boatman shoved off with his paddle. When they had pushed out a little way, he indicated that Caradoc should throw out the rope. The stick-end landed on the mud and Cynric snatched it up in his jaws, floundered out into the water and began paddling as if he was born to it.

Geraint heard the old boatman instructing Caradoc to keep the rope slack so that the dog's struggles would not drag the boat down. He watched as the boat cleared the reeds and shallows and bobbed out into the clearer stretch of the Abona, the black head of the dog just visible. At once he felt very alone. Suppose the boat overturned and his brother was drowned? It did not look very stable, more like an oversized platter thrown onto the water. Suppose that, once they reached the other side, the ferryman refused to return? But then he would not be paid. Geraint did not believe that Brennus would be able to overpower Caradoc, his older, stronger brother, equipped with knife and sword. He breathed deeply, taking in cool draughts of evening air. He gazed back at the willows and poplars that fringed the shore.

By the time he looked again across the river it was to see Caradoc clambering out of the little boat on the far bank, followed a few moments later by Cynric. Geraint sensed rather than saw the dog shaking itself violently, sending spray everywhere. Then the boat, paddled by Brennus, was making progress back over the water. With one hand Geraint grasped his sword hilt, while the other kept firm hold on the pouch attached to his belt. Inside was his tribute, intended for some purpose that he did not yet know. He was tempted for an instant to unfasten the pouch, to unwrap the precious item, examine it once more in the twilight. But, hearing the splash of the paddle as the boat pushed through the outermost reeds on this side, he resisted the temptation. He glanced at the ground and noticed the white, blood-speckled front of the dead rabbit. Caradoc had forgotten his contribution to the supper that they hoped to get on arrival. Geraint picked up the dead animal by its stiff hind legs. Carrying it somehow distracted attention from the contents of the pouch.

Brennus grounded the boat once more in the mud of the shore.

'Come on, sir,' he said. 'No time to waste. We must get across before nightfall.'

Geraint stepped in the boat and sat down clumsily as Caradoc had done.

For the second time, the boatman used the paddle to push them off the bank and the craft bobbled its way out into the open.

The river seemed immense once you were in the middle of it and the willow frame and stretched skin of the boat offered very thin protection. The current carried them at an angle, but Brennus was familiar with its twists and turns for, with a slight touch or stroke of the paddle, he aimed for the point at which Geraint could see his brother standing with the dog. The rushing of the water threatened to swamp the boat but it was more stable than it looked and, after a time, Geraint started to relax and study Brennus, helped by the fact that the boatman's face was half averted. He wondered what the man did for a living. Ferrying travellers across the Abona? Fishing? Certainly a strong, disagreeable odour of fish came off him now that he was at close quarters.

Then the boat came to a halt or, rather, began to spin about in a slow circular motion as if they were trapped on the edge of a whirlpool. Geraint found himself looking at the bank they'd left behind. Brennus withdrew his paddle from the water and laid it, dripping, across his bony knees. He reached over and stroked the fur of the rabbit, which Geraint was holding. The young man suddenly felt foolish for bringing this insignificant dead tribute.

'I've changed my mind, sir,' said Brennus. His voice grew higher, more disagreeable and grating. 'The coin your brother is offering is only enough for one passage. I need something more before I take you to the other side.'

'I haven't got anything,' said Geraint, somehow unsurprised by this new demand. He had not trusted Brennus from the instant the boatman slid out of the reeds. He indicated the rabbit that nestled in his lap. 'Nothing except this cony. You are welcome to it.'

'I want more than a dead thing,' said Brennus. 'You have got something else on your very person. I saw the way your hand went towards your belt on the bank earlier. I see the way you're gripping that pouch on your belt even now.'

It was true. Geraint was holding on to the leather pouch even more tightly than he was using his other hand to cling to the side of the boat. He had his short sword, but it was tucked awkwardly down by his side and would be slow to draw. Besides, he had never used it in anger, scarcely knew how to wield it.

'Can you swim?' said the boatman.

'Yes,' said Geraint promptly.

'You're a liar, and a bad one at that. Whatever you say, you *have* got something in that pouch of yours and, whatever else you say, you cannot swim. Not one in a hundred men can swim. I'll turn the boat over and you'll sink like a stone.'

'Then you lose whatever I'm carrying. You lose your boat.'

'Boats float,' said Brennus. 'And you will lose rather more when you're at the bottom of the river.'

Geraint sensed that Brennus was enjoying this: the teasing, the control of what was happening on his boat. He looked towards the far bank where Caradoc and Cynric were standing expectantly. He thought of shouting out, but what could his brother do? Then he noticed that although they were still spinning round, the figure of his brother was growing larger. The current was gradually pushing them to the other shore while the boatman, intent on his threats, was neglecting to use the paddle to keep them in the centre of the stream. If he could only manage to distract Brennus for a little longer . . .

'So *you* are able to swim?' he said.

'Like a fish. Come on now, just open up your pouch and hand whatever's inside it to me. I'll take it in exchange for a safe landing. A blind bargain on my side, can't say fairer than that.'

'It is a keepsake from my mother,' said Geraint.

This was a lie too, more or less, but one the boatman seemed eager to accept.

'Then she'd be pleased if you handed it over to save yourself from death by water.'

'She is dead now, my mother,' said Geraint, his eyes growing moist as he said the words but still seeing the outline of Caradoc, standing rigid on the bank. From his posture, Geraint's brother knew something was wrong.

'I don't care what she is,' said the boatman, tiring of his chat. 'Give me what you're carrying or you'll be dead alongside her.'

'Here you are then,' said Geraint, angry now. He made to open the leather pouch. Instead he seized the rabbit by the hind legs and swung it straight at Brennus's face. It connected with a satisfying thwack. The dead cony was no club but the shock of the blow was enough to surprise and distract the boatman, who jerked back and put up his hands to protect himself. Geraint rose to his feet, the boat swaying wildly beneath him, and before he should lose his balance altogether he pressed down against the side of the shallow craft and made to leap into a clump of feathery reeds, one of several outcrops not so far from the bank. He felt something holding him and realised that Brennus had made a grab at the region of his waist. There was a tearing sound and Geraint toppled rather than jumped into the water.

His body sank through the reeds into the murk. His mouth filled with choking water and his feet flailed for the bottom.

13

Through his mind flashed the image he'd glimpsed on the villa floor, the sea with the strange beasts that lived there, and he wondered whether his final moments had come. He could not swim, that was no lie. Then his feet came to rest on something that was neither hard nor soft, perhaps a submerged clump of vegetation, and it gave him enough purchase to push himself above the surface of the water. Gasping for air, he scrabbled about among the reeds, pulling himself forward, kicking out with his legs and feeling his wool clothes growing heavier by the second.

He touched bottom but, far from giving him support, the mud of the river-bed grabbed at his boots as if it wanted to tear them from his feet. His head was above the surface but he could not keep upright. Something struck him in the face and he heard shouting. At first he thought it was the boatman, but then he recognised his brother. He was calling out, 'Take hold! Take hold!' Caradoc was too far off to reach Geraint but he had tossed out the boatman's rope to which was still fastened the stick the dog had used. Geraint grabbed it and, half by dint of his own struggling, half by being tugged in on the rope, found himself drawn up onto the bank, the last few feet in his brother's hands.

He lay on his front, a landed fish, water pouring from his hair, his eyes, his garments. The black shape of Cynric panted above him while his brother stood off a distance to allow him to recover. Geraint sat up. He wiped his eyes and looked out across the Abona. He glanced at the bank on either side of him. He half expected to see the treacherous boatman emerging from the river, dripping wet and vengeful. It was only then that he realised, in the struggle, the pouch had been torn away from his belt. It was lost, presumably at the bottom of the river. Or in the watery grasp of the boatman.

He felt more angry than he could remember feeling in his
life. He would have attacked the boatman with his bare
hands if he had appeared onshore. But of Brennus there
was no sign, not an arm or head visible in the twilight above
the swirling current. Then he caught sight of the man's
upturned boat, like a giant's hat in midstream. Boats float.
But he prayed that Brennus had gone to the bottom.

'What in God's name was going on out there?' said
Caradoc. He sounded more irritated than relieved.

'He tried to rob me,' said Geraint. 'He said the coin you'd
promised him wasn't enough. He thought I was carrying
something of value.'

Caradoc looked curiously at his brother. He made to say
something but stopped himself. Geraint stood up. His clothes
clung to him. The anger had gone and now he was cold and
shivery.

'At least you have saved yourself a silver coin.' The bitterness of losing his pouch and its contents was like a bad
taste in Geraint's mouth. He said nothing of the loss to his
brother.

'And I have got the man's rope,' said Caradoc, rolling it up
into a coil.

'We should use it to hang him with if we find him again.'

'I see there's some spark in you after all, brother. Save it for
the Saxons. Come on.'

They tramped across the fields to the nearest encampment, marked by fires and makeshift shelters. They struck
lucky almost straight away. Caradoc did not give the name
of their village or steading – a place-name that few were
likely to know or remember among the occupants of so
many villages that had flocked to Aquae Sulis – but he
spoke instead of a very tall man with reddish hair by the
name of Aelric. The second person to whom he mentioned

Aelric indicated a dilapidated farm building in the twilight next to a cluster of willows. Approaching, Geraint and Caradoc saw a cluster of men sprawled about a fire by the entrance. Hobbled horses champed the grass close by. Red-headed Aelric seemed surprised to see them but grudgingly welcomed the young brothers to the circle. Geraint was ribbed about his wet clothes but allowed to get close to the fire.

It was only later, after the food and drink and the talk, that Geraint, now lying at a little distance from the cooking fire, finally began to think of what he had lost or had been snatched from him. The pouch that hung from his belt and the precious object that he had been carrying for three days on his journey from the south. Although he had been guarding it for longer than that.

II

It was on his third and last visit to the old woman that Geraint was presented with the gift. She lived inside one of the hollowed-out mounds that dotted a flat area of ground not far from the village. The field, with its tussocky hummocks, was a place that the villagers avoided because it was believed to hold the dead. Not their dead, the recent ones, but the dead of long ago. At least, that was what was suggested by the things that had been discovered (and allowed to remain undisturbed) within the hummocks: the remains of skeletons and scraps of old leather and potsherds; even knives and axe-heads fashioned from stone.

There must have been some powerful magic preventing the villagers from using these places for shelter or storage, since they were dry and warm in winter, as well as cool in summer. Perhaps it was not only the partial skeletons but the presence of the woman that frightened people. She had flowing white hair and a face through which the bones showed as if she was more than half-way towards joining her underground companions for ever. She was so tall that, when she stood, she had to stoop within the quite generous confines of the burial chambers. At first, Geraint had not realised she was blind. There was a little light by the outer parts of the old woman's lair because during the day she was in the habit of sitting near the entrance, which was made out of two stone uprights and a crosspiece. Geraint thought she sat there because she wanted to see who was coming, before he realised that there was no sight in her large, glazed eyes. And then he understood that she did not need to see in order to know who was coming. She had, after all, greeted him by name on his first visit.

Geraint was not frightened. He did not see why he should be frightened. Unlike the other villagers – unlike his brother, Caradoc, for example – he did not question why the woman – she had no name, she was simply the *woman* – should not live there in the place of the dead, by herself. If she really was alone. Once or twice during their conversations, Geraint had caught the tremor and sound of movement further back in the chamber, not some animal but human, he thought. Who it was he never discovered.

But the woman already knew much about Geraint. Knew that his mother was ill and must shortly die, knew that his father had been killed in a skirmish with the Saxons when Geraint was little, knew that he regarded his only surviving brother with a mixture of respect and love and resentment. Above all, she knew of his waking dreams, of those moments when something seemed to slide between him and the reality surrounding him. When he first began to experience these, around the time of his father's death, Geraint had been truly frightened. He told no one and suffered in silence.

In one vision he saw two men tussling on the bank of a nearby river. One fell in, or was pushed, and the other stumbled after him. He recognised the two men. Geraint was actually within sight of the river but by the time he plucked up the courage to go closer, they had disappeared. The death by drowning – which occurred a few days later – was accounted an accident but Geraint had seen in his vision the way in which Deri's opponent, who desired Deri's wife, had held his rival's head underwater. Perhaps he did not intend to get rid of Deri but had taken the opportunity as it arose. The man who held the other underwater was red-headed Aelric, the head of the village. Later Geraint heard Aelric describe to the other villagers how he had been several fields away when Deri drowned, and this seemed to allay any suspicions they might have. Geraint said nothing to contradict him but, afterwards, he was more wary and frightened of Aelric than ever.

On another occasion during the winter Geraint dreamed several times of a sunless summer of cloud and constant rain, and how the village went hungry when the crops failed. Sure enough, it happened and the village sent petitioners to Cadwys for help.

When, on his second visit to the burial ground, he started to tell the woman who lived there of these things – and he had never mentioned them to anyone before – she merely nodded and grasped his arm with her claw-like hand. She reassured Geraint, telling him he was possessed by a gift, not a curse. All men and women could see with their eyes, she said, save those few unfortunates like herself who lacked sight. And everyone, even the blind, was able to see backwards in time thanks to the gift of memory. A few, a lucky few, had the ability also to see *forwards* in time.

'What can I do with it, this gift?' said Geraint. 'I should have warned Deri that his neighbour was going to kill him.'

'You would not have been believed.'

'I could have told the others that the crops would fail.'

'You would not have been believed.'

'So what use is it?'

'Everything has a place,' she said, 'but not everything has a use.'

The third time he visited the burial place the woman told Geraint that he would soon be leaving the village where he had been born; he and most of the other able-bodied men. Geraint was pleased to be thought a man. It put him on the same level as his brother, Caradoc. A great crisis was coming, the woman said. They would be summoned away to face it. Geraint knew nothing of this but accepted the truth of her words without question. He wanted to ask if he and the others would ever return but he was afraid of the answer. The woman sensed his mood and said that it was a time of danger but also of hope. Geraint would experience grief but gladness as well. There is no victory without tears, she said.

'Will Caradoc go too?'

'He will accompany you,' she said.

She had a gift for him. He was to take it on his journey when the call came. She reached into a bag that lay at her side and extracted a small object. He was surprised to see that it was a knife, but small, almost ornamental, rather than practical. She held it in the palm of one hand and ran the fingers of the other across the surface of the hilt before passing it to Geraint. The blade glinted with a metallic blue threat but the hilt was finely worked. It was made from some off-white substance that Geraint did not recognise, like stone but with a smooth, living feel to it that stone did not possess. The hilt depicted an animal that Geraint also didn't recognise. The beast stood on its hind legs with its forelegs wrapped around the trunk of a tree. Its upright posture was disturbing, neither man-like nor animal.

'What is the beast on the hilt?'

'A bear.'

'I have never seen one.'

'Are you sure of that?'

Geraint did not answer. Instead he said, 'What am I to do with it?'

'Keep it with you, safe. Take it with you when you are called away. You will know what to do with it when the time comes.'

And Geraint had to be content with that. A few weeks afterwards the call came. Arthur was summoning his countrymen to confront the Saxon hordes at a place several days' travel from the village, near the old Roman town of Aquae Sulis. Caradoc explained what was happening. It all might have been rumour but he told his younger brother as if it were fact (which it was, more or less). Caradoc said that for many months Arthur, using pedlars and paid informants as well as reputable travelling merchants, had caused a story to be spread among the Saxon enemy. The story was that the Picts, the people of the far north, were preparing to march south as soon as the winter retreated. Arthur had made a great show of sending some of his men north, apparently to face the Pictish threat and leaving the southlands undefended. But the British army had halted near the mouth of the Sabrina, far from their supposed destination. The Saxons, deceived, saw their chance to swing round and cut the country in two, like a woodman cleaving an upturned log at a single stroke. They massed to march west and south towards the river Abona, ignorant of the existence of the army lying hidden at their heels.

When Arthur received news of the Saxon preparation to march, he made the general call to arms. It was the final crisis, as predicted by the woman in the burial ground. If the Saxons were not dealt with now, they would surely over-run the whole land.

Caradoc and Geraint might have left with the other men of the village although they had not got the explicit permis-sion of Aelric to go. But, as it happened, they had to delay their departure by a couple of days since their mother, so long dying during the spring and early summer, was now at the very point of extinction. They departed on the morning following her death, each young man sunk in his thoughts and letting the breeze dry the occasional tear. Hence it was that they eventually arrived near Aquae Sulis, accompanied by the dog Cynric, but behind the rest of their neighbours.

Now Geraint sat not far from the men's campfire and wondered about the coming battle. He heard the sound of his brother's voice, protesting amid some laughter that he did know how to use the sword and knife that he carried. Geraint remembered the knife and its ornamental hilt. The bear with its arms clasped around the tree trunk. *You will know what to do with it when the time comes.* What would he have to do? When? Too late now. He had been robbed by the old boatman. The leather pouch and the knife were at the bottom of the river Abona. He had failed. He felt ashamed.

His thoughts were interrupted by the arrival of a tall man near the dying fire. Aelric welcomed him and asked him where he was from. The man said, 'I am with the Company of the Bear.'

Geraint started at the words, since they chimed with his recent thoughts. The newcomer settled himself close to the embers as if he had a right to be there and the others accepted him without question. He was wearing a hooded mantle, grey, and his great height was evident even though he carried himself with a stoop.

'What news?' he said to no one in particular.

Aelric said, 'The enemy draws nearer.'

'And what are our chances?'

It was either a foolish or an inappropriate question for there was an uneasy shifting among the group by the fire.

Then Caradoc piped up, 'Under our leader, how can we fail?'

'You mean Arthur guards us against defeat?'

There was a general mutter of agreement at this but the man was firm in contradicting his own question. 'No, each man must guard himself against defeat. Arthur is not one of the gods, as in the religion of the olden days.'

'He is not an ordinary man,' said Aelric. 'You, of all people, must know that if you are truly with the Company of the Bear.'

'Perhaps so,' said the newcomer, 'but the outcome of battle is always uncertain. What do you think, you over there? Do you expect victory?'

As he said these last words he turned to look at Geraint, who was sitting in shadow. Disconcertingly Geraint could see nothing of the face under the hood except the glitter of the man's eyes – that and a grizzled beard.

'No victory without tears,' said Geraint, repeating what the sightless woman in the burial ground had told him.

'True enough,' said the man.

'That is my young brother, Geraint,' said Caradoc.

'Whoever he is, he speaks sense,' said the man.

After that the group about the fire fell silent and after a time the man got up and, with a muttered farewell, left them.

III

The next morning Geraint woke early, cramped and stiff from where he'd been sleeping on the rough ground. There was a thin mist lying across the valley and the damp had crept under his clothes. He clambered to his feet. Cynric, who had edged himself close to the dying fire during the night, staggered up, looking expectantly at Geraint. No one else was awake, not even Caradoc.

Geraint and the dog wandered away to stretch their legs. Quite soon Geraint heard the sound of the river, although at first he saw nothing but the blurred outline of the willows along the bank. He pushed through some low-lying shrubs and entered a flat, grassy area fronting the water. Suddenly Cynric stopped and the hackles on his back rose. Through the mist Geraint strained to see what the dog had sensed. A few yards in front of him a man was sitting on the edge of the water. His knees were drawn up under him and his head was bowed. He looked like a large grey stone. Something about his posture and the cowl that covered his head reminded Geraint of the individual who'd joined them at the campfire the previous evening. He gave no sign of being aware of their presence. Perhaps he was asleep or praying.

Geraint was about to move away. Then out of the corner of his eye he saw movement on the far side of the clearing. Another man was emerging from the undergrowth. This one Geraint also recognized, and his heart thumped and his mouth went dry. It was the boatman, Brennus. He had survived the spill from his coracle! Moving through the long grass with exaggerated gestures, raising his legs high with each step, he advanced towards the man on the bank, who remained still as a stone. In his hand he held a knife. Geraint recognised this too. It was his, the knife with the bear-hilt.

The treacherous boatman was within a few strides of the other, the one huddled up on the bank. His intention was plain: to take the other by surprise, to stab him in the back or the neck.

Geraint had no weapon. His sword was left, carelessly, inexcusably, where he had been sleeping. But his unarmed state did not cross his mind. Seeing Brennus once more, stepping like a malevolent spirit through the tendrils of mist, grasping *his* bear-knife, was sufficient to cause Geraint to launch himself across the clearing. He almost took Brennus by surprise but the wrinkled man turned just in time and slashed out with the knife. He was aiming too high and the sweeping stroke passed over Geraint's back as the lad hit him around the knees. Both of them tumbled into the dank grass and rolled over, now one on top, now the other. Geraint seized hold of Brennus's forearm and exerted all his strength to keep the knife blade away from his face and eyes. His nostrils filled with the stench of fish from the boatman.

Cynric joined in but he was no dog for a fight. Rather, he lunged at the tangle of legs and impeded Geraint instead of helping him. Brennus might have been old but he was tough and wiry as a strip of tanned leather. At one moment, Geraint levered himself up and sat astride Brennus. As he did so, his grip on the other's knife-hand slackened. The boatman's arm wriggled away and would have slashed Geraint across the face had he not raised his own arm to protect himself. So instead the blade sliced through the coarse fabric of Geraint's sleeve and ripped down the underside of his arm. He was conscious of no pain but the blood welled through the cloth and blotted Brennus's withered face. Wounded with his own weapon, Geraint managed to seize the other's knife-hand once again but his hold was not as tight as it had been. Now the boatman had the advantage and, arching his back, he threw Geraint off. Positions were reversed, with the boatman lying at an angle across the younger man and attempting to twist his hand and arm about so that he might pierce Geraint in the flank.

Then there loomed above them both a man's shape, a very tall man in cloak and hood. With one hand, it seemed, he grabbed Brennus about the nape of his neck and lifted him clear of Geraint. He held the boatman at a distance as one would a poisonous viper, and his grip on the other's neck was so firm that Brennus appeared to hang like a sack from the man's hand.

With his other arm and in almost leisurely fashion, the tall man reached about and twisted the knife-hand of the boatman. Twisted it so sharply Geraint could have sworn he heard the crack of bone. Brennus gave a screech like a bird and let go of the bear-knife. The man dropped the boat-man on the ground and then planted a foot on the side of his head. All this time he looked not at Brennus, who might have been so much discarded rubbish, but at Geraint. The lad was standing up by this time but felt very unsteady. It was not only as a consequence of his wound but also because he recognised the man for certain. In the struggle his hood had fallen away and Geraint realised this was indeed the individual from the night before, the man with glittering eyes and grizzled beard. His stooping posture then had disguised his true height: he was almost a giant, in Geraint's eyes. Cynric the dog crouched uneasily at the edge of the clearing, watching the trio.

'Thank you,' said the man. 'You have protected me. I know this traitor. He would have killed me while I was sunk deep in my thoughts and was lost to the world. Each man must guard himself, I said, but I forgot my own teaching.'

'Thoughts about the battle – the battle to come?' said Geraint, surprising himself by the evenness of his voice. But he could not look at the tall man and instead cast his glance down to where Brennus, writhing, was pinned under the other's foot.

'Yes. I was thinking of the battle.'

'I am here to take part,' said Geraint.

'How old are you?'

'Old enough to fight,' he said, then, seeing the man staring hard at him, 'Twelve years, I think.'

'And your brother, the one who identified you last night?'

'I do not know,' said Geraint. 'Two years older maybe.'

The man seemed about to say something then turned his head to one side. 'You must be attended to,' he said.

By now blood was beginning to issue from his arm in some quantity and, before he knew it, Geraint was sitting back on the rank grass and then lying down as he heard rather than saw a rush of people enter the clearing. Then the morning mist seemed to enter his own mind too.

Geraint dreamed he was in a desperate fight but, even though he was once again equipped with the bear-knife, he could not lift his arm to strike out against his unseen enemy, who was jabbing at him out of a mist. Then he woke and when he glanced sideways at his arm he saw it was swathed in blood-soaked bandages and, although it was throbbing slightly, it seemed not to be part of him. He was lying on a plain bed in a plain room, illuminated by sun pouring through a high narrow aperture. Caradoc was standing nearby, awkward.

'Brother,' he said simply.

He squatted down on his hams so that he almost on a level with Geraint.

In a corner of the room lay Cynric. The dog's tail fluttered to see Geraint awake. It was cool and dry in the chamber.

'This is a storage room of one of the villas in Aquae Sulis,' said Caradoc. 'You have been brought here to recover. One of the women of the town has been ordered to tend to you.'

'It is my fighting arm,' said Geraint.

'You will not be doing any fighting for a while,' said Caradoc, and the remark sounded like something he had heard someone else say.

'What happened? Did you see Brennus?'

'Who? Oh, the boatman. Yes, he has been . . . questioned. It seems he was more than a petty thief and ferryman. He was in the pay of the Saxons. We have agents among them and they keep traitors among us.'

'Brennus was trying to attack the man by the river. The hooded man.'

'Thanks to you he did not succeed. You know who the hooded man is?'

'Arthur,' said Geraint, remembering the time when he had seen him near Cadwy's Fort. On that occasion he had ridden past in splendour, high and easy, like a god. Very different from the man still as stone in a grey mantle by the river-bank. 'Arthur, our leader.'

'Arthur knew Brennus of old. He was a steward at Cadwy's Fort. He had stolen from the stores and kept false records. Arthur showed mercy by driving him from the realm in disgrace instead of taking his life. He was not grateful but twisted with bitterness. He would have harmed Arthur.'

'Arthur was the stranger by the fire last night. The one who said he was not a god.'

'It is his custom, they say, to walk unknown among his men and listen to what they are saying.'

'We are his men,' said Geraint.

'Yes,' said Caradoc. 'Boys no longer.'

There was an awkward pause before Caradoc said, 'He told me to return something to you. Arthur spoke to me! I could scarcely meet his gaze. He told me to give this back to you. He assured me it was your property even though I have never seen it before.' He fumbled in his garments and produced the knife with the bear-hilt. Geraint took it with his good hand. 'Where did it come from? It is not our father's.'

'The bear is Arthur's image, isn't it?' said Geraint, not replying to his brother's question. 'The Company of the Bear. Brennus could surely not have killed Arthur with a weapon bearing his own image on the hilt.'

'In any case, you alerted him.'

'He was deep in thought. Or he was praying for success in battle.'

'The battle that is coming,' said Caradoc.

'I am afraid for you,' said Geraint, struggling to rise from the narrow bed.

'Be still, little brother. Recover your strength and the use of your arm.'

The battle of Badon Hill, which Geraint had witnessed as plumes of smoke and cries and screams, began within a matter of days. The Saxons were ambushed by Arthur's men as they approached Aquae Sulis, in a pass between the hills to the east of the Roman town. Taken by surprise and temporarily overwhelmed, they retreated to the old fortified hill top called Badon and there the Britons laid siege to them. The hill top was barren, without water or any resources.

When the enemy was weakened by hunger and thirst and constant harrying, Arthur's men stormed the bare slopes and swept over the plateau with sword and fire.

It was a great struggle, and a great victory for Arthur and the Britons against the Saxons. Arthur was reputed to have slain over nine hundred of the foe single-handed – or so the story went centuries later when he was no longer a mere man but a god once more. There were losses on the British side too, among them red-headed Aelric and young Caradoc from an anonymous village not far from Cadwy's.

Geraint, kept from the battle by his wound, knew of Caradoc's death before the woman who was tending to him informed him of it. He knew of it not because of any vision but because one morning Cynric, who stayed in the store-room and would not leave Geraint's side, was restless for hours and then raised the hairs on the boy's neck with a long-drawn-out ghostly howl. Geraint turned his head to one side and wept for his brother, following so hard at the heels of their departed mother.

He might be glad of the happy outcome of the battle but he grieved for the loss of Caradoc. In commemoration of his brother and before returning to his village, Geraint went to the hill of Badon outside the town. The day was overcast and the clouds pressed down low. Geraint did not walk to the very top of the hill from which smoke drifted, acrid, smelling of meat. The dead were still burning, the corpses of Saxons and the Britons, or it was merely the carcasses of the horses. Nevertheless Geraint did not want to climb any higher. He did not want to go searching for the exact spot where Caradoc had fallen. He did not want the possibility of glimpsing his brother's mangled, roasting corpse among the slain.

Instead he faced about to the south-west in the direction

of his village. The gentle hills slept under the low sky. Geraint saw no vision of any battle to come. Perhaps the talk that he had heard while he was recovering his strength was true: that the battle of Badon was the last battle, or the last for many years. The Saxons were routed. For all the bitter scent in his nostrils, thought Geraint, perhaps the Saxon threat was sleeping or even at an end. Then, in the company of the dog Cynric and, choosing a secluded spot on the slope, Geraint buried the dagger with the ivory bear-hilt.

ACT ONE

I

Bath Abbey, September 1199

Something rotten was unfolding in Bath. Two good men were dead, and Prior Hugh suspected murder. The first had happened eight years ago, when the saintly Bishop Reginald had died *en route* to Canterbury, where he was to have been invested as archbishop; his body had been returned to Bath, and over the last few weeks, miracles had been occurring at his tomb. And second, there was Adam.

Adam had not wanted to be Master of St John's Hospital, but Reginald's successor, Bishop Savaric, had been insistent. And no one refused the ruthless, uncompromising Savaric. Adam had been a talented healer, but he had not enjoyed running a large and busy foundation, and it had probably been a desire for peace that had led him up Solsbury Hill a month before.

No one knew exactly what had happened, but Adam's torn body had been found at the foot of the hill the following morning. Opinions in the abbey were divided: some monks thought a wolf was at large, while others believed Adam had fallen to his death. Fallen! Savaric had been the one to propose that ridiculous notion, determined – suspiciously, as far as Hugh was concerned – that the matter should be dismissed as a tragic accident.

Hugh stood with difficulty. He had been sitting in the cloister all afternoon, thinking, and his legs were stiff. A walk
would ease them, though, and he brightened at the prospect.
It was a pretty evening for a stroll. He stifled a sigh when
his sacrist stepped to intercept him. Robert was a portly,
smiling man who always gave the impression of great piety;
Hugh had yet to be convinced that it was sincere.

'You seem troubled, Father Prior,' Robert said, all kindly
concern. 'May I help?'

Hugh itched to tell him to mind his own business, but several other monks were listening, and Robert was popular –
unlike Hugh himself, who was resented for the strict way he
ran his abbey. Rebuking the sacrist would be more trouble
than it was worth.

'Adam,' he explained, forcing a patient smile. 'I am sure he
died unlawfully, no matter what our bishop says.'

Robert shrugged. 'Then go to Solsbury Hill, and look for
clues.'

Hugh regarded him askance. 'It will be dark soon. Besides,
I must prepare for vespers.'

'I will lead vespers,' offered Robert eagerly.

He was always trying to preside over sacred offices, a habit
Hugh found intensely annoying. The prior forced another
smile.

'Thank you, Robert. However, I cannot visit Solsbury so
near dusk. Adam did, and look what happened to him.'

'Adam went considerably later,' argued Robert. 'I am sure
you will be quite safe. And if you do believe he was murdered, you have a moral obligation to prove it.'

Hugh felt his jaw drop that the sacrist should dare lecture
him, and was about to put him in his place when he became
aware that the other monks were waiting with interest for his
answer. He knew why, of course: recently, a rumour had

started about Solsbury Hill – one that said only the pure in heart could survive a night there when the moon was full. There was a full moon that night, so declining to accept Robert's challenge was tantamount to admitting to some serious personal flaws.

Normally, Hugh would not have cared what the eaves-droppers thought, but Bishop Savaric was eager to dismiss him and appoint a more malleable prior – and Hugh's strict rule meant the monks were on Savaric's side. Any hint of impropriety might be used against him, even gossip that said he was too steeped in sin to brave Solsbury Hill.

'Then I shall go,' he said, thinking that if he walked fast, he could be back before nightfall. While not superstitious, he had no wish to loiter in a place where a man had died. 'Will you come with me?'

'No,' replied Robert with a smile that Hugh thought sly. 'I shall pray for Adam's soul.'

One of the abbey's many sources of income was the tolls paid by those wishing to sell their goods in the market. These were collected at the town gates by lay-brothers, and the one on duty that day was named Eldred. As Hugh strode through the gate, he recalled that it had been Eldred who had found Adam's body. He was surprised to note that Eldred was with Brother Walter, though. Walter was well known for being Savaric's spy, which meant most of the abbey's staff gave him a wide berth.

'What are you doing here, Walter?' The question emerged more sharply than Hugh had intended, and he saw resent-ment flash in Walter's eyes.

'Just talking,' Walter replied coolly. 'About Adam and Reginald.'

'We were saying how much we miss them,' elaborated

Eldred. 'Especially Adam. I still have not recovered from the shock of finding his poor, torn body.'

So Walter had gone to gossip, thought Hugh disapprovingly. Yet Walter's unseemly penchant for chatter had its advantages. In this case, it provided an opportunity to solicit a few opinions, and Hugh desperately needed new information if he were to unmask a killer.

'How do *you* think Adam died?' he asked, looking at each man in turn.

'A wolf,' replied Eldred promptly.

'There are no wolves in Bath,' countered Walter scornfully. 'I believe the bishop's theory: that Adam lost his footing and fell.'

He smiled insincerely, and the expression sent a shiver down Hugh's spine. Did Walter know more than he was telling about Adam's fate?

Unhappy and agitated, Hugh resumed his walk. Eventually, he reached Solsbury Hill, and the path that wound steeply towards its summit. When he arrived, he sat to catch his breath, then automatically began reviewing his suspects again.

At the top of the list for involvement in the two deaths was Bishop Savaric, first for being so determined that Adam's demise should be seen as accidental, and second because he had inherited a lot of money from Reginald – the two had been cousins. Hugh found Savaric's brazen ambition distasteful, particularly in his actions regarding Glastonbury: Savaric had contrived to have its abbot promoted, then declared *himself* its new head, styling himself 'Bishop of Bath and Glastonbury'. As a Glastonbury man himself, Hugh thought closer relations between the two foundations was a good thing, but Savaric had gone about it far too aggressively.

The bishop would not have soiled his own hands with murder, of course. His henchmen, Sir Osmun and Sir Fevil, would have done it for him. These two loutish knights had, Hugh was sure, organised 'accidents' before.

Next on the list was someone who had argued bitterly with both Adam and Reginald, and who made no secret of his dislike. His name was William Pica, a fierce bantam of a fellow, whom the monks at Glastonbury had elected as their new abbot – an election that was their way of saying they did not recognise Savaric's claim. They had chosen Pica not because he was popular, but because he was one of few men who was not afraid of Savaric.

Then Hugh had two suspects in his own abbey – the slippery Walter and the nauseatingly pious Robert. Both had been in the party that had been escorting Reginald to Canterbury, and neither could account for his whereabouts on the night that Adam had died. They had no obvious motive for either murder, but there was something about both that Hugh found unsettling. And he had not reached his lofty position by ignoring his instincts.

And finally, there was Reginald's chaplain. Dacus had been distraught when his bishop had died, so much so that Hugh had feared for his sanity. Had guilt prompted his wild display of mourning – that he had not loved Reginald as much as he had claimed, and had killed him for some warped reason known only to himself? By contrast, Dacus had received the news of Adam's death with an indifferent shrug. Hugh could not fathom the man at all, but wished Savaric had not appointed him as Adam's replacement at the hospital. Compassionate and patient Dacus might be, but Hugh considered him unstable.

He came out of his reverie when he noticed that the sun had set. He swore softly. He was supposed to be looking for clues to tell him what had happened to Adam, not sitting around doing more brooding. And now it was too late – it would be dark soon. With an irritable sigh, he stood, and started to make his way back down the path.

He stopped when he heard a sound behind him. It sounded like panting. He peered into the shadows, but there was nothing to see. Had he imagined it? He began walking again, more quickly this time, then whipped around a second time when a grunt told him he was not alone.

'Who is there?' he demanded.

The only reply was a growl that made his blood run cold. He turned and ran, stumbling over the uneven ground. Then he fell, and when he stopped rolling, something was looming over him. Sobbing his terror, he tried to push it away, but it was too strong. He opened his mouth to scream, but no sound came, and all he could hear was enraged snarls as teeth fastened around his throat.

II

October 1199

Winter had come early, bringing with it biting winds, slashing rain and even the odd flurry of snow. Gwenllian shivered, and wished she could have stayed in Carmarthen, the great castle her husband was building in west Wales. She glanced at him as he rode beside her. He seemed oblivious to the foul weather, and was humming under his breath.

'You are enjoying yourself!' she said accusingly. 'We leave our comfortable home and our baby son, to spend days trudging along dreary roads to Bath, and you are happy!'

'No,' he replied, although his guilty expression said otherwise. Sir Symon Cole was a terrible liar, which was one of the reasons Gwenllian loved him.

Of course, she thought wryly, it was his inability to prevaricate that had made their journey necessary in the first place. Other knights would have been able to look John – recently crowned King, following the death of his brother, Richard – in the eye and shower him with compliments, but not Cole. He considered the new monarch weak, treacherous and incompetent, and had elected to stay silent rather than say things he did not believe.

Unfortunately, John knew exactly what Cole thought, and was keen to replace him with one of his sycophants. Luckily for Cole, Gwenllian was the daughter of a powerful Welsh prince, and dismissing Cole without good cause would offend too many of her volatile kinsmen. So John had set him a challenge instead: if he could discover who had murdered Bath's prior, he could keep Carmarthen; if he failed, he was to resign.

'I miss Meurig,' Gwenllian said, pulling her mind from politics. 'By the time we go home, he will not know us.'

'You think he is lacking in wits, then?' asked Cole. 'Like his father?'

Gwenllian knew what had prompted that remark. *She* was the clever one, who would catch the prior's killer. Prudently, she changed the subject. 'Will we reach Bath before dark?'

Cole squinted at the sky. 'Yes, and I am looking forward to seeing the Master of St John's Hospital again. You will like him, Gwen.'

Gwenllian decided to reserve judgement on that. Cole liked most people, and more villains than she cared to remember had been introduced with the earnest assurance that they were decent men.

'Tell me again how you met,' she said, to avoid passing comment.

'I was injured during an ambush some years ago, and he helped me recover. He was a monk at Glastonbury, and was there when King Arthur's relics were discovered.'

They exchanged a glance. They knew a great deal about King Arthur's bones, and what had happened to them after they had been excavated.* Gwenllian eased her horse towards him, so they would not be overheard by Sergeant Iefan, who was riding behind.

'I know the master of this hospital is your friend, but King John's letter implied that Prior Hugh may have been murdered by a colleague. This master will be a colleague ...'

Cole shook his head firmly. 'He is the kindest, most generous man alive. I know I have said that about other people, but it really is true of him.'

Gwenllian stifled a sigh. Loyalty to friends was another of Cole's virtues, but she hoped it would not impede their investigation. John's determination to discredit him meant it was imperative that she solved the mystery, and she could not afford to be hindered by his blind affection for an old comrade.

Bath was a pretty place, its cluster of buildings dominated by the mighty abbey church. Its roads were well drained, and someone paid for them to be swept regularly, because they were almost as clean as Carmarthen's. Cole led the way along the shop-lined main street.

'I wish you *had* told the King what he wanted to hear.' Gwenllian had never enjoyed travelling, and could not recall

---

*See *King Arthur's Bones*, The Medieval Murderers

a time when she had been colder, wetter or more tired. 'It would have saved a lot of trouble.'

'Yes.' Cole tried to sound apologetic, but he had a Norman's love of horses, and for him, the prospect of days in the saddle was a delight. He liked dogs, too, and if she had not objected, he would have brought several with him and prolonged the journey by hunting.

He reined in outside a building with gracefully arched windows and a carving of St John the Baptist above the door.

'This is the hospital. We shall visit it now, and find an inn afterwards – we cannot stay in the abbey, given that one of its monks might be a murderer.'

'I would rather find an inn first,' objected Gwenllian. 'I am too wet and dirty for—'

'No one will mind,' said Cole, reaching up to lift her from the saddle.

He had opened the door before she could inform him that she had been thinking about her own comfort, not the impression she might make on Bath's residents. She stepped inside reluctantly. The hospital was a pleasant building, and no expense had been spared on its construction. It comprised a chapel with a hall to house inmates on one side, and a chamber containing a pool of greenish water on the other. A corridor led to a yard at the back.

'Bishop Reginald founded it,' Cole explained, while they waited for someone to come to attend to them. 'For the sick to enjoy the healing springs. He died eight years ago, and people have prayed at his tomb ever since. The merchant we met last night said that miracles started occurring there two months ago, beginning with the return of Bishop Savaric's crosier.'

Gwenllian regarded him in confusion. 'You mean his crook?'

Cole nodded. 'It was stolen, apparently, but he prayed to
Reginald, and the very next day, it appeared on the high
altar. Since then, a number of people have been cured or
granted boons. I intend to pray there myself – I should like
our son to have a sister.'

His words startled Gwenllian enough that she was gaping
when a priest arrived. He was a large, bulky fellow with a
mane of black hair and wild eyes.

'What do you want?' he demanded.

'To see Adam,' replied Cole, unruffled by the hostile greeting. 'He is an old friend.'

'He is dead,' said the priest, spite supplanting churlish-
ness. 'And it served him right. He was an evil man, and he
came to an evil end.'

The announcement caused the colour to drain from Cole's
face. 'He cannot be dead! And he is not evil, either. He is a
healer!'

'He was skilled at medicine,' conceded the priest grudgingly. 'But he was wicked in all else. I suppose you are the
man charged to find out what happened to Prior Hugh? You
took your time coming. We were beginning to think you had
decided not to bother.'

'The weather was bad,' explained Cole shortly. 'But who
are you? And why—'

'I am Dacus, Adam's successor. He died two months ago,
which was not a moment too soon, as far as I was concerned.
Bath is a better place without his tainted presence in it.'

Cole stepped forward angrily, but Dacus did not shy away,
as most people would have done when faced with an irate
Norman warrior, and Gwenllian wondered whether he was
entirely sane. She interposed herself between them, loath
for the investigation to begin with violence.

'If he really is dead, show us where he is buried,' she ordered.

Dacus made a peculiar curtsy that made her even more convinced that something was awry, then led them to the yard. It was an odd combination of vegetable plot and cemetery, with graves in a line along the wall. He pointed to one in the corner.

'How did he die?' asked Cole hoarsely.

'Throat torn out by a wolf,' replied Dacus. 'He was rash enough to visit Solsbury Hill on a full moon, and his body was found the following morning. Hugh died the same way, although I imagine you already know that.'

'There are no wolves in England,' said Gwenllian. 'What really happened?'

Dacus glowered and became childishly sullen. 'There *are* – ask anyone. Hugh was stupid to have lingered there after dark. Especially given what had happened to Adam.'

'My wife is right,' said Cole stiffly. 'There are no wolves here, and if Adam and Hugh did die in the way you suggest, then some other beast did it. A dog, perhaps. Although it would take a monster to train one to act in such a way . . .'

Dacus laughed mockingly. 'The manner of Hugh's demise is news to you! I thought the King's officer would have been better informed.'

'Then enlighten us,' suggested Gwenllian, reaching out to prevent Cole from grabbing the priest. 'You can start by telling us about Solsbury Hill.'

Dacus pointed over the wall to a mound about three miles distant. His voice grew curiously singsong. 'It is a malevolent place, and only those with pure souls can survive a night there. Adam and Hugh took the test, but failed.'

'Hugh was not pure?' asked Gwenllian, gripping Cole's

arm more tightly. Dacus was providing information, and she was willing to accept intelligence from anyone willing to talk, no matter how objectionable they were.

'No,' replied Dacus airily, 'because otherwise he would have lived. Will you take the test, King's man? There is a full moon on Thursday – three days' time. Go to Solsbury then, and if you are honourable, God will protect you. But if you are sinful, you will die. Of course, you will have to do it alone.'

'How do you know a wolf killed Adam and Hugh?' asked Gwenllian quickly, before Cole was goaded into accepting the challenge.

'It savaged them, but it was God who decided they should die,' declared Dacus. 'Of course, there was no need for avenging wolves in Bishop Reginald's day. *He* was a saint, who kept good order in Bath. He should have been an archbishop, you know.'

'He was offered the post,' explained Cole, seeing Gwenllian's eyebrows rise at the claim, 'but he died on his way to Canterbury. He considered himself unworthy, and God apparently agreed, because he was struck down as he—'

'How dare you say God killed Reginald!' shrieked Dacus, lurching forward suddenly. 'You stupid Norman! He was *murdered*. I was his chaplain, and I was there – I *know*.'

One of his fists shot out, but Cole had no trouble evading it. Dacus tried again, so Cole caught his arm and twisted it behind his back. Dacus struggled frantically, then began to weep and curse in equal measure.

'He is demented,' said Gwenllian quietly. 'He does not know what he—'

'I do know,' shrieked Dacus. 'I am glad Adam is dead. He was *evil*! He deserved to die.'

When the priest's rage was spent, Cole released him. Dacus crawled into a corner and began to whisper to himself. Cole watched for a moment, then turned on his heel and strode outside. Gwenllian followed.

'Do not let him upset you,' she said gently. 'His wits are awry, and—'

'He would not have been appointed master of a hospital if he was truly mad,' interrupted Cole tightly. 'And it is obvious what happened: he hated Adam and Hugh, so *he* murdered them.'

Gwenllian gazed at him. 'Symon! There is no evidence for—'

'He killed Adam because he wanted his job, and he killed Hugh to prevent him from telling anyone. And he challenged me to go to Solsbury Hill on Thursday, because he intends to kill me, too. It is why he told me to go alone.'

Gwenllian regarded him askance. 'Our task here will be difficult enough without you jumping to wild conclusions—'

'Dacus murdered Adam,' repeated Cole, in a tone of voice that she had never heard him use before. 'I can see it in his eyes.'

'Perhaps,' she said soothingly. 'But you will need evidence to bring charges against him.'

'Then I shall find it.' Cole sprang into his saddle, and wheeled the destrier round in a savage arc. 'See Gwen settled in a decent inn, Iefan. I will join her later.'

'Where are you going?' asked Gwenllian, alarmed.

'To do as you suggest.' Cole's next words were called over his shoulder as he kicked the horse into a canter. 'To find evidence that Dacus killed Adam.'

Gwenllian stared after him in astonishment. He did not usually abandon her in strange towns. Moreover, what sort of evidence did he think he was going to find, on horseback when daylight was fading? Regardless, she hoped he would do nothing rash.

Iefan regarded her rather helplessly – his English was not good enough to question passers-by about suitable accommodation – so Gwenllian waylaid two Benedictines, and asked them to recommend some. The first was a portly fellow with a beatific expression, and the second, who was thin with sly eyes, haughtily informed her that he was Prior Walter.

'Hugh's successor?' asked Gwenllian.

Walter nodded as he led the way along a lane. 'Bishop Savaric appointed me. He and I have always enjoyed an easy relationship, so I was the obvious choice. There is no unseemly wrangling between diocese and abbey with *me* in charge.'

'No,' agreed his chubby companion, rather ambiguously.

'That knight who almost rode us down just now,' said Walter, choosing to ignore the remark. 'Is he the man charged to look into Hugh's death?'

Gwenllian nodded. 'Do you know anything that might help him?'

'No,' replied Walter. 'Although we still grieve.' He did not sound sincere.

'We do,' agreed the fat one. 'Hugh was strict, cold and humourless, but we miss him.'

'He was a decent man,' countered Walter. 'Of course, he was nothing compared to Bishop Reginald. Will you visit Reginald's tomb, lady? He is granting petitions aplenty at the moment. For example, I prayed for more money for the abbey last month, and within a week, a benefactor died, leaving us a house. Now that is the kind of miracle I like!'

'I see,' said Gwenllian, not sure a benefactor's death was something a monk should welcome so brazenly.

'Tell her, Brother Robert,' Walter urged. 'Tell her of all the wonders that have occurred. You spend more time in the church than anyone else, so you have witnessed most of them.' He smiled at Gwenllian. 'Robert is our sacrist, you see.'

'People have been healed,' obliged Robert. 'Back pains cured, headaches eased, lost items found—'

'Like Bishop Savaric's crosier,' put in Walter.

'Quite,' agreed Robert. 'He was distraught when it disappeared, because it had been a gift from Reginald himself. Its return was the first miracle.'

Gwenllian nodded politely, although none of the 'miracles' seemed especially dazzling to her – cured headaches and backaches were difficult to verify, while 'lost' objects reappeared all the time.

'Tell me about Hugh,' she said. 'I understand he died on Solsbury Hill, as did Master Adam. Do you know what happened to them?'

'Our bishop guessed it immediately,' nodded Walter. 'They fell, and the wounds to their throats were caused by sharp rocks.'

'That is one interpretation,' said Robert, earning an irritable glance from his prior. 'However, I suspect murder, because it is not possible to die falling down Solsbury Hill. Not from those sorts of injuries, at least.'

'Then who killed them?' asked Gwenllian.

'I do not know,' replied Robert, although Gwenllian did not miss the look he flicked towards his prior. She tried to guess what it meant. Did he think Walter had killed Hugh? Or was he trying to mislead her?

She was about to resume her questions when two priests

materialised out of the darkness. One looked like a pig, with small eyes and a snout-like nose, while the other was more warrior than cleric – he wore a dagger and carried a mace.

'Good evening, Walter,' said the pig. 'I thought it was time for vespers. You will be late.'

'I will oversee the ceremony,' offered Robert eagerly. 'It will be no trouble.'

'I am sure it will not,' said Walter coolly. 'But our brethren can wait until we have escorted our guest to the Swan Inn.' He turned to Gwenllian. 'Allow me to introduce Canon Lechlade and Canon Trotman. They are from Wells Cathedral, here on business with the bishop.'

The pig bowed. 'We heard the King's agents had arrived – news travels fast in Bath. But you cannot install them in the Swan, Father Prior. It has fleas. They must go to the Angel. But you two go to vespers – Lechlade and I will take her there.'

Robert smiled gratefully. 'Thank you. It is kind—'

'I will do it,' said Walter sharply. Then he grimaced. 'Although it is late, so I suppose Robert had better take vespers in my stead.'

'It will be my pleasure,' gushed Robert smugly.

Gwenllian was glad of Iefan's reassuring presence at her side as she followed the three clerics, and wished Cole had not abandoned her. Supposing one of *them* was the murderer? Trotman was chatting about Bath's healing waters, an innocuous subject that should have put her at ease. It did not, and she became more uneasy with every step. When a dog barked suddenly, she jumped in alarm.

'There is no need to be frightened,' said Walter, smirking. 'Bath is quite safe. Bishop Savaric sees to that.'

'Does he?' asked Gwenllian, heart hammering in her chest. 'How?'

'With henchmen,' explained Trotman. He raised his hands defensively when Walter started to object. 'They *are* henchmen. How else would you describe Osmun and Fevil?'

'Knightly advisers,' replied Walter shortly. 'And please do not make disparaging remarks about Savaric. He is a fine man, and I am proud to serve him.'

'Serve him?' pounced Lechlade disapprovingly. 'A prior should not serve anyone except God.'

'I serve my King,' Walter flashed back. 'And Savaric is one of his favourite prelates.'

'No one can deny that,' agreed Trotman pointedly. 'There is nothing Savaric would not do for John. And nothing John would not do in return.'

Gwenllian was not sure what was meant by the remark, but it was enough to tell her that she would need to be careful when she met the bishop the following day.

'You are no doubt wondering why two canons from Wells should be in Bath,' said Lechlade pleasantly, although the question could not have been further from her mind. 'We are here to tell Savaric that he has no right to declare himself "Bishop of Bath and Glastonbury" without *our* approval.'

'Wells is supposed to be consulted on all major decisions, you see,' explained Trotman. 'But Savaric made this one alone – and we do not approve. Glastonbury does not want him, for a start. They have elected their own abbot. His name is Pica, although Savaric refuses to recognise him.'

'Who cares what Glastonbury wants?' shrugged Walter. 'Ever since King Arthur's bones were discovered, they have been getting ideas above their station. Personally, I am delighted that Savaric cut them down to size by making them subordinate to Bath.'

'He only did it because he wants to control their coffers,' countered Lechlade acidly. 'But they should decide who rules them, not him.'

'The King and the Pope disagree,' argued Walter. 'They both support what he did.'

'That Pope is now dead,' snapped Lechlade. 'And the King only gave his blessing to the scheme because Savaric offered him a share of Glastonbury's profits in return. Do not deny it, Walter – you know it is true.'

'Walter has been telling me about Prior Hugh,' said Gwenllian, speaking before the quarrel could escalate further – she wanted to hear about Bath, not Glastonbury. 'And about Master Adam and Bishop Reginald.'

'All dead before their time,' said Trotman sadly. 'There are rumours of murder, but I do not believe them. Adam and Hugh were called by God. Well, by seraphim, to be precise.'

'Seraphim?' echoed Gwenllian, startled.

Trotman nodded keenly. 'There are fiendishly sharp claws on every one of a seraph's six wings, and God sent them after Adam and Hugh, although I cannot tell you why – they seemed like decent men to me. However, seraphim did not kill Reginald – he died of a fever. I know this for a fact, because Lechlade and I were there.'

'Lots of people were there,' elaborated Walter. 'Reginald wanted friends from Glastonbury, Bath *and* Wells to see him enthroned in Canterbury. Naturally, I was among his honoured guests. So were Robert, Pica, Sir Fevil and Dacus.'

'Dacus?' asked Gwenllian. 'We just met a man named Dacus. He told my husband to go to Solsbury Hill on Thursday, when there will be a full moon . . .'

Trotman grimaced. 'Dacus has not been in his right mind since Reginald died. Savaric was wrong to have made him Master of the Hospital.'

'He did it because he thought the responsibility might help Dacus regain his wits,' explained Walter defensively. Then he sighed ruefully. 'Although it does not seem to be working.'

'Did Dacus tell you that spending a night on Solsbury will prove your virtue?' asked Trotman, adding when Gwenllian nodded, 'Then do not take the challenge lightly. If you go in an irreverent frame of mind, you will die. Seraphim do not approve of levity.'

The Angel was a pleasant inn that smelled of burning pine cones and fresh rushes. Gwenllian was allocated a chamber that was clean, warm and inviting. Hot water was available for washing, along with a meal of bread and roasted meat.

She was exhausted, but refused to sleep until Cole returned. He was quite capable of looking after himself, but her anxiety still increased as the night wore on, and she was near to panic by midnight, when he eventually appeared.

'Where have you been?' she demanded angrily. 'I have been worried!'

'There was no need.' He went to kneel by the fire; its faint light showed him to be wet, scratched and muddy.

She narrowed her eyes. 'What have you been doing, to get so bedraggled?'

'I went to Solsbury Hill. But it was devoid of wolves.'

'Of course it was! Even if one is in the area, it will not frequent the place regularly, or people would kill it.' Gwenllian regarded him coolly. 'Or was it a different kind of wolf you were hoping to meet? Dacus, for example?'

Cole winced that she should read him so easily. 'I thought he might appear, after tempting me there with all those remarks about the danger.'

'I think they were intended to frighten, not entice you! Besides, he suggested you go on Thursday, when the moon is full – presumably so he can see what he is doing as he kills you.'

Cole began to remove his sodden boots. 'He has had his chance. I am not climbing up there again. It was not a comfortable jaunt, especially in the rain.'

'Did you learn anything that might tell us what happened to Prior Hugh?'

Cole nodded. 'The same thing that happened to Adam: Dacus lured him up there, then set some savage beast on him.'

'And why would Dacus do that?' asked Gwenllian tiredly.

'Presumably because he had decided that they were evil. We both heard him say so.'

'We shall bear it in mind – but not to the point where we are blind to other possibilities.'

'There are no other possibilities. I *know* Dacus killed Adam, which means he killed Hugh, too. All you need to do is prove it.'

'I shall do my best,' said Gwenllian wearily. 'However, there are other suspects. Walter, who succeeded Hugh as prior, is Savaric's creature – perhaps they conspired to be rid of an awkward customer. Meanwhile, Brother Robert is nauseatingly pious, and I am always wary of such men. Then there is Reginald to consider.'

'He died years ago,' said Cole, startled. 'He cannot be a suspect.'

'I meant we cannot overlook the possibility that Dacus is right, and *he* was murdered, too,' explained Gwenllian patiently. 'Which means we have three odd deaths to investigate.'

'I disagree. The King mentioned neither Adam nor Reginald in his letter.'

'No,' agreed Gwenllian acidly. 'Although I imagine he has certainly heard the rumours of foul play. But let John play his sly games – he will not best us.'

'We had better pay our respects to the bishop this morning,' said Gwenllian, after a breakfast of smoked pork, eggs and dried fruit. 'We do not want to offend him by delaying.'

'Very well,' said Cole unenthusiastically. He rarely enjoyed the company of senior clerics, mostly because they tended to be deficient in their knowledge of horses and dogs.

The Bishop's Palace was an elegantly appointed mansion in the southern quarter of the abbey precinct, which boasted windows of real glass. There were also arrow slits in the walls, and a crenellated roof. Cole surveyed it with a professional eye.

'It is better defended than Carmarthen Castle! I could hold out for months here.'

Gwenllian was less impressed. 'So Savaric feels the need for defence. I wonder what he does that makes him unpopular.'

They were ushered into a solar, where two knights were waiting, both wearing leather leggings and mail tunics. Gwenllian could not suppress a shudder when her eyes met those of the first. They were pale green, like a serpent's, and she did not think she had ever seen a colder expression. He was Cole's height, but thinner. His companion was a giant, with the blankly stupid expression of a man who followed orders without question. Instinctively, she sensed that neither was a man to be crossed.

'Carmarthen's castellan,' said Reptile Eyes, treating Cole to a smile that was far from friendly. 'Why have you brought your wife? Do you plan to be here a while?'

'As long as it takes,' replied Cole evenly, although

Gwenllian bristled at the man's tone. 'We will not leave without seeing a murderer brought to justice.'

The pair exchanged glances that were easy to read: alarm. Gwenllian wondered why.

'I see.' Reptile Eyes cleared his throat. 'I am Sir Osmun d'Avranches, and my companion is Sir Fevil. We had the honour of escorting King Richard to Acre on the last Crusade, where we played a vital part in breaking the siege. Now we are advisers to Bishop Savaric.'

'Advisers?' Gwenllian wondered what kind of advice these brutes could offer a prelate.

'He values our opinions,' elaborated Osmun, while behind him Fevil scowled, sensing an insult in the question, but not quite sure what to do about it.

'I was at the Siege of Acre, too,' said Cole. 'Did you see the red and white striped walls?'

'Of course,' replied Osmun. 'They are very fine. But we had better save our reminiscing for when the bishop is not waiting. We shall take you to him.'

'Tell us what you know of Hugh's death,' said Cole, as they walked along corridors that told them the Bishop's Palace was large as well as elegant. 'And Adam's.'

'Why?' asked Osmun suspiciously.

'Because we respect the views of knights who advise the bishop,' lied Gwenllian. She favoured him with a disarming smile, although it was not easy to simper at such a man.

Osmun was flattered. 'Then you shall have them. There is a rumour that Hugh and Adam were savaged by an animal, but Fevil and I do not believe it – there are no wolves in Bath. It is our contention that they fell, and caught their necks against jagged rocks.'

'What, both of them?' asked Gwenllian incredulously.

'Yes, both of them,' replied Osmun smoothly.

'We have been told that a seraph is the culprit,' said Cole.

Osmun laughed. 'I doubt they were wicked enough to warrant the attentions of seraphim. When others fail Solsbury's test, they are just sent home screaming, not harmed physically.'

'Do many folk accept this challenge, then?' asked Cole.

Osmun smirked. 'Yes, but few pass. Fevil and I did, though. We took it when we first arrived, and our success means we are courageous, true and bold.'

Gwenllian decided to reserve judgement on that. 'Did you see the bodies?'

Both men nodded, although it was Osmun who answered again, and Gwenllian began to wonder whether Fevil was capable of forming a sentence.

'Their throats were terribly mangled – they must have rolled a long way. But necks are vulnerable. I know, because I usually aim for them when I dispatch my enemies.'

The smile he gave Cole made Gwenllian shudder. 'Where were you when these men died?' she asked.

Osmun's grin did not falter. 'Playing dice together, on both occasions.'

At that point, he and Fevil were distracted by a messenger from the King. The exchange that followed told Gwenllian that monarch and bishop were in regular contact, which confirmed what Trotman had said: they were allies. She would indeed need to be careful when dealing with Savaric.

'They were not at Acre,' whispered Cole.

'How do you know?' she whispered back.

'Because Constantinople has striped walls, not Acre. And any real crusader knows it.'

'What made you want to catch them out?'

'You told me not to trust anyone, so I decided to test their truthfulness. They are liars, Gwen, and we should not believe them when they say Adam and Hugh fell.'

'I agree. Osmun and Fevil are suspects, as far as I am concerned.'

'I suppose they *might* have helped Dacus.' Cole shrugged at her exasperation. 'I *am* keeping an open mind, Gwen. I am quite happy to believe that Dacus had accomplices.'

The bishop was in a magnificent hall, which was decked out in hangings of purple and red. He was a handsome man, with dark eyes, smooth olive skin and silver hair, and when he stood to greet his guests, he moved with a haughty grace.

'I am afraid you have had a wasted journey,' he said. 'Poor Hugh wandered up Solsbury Hill in the dark, and his death was an accident. There is no mystery to solve.'

'Your monks do not think so,' said Cole. 'Two of them told my wife that Hugh was murdered. So was Adam, for that matter, and he was my friend.'

Savaric's lips compressed into a hard, thin line, and Gwenllian glimpsed ruthlessness behind the suave exterior. 'Then they are mistaken.'

'We have also been told that these deaths were acts of God,' added Gwenllian.

'Now that *is* possible,' nodded Savaric. 'I liked Adam, but he was vain about his medical skills, while Hugh was dour and sanctimonious. The Almighty may well have decided to provide me with an opportunity to appoint better men.'

'Dacus is not better than Adam,' declared Cole indignantly.

Savaric regarded him silently for a moment. 'Perhaps "better" was the wrong word to have used, when what I meant was "different". As I said, I liked Adam.'

'Do you like Dacus?' asked Cole, a little dangerously.

'Not particularly. But he is a good *medicus*, and he was a devoted chaplain to Reginald – my cousin. He was mad with grief after Reginald's death, but he is well again now.'

'But you believe Walter is a better man than Hugh?' asked Gwenllian, thinking that Dacus must have been raving indeed, if he was now considered to have recovered.

'Without question. Bath is a much happier place now. It will be happier still when the business involving Glastonbury is resolved, and its monks accept *me* as their rightful ruler. But what do you intend to do here, Sir Symon? Or will you take my word that nothing untoward has happened, and leave us in peace?'

'Is that what you would like us to do?' asked Gwenllian probingly.

Savaric continued to address Cole, dismissing her as of no importance. 'Tell the King the truth: Hugh had an accident. I am sure we can find a little something to make your journey home more agreeable.'

Cole gaped at him. 'Are you trying to bribe me?'

Savaric looked pained, clearly unused to dealing with plain-speaking men. 'I am suggesting ways in which your commission can be discharged to our mutual advantage. The King will be delighted to learn that Hugh's death was unavoidable, and I always aim to please him. I assume you are similarly loyal?'

Cole hesitated, not sure how to answer without condemning himself.

Gwenllian came to his rescue. 'We shall do what is appropriate.'

Savaric frowned at the ambiguity of her response. 'Keep me apprised of your progress, then. However, do not forget that Bath is a holy place, and *I* am the favoured recipient of a miracle. Have you heard about my crosier? Here it is – I always keep it in this hall.'

The staff was unexpectedly plain to be the property of so vain and grand a man, although there were three large jewels in its handle. Gwenllian inspected them.

'But they are only glass,' she blurted in surprise.

Savaric nodded. 'It belonged to Reginald, and he was a man of simple tastes. I was appalled and shocked when it dis-appeared.'

'Was it stolen?' asked Cole.

'Possibly. All I can tell you is that it was here one day, and gone the next. But I prayed to Reginald for its safe return, and it appeared on the high altar the following morning.'

'Did it now?' murmured Gwenllian sceptically.

'It was the first miracle of many,' Savaric went on happily. 'Pilgrims pay a fortune to pray at his tomb now.'

'Your knights claim to have had their virtue proved on Solsbury Hill,' began Cole. 'Do you think Adam and Hugh were—'

Savaric snorted his disdain. 'Superstitious nonsense! My monks are always clamouring at me to be tested – especially that pious Robert – but I am not a man for grubbing about in the dark. Besides, I have no wish to see seraphim. I do not like the sound of them at all.'

'What about wolves?' asked Cole.

'Not those, either. However—' At this point, Savaric was interrupted by a commotion outside. He closed his eyes wearily. 'Will that damned villain never leave me in peace?'

The 'damned villain' entered the hall in a flurry of snarling words and jabbing elbows. Osmun and Fevil tried to stop him, but – although only half their size – he simply put his head down and battered his way past them. The newcomer was a Benedictine, and he was quivering with rage, small fists clenched at his sides.

'This is William Pica,' explained Savaric heavily. 'From Glastonbury.'

'*Abbot* Pica,' spat Pica. 'Legally elected. You have stolen my title, but you will not keep it. I shall travel to Rome, and the new Pope will condemn your vile behaviour. You only want Glastonbury because we have King Arthur's bones, and they are proving to be lucrative.'

'Nonsense! It makes good administrative sense for Glastonbury and Bath to be united,' argued Savaric. 'Besides, Reginald wanted me to join the abbeys. He said so on his deathbed.'

'Lies!' screeched Pica. 'I was with him – and he did not sully his lips with *your* name.'

'And was that because he was poisoned, so could not speak?' demanded Savaric, suave demeanour evaporating. 'There are tales that say he did not die a natural death, and I have not forgotten that *you* were present. I have not forgotten that you happened to be in Bath when Hugh and Adam perished, either. You claim you were asleep, but you cannot prove it.'

Pica turned purple with rage, and while he spluttered incoherently, Gwenllian addressed the bishop.

'You just told us that those three deaths were not suspicious. Yet now you accuse Pica of being complicit in them?'

'Forgive me,' said Savaric shortly, taking a deep breath to compose himself. 'Pica always goads me into saying things I do not mean.'

'Is that so?' shrieked Pica. 'Because I suspect *you* of killing them. One of your minions poisoned Reginald, while you have no alibi for when Adam and Hugh died, either.'

'Yes, I do,' snapped Savaric. 'I was praying. God is my witness.'

'Then tell Him to say so to the King's officer,' snarled Pica, waving a hand at Cole, who looked alarmed by the prospect. 'Ask for a divine sign.'

'There has already been one,' argued Savaric, becoming angry again. 'My crosier would not have been returned to me if I did not own God's favour.'

Pica was evidently unwilling to argue with this, because he changed the subject. 'Then tell the King's officer what Hugh was doing when he died. Let us see what he makes of *that*.'

Savaric sighed as he addressed Cole. 'Hugh thought there was something odd about the deaths of Reginald and Adam, and had been pondering and asking questions—'

'He was investigating their murders,' interrupted Pica harshly. 'Personally, I suspect he learned something that implicated Savaric, but was killed before he could make his findings public. It is a pity he did not write anything down.'

'Do either of you know why Hugh went to Solsbury Hill?' asked Cole. 'Was it to be tested for—'

'Hugh was not a fool,' snapped Pica. 'Only saintly men, like me, dare take that challenge. He would not have risked it, and neither would Adam. Savaric has never tried it, of course.'

'The test is a lot of nonsense,' said Savaric, flushing angrily. 'Moreover, Reginald died of a fever, and Hugh and Adam had accidents. And anyone who disagrees with me is a fool.'

There was no more to be learned at the Bishop's Palace, so Gwenllian and Cole spent the rest of the morning and much of the afternoon talking to Bath's monks, lay brothers and servants. These numbered more than two hundred people, but Gwenllian had not questioned a third of them before Cole decided he had had enough.

'We cannot stop yet, *cariad*,' she said reproachfully. 'We do not have any answers.'

'We have the only answer we need: that Dacus murdered Reginald, Adam and Hugh. And tomorrow, we shall confront him with the evidence.'

'What evidence?' asked Gwenllian, exasperated. 'However, we may learn something useful if we speak to the man who found Adam and Hugh's bodies.'

'A lay brother named Eldred,' mused Cole. 'I suppose we could interview him today, although it is tedious work, and I would rather tend my horse.'

'It will not take long. And the sooner we have answers, the sooner we can go home.'

Enquiries revealed that Eldred was collecting tolls on one of the city gates.

'Yes, I found Hugh and Adam,' he nodded. '*And* I was in Reginald's retinue when he died. Now there was a sad day. Personally, I suspect Savaric had him poisoned, because he was jealous of his goodness.'

'On what grounds do you make such an accusation?' asked Gwenllian. 'Did you see one of Savaric's minions administer a toxin? Or overhear a confession by the killer?'

'Well, no,' admitted Eldred. 'But Savaric would not have hired a fool for such a task. He would have chosen a villain who knew how to be careful.'

Gwenllian supposed that was true, but even so, she was inclined to dismiss the testimony as yet more gossipy speculation. Cole was thoughtful, though.

'A number of people accompanied Reginald on his fatal journey to Canterbury – Dacus as his chaplain, Fevil, Pica, Robert, the two canons from Wells, you ...'

Eldred nodded. 'And any one of them might have killed

Reginald on Savaric's orders. Except Dacus. He loved Reginald dearly.'

'What about Prior Hugh?' asked Gwenllian, frustrated that the lay brother's testimony was so light on facts, and heavy on unfounded opinion. 'What happened to him?'

'He had been sitting in the cloister all afternoon, fretting about the deaths of Adam and Reginald. So Robert suggested he go to Solsbury Hill, to look for evidence of foul play. Robert also offered to take vespers for him, which was nice.'

'Robert did?' asked Cole, exchanging a glance with Gwenllian. Was this evidence of a victim being manoeuvred into a desired location?

Eldred nodded. 'Prior Hugh stopped by this gate for a moment, to chat with me, then he went on his way. Walter was here, too.'

'What did Hugh say?' asked Cole.

'He asked about Adam. I said I thought a wolf had killed him, although Walter disagreed, and repeated the bishop's theory about an accident. But Hugh did not believe that nonsense – he was not stupid. And Adam's wounds were *not* caused by falling on sharp stones. They were made by teeth. Wolf's teeth.'

'How do you know it was not a dog?' asked Cole.

'I just do,' replied Eldred firmly. 'And the same beast killed Hugh, because there cannot be two such creatures in the area.'

Gwenllian regarded him sceptically. 'Are you not afraid to be out here, then?'

'I am safe enough in daylight. But there is a full moon the day after tomorrow, and wild horses will not drag me outside the abbey then.'

*

Cole and Gwenllian argued about what they had learned as they walked back to the Angel. He was of the opinion that Dacus had trained an animal to kill. She believed the injuries could have been made by a weapon, and felt Savaric and his henchmen, the smugly pious Robert, Walter and the belligerent Pica made far more convincing suspects.

'I *know* dogs,' Cole insisted. 'And I have Dacus' measure, too. I am right, Gwen.'

'But Bath is a small town. How could Dacus keep such a beast hidden? Someone would see it, and the game would be over.'

He had no answer, and they walked the rest of the way in silence. A group of minstrels was singing near the abbey gates, and it was apparently an unusual event, because a crowd had gathered to listen. It included all their suspects. Frustrated by their lack of progress, Cole advanced on Bishop Savaric before Gwenllian could stop him.

'Hugh's throat was torn out,' he said bluntly. 'So was Adam's. Yet you claim their deaths were accidental. Surely, you must see that is unlikely?'

'Unlikely, but not impossible,' replied Savaric curtly. 'Besides, there are no wolves in Bath. You are wasting your time here, and I strongly advise you to leave the matter alone.'

'You heard him,' said Osmun, coming to loom menacingly. Fevil did the same, crowding forward in an effort to intimidate. Cole turned on him.

'You accompanied Reginald to Canterbury, but you did not protect him from—'

'How could he protect Reginald from a fever?' sneered Osmun, interposing himself between them. 'And it *was* a fever, not poison, before you make any unfounded accusations.'

'We have already discussed this,' said Savaric quickly, as hands dropped to the hilts of swords. 'But I will repeat it. There is nothing suspicious about the deaths of Reginald, Adam or Hugh, no matter what the gossips tell you.'

Cole stared at him for a moment, then stalked towards a gaggle of clerics that included Robert, Walter, Pica, Trotman and Lechlade. Savaric rolled his eyes when he saw his assurances had not been believed, and Osmun and Fevil exchanged furious glances. Gwenllian stifled a sigh. Antagonising men who might be murderers was reckless, and she wished her husband would leave the talking to her.

'You told Hugh to climb Solsbury Hill,' Cole said, homing in on Robert. 'Why?'

The sacrist jumped at the irate voice behind him, but quickly regained his composure. 'Because he had spent the day agonising over Adam and Reginald. I suggested a walk to clear his head. Unfortunately, someone – or something – was waiting for him.'

'Seraphim,' nodded Trotman, pig-like face earnest. 'With sharp claws.'

'Nonsense,' declared Pica. 'Savaric killed them, just as he killed Reginald. He never saw eye to eye with Hugh, while Adam's virtue put him in a bad light. He – or his henchmen – dispatched all three.'

'No,' said Robert quietly. 'Reginald died of a fever. However, Adam and Hugh *were* murdered, although I cannot believe the bishop did it. It must be someone else.'

'Dacus?' asked Cole, looking to where the master of the hospital stood with his patients. He was solicitously gentle with them, wholly different from the man who had broken the news of Adam's death with such calculated cruelty.

'Definitely not Dacus,' said Robert. 'He speaks hotly, but

there is no harm in him. If he has offended you, ignore it. He cannot help his untamed tongue.'

'There *is* harm in him – he is responsible for the rumour that Reginald was murdered,' countered Trotman. 'He has never accepted that Reginald died of natural causes.'

'His claims are a nuisance,' agreed Walter. 'And I wish he would not waylay strangers and challenge them to visit Solsbury on a full moon, either. It creates a bad first impression of our town. But his virtues outweigh his faults. Look at how his patients love him.'

They turned, and even Cole was forced to acknowledge that Dacus had a way with his charges. They jostled for his attention, and the affection they felt was clear in their faces. Cole watched for a while, then turned to leave, but Walter caught his sleeve.

'Listen to Savaric,' he whispered. 'The King ordered you here because he had to appoint someone to assess what happened to Prior Hugh, but he is not interested in the truth. All he wants is a verdict of accidental death, so he can put the matter from his mind.'

Cole freed his arm. 'What are you saying? That Hugh *was* murdered?'

Walter grimaced. 'No! It was an accident, as I have already told you. I merely suggest that you give John what he wants. No good will come of doing otherwise – not for you, and not for Bath, either.'

Cole watched him slink away, then turned to Gwenllian. 'When I hear remarks like that, it makes me even more determined to uncover what really happened.'

'We have a number of suspects for these murders,' said Gwenllian as they sat in their room at the Angel that night. It was late, because Cole had been trawling the taverns for information, although with scant success. 'And Adam and Hugh *were* murdered, no matter what else we are told. I am not sure what to think about Reginald, though.'

'I have one suspect,' said Cole. 'Dacus.'

'Dacus is on the list,' said Gwenllian, more to humour him than because she believed it. 'So is Savaric. He does not want us here, and maintains, suspiciously, that Hugh and Adam had accidents. He also benefited from Reginald's will. I doubt he killed anyone himself, but he may have ordered Osmun and Fevil to do it. They claim to have been dicing together when Hugh and Adam died, which is no alibi at all.'

'Dacus may have enlisted them as accomplices,' conceded Cole. 'Or Pica, who claims to have been sleeping when Adam and Hugh were killed. Moreover, Pica was also in Reginald's retinue on that fateful journey to Canterbury.'

Gwenllian nodded. 'Pica wants to be Abbot of Glastonbury, and it would not be the first time an ambitious man has killed to achieve his objective. I am suspicious of Robert, too. He was the one who told Hugh to walk up Solsbury Hill – an excursion that cost the prior his life.'

'But if Robert were guilty, he would not be insisting that Adam and Hugh were murdered,' Cole pointed out. 'He would be saying it was an accident or seraphim, like everyone else. Moreover, I am under the impression that he suspects Walter of the crime.'

'Walter is a strong contender,' acknowledged Gwenllian. 'His grief for Hugh is insincere, he is Savaric's toady, and he was made prior the moment Hugh died. He has plenty of reasons to kill, but no reliable alibi—'

Suddenly, Cole leaped to his feet, grabbed his sword and kicked over the lantern, plunging the room into inky darkness. An instant later, the door flew open and an arrow thudded into the mattress. Instinctively, Gwenllian dived for safety beneath the bed.

There followed the sounds of a clumsy skirmish – swords whipping through the air, mostly failing to connect but occasionally resulting in a clash or a grunt, and muttered curses. There was another sound, too: a deep, guttural growl. Had the invaders brought an animal? Gwenllian's blood ran cold at the notion.

'Kill him quickly!' came a furious hiss. 'You are making too much noise.'

Gwenllian tried to identify the voice, but she had never been good at recognising whispers. Sparks flew when a sword struck the stone wall. Then she heard a cudgel land with a sickening thud, and Cole gasped in pain. A second blow followed, and she sensed his assailants home in on the sound. Unwilling to cower while he was battered to death, she began to scream as loudly as she could.

'Silence her!' came the frantic voice.

Gwenllian kept yelling, punching away the hands that tried to lay hold of her. Then footsteps hammered on the stairs. Rescue! A sudden draught told her a window had been opened. The hands withdrew, and she scrambled from under the bed just in time to see three shadows jostling with each other to make their escape.

Cole struggled to his feet and started to follow, but reeled dizzily. Iefan jerked him back before he could tumble out.

'You cannot fight with a broken sword,' the sergeant said gruffly. 'I will go.'

Cole glanced at the weapon in his hand, and swore when he saw the tip of the blade had sheared off. He sat on the bed, hand to his side, and smiled wanly at Gwenllian.

'I thought I was dead once they had knocked me down, but your howls drove them off.'

Gwenllian inspected his ribs. The cudgel's imprints were etched clearly into his skin, long red marks already darkening into bruises. There were lacerations at one end, too, where she assumed sharp objects had been hammered into it, to render it more deadly.

Eventually, Iefan returned to report that their attackers had escaped him. Tracking was difficult at night, and the culprits knew the city better than he. Then the landlord arrived, all horrified concern. Nothing like it had ever happened before, he told them; Gwenllian was sure he was telling the truth. He refused to leave until he was sure they believed him, so it was some time before she and Cole were alone again.

'It was too dark to see, but they had an animal,' she said. 'I heard snarls . . .'

'A dog,' nodded Cole. 'I heard it, too. And they were professional warriors – I could tell by the way they fought.'

'Osmun and Fevil? Or soldiers hired by someone else? Regardless, it tells us that someone does not want us asking questions.'

Gwenllian dozed fitfully for the rest of the night, while Cole declined to sleep at all; he stood guard by the door, honing a dagger to keep himself awake. As soon as it was light, they went to find a smith who could mend his sword.

They were directed to a man who had set up business by one of the springs, the stench of hot metal vying with the sulphurous odour of steaming water. He was chewing a stick of dried meat, which he was evidently in the habit of sharing with local dogs, because a pack had gathered by his door. Gwenllian gave them a wide berth, but Cole stopped to pet a couple; they swarmed around him, tails wagging.

Once the smith had assured Cole that the sword would be

repaired by the following day, they left for the abbey. Gwenllian wanted to see Reginald's grave, although Cole grumbled that they would be better off confronting Dacus.

The tomb was a simple one, near the high altar, and was surrounded by pilgrims. Robert detached himself from the throng, and came to greet them.

'The miracles started here two months ago,' he said proudly. 'Beginning with the return of Savaric's crosier.'

'But Reginald has been dead for eight years,' said Gwenllian. 'Why the delay?'

'Who knows the minds of the saints?' Robert turned his gaze heavenward.

'Perhaps these miracles should be attributed to Adam, not Reginald,' suggested Cole. 'They coincide with *his* murder, after all.'

Robert's beatific expression slipped a little. 'I doubt Adam would have returned Savaric's crosier. He was generally sympathetic to thieves – he often tended them in his hospital.'

'Assuming the crosier was stolen in the first place,' muttered Gwenllian.

'What are you saying?' cried Robert, loudly enough to attract the attention of Walter, who was collecting coins from hopeful penitents. 'Of course it was stolen!'

'It was,' agreed Walter, coming to join them. 'And to suggest otherwise infers that Reginald's cult is based on deception.'

'Do either of you own a vicious dog?' asked Cole, changing the subject abruptly enough to make both monks blink their surprise.

'No, of course not!' replied Walter irritably. 'I do not allow fierce creatures in my abbey.'

'But Reginald kept hounds,' mused Robert. 'He had kennels built in the Prior's Garden. These days, we use them to store the urine we shall use for tanning leather this winter.'

'The wind blows the stench away from my house,' said Walter. Then he added with a grimace, 'Most of the time, at least. Would you like to see them? I can provide pomanders.'

'No, thank you,' said Gwenllian in distaste.

'As you wish,' said Walter. 'What prompted you to ask about dogs?'

'They probably think one was used to kill Adam and Hugh,' explained Robert. He turned back to Cole. 'Osmun and Fevil keep hounds – an entire pack of them.'

'I doubt *those* animals are responsible,' countered Walter. 'They are used for hunting.'

'Visit them, and decide for yourself,' said Robert slyly, ignoring his prior's immediate glare at the suggestion. Then he gave a small bow. 'But you must excuse me: I have religious duties to perform.'

He hurried back to the pilgrims, and Walter followed, apparently unwilling to be seen as less devout than his sacrist. After a moment, Cole went to kneel at the tomb. When he had finished his prayers, Walter was ready with a bowl for his donation.

Cole took a deep, careful breath as they left the abbey, then winced. 'It still hurts,' he complained. 'And if you are not pregnant by the time we leave, I am getting my money back.'

Gwenllian regarded him askance. 'What did you—'

'Can we look for this dangerous dog now?' interrupted Cole impatiently. 'When we have it, we shall know our killer. We shall begin with Dacus, at the hospital.'

Dacus was supervising his elderly charges as they took the healing waters. They splashed and wallowed like children, and he smiled indulgently as he sat in a chair, a fat ginger cat in his lap. His contented expression evaporated when he saw Cole.

'The man who admits to befriending Evil Adam,' he sneered, standing abruptly. The cat hissed its disapproval as it was deposited on the floor. 'What do you want?'

'Do you own a dog?' asked Cole, manfully overlooking the slur on his friend.

'I prefer cats.' Dacus' eyes narrowed suddenly. 'Why? Is it because the wolf came after you last night, and you are eager to know who controls it?'

'How do you know what happened last night?' demanded Cole suspiciously.

'News travels fast in Bath. But there is no wolf here at the hospital. Try asking Osmun and Fevil – they like savage beasts. Savaric has one, too; Pica gave it to him.'

'Why would Pica give Savaric a gift?' asked Cole, bemused. 'They dislike each other.'

Dacus' voice took on the curious singsong quality he had used the first time they had met. It made him sound demented. 'It was a bribe, presented three months ago, to encourage Savaric to relinquish his claim on Glastonbury. It did not work, of course.'

'Pica gave Savaric a dog?'

'A big fierce one.' Dacus laughed suddenly. 'Do you think Savaric set it on you? He might have done. It is common knowledge that he does not want you here. But he should have waited until tomorrow.'

'Why?'

'Because dogs become wolves when the moon is full,' chanted Dacus. He poked Cole in the chest, a liberty few dared take with Norman warriors, which told Gwenllian for certain that he was fey-witted. 'Will you go to Solsbury tomorrow? Or are you as sinful as Adam, so fear to take the challenge?'

'He will not,' said Gwenllian, before Cole could reply for

himself. 'He does not believe these ridiculous tales of wolves, seraphim and full moons.'

Dacus regarded Cole with utter disdain. 'Coward!'

'We have the proof we need now,' said Cole, the moment he and Gwenllian were outside. 'Dacus denies owning a dog, but there were hairs all over his habit. Did you see them?'

'I saw a cat in his lap. I imagine those came from her.'

'No,' stated Cole emphatically. 'Cat hairs and dog hairs are not the same.'

Gwenllian doubted he could tell the difference. 'Do you really think a cat would stay if a savage dog was at large?' she asked, trying to keep the impatience from her voice.

'Clearly, he keeps it tethered. I shall break into the hospital after dark tonight, and look for it.'

'No! If you are caught committing burglary, the King will use it as an excuse to seize Carmarthen. Besides, we should inspect the dogs owned by Savaric, Osmun and Fevil, first.'

'To eliminate them, thus reinforcing our case against Dacus,' nodded Cole. 'Good idea.'

Although Gwenllian was used to her husband's occasionally stubborn moods, she wished he had not chosen to indulge in one when so much was at stake. It meant she was effectively investigating alone, and she was silent as they walked, hoping he would sense her irritation and adopt a more reasonable attitude. Unfortunately, he did not seem to notice.

Pica was in Savaric's hall when they arrived. He was apoplectic with rage, and Osmun and Fevil had unsheathed their swords.

'How dare you?' he was howling. 'You cannot excommunicate me! I am Abbot Elect.'

'Your election was unlawful – the King says so,' said Savaric. 'And I would not have to excommunicate you had you shown a shred of restraint. But you strut about the city making disparaging remarks about me.'

Without further ado, he began reading the words that would banish Pica from the Church. Pica surged forward, his face dangerously red, but all he did was wag a shaking finger in Savaric's face before storming out.

'There,' said Savaric, closing the book in satisfaction. 'Let us see how he likes *that*. But what can I do for you, Sir Symon? Or are you here to tell me that you are going home?'

'I want to see your dogs,' said Cole bluntly.

Savaric blinked. 'I do not have any. All dogs in the Bishop's Palace belong to Osmun or Fevil. You may view those, if you wish.'

He led the way to a yard, where two outbuildings had been given over to the care of hounds. Fevil opened the door to the first, and Cole immediately forgot that he was meant to be looking for one that killed people, and waded among them in delight, calling compliments to their owners. His praise was effusive enough to make even the sour Fevil smile. Savaric watched in disdain.

'I cannot abide dogs,' he said to Gwenllian. 'All they do is eat, bark, bite and shove their noses in embarrassing places.'

Gwenllian suspected that might be true of Osmun and Fevil's collection; they seemed an unappealing pack to her.

'These are all we have,' said Osmun quickly, when Cole started to move towards the second shed. 'Look at these pups. Their dam is that brindled bitch in the corner.'

While Cole was distracted, Gwenllian turned back to Savaric. 'Which one is Pica's gift?'

'That thing is dead, thank God! Osmun, tell the good lady what you did with that vicious beast Pica had the temerity to press on me. That grey creation with the nasty yellow teeth.'

'Fevil slit its throat, and we served it to Pica in a pie.' Osmun's reptilian gaze was bland, so Gwenllian had no idea whether he was telling the truth.

There was no more to be learned, so she indicated it was time to leave.

'That was a waste of time,' she said in disgust, once they were outside. 'I have no idea whether the animal Pica gave Savaric is dead or alive, while you were more interested in admiring the quality of their breeding bitches than in assessing whether any were killers.'

'I *did* assess them – none is savage. However, Osmun offered me a pup if we left Bath today. The fact that he tried to bribe me says he has something to hide.'

'Yes,' agreed Gwenllian. 'But what?'

They decided to visit Pica next. They found him near the Chapter House, braying his fury to Walter and Robert about his treatment at Savaric's hands.

'It is your fault!' he raged, stabbing a finger at Cole. 'Savaric says he has no time for my complaints, because he is busy with you. It is *your* fault he excommunicated me.'

'He excommunicated you because you rail at him,' countered Cole shortly. 'Besides we have spent very little time in his company since we arrived. He is fobbing you off with excuses.'

'I am sure he will lift the interdict if you ask nicely,' said Robert soothingly.

'Offer him a little something to gain his favour,' suggested Walter. 'But make sure you say it is for the abbey. If you imply it is for him personally, the price will go up.'

Cole laughed, although Walter had apparently not intended to be amusing, because he looked too startled.

'We are here to ask about another bribe, as it happens,' Cole said. 'A dog.'

'I presented one to him three months ago.' Pica scowled. 'It cost me a fortune, but the gesture did nothing to make him more kindly disposed towards me. I should have kept it myself, because it was a lovely creature.'

'We were told it was savage,' said Cole. 'Did you give it to him in the hope that he would be bitten?'

'No,' said Pica, in a way that told even Cole, who tended to take such remarks at face value, that he was lying.

'Then did you eat a pie with him not long afterwards?'

'I do not recall,' replied Pica, frowning his puzzlement. 'What a peculiar thing to ask!'

'Have you seen the dog recently?'

Pica glared. 'No, and I resent all these questions. What are you going to do about this excommunication? You must abandon your enquiries and intervene. In the King's name!'

'Meddle, and you will be sorry,' warned Walter. 'It is none of your concern.'

'I disagree,' said Robert softly. 'No bishop should excommunicate someone over a private quarrel. Sir Symon *should* postpone his investigation, and attend to this matter.'

He and Walter began to argue, Pica interrupting angrily every few words. Gwenllian and Cole took the opportunity to slip away.

'Savaric, Pica and Robert urge us to abandon our enquiries, Osmun offers you a new dog, and Walter threatens us,' she mused. 'I wonder what inferences we can draw from that.'

Cole had no answer. As they still had monks to interview, Gwenllian suggested returning to the abbey. Cole yawned hugely, weary after two nights of interrupted sleep, so she suggested he go back to the Angel, to rest.

'And I mean rest. That does not entail confronting Dacus.'

'I will attend Mass,' he said, using the airy tone that told her he was lying. 'But the abbey is too noisy, so I will go to St Michael's instead.'

As St Michael's was near where his horse was stabled, Gwenllian suspected he intended to spend time with it, but did not want her to think he was leaving her to do all the work. As it happened, she did not mind: the monks were more likely to confide in her without a bored knight looming over them.

Just before they parted ways, Trotman intercepted them, to express his shock over what had happened the previous night.

'Perhaps you will join me in a prayer of thanks for your deliverance,' the canon said. 'I am going to meet Pica in the abbey, and you are welcome to join us. Ah! Here he is now.'

'My husband has made arrangements to visit St Michael's instead,' said Gwenllian, before Cole could respond with a more pithily worded refusal. 'He will—'

'Good,' said Pica unpleasantly. 'Let us hope God tells him to ditch his stupid enquiries about Hugh, and take up *my* cause instead.'

It was dark by the time Gwenllian had finished. Iefan was waiting to escort her back to the inn, and they were just passing St Michael's when they heard a commotion. They joined a crowd of people hurrying to see what was amiss.

Lechlade was lying on the ground, dead from a wound near the groin.

Those in authority did not take long to arrive. Walter was first. He had brought a lantern, and Gwenllian looked away when she saw the amount of blood that had been spilled. Next came Trotman, Robert at his side. Trotman dropped to his knees and began to weep when he saw his friend's corpse, and Robert laid a comforting hand on his shoulder. Then the bishop appeared, his henchman-knights slouching behind him.

Cole arrived, holding the tool he used for paring hoofs. Dacus was not far behind, and Gwenllian realised the stables were near the hospital; Cole might have been tending his horse, but he had also been monitoring the man he considered a villain.

'Lechlade was killed with a sword,' Cole said, kneeling next to the body. As a soldier, he was familiar with such injuries and well qualified to judge.

'Who would do such a thing?' wailed Trotman. 'And why did Lechlade not fight back? He always carried a dagger and a mace when away from Wells.'

'He must have been taken by surprise,' replied Cole. 'His weapons are still in his belt.'

'A knight did it,' stated Osmun. 'Who else wears a sword? Fevil and I have been with the bishop all afternoon, so we are not responsible. It is *another* knight.'

His reptilian gaze settled on Cole, and Gwenllian's stomach lurched. Was this how they would thwart the investigation, given that cajolery, bribes and threats had not worked?

'No!' said Trotman unsteadily. 'Sir Symon has been in St Michael's, attending Mass.'

'And where are we now?' demanded Walter archly. 'Outside St Michael's! Obviously, he said his prayers first, and murdered Lechlade afterwards.'

Gwenllian watched in horror as Osmun and Fevil drew their swords. Cole started to do the same, but his scabbard was empty.

'Symon cannot be the culprit,' she said, seizing in relief the way to exonerate him. 'His blade was broken in last night's attack, and it is with the smith. You can see he is unarmed.'

'Then he used another one,' snapped Osmun. 'There are plenty available in Bath.'

'But you just said only knights wear swords,' said Robert. 'You cannot have it both—'

'Arrest him,' chanted Dacus. He began to dance in small circles. 'He is an evil killer, who refuses to face the wolf on Solsbury Hill. Throw him in prison! Hang him in chains!'

'What is going on?' came an imperious voice. It was Pica. He stopped dead in his tracks when he saw Lechlade, and his hands flew to his mouth. 'God save us! What happened?'

'A knight has murdered Lechlade,' explained Trotman brokenly. 'But Sir Symon's sword is broken, which means Savaric's henchmen—'

'Now just a moment,' began Savaric. 'My advisers have no reason to harm Lechlade. Besides, they have an alibi in me, whereas Cole has been alone in the stables.'

'How do you know he was alone in the stables?' pounced Gwenllian. 'Have you been spying on him?'

'I may have ordered him monitored,' acknowledged Savaric reluctantly. 'For his own safety. He was almost killed last night, in case you had forgotten.'

'I had not,' said Gwenllian coldly. 'However, your confession is excellent news. Let this spy step forward. *He* will tell you Symon is innocent.'

'Fair enough,' said Savaric. He turned to Walter. 'Well? Speak.'

Walter grimaced that the bishop should so blithely reveal the demeaning way in which he had spent his afternoon, while Gwenllian experienced a pang of alarm. Walter was Savaric's toady. Would he tell the truth, or lie to curry his master's favour?

'Cole never left the stables,' Walter said eventually,

although it was clear he wished he could have reported something different. 'He did not murder Lechlade.'

'You might have mentioned it sooner,' sighed Savaric irritably. 'Osmun was on the verge of arresting him, and the King does not like his officers imprisoned without a decent pretext.'

'Arrest him anyway,' sang Dacus, then laughed wildly. 'He deserves it. He is evil, like Adam and Hugh. Throw him in the dungeons and lose the key.'

'I had better take Dacus home,' said Walter, clearly thankful for an excuse to be away from the bishop's admonishing glare. 'Incidents like this distress him.'

'He does not look distressed to me,' muttered Cole to Gwenllian, as the master of the hospital was ushered back to his domain. 'He looks vengeful.'

But Gwenllian was more interested in Walter. Had *he* abandoned his surveillance to go a-killing? But what reason could he have for stabbing Lechlade? When Walter and Dacus had gone, she turned her attention to the others who had gathered.

Savaric was angry, although it was unclear whether it was because another murder had been committed, or because Cole was still free to pursue his investigation. Meanwhile, Robert was comforting Trotman, but seemed distracted. Osmun and Fevil were impossible to read, and Gwenllian was disinclined to believe that they had been with the bishop. And Pica, white and shocked, was uncharacteristically subdued. Was guilt responsible for the change?

She sighed. Any of them might be the culprit.

There were no attacks that night, although Gwenllian slept poorly, despite the fact that Iefan was standing guard outside. She woke when it was still dark, and opened the window to

see the moon bright and clear in a cloudless sky. The next
night would see it full, and she recalled the challenge Dacus
had issued.

When she sensed dawn was near, she nudged her husband
awake. He snapped into instant wakefulness, and reached
for his sword, cursing softly when he found it was not there.

'We need to review what we have learned,' she said.
'Perhaps discussing it will see answers emerge.'

Cole looked as if he would rather go back to sleep, but
nodded acquiescence.

'We have four deaths,' she began. 'First, Reginald may
have been poisoned. His cousin Savaric is the obvious suspect, because he was a beneficiary of his will. Of course,
Walter, Robert, Pica and God knows how many others were
with him when he died. He was a good man, and miracles
have been occurring at his tomb, although only in the last
two months.'

'Which coincides with Adam's murder. *He* was a good
man, too.'

'Adam died second,' nodded Gwenllian. 'And Hugh third.
Both had their throats torn out on Solsbury Hill. Rumours
say they were savaged by a wolf, but some dogs look like
wolves, and they can be trained to kill.'

'They can. And that explanation makes a lot more sense
than seraphim.'

'So let us consider dogs. Pica gave one to Savaric, the
whereabouts of which is unknown to us; and Osmun and
Fevil have a pack of them, including some they declined to
show you.'

'Dacus will have one, too. There were hairs on his habit,
and his hospital has grounds and outhouses aplenty for concealing such an animal. If you had let me search them last
night, we would not be having this conversation.'

Gwenllian ignored him. 'As regards motive for killing Hugh, Walter is at the top of my list, because he was awarded Hugh's post. However, it was Robert who encouraged Hugh to walk up the hill in the first place. Then there is Savaric, who was at loggerheads with Hugh, and who has the dubious talents of Osmun and Fevil at his disposal.'

'What about their motive for killing Adam? He and Hugh died in identical manners, so I think we can assume a single culprit.' Cole looked triumphant when Gwenllian was unable to answer. 'Dacus hated Adam, and the moment he was dead, *he* became master of the hospital. And he does not have alibis, either.'

'He is barely sane,' said Gwenllian irritably. 'Do you really believe he is wily enough to commit murder and conceal the evidence?'

'Of course. He may not be clever, but he has an animal's cunning.'

There was no point arguing. 'Lechlade is the last victim, killed with a sword. Osmun said only a knight would use such a weapon, but then claimed they are readily available in Bath. If his second remark is true, then any of our suspects might be responsible. And so might Trotman, for that matter. He wept bitterly over the corpse, but perhaps it was an act.'

'No – his grief was sincere. But even if I am wrong, he would not have dispatched an ally from Wells, because it leaves him battling Savaric alone. And I do not believe Robert would be so callous as to comfort him if he was the killer, either.'

Gwenllian supposed he was right. 'So who do you think murdered Lechlade? And please do not say Dacus.'

'It was not Dacus,' said Cole, albeit reluctantly. 'I spent the afternoon watching him, and would have noticed. Walter did not do it, either – not if he was following me.'

'So, we have eliminated Dacus, Walter, Robert and Trotman. That leaves Pica, Savaric and the henchmen.'

'It was not Osmun or Fevil.' Cole feinted with an imaginary blade. 'The fatal blow was inflicted clumsily and awkwardly, not the work of a professional warrior.'

Gwenllian sighed. 'Then we can eliminate Savaric, too, because I do not think he would bloody his own hands. That leaves Pica.'

'He certainly has a temper. So is that the answer? Pica?'

Gwenllian nodded. 'We shall speak to him as soon as it is light.'

'Savaric will be delighted when we tell him Glastonbury's Abbot Elect is a killer.'

'Yes,' agreed Gwenllian soberly. 'He will.'

The sun was shining by the time they left the inn, and the only clouds were high and wispy. Unfortunately, the fine weather did nothing to ease Gwenllian's growing sense of disquiet, and her nervousness transmitted itself to Cole, who insisted on collecting his sword before tackling Pica. He was not pleased with the result: the blade was unbalanced and nowhere near sharp enough. There was a sly look in the smith's eye when he offered to make amends, and Gwenllian stared at him. Had he been paid to ensure Cole continued to be unarmed?

'Borrow Iefan's,' she whispered. 'I have a bad feeling about today.'

Cole did not question her, and it was not long before he was buckling his sergeant's weapon around his waist. As they left the inn a second time, they met Trotman.

'I am leaving today.' The canon's piggy eyes were red, as if he had spent the night crying. 'I must take the news of Lechlade's death to Wells. I wish you well in your investigation, but be careful what you tell the King. John is the kind of man to mangle words and use them to harm you later. Write your dispatches with care.'

Gwenllian stared after him, suspecting they had just been given some very sound advice, then she and Cole began to walk towards the abbey.

'Pica was with Reginald when he died,' Cole began tentatively. 'Do you think he killed him, as well as Lechlade?'

'It is possible, although poison seems too discreet a weapon for him . . .'

But the question had sparked the germ of an answer, and by the time they arrived, she had at least part of a solution. Pica's responses would determine the rest. They found the feisty little man in the abbey's guesthouse, pacing back and forth.

'What do you want?' he demanded. 'I have nothing to say to people who stood by and did nothing while Savaric excommunicated me.'

'But we have something to say to you,' said Gwenllian quietly. 'You stabbed Lechlade, although we know it was a mistake.'

'We do?' blurted Cole, startled.

Pica stared at Gwenllian. 'I did not stab Lechlade.'

'You did,' said Gwenllian in the same calm voice. Pica was volatile, and she did not want to precipitate an attack: it would not look good for Symon to engage in fisticuffs with senior clerics. 'You were angry because Savaric is using us as an excuse to postpone discussions—'

'Of course I am angry,' snarled Pica. 'But that does not make me Lechlade's killer.'

'Symon said he was going to St Michael's Church, but the truth was that he wanted to spend time with his horse. You waited until dark, and you struck the man who emerged. Unfortunately for you, it was someone else.'

81

'Pica wanted to kill me?' asked Cole, shocked.

'No,' said Pica, although his face was white. 'She cannot prove these nasty allegations.'

'I can. You see, you and Trotman were the only people who knew where Symon was going, and we know Trotman did not kill his friend. Then there was your horror when you saw Lechlade's body – your realisation that you had claimed the wrong victim.'

'No,' said Pica again, but unsteadily. 'I am not a fool, to attack a Norman warrior.'

'Which is why you waited until dark,' Gwenllian pressed on. 'To give yourself the advantage of surprise. Moreover, you held back until your victim left the church – good monk that you are, you did not want to spill blood on holy ground.'

'Lechlade's injury!' exclaimed Cole suddenly. 'I see how it happened now.'

He crouched, which made him Pica's height, and stabbed with Iefan's sword, using Gwenllian as his 'victim'. The wound he would have inflicted, had he been in earnest, was exactly where Lechlade had been struck.

'I would never . . .' stammered Pica. 'I do not . . .'

'Symon is following the King's orders, and you were going to murder him for it,' said Gwenllian coldly. 'Just to deprive Savaric of an excuse to procrastinate. As it is, you killed an innocent man instead.'

Pica closed his eyes. 'I did not mean to kill, only incapacitate. But surely, you understand? I cannot wait days until your investigation is complete, when every hour that passes sees Savaric grow more powerful, to Glastonbury's detriment. Something had to be done.'

'What about Reginald?' asked Cole. 'Did you murder him, too?

'Reginald was not poisoned, no matter what the gossips claim,' said Pica wretchedly. 'He died of a fever.'

'Then what about Hugh and Adam?' asked Gwenllian. 'They were killed by a dog that tore out their throats. And you gave Savaric a large grey animal – one that looked like a wolf.'

Pica stared at her. 'If that dog did attack Hugh and Adam, you cannot hold *me* responsible. Perhaps it was a little more savage than I led Savaric to believe, but Osmun and Fevil should have been able to control it. Besides, they told me yesterday that they had turned it into a pie weeks ago.'

'They said the same to us,' acknowledged Gwenllian. 'But we cannot be sure they were telling the truth.'

'If the creature is alive, then I know nothing about it,' stated Pica. 'I admit to stabbing Lechlade, but it was a mistake, and any court of law will see it.'

'A mistake because you were aiming to kill the King's officer?' asked Gwenllian icily.

'A mistake because Savaric fosters an atmosphere of fear and mistrust,' countered Pica, finally regaining his composure. 'Bath has an unsettled and dangerous feel, and I struck out in self-defence. That is what I shall say, and no one will be able to disprove it.'

'Pica is right, you know,' said Gwenllian, as she and Cole watched him escorted to the abbey cells. 'It was dark, and Lechlade was armed. No one can prove he did not act in self-defence.'

'Lechlade's weapons were still in his belt. Of course it was not self-defence!'

'I know that, but do not expect justice to be served for this particular crime. Royal pardons can be purchased, and Glastonbury is a wealthy foundation.'

'So is Wells. Trotman will want Lechlade avenged.'

'But Glastonbury has the revenues from King Arthur's bones. It is richer and stronger.'

'We could speak out – make sure the truth is known.'

'Then John will arrest you for questioning the judiciousness of his pardons, and will give Carmarthen to one of his cronies. It is better to stay silent.'

'Very well, but I will not look the other way while *Adam's* killer walks free.'

Gwenllian sighed. 'I know. But we had better give an account of our findings to Savaric now. He will want details of Pica's crime, and we cannot afford to offend him.'

They walked to the Bishop's Palace, where Savaric was eating breakfast with Walter; Osmun and Fevil were by the window, honing daggers. As Cole explained how they had cornered Pica, Gwenllian noticed that the famous crosier – which Savaric claimed was always kept in the hall – was missing. Another piece of the mystery snapped clear in her mind.

'Where is your staff?' she asked.

Savaric's eyebrows went up at the question, but he went to the place where it was kept. His jaw dropped in dismay when he saw it had gone, but Walter hurried forward.

'Here it is,' he said soothingly, reaching behind a curtain. 'I noticed it had been moved yesterday. One of the servants must have done it.'

Relieved, Savaric held out his hand.

'Allow me to see it restored to its proper position,' said Walter ingratiatingly, declining to pass it to him.

'May I see it first?' asked Gwenllian.

'Certainly not,' said Walter, holding it to his chest. 'It is too holy to be pawed by women.'

'I touched it the other day,' she challenged. 'And I want to see it again now.'

When Osmun and Fevil whipped out their swords, Gwenllian knew her suspicions were correct. She also saw that making them known had been a terrible mistake. Bewildered, Cole drew his own weapon.

'Osmun, see to Cole!' Walter bellowed, lashing out with the staff so suddenly that Gwenllian only just managed to avoid being brained with it. 'I will deal with his wife.'

'What are you doing?' cried Savaric, aghast. 'Put that down at once!'

'Trust me!' snapped Walter, gripping the crook more firmly. 'I am acting in your best interests, just as I always have.'

He advanced on Gwenllian again, but she darted behind the startled prelate. On the other side of the room, Cole was engaged in a fierce battle with Osmun and Fevil. The clang of steel was deafening, and she wondered fleetingly how disadvantaged he would be with an unfamiliar sword. But she could not dwell on his predicament, because she had her own troubles. Walter grabbed her cloak and yanked her towards him. She drew a small knife and brandished it, causing him to leap back in alarm.

'Afraid to fight me?' she jeered. 'Or do you only strike your victims when it is dark, and no one can see?'

'What is she talking about?' demanded Savaric. 'Osmun, Fevil! Desist immediately!'

The two knights had Cole backed into a corner and were taking it in turns to attack. They ignored Savaric's order.

'What you do not know cannot harm you,' said Walter to the bishop, lunging for Gwenllian again. 'Look the other way, and pretend this is not happening.'

'Overlook the slaughter of the King's officer and his wife in my own hall?' cried Savaric, aghast. 'Do not be a fool, man! And give me my crosier before you damage it. It is a holy thing, touched by a miracle—'

'Oh, come,' scoffed Walter. 'Do not tell me you believe that? You left the damned thing in the cloisters, and it was I who put it on the altar.'

Savaric's jaw dropped a second time. 'No! But Reginald . . . He *cured* people!'

'After the so-called Miracle of the Crosier, I paid a beggar to say he was healed, and subsequently, people thought they were better because they *wanted* to be. But the ruse has earned our abbey a fortune, so I have no regrets.'

Savaric's face was ashen. 'I do not believe you would stoop to such a vile deception!'

'No? Then why did you make me prior, if not as a reward for devising the plan that has generated so much money?'

'Because my only other choice was Robert, and his piety makes me look irreligious,' explained Savaric weakly. 'Now give me my crosier before—'

'No!' snarled Walter, trying again to grab Gwenllian. 'Let me resolve this matter as I deem fit, and we shall say no more about it. I know what I am doing.'

'Walter will not let you see your staff because there is blood on it,' said Gwenllian to Savaric, retreating further behind him. 'Which is why it was hidden behind the curtain. He has not had time to clean it.'

'Whose blood?' whispered Savaric.

'My husband's. Walter and your two henchmen came to the Angel to kill him. But he is quick-witted in that sort of situation. He kicked over the lamp, and darkness prevented them from committing murder.'

'What?' cried Savaric, more appalled than ever. 'But he is the King's officer! You cannot kill him, Walter – especially with my crosier! It is a religious artefact, not a cudgel.'

Cole was tiring from the vicious two-pronged attack, and

Gwenllian saw that unless she did something soon, the knights would kill him.

'Symon has bruises that match your staff precisely,' she said desperately. 'Even down to the puncture marks caused by its three glass jewels. Tell your men to lay down their weapons, and he will show you.'

'Osmun, stop!' shouted Savaric. 'End this madness at once.'

'Keep fighting!' Walter turned to Savaric. 'It is them or you. If they live, they will accuse you of murder.'

Savaric gazed at him. 'Murder? *Me*? What are you talking about?'

'They think you killed Adam and Hugh,' explained Gwenllian, 'using Pica's dog.'

'What?' exploded Savaric. 'That vile creature? I assure you, I—'

'You do not need to pretend with us,' interrupted Walter briskly. 'We know it was the dog Pica gave you that dispatched Adam and Hugh. We saw its hairs on their bodies.'

Savaric was horrified. 'If that beast *was* responsible, then it had nothing to do with me! I thought Osmun had destroyed the thing. I swear on holy Reginald's tomb that I had nothing to do with what happened to Adam and Hugh!'

The oath made Osmun falter, and it was enough for Cole to strike him on the side of the head with the hilt of his sword. Osmun staggered backwards, then collapsed in a heap. Fevil issued a peculiar growl, and Gwenllian stared at him.

'The animal we heard in the Angel!' she exclaimed. 'It was you!'

'Fevil cannot help the sounds he makes,' said Savaric. He spoke distractedly, still trying to process what Walter had told him. 'You would fare no better if you had no tongue.'

'For God's sake, Fevil!' howled Walter, as the big man faltered. 'We will lose everything if Savaric surrenders. Finish Cole!'

'Wait!' It was Osmun, climbing slowly to his feet. Fevil obeyed instantly, and Cole backed away, using the opportunity to catch his breath. Osmun addressed the bishop. 'Are you saying you are innocent of killing Adam and Hugh?'

'Of course I am innocent!' cried Savaric. 'What do you think I am?'

Osmun gazed at him in confusion. 'But you used bribery *and* coercion to make Cole abandon his investigation. Why would you do that if you had nothing to hide?'

'Because the King does not want me to co-operate,' explained Savaric, clearly affronted. 'But I had nothing to hide personally.'

Gwenllian grimaced. The news of John's duplicity came as no surprise.

Walter was also staring at Savaric, his expression one of confusion. 'But the dog was yours, and if you did not set it on Adam and Hugh, then who did?'

'You should choose your followers more carefully,' said Gwenllian to Savaric in the silence that followed Walter's question. 'They believe you capable of terrible things.'

'My immortal soul may be stained with many sins, but murder is not one of them,' said Savaric firmly.

Osmun exchanged a glance with Fevil, who nodded. 'We believe you.'

'Good,' said the bishop drily. He glared at Walter. 'And now *you* have some explaining to do. You can begin by telling me why you tried to kill Sir Symon with my crosier. Because his wife is right: there is blood on it.'

'I planned to rinse it off,' said Walter bitterly. 'But I was shaken after our narrow escape in the Angel, and then I forgot.'

'That does not explain why you took it in the first place,' said Savaric angrily.

'Because I needed something to defend myself with,' snapped Walter. 'Cole is a skilled warrior. And it was the only thing to hand.'

'Beating him with it was not defending yourself,' said Gwenllian icily.

'I was frightened,' said Walter sullenly. 'We were supposed to shoot him while he was asleep. Instead, he was awake and fighting with terrifying ferocity.'

'A misunderstanding, then.' Savaric raised his hand when Gwenllian started to object.

Walter nodded eagerly. 'Yes, and we did it for you. They had learned that a dog killed Hugh and Adam, and it was only a matter of time before they also learned that Pica had given you an especially savage one. We decided that if they died during a raid by robbers ...'

'The King would be unlikely to launch a second enquiry to Hugh's death, and I would be spared,' finished Savaric.

'He was going to try to murder Symon again,' said Gwenllian, angry that the matter was going to be 'forgotten'. She regarded Walter contemptuously. 'How much did you pay the smith to keep my husband's sword, to ensure he was unarmed today?'

'Too much,' muttered Osmun. 'Given that Cole just went out and borrowed another.'

But the knights and Walter were more interested in regaining Savaric's approval than in answering Gwenllian's accusations. When they went to clamour at him, she stood next to Cole, her mind working fast.

'We now know that Walter, Osmun and Fevil are innocent,'

she said. 'They would not have felt the need to protect Savaric if they were the culprits. And Savaric is innocent, too – his denials were convincing, and so was the oath he swore. So who is left?'

'Dacus,' replied Cole shortly.

'And Robert, the man who sent Hugh to Solsbury Hill. And Pica.'

'If you thought Pica was guilty, you should have raised the matter when we cornered him about Lechlade.'

'It did not occur to me. However, he has no alibi for either death, and he was the one who brought this fierce grey dog to Bath.'

'The dog,' said Cole thoughtfully. 'If Osmun and Fevil are innocent, then so are their hounds. *Ergo*, perhaps Pica's grey hound *is* the animal that—'

'Join me for a cup of wine,' called Savaric, breaking into their discussion. He nodded that Walter, Osmun and Fevil were to leave; they did so reluctantly. 'We must assess this situation, and discuss how it can be resolved to our mutual advantage.'

'No,' said Cole immediately. 'I will not do anything against my conscience.'

Savaric gazed at him wonderingly, and shook his head. 'No wonder the King wants rid of you! Conscience indeed!'

Gwenllian's eyes narrowed. 'What makes you think John wants rid of him? Did he say so when he wrote the letter asking you not to co-operate with his investigation?'

Savaric shot her a patronising glance. 'He would never commit such a request to parchment! I deduced it from the fact that he sent Sir Symon here in the first place – too much time has passed since Hugh's death, and there is no evidence to convict a culprit. The case is unsolvable, and John knows it. So of course he does not want me to co-operate.'

'Then why did he order me to try?' asked Cole, confused.

'I imagine you have done something to annoy him – he wants an excuse to oust you.'

'The solution lies in the grey dog,' said Gwenllian to Savaric, as Cole winced. 'Pica gave it to you, but now neither you nor your knights can tell us its whereabouts. I believe Pica took it back, and used it to kill.'

'Pica!' exclaimed Savaric, eyes gleaming. 'I might have known! And his motive is obvious, of course: Adam and Hugh both thought Glastonbury and Bath should be united. They haled from Glastonbury themselves, and wanted to foster closer relations.'

'Adam was from Glastonbury,' acknowledged Cole. 'But . . .' He trailed off, and reluctantly began considering the possibility that Dacus might not be the culprit after all.

'So now comes the difficult part.' Savaric addressed Gwenllian, recognising her as the one with whom business could be done. 'If you tell John that you have solved the case, he will be livid. In essence, you will have outwitted him. However, Pica is a thorn in my side, and I would like him gone. Another charge of murder against him would suit me very well.'

'So what do you suggest?' asked Gwenllian.

'I own some skill in politics,' said Savaric with a modest shrug. 'So *I* shall draft the letter you will send the King. I shall phrase your findings in a way that will condemn Pica, but that will not antagonise John. Then we shall both have achieved our objective.'

'No,' said Cole uneasily. 'It smacks of dishonesty and sly dealing.'

Gwenllian laid a gentle hand on his shoulder. 'Consider our choices, Symon. We can submit our own report, and let John expel you from Carmarthen. Or we can accept

Savaric's help. I do not want to leave our home, and it is not just us who will suffer if you are ejected. The town deserves better than to be ruled by one of John's creatures.'

Cole nodded reluctant agreement. Then he sat in the window, staring moodily into the street, while Gwenllian and the bishop worked.

Gwenllian felt vaguely tainted by the time they left the Bishop's Palace. Cole did, too, and was angry about it.

'What we have done is wrong. Your letter lists all the evidence that proves Pica stabbed Lechlade, but only *hints* that he murdered Adam and Hugh. *Ergo*, he will be charged only with Lechlade's death – for which he will claim self-defence. And he will go free.'

Gwenllian sighed. 'Very possibly, but he will never be Abbot of Glastonbury, and *that* will be his real punishment. I hate to admit it, but Savaric's letter is a masterpiece of duplicity: it lets John know we solved the case, so he cannot accuse us of disobedience, but it does so in such a way that even he cannot take offence. We may keep Carmarthen yet.'

Cole pulled a face to register his distaste. 'I wish Richard had not died. He was not much of a King, but he was better than the scheming devil we have now.'

'Not so loud, *cariad*!'

'I do not care,' said Cole sullenly. 'I hate devious politics.'

'So do I, but we will go home tomorrow, and then we can forget about Bath. However, there is one question we have not yet answered: where did Pica keep this dog? He sleeps in the abbey guesthouse, and someone would have noticed if it was there.'

'There is only one place it can be – the Prior's Garden. Do you remember Walter telling us how Reginald built kennels there?'

'Yes, but he also said they are used for storing the urine that will be used for tanning hides over the winter.'

'Precisely! A dog will stink if kept in close confinement, and what better than urine to conceal it? Besides, such an unpleasant place will deter visitors. Shall we go there now?'

He led the way to an attractive arbour that was separated from the rest of the precinct by a wall. Once inside, it did not take them long to locate the row of sheds. They reeked, and Gwenllian gagged. Cole opened a door, and was greeted by a medley of snarls and grunts.

'It has been starved,' he said, disgusted, 'and kept close-chained. It is muzzled, too, so it cannot bark. Pica is a monster to have done such a thing.'

Gwenllian poked her head around the door and saw an enormous grey animal. Before she could advise against it, Cole had removed the muzzle and was feeding it scraps of the dried meat he always carried with him – no soldier liked to be without supplies.

'Please do not let it off the leash,' she begged. 'It looks half mad to me.'

'It will have to be destroyed,' said Cole sadly. 'What a pity! It was once a fine animal.'

Walter's eyebrows shot up in astonishment when he learned what had been happening in his domain, although his surprise quickly turned to indignation.

'How dare Pica use my outbuildings for his private menagerie – especially for a beast that has claimed the lives of two men. What if it had escaped? It might have attacked me.'

'Yes,' said Cole, and Gwenllian was under the impression that he wished it had. 'But it would have been Pica's fault, not the dog's.'

'I suppose it would.' Walter softened. 'I shall tell Eldred to feed it well tonight, and dispatch it tomorrow. Do not worry, he will not let it suffer.'

Cole nodded, although Gwenllian could see he was not much comforted. They left the abbey in silence, and it was some time before he spoke.

'Are you sure Pica is the culprit? Dacus seems a much more likely candidate for abusing animals than he.'

'He does,' agreed Gwenllian, taking his arm sympathetically. 'But yes, I am sure.'

'Then I suppose you must be right,' said Cole, a little resentfully. 'You usually are.'

It was the deepest part of the night when Gwenllian woke to find herself alone. There was a full moon, and its silvery rays had fallen on her face. She rose and dressed, supposing Cole was in the tavern downstairs, drinking to wash away the dirty taste of politics, but the place was empty. Her stomach lurched when she realised where he had gone. She hurried to Iefan, and shook him awake.

'I think Symon has gone up Solsbury Hill.'

Iefan blinked. 'Why would he do that?'

'Because Dacus challenged him to go. He was unhappy earlier, and I am afraid that if Dacus is there and makes wild remarks about Adam ... Will you come with me?'

As Cole still had Iefan's sword, the sergeant borrowed another, and they set off to where the hill was a black mass against the night sky. The moonlight made walking easy, and it was not long before they reached the bottom. Then there was a peculiar howl.

'Was that a wolf?' asked Iefan uneasily.

'Hurry!' urged Gwenllian, breaking into a run.

They were breathless by the time they reached the top.

Cole was there, sword in his hand, and at first, Gwenllian assumed he was alone, but then she glimpsed a movement in the shadows. It was Dacus, gripping the leash of Pica's dog. She was glad it was upwind of her, sure it would attack if it could sense her fear. She crouched down, straining to hear what was being said. The wind that kept the dog from catching their scent also blew the words towards her.

'You came,' Dacus was saying. 'I did not think you would have the courage. I thought I would have to find another way to kill you.'

'Why would you want to kill me?' Cole asked quietly.

'Because you are corrupt.' Dacus' voice was hard and cold. 'I know what you did today. You helped Savaric concoct a tale that will conceal the unsavoury happenings at Bath and let Pica take the blame. But you are Adam's friend, so what else should I expect?'

'Adam was not corrupt.'

'He was evil!' Dacus' anguished cry set the dog growling. 'He poisoned Reginald. I know – I was there.'

'He was a healer. He would never—'

'He *was* a healer, and that is why he itched to be master of the hospital. But Reginald was master as well as bishop. So Adam killed him.'

'But Adam did not want that post,' argued Cole. 'He wrote and told me. He was old and tired, and wanted to spend his final days in prayer.'

'You are wrong! He was evil and a killer.'

'My wife always insists on evidence to support that sort of claim. So what is yours? Did you find toxins in his possession? Did you see him administer a dose of—'

Dacus made a curious hissing sound, and jerked the dog's leash. 'I do not need evidence. I know a guilty man when I see one. But you will regret coming here tonight. Like Adam

95

and Hugh, you will be tested and found lacking. I will kill you, just as I killed them.'

In the darkness, Gwenllian gaped in disbelief.

'But there cannot be a third man found with his throat ripped out,' Dacus went on. 'So I have dug you a grave.'

He nodded to a gaping pit Gwenllian had not noticed before. It was black and sinister in the moonlight, like an opening to Hell.

'I knew you had murdered Adam from the first time we met,' said Cole. 'My wife said they were cat hairs on your habit, but I knew they belonged to a dog.'

'It is not a dog, it is a wolf.' Dacus ruffled the beast's fur. It twisted around, as if to bite, and he tightened his grip on its collar. 'And when I saw Pica training it to kill lambs, I knew what I had to do. I stole it from Savaric's palace.'

'Pica must have hoped it would hurt the bishop,' muttered Gwenllian to Iefan. 'He may be innocent of killing Hugh and Adam, but he has committed many other crimes.'

'You hid it in Reginald's kennels,' said Cole. 'Muzzling it, so it could not bark—'

'I have not fed it since you arrived,' interrupted Dacus, tightening the lead savagely. 'It is ravenous. It will tear your throat out, and I will dance in your blood.'

To Gwenllian's horror, Cole laid his sword in the grass, then raised his hands to show he was unarmed. 'Enough, Dacus. Listen to me. Adam did not kill Reginald. No one did. It *was* a fever. I spoke to his physicians yesterday, and—'

'Liar!' hissed Dacus. 'God thought I was right to kill Adam, because He immediately started granting miracles at Reginald's tomb. Reginald was like a father to me, and Adam *deserved* to die for killing him. And so did Hugh, for asking too many questions.'

'Neither of them—'

'Kill him!' screamed Dacus, unhooking the leash. He kicked the dog to start it moving.

Cole did not move as the animal bounded towards him. Dacus was hot on its heels, whipping it with the lead. At that moment, the moon went behind a cloud. Gwenllian abandoned her hiding place and stumbled forward, fighting off Iefan's restraining hands. She could see nothing in the sudden darkness, but there were snarls, an agonised scream, a yelp and silence. The moon emerged again to reveal Cole standing in the same place, and Dacus on the ground with the dog lying across him. She hurried forward, Iefan close behind her. Cole spun around in alarm at the sound of their footsteps.

'You should not be here!' he cried in horror. 'It might have attacked you.'

'Iefan has a sword to protect us,' countered Gwenllian. She glared at him. 'Unlike you.'

Cole showed her the dagger he had concealed in his hand. 'It posed no threat to me. Besides, Dacus maltreated it, and it was only a matter of time before it turned on him.'

'But you could not have known that would happen tonight,' shouted Gwenllian, angry with him. 'You took a foolish, reckless risk.'

Cole regarded her irritably. 'I did nothing of the kind. I *know* dogs, and as long as I posed no threat, I was safe enough. However, I imagine Hugh and Adam ran when they saw it, and it instinctively homed in on a moving target. And tonight, it was Dacus who was running.'

Gwenllian was unconvinced, and was about to say so when Iefan spoke.

'It will not be biting anyone else,' he said, struggling to haul the carcass from Dacus' body. 'He stabbed it with this peculiar knife.'

Cole took the weapon from him, and inspected it in the moonlight. Its blade was of such fine steel that it was almost blue, and the handle was ivory, carved with what appeared to be a bear climbing a tree. 'It is soil-stained – he must have unearthed it when he dug the grave.'

But Gwenllian was more interested in Dacus. She knelt next to him, fighting off her revulsion for him and what he had done. 'Help me, Symon. He still breathes.'

'You passed Solsbury's test,' Dacus whispered weakly, as Cole crouched by his side. 'I was wrong ... about you. Will you ... do something for me?'

'Very well,' agreed Cole, before Gwenllian could urge caution. 'What?'

'Do not bury me ... near Adam. Somewhere else.'

He closed his eyes, and the breath left him in a hiss.

For a moment, no one spoke, then Cole stood and lifted Dacus in his arms. Gwenllian thought he was going to carry him back to the town, but he stopped next to the pit.

'Is this a good idea?' she asked nervously, as he laid Dacus in the hole and placed the dog at his side. 'If anyone were to find him ...'

'No one will find him,' said Cole, setting the peculiar weapon on Dacus' chest and picking up a spade. 'And it is time he had some peace.'

III

Carmarthen

The return journey was quicker and more comfortable than the outward one, and Gwenllian's spirits soared when she saw Carmarthen's familiar walls and roofs in the distance.

There had been no word from the King, and while Cole believed this to be a sign that Savaric's letter had worked, she was uneasy. John was vengeful, and she knew it was only a matter of time before he remembered that Carmarthen was held by a man who had declined to flatter him.

'I should have listened to you,' she said, as they travelled the last mile. 'Your instincts about Dacus were right, and my logic was wrong. However, I am still vexed with you for going up Solsbury Hill to confront that wolf.'

'It was a dog. Still, I suppose some good came out of our investigation. Savaric dismissed Walter, and appointed Robert as prior instead.'

'Robert is a better man. Although I still think his piety is insincere.'

'Others think so, too,' said Cole with a conspiratorial grin. 'On the grounds that there have been no miracles at Reginald's tomb since he was appointed.'

Gwenllian hesitated, but then forged on. 'There is something I should tell you. I did not mention it sooner, because I did not want to return to Bath ...'

'What?' asked Cole uneasily. 'Was it something in that letter you received in Brecon – the one you told me contained only a copy of the message we sent to John?'

Gwenllian nodded. 'It was from Savaric. Pica managed to escape from the abbey cells, and is on his way to tell the Pope that he is innocent of killing Lechlade – and that he should be Abbot of Glastonbury into the bargain.'

Cole reined in. 'Should we go after him? The man is a killer.'

'Savaric sent Walter to do it.'

'And Walter agreed?'

'Of course – hoping to grease his way back into favour.' Gwenllian indicated that Cole should begin riding again.

'And the matter is no longer our concern, anyway. We did what the King asked, and we are likely to bring ourselves trouble if we dabble further.'

They rode in silence for a while. Then Cole pointed suddenly. 'Look!'

A small party of riders was coming to welcome them home, and Gwenllian was sure she could see one of the soldiers carrying their infant son.

'I know Walter confessed to fabricating those miracles,' said Cole, 'and that nothing divine has ever happened at Reginald's tomb. But before we left, I asked Reginald a second time to provide us with a daughter, and I think he will oblige.'

Gwenllian regarded him askance. 'You do? Why?'

'Because I buried Dacus on Solsbury Hill for *his* sake – to spare the reputation of a chaplain he loved. And then you explained Dacus' disappearance by telling everyone that he had gone on a pilgrimage. Reginald will be grateful to us, so I imagine you will have some good news for me soon.'

Gwenllian stared at him, wondering whether the queasiness she had been suffering these past few mornings could be a new life beginning inside her, and not something she had eaten, as she had assumed. She did some rapid calculations. It was certainly possible.

Rome, 1200

It had taken Walter some time to catch up with Pica, but he had done it in the end, intercepting him just as he was about to enter the Holy City. He watched dispassionately as Pica grabbed the poisoned goblet and raised it to his lips. The feisty Abbot Elect drained the contents in a single swallow, and set it back on the table with an impatient clatter.

Walter smiled. Life had been so much better since he had manipulated the unstable Dacus into believing that Adam had killed Reginald. Walter had hoped to be appointed master of the hospital himself, but when he had seen Adam's murder pass virtually unremarked, he had decided to try for an even greater prize. Again, it had been easy to persuade Dacus that Hugh was close to learning the truth about Adam's murder, and within days, Walter was prior.

Of course, Savaric could hardly keep him in post after Gwenllian had exposed his role in the tavern attack – although mercifully, no one had guessed that *he* was the power behind Dacus as well. He had been in the process of urging Dacus to kill Cole, too – the death of her husband would be Gwenllian's punishment – but Dacus had selfishly disappeared on a pilgrimage, so revenge would have to wait until both returned to Bath.

Walter's fortunes had taken something of a downward turn since then, but he was not unduly worried. Savaric had shown his continued favour by giving him another mission, and would be delighted to learn that the belligerent Pica would no longer be a problem. Walter licked his lips as he anticipated the riches and high offices that would soon be his.

He watched Pica sit suddenly and raise a hand to his head. It looked like the beginnings of a fever – and Walter knew, because that was what had happened after he had fed a similar substance to Reginald. Of course, Savaric did not know who had been responsible for *that* particular deed; for all this ambition, Savaric had loved his cousin dearly. Walter, though, had found the man's piety irritating, and it had been deeply satisfying to poison him before he could be made Archbishop of Canterbury.

Walter did not wait to see Pica die, because a pouch had arrived that morning along with instructions that it was not to be opened until he had completed his duties. He was eager to know what it contained, because he could certainly hear the jingle of coins within. As Pica was already as good as dead, he fumbled with the seals, excitement making his fingers clumsy. He grinned his delight when several gold nobles spilled into his eager hands. There was also a letter.

He tore it open, and read the message within – Savaric thanking him for getting rid of a man who had been such a thorn in his side. Walter regarded it in alarm. Was the bishop mad to put such thoughts in writing? What if the pouch had fallen into the wrong hands? It would have sealed both their fates!

Then he became aware of raised voices and looked up to see that the people who had gathered around the dying Pica were staring at him. Pica raised a shaking hand and pointed. Immediately, three monks started to run towards him. Appalled, Walter tried to hide the letter, first slipping it up his sleeve, and then, in frantic desperation, stuffing it in his mouth.

It was no good. The monks forced him to spit it out, and their faces paled with shock when they read what was written. They grabbed his arms, so he could not escape, at which point, the coins dropped from his fingers. He tried to protest his innocence, but he had neglected to throw away the phial that had contained the poison, and they found it in his bag. That, with the letter and the gold, would be more than enough to convict him. Would it convict Savaric, too? Walter, full of frustrated spite, sincerely hoped so. But then he happened to glance at Pica, who still clung to the vestiges of life.

Pica was smiling. It was an unusual enough sight that Walter gaped. But then he understood. Clever Pica! He had guessed that he might not reach Rome alive, so he had staged his own revenge on the men he thought might kill him. Savaric had written no letter. Of course he had not – he was far too astute for such a blunder. It was Pica!

But would it succeed in destroying Savaric, or would the bishop's denials be enough to let him keep the kingdom he had carved for himself in Bath and Glastonbury? Walter could have wept with pity for himself when he realised that he would never know.

Historical Note

There has been an abbey in Bath since Saxon times. Originally, an abbot was in charge, but this changed in 1098, when the then Bishop of Wells moved his seat there. The abbey became a cathedral priory, with a prior as its head. Hugh was prior from 1174; Prior Walter died in 1198; and Prior Robert stayed in office until being elected Abbot of Glastonbury in 1223.

In 1191, Savaric fitz Geldwin became Bishop of Bath, following the promotion of his cousin, Reginald fitz Jocelyn, to the Archbishopric of Canterbury. Reginald died *en route* to his installation, and his body was returned to Bath, where it was buried in the abbey church. He was popular, founding the Hospital of St John the Baptist (one of its early masters was named Adam), and several miracles were later said to have occurred at his tomb.

No such saintliness was attributed to Savaric, however. Greedy and ambitious, he contrived to have Hugh de Sully, Abbot of Glastonbury, appointed Bishop of Worcester, and then announced to Glastonbury's astonished monks that he was their master now. Needless to say they objected, and immediately appealed against him to Richard I and the Pope. Unfortunately for them, both supported Savaric, although Richard later recanted, and claimed he had been coerced.

The Dean and Chapter of Wells were also outraged by Savaric's high handedness in changing his title from 'Bishop of Bath' to 'Bishop of Bath and Glastonbury'. Canons Ralph de Lechlade and Jocelin Trotman were the two representatives who travelled to Bath to make their objections known.

In 1198, the Pope died, Richard withdrew his support from Savaric, and the Glastonbury monks elected William Pica as abbot. Savaric promptly excommunicated Pica. Another twist in the tale occurred in 1199, when King Richard was succeeded by his brother John, who allowed Savaric to buy his support. Armed with John's backing, Savaric invaded Glastonbury with a mob of henchmen, and forcibly enthroned himself. Several monks were injured in the resulting mêlée.

Outraged, Pica left for Rome. He died on the journey, and Glastonbury's monks claimed that Savaric had had him poisoned. Glastonbury did not win its independence from Bath until 1219. Savaric weathered the accusations, and died a wealthy and successful man in 1205. He was succeeded as bishop by none other than Canon Trotman, who remained in post until 1242.

ACT TWO

September 1204

The lay brother set the wooden tray on the floor at his feet and stretched himself, hands pressed against his aching back. He had been bending for the last ten minutes, polishing the brass feet of a lectern until he could see his face in the gleaming metal.

Eldred took an almost proprietorial pride in his part of the great abbey church and now gazed around fondly in the peaceful noon-time, glad to be alone while the priests, monks and deacons were eating in the refectory. He was a slight, fair man of thirty, with an open face and an inoffensive manner to match.

He had been tending the fabric of Bath's cathedral for the past ten years and had graduated from being a lowly cleaner down in the nave, to being responsible for this upper part of the building, the most sanctified area of the choir, the presbytery and the sanctuary, the space that held the high altar.

Picking up his tray of cleaning cloths and beeswax polish, Eldred moved to the centre and genuflected towards the altar, a long table covered with a lace-edged linen cloth of spotless white, on which was a bronze cross and a pair of tall candlesticks. He crossed to the north side of the presbytery, the space between choir and sanctuary. As he went, he looked briefly down through the rows of choir stalls. Beyond them, he saw the carved rood screen that shielded the holiest area from the nave and the rude stares of the townsfolk, when they came to stand there for Sunday worship. There was still no sign of anyone returning from their midday meal, so Eldred decided to give a quick polish to the sacred vessels – his favourite task, as it allowed him to handle the most venerated objects in the abbey.

Padding across the tiled floor in his sandals, he went to the aumbry, a cupboard set in the thickness of the wall between the presbytery and the ambulatory, the corridor that ran around inside the east end of the church.

The two doors of the aumbry were of polished oak with brass corners, an ornate ivory cross set into each panel. They were closed by a large brass hasp and staple, with a padlock securing them. Eldred fumbled for the ring of keys that hung on a chain from the leather belt around his long brown robe. By touch alone, he chose one that he had handled virtually daily for the past four years and advanced on the lock.

It was then that warning bells began to ring inside his head. As he touched the lock to push the key into the hole, the hasp swung slackly back on its hinge, the staple from the other door coming away with it. Almost unwilling to believe his eyes, Eldred saw that the four long rivets that had held the staple to the oak were drooping from the brass plate, scraps of torn wood falling to the floor beneath. In a frenzy of concern, he pulled open both doors, still hoping that this was some explicable happening, like dry rot or woodworm – a foolish thought, but better than the obvious alternative.

Inside, there were two shelves, the lower one carrying vials of oil and unguents, as well as the service books, sheets of parchment bound between wooden covers. Nothing there was amiss, but the upper shelf was almost bare. A couple of silver patens remained, on which the consecrated host was carried to those taking communion, but the pride of the abbey, the golden chalice and the pyx, had gone!

Sweat began to pour from Eldred's brow. He knew he would get the blame for this, as he was the only one with access to the aumbry, apart from Hubert, the sacrist, responsible for setting up the arrangements for each Mass, who was his direct superior, and Brother Gilbert, the cellarer, who was responsible for the material contents of the abbey. Even Prior Robert did not possess a key. That the aumbry had been forcibly broken into would not help Eldred, unless the real culprit was rapidly discovered, as the prior disliked him and would be only too ready to make him the scapegoat.

As the first horror of the situation subsided into a deadening acceptance, the lay brother knew that he had to report the theft immediately. The chalice, though small, was solid gold, a legacy of the first monastery on this site, many hundreds of years earlier. Eldred was not an educated man – he could neither read nor write – but had been around the abbey for many years and had picked up something of its history from listening to others. The chalice, given by Offa, King of Mercia in the eighth century, was probably made from gold stolen from the Welsh by the Saxons. The pyx, a small gold-lined silver box, was for holding the 'reserved sacrament', communion wafers that had been consecrated ready for use.

With feet of lead, Eldred made his way to the steps that led to the south transept, after first pushing the rivets back into the shattered holes in the door of the aumbry. For a moment, he contemplated leaving it as he had found it and letting someone else discover the catastrophe, denying any knowledge of it. But that would be futile, he recognised.

Everyone knew that Eldred spent much of his time in the chancel, cleaning and polishing.

He began to hurry and reached the small door set just beyond the south transept, which led directly out into the cloisters. The clergy were thronging the cloister, gossiping as they came out of the refectory into the pillared arcade.

Almost immediately, Eldred saw the skinny figure of the sacrist approaching. Hubert of Frome, the monk responsible for the fabric and furnishings of the abbey, was a small, weasely fellow with a sallow complexion and a turn in his left eye. The black Benedictine habit hung badly on his meagre frame and his permanently irritable expression made him even more unattractive. His first words set the tone for a fraught encounter.

'Eldred, what are you doing here?' he rasped. 'Why have you left your duties?'

There were a dozen monks within hearing distance and Eldred sidled up to the sacrist to murmur in his ear, 'You must come to the presbytery at once, brother! An evil thing has happened!'

Hubert scowled at his lowly assistant, but something in Eldred's voice persuaded him not to make a public issue of it in the cloister. He followed Eldred as he scurried back to the presbytery and crossed to the other side without acknowledging the high altar. Hubert crossed himself as he bent a knee, then prepared to berate the other man for not doing the same. But his protests died in his throat as Eldred reached the aumbry and with a dramatic gesture, pulled open the doors to display the broken lock and the bare shelf.

'The chalice and the pyx, Master! Gone!'

The sacrist was speechless. Then with a moan, he dropped to his knees and peered inside the aumbry. His hand groped blindly at the back of the upper shelf, as if his sense of touch might reassure him that his sight was defective. When he rose to his feet, his normally pallid features were almost dead white with shock.

'How can this be? What have you done, fellow?'

'Nothing, Master! I found it like this, not ten minutes ago,' wailed Eldred. 'See, the staple has been torn from the wood!'

With trembling fingers, Hubert rattled the still-closed padlock and prodded the long rivets hanging loosely from the staple.

'You swear by Almighty God that you had no hand in this?' he hissed. He would liked to have yelled at the top of his voice, but the sanctity of this place overcame even the horror of the situation.

'Of course, Master!' said the terrified but still outraged Eldred. 'I carry a key – why should I break the doors?'

Hubert of Frome managed to pull himself together and his pallor began to change to a rising flush as anger and fear of retribution flooded his system.

'Prior Robert must be told at once! The chalice was priceless, as well as being a historic legacy. And the pyx ...!' A sudden thought occurred to him and his face blanched once again. 'Holy Mary! Was there Blessed Host within it?'

Eldred shook his head emphatically. 'None was reserved after the last Mass – it was all used.'

Hubert puffed out a long breath of relief. 'Thank God for that!' he sighed, crossing himself fervently. If consecrated wafers had been stolen along with the sacred vessels, not only would it have been a greater sacrilege, but the pillaged Host would have had a high monetary value. Witches and necromancers set great store by such rare material for their evil rituals and spells.

With sudden resolve, the sacrist grabbed the loose sleeve

of Eldred's robe and pulled him towards the doorway into the side passage.

'Come with me, we must find the prior immediately!' he brayed, releasing Eldred's arm and padding ahead of him back to the cloister door. The unhappy lay brother followed him, his feet slapping on the flagstones as they went into the cloister. The sacrist grabbed the ring of a nearby door, which led into the stores.

'I saw the prior go in here after dinner. He was seeking Brother Gilbert,' he said in a voice trembling with agitation, as he pushed the stout door open. Inside it was gloomy, the only light coming from small apertures high up on the walls, laced with wicker mesh to prevent birds from entering to steal the grain that was stored in large tubs. Partitions divided the long chamber into sections, but left a central aisle running its full length.

'He will be down at the end, in Brother Gilbert's cell,' muttered Hubert, pattering down the aisle, past cubicles piled with flour, oats, wheat and fresh vegetables, others containing bales of coarse cloth, kegs of French wine, furniture, candles and all the provisions necessary to sustain a monastic house.

At the end was an arch, beyond which was a chamber stretching across the width of the building, with double doors on the right leading into the abbey yard. A large table was set in the centre, and to the left was a desk where another monk was perched on a high stool. He was busily writing lists of merchandise with a quill on sheets of parchment, held flat with small pebbles from the nearby River Avon.

The sacrist marched up to the table, where two more monks were hunched over a large pile of silver pennies, counting them into leather bags. One was the cellarer, Brother Gilbert, a squat, heavily built man, with black hair shaved high on the back of his neck and temples in the Norman style, leaving a dense rim below his tonsure. The other was Prior Robert, the dictatorial head of the abbey. Though an abbey should have been led by an abbot, the monastery had reverted to a priory a century before, when John of Tours, King William Rufus' physician, moved the bishopric of Somerset from Wells to Bath and built a great new cathedral on the site.

The present prior was a corpulent man with wiry dark hair. His chubby face carried an almost permanent benign smile, but the responsibilities of his office had eroded his patience so that if he was crossed, this could vanish, to be replaced by a show of temper. At the sound of some-one approaching, his bag of money dropped with a clunk onto the table, as he turned his head to beam at his sacrist, whose job he had held himself before his elevation to prior.

'Dear Brother Hubert, you seem in a hurry! I cannot be disturbed now, we are accounting for the wool sales.'

'Prior, you must come at once!' the agitated sacrist cried. He clutched the prior's arm with his hand, which Robert shook off irritably, but before he could protest further, Hubert gabbled out the story of the missing treasures.

The sanctimonious prior placed the palms of his hands together high before his face in an attitude of prayer and rolled his eyes upwards towards heaven.

'O Lord my God, I beseech Thee to assure me that this is some grave mistake. Surely this cannot be!'

Then he dropped his hands and spun round, snarling at both Hubert and Eldred, who was cowering behind the sac-rist.

'What have you done, you wretched souls? Which of you has stolen these priceless relics – or forgotten to lock the aumbry, eh?' He was quivering with rage, arms upraised, his fingers clawing the air.

'The fastenings have been smashed, Prior,' quavered Hubert. 'You must come and see for yourself!'

Robert shoved the two men aside and stormed ahead of them to the cloister door, with the others, including the cellarer, hurrying after him, leaving the young clerk Maurice to guard the bags of money on the table. In the presbytery, it was a matter of a moment for the prior to confirm both that the staple had been wrenched out of the door and that the top shelf was empty.

. 'I possess a key, Prior!' whined Hubert, determined to get his alibi in first. 'So I could not be involved in this sacrilege!'

'Nor I, for I too hold one,' boomed Brother Gilbert, aggressively. He was a short-tempered man, as most of the residents of the abbey could testify.

The three monks swivelled to glower at Eldred, who nervously grabbed the ring on his belt and held up his own key.

'I also have a key! It is my task to clean those blessed vessels,' he said timorously. 'Which I have done faithfully these past four years,' he added.

The prior took one last desperate look into the aumbry, as if the chalice and pyx might have miraculously reappeared during the last half-minute. Then he moved to the centre of the presbytery and dropped to his knees before the altar. Once again lifting his supplicant hands before his face, he prayed in loud high-pitched voice for God, his Son, the Holy Mary and all the saints and angels to reveal who had done this awful act and to restore the sacred vessels to them, so that their humble servants might continue to worship in the manner to which they were accustomed.

The others, well aware of Prior Robert's ostentatious show of piety, listened with varying degrees of impatience, more concerned with their own vulnerability when the prior unleashed his ire upon them. They had not long to wait, for as soon as Robert had finished talking to his Creator, he rose to his feet and with a face like thunder, pointed a quivering finger at Eldred.

'Sacrist, send for the proctor's men to seize this fellow!'

The fact that Eldred had suspected that he would be made the scapegoat did not lessen the terror with which he heard these words.

'Prior, I am innocent!' he screamed. 'It was I who ran to tell the sacrist. I handle those holy things almost every day! Why should I steal them after all this time?'

Surprisingly, Hubert spoke up for him. 'Prior, he does have a key. Why would he break the fastenings?'

Robert ignored him. 'Send for the proctors, I say! Let the processes of canon law and the judgement of Almighty God decide on his guilt.' He crossed himself vigorously again. 'And now, set up a search throughout the abbey . . . throughout the whole town! Go, marshal every monk, every lay brother, every kitchen boy to leave no stone unturned! We must find those sacred treasures!'

The two proctor's men were what passed for the police force of the abbey, keeping order amongst the lay brothers, the servants and, less often, the monks themselves. They were nominally lay brothers in that they enjoyed the Church's protection from the secular law, but in reality were a pair of strong-arm men not over-imbued with intelligence. The actual proctors were a pair of the more senior monks, charged with the discipline of the brethren, but it was their two servants who carried out the day-to-day policing of the large abbey compound, which behind its high wall, occupied most of the south-eastern quarter of the city.

Within minutes of the prior's peremptory command, they had grabbed Eldred and marched him off to the detention cell, a small outhouse built on to the end of the stable block at the south end of the abbey yard. As well as for the storage of animal fodder, it was used mostly for housing drunks, beggars and troublemakers found in the abbey yard, which was open to the public.

Servants, lay brothers and even novitiate monks who had transgressed the rules were also incarcerated in the cell on a diet of bread and water until they had expiated their sins. The Church jealously guarded its independence from the legal apparatus of the State, strengthened by old King Henry's penitent promise after the murder of Thomas Becket.

After the first shock of arrest had passed off, Eldred became more philosophical about his plight, as he was sure that his innocence would soon become apparent. Although it was well over a century since King William the Bastard had conquered England, there was still a prejudice against Saxons such as himself, even though generations of inter-marriage had blurred the distinction. He was being set up as the villain by the largely Norman Church, mainly because of his name and fair Saxon hair and complexion.

Despondently, he sat on the bare board that formed the bed and looked at the rest of the furnishings – a pile of hay, a battered leather bucket for his ablutions and a large wooden cross on the wall, set there by the pious Robert to remind prisoners that the Almighty was always watching them. There was nothing else to comfort him, apart from a rough blanket folded on the end of the bench. There was no window and the only light came through a gap above the heavy oaken door, which also admitted a strong stench of horse manure from the adjacent stables.

Eldred's first concern was for his wife, Gytha. Before he was dragged away, he had managed to plead with Hubert to let her know of his arrest, so that when he failed to return home that night, she would not think that he was either dead or had abandoned her. The Abbey did not oblige lay brothers to be either celibate or resident, and Eldred and his wife lodged with two other families in a small house in Binnebury Lane, only a few hundred paces away from the main abbey gate. They had no living children and their one half of a room, divided by a curtain from a family of four, was enough for them to be content with their lot.

A few hours passed and no one came near him. As the afternoon waned, he heard the bells of the abbey church tolling for compline. It was hot and stuffy in the little room, but there was no water to drink. Eldred assumed that the prior was not going to starve him to death, or until he confessed to a crime he had not committed, but he was getting hungry, having missed his midday meal in the servants' hall.

The thick door had no cracks for him to peer through, so he had only sounds to tell him what was happening outside. The abbey yard was a busy place, as townsfolk came in on many errands, and it was a focus for gossip and business dealings. Goods came constantly to the cellararium, oxwagons and handcarts bringing supplies to feed and clothe the many inhabitants of the abbey. Horses whinnied nearby as they were taken in and out of the stables and the shouts of yard boys rang out as they sluiced down the soiled floors. Farriers came to shoe horses at the forge opposite, and the saddlery at the other end of the stables was always busy. But no one came near Eldred and he began to wonder if he had been totally forgotten.

His dry tongue was cleaving to the roof of his mouth and his empty stomach was rumbling before he heard the noise

of the bar being lifted from its sockets on the outside of the
door. Almost blinded by the light of the early evening sun, he
squinted as the welcome figure of Gytha was silhouetted in
the doorway. Behind her, he saw the burly figure of William,
one of the proctor's men, who pushed her inside and
slammed the door, though he did not replace the bar.

'I'll give you a couple of minutes, that's all!' he yelled from
outside.

The plump goodwife of about thirty, another fair-haired
Saxon, put a basket on the floor, then threw her arms around
Eldred.

'What have you been up to, you silly man?' she cried, with
an attempt to cover her distress with scolding bravado. 'I've
brought you a skin of ale and some bread and meat. Now tell
me what's been going on!'

They sat down side by side on the board and he explained
how he had been unjustly accused of the theft.

'It counts as sacrilege and a mortal sin!' he wailed. 'Unless
I can prove my innocence, Prior Robert will probably hand
me over to the sheriff, for it's common knowledge that the
Chapter despises us Saxon servants. Then I'll hang, that's
for sure.'

Gytha tried to console him, saying that his status as a lay
brother would protect him through 'benefit of clergy', but
Eldred was pessimistic. 'The bishop's Court can't hang me
if they find me guilty, but they can choose to hand me over
to the King's men for sentence and execution.'

Again his wife tried to soothe him. 'When I leave here,
I'll go straight to Selwyn and ask him for help. He'll think of
something!'

Selwyn was Eldred's best friend – in fact, almost his only
friend, for in the restricted orbit of his life, he was confined
to work in the abbey for twelve hours a day and spent most

of the remainder on his bed. Selwyn was a servant in the
King's House, a substantial residence built in the abbey
precinct three years before by the new King John. The
monarch rarely visited it, but used it when his country-wide
perambulations brought him to this part of the West
Country. More often, it was loaned to other favourites in his
court, so a permanent staff was kept there and Selwyn was
one of the two stewards who maintained it. Though not a
Saxon himself, he had struck up a friendship with Eldred,
who often visited him in the kitchen of the King's House
and shared a pot of ale and a gossip.

Before Gytha could elaborate on how Selwyn might be
able to help, the door was flung open and William hustled
her out. Before it was slammed shut again, she called out
that she would bring him more food and drink in the morning.

Eldred ate and drank the simple fare that Gytha had
brought. Then, though it was still early, he settled down on
the hay in preference to the hard bed, more hopeful now
that his faithful wife was seeking some aid for him.

When Gytha left her husband, she went straight to the
King's House to seek Eldred's friend, Selwyn Vassel.

Gytha was a determined woman who loved her husband,
and she was grimly set upon rescuing him from the unjust
predicament in which he now found himself. She marched
across the abbey yard beside the high wall that separated it
from the bishop's palace, which occupied the south-western
corner of the precinct. This barrier turned sharply left to
reach the abbey's outer curtain wall. The King had built his
house against this, almost opposite the West Front of the
cathedral.

At the front of the house was a wide flight of steps leading up to the main door, used only by the King himself or his invited guests. Gytha used a small door for servants and tradesmen on the further side. This led into a scullery and storeroom, beyond which was a large kitchen, where Selwyn was usually to be found. As the house was presently unoccupied by any of the nobility, none of the other servants was present, his fellow steward being away visiting his parents in Cheddar.

Selwyn was a tall, erect man of forty years, with powerful shoulders and dark hair cropped short. He had a handsome and kindly face and as soon as Gytha entered, he jumped from his stool by the fire and sat her down opposite, giving her a pot of small ale to match his own. She hastily poured out her story and beseeched Selwyn to help his friend, swearing that he was innocent of the baseless accusation.

'But they'll hang him, I know!' she wailed. 'They have no idea who did this awful thing, but they need a scapegoat to satisfy the bishop.'

Selwyn did his best to soothe her agitation and promised to do all he could to help. Eventually he rose and went to the door.

'You bide here, Gytha. I'm off to talk to people around the abbey and see what the latest news might be.'

He vanished, leaving the goodwife sitting anxiously by the small fire that burned in the hearth. When he returned half an hour later his face bore a grave expression, which further increased Gytha's concern.

'Virtually all the monks and servants have been searching the precinct, looking for the stolen vessels,' he said. 'This must be the only place they have not visited, as it is the King's property.'

'They found nothing? Have they been to our home?'

Selwyn nodded. 'Yes, I spoke to one of the proctor's

bailiffs. Your dwelling was one of the first places they searched.'

'It would take them no more than a minute to discover there was nothing in our part of that humble room,' she said bitterly. 'So what happens now?'

'Eldred will be interrogated by the prior and other members of the Chapter this evening. Then if he does not confess and tell them where the treasure is hidden, he will be sent before the consistory court tomorrow.' Selwyn sighed. 'I know that Bishop Savaric is returning in the morning. I fear it will go badly with poor Eldred when he is hauled before him.'

Gytha sobbed quietly. 'If they hand him over to the sheriff and his gang of ruffians, it will be the end of him. Maybe they will torture him to get him reveal where he put the stolen vessels – but how can he tell them what he does not know?'

The tall steward paced up and down the kitchen, where clean cooking pots and ladles awaited the next batch of guests.

'We must get him out of the abbey and hide him until the real culprits are found. You go home now, Gytha, and stay quietly until I come to you with news. It is best if you know nothing of this; then you cannot be accused of being involved.'

She nodded mutely, trusting this good friend even with her husband's life. As she went to the door to leave, she had one further question.

'Can you do this alone, Selwyn? Can you not find help?'

He nodded. 'Eldred has another good friend. I will ask Riocas to share this task.'

It was getting dusk when they eventually came for him. The two proctor's men grabbed him by the elbows and hauled him off to the Chapter House, a semi-circular building attached to the back of the monks' dormitory, near the south transept. This was where the abbey's hierarchy met daily to settle their business, but this evening, only five of them were there when the guards hustled Eldred inside to stand before them. The half-circle of benches was empty and the interrogators sat on chairs on the low dais at the front, near the lectern from which a chapter of the Rule of St Benedict was read before each meeting, a ritual that gave the place its name.

Prior Robert, from his seat in the centre, began the proceedings.

'You wretched man, tell us where you have hidden those sacred vessels!' he demanded. Tonight, there was no trace of his usual oily benevolence, and he glowered at Eldred with a face like thunder. 'We have searched everywhere, but there is no sign of them.'

'You must have taken them out of the abbey, into the city,' rasped Brother Gilbert, the cellarer. 'Tell us what you did with them, if you want any chance of saving your neck!'

Two of the others also had their turn at haranguing the luckless lay brother, threatening him with every penalty from excommunication to flaying alive. One was Brother Thomas, the treasurer, the other the precentor, Brother Seymour, who was responsible for organising the cathedral services.

The only one of the five who did not castigate Eldred was Hubert of Frome, under whose supervision the lay brother worked. The sacrist looked sadly at him, either from sorrow at the man's present plight or disillusionment at his presumed treachery. Though usually a miserable, carping fellow, Hubert now seemed inclined to defend his lowly assistant.

Eldred had done all he could to protest his innocence, but

he could hardly get a word in between the harsh accusations pouring from the senior monks. Only when their vituperations eased off from lack of breath, did the sacrist manage to speak on Eldred's behalf.

'Brothers, I fail to see what evidence we have of this man's guilt,' he offered tentatively. 'As he pointed out, he has a key, so why should he break the lock?'

'For the very reason that you are making the suggestion, Hubert,' ranted the cellarer. 'It is a device to mislead us. I too have a key, but if I were to pillage the aumbry, I would also break it open to deflect suspicion.'

'That is a very illogical argument, Brother Gilbert,' answered Hubert, stubbornly. 'Eldred has not left the abbey since the theft and he has had no chance to secrete the stolen items, as he was arrested straight away.'

'You too are lacking in logic,' snapped the prior. 'How do we know when the treasures were stolen? He could have taken them during the night and only claimed to have discovered their disappearance today.'

'That would have given him plenty of opportunity to hide them away,' agreed the precentor, a stout, blustering *émigré* from Brittany.

The bad-tempered dispute went on for a time, again with no chance for Eldred to protest his innocence. Eventually, Prior Robert tired of their attempt to bully a confession from him and brought the meeting to a close.

'The bishop returns tomorrow and he will be appalled to hear of this loss. I will ask him to hold an immediate session of the Consistory Court to try this miserable wretch. Eldred, you have until the morning to confess your great sin and to tell us what you have done with those priceless relics. Bailiffs, take him back to his cell!'

*

Riocas of Dinan was a Breton who had lived in Bath for many years, since he had been chased out of his home town over the Channel for seducing the daughter of the harbour master.

He had a shop-house and a stall in the street market selling cheap fur linings and trimmings, mainly coney, squirrel, otter and cat. In fact, he was known locally as 'Riocas the Cat-Catcher', as this was how he obtained much of his stock.

Selwyn found him in one his usual evening haunts, the Black Ox alehouse in Fish Lane, an alley off High Street. They met there once or twice a week to grumble and put the world to rights over quarts of thin ale. Tonight, Riocas was sitting on a plank seat below a small window in the crowded taproom, staring out at the twilight. Selwyn dropped down alongside him and signalled a slatternly girl to bring him a pot of ale.

'We have a problem, friend,' he began without any preamble, then went on to tell the cat-catcher about Eldred's predicament and Gytha's plea for help. He paused as the serving wench, who looked about ten years old, banged an empty pewter pot on the window sill and filled it from a large earthenware jug, before topping up Riocas' half-empty quart. When she had moved away, Selwyn explained that they needed to get Eldred out of the abbey that very night.

'Unless we do, the next time we see him might well be from the foot of the gallows!' he concluded in sombre tones.

His companion nodded gravely. 'We can't let the poor little devil swing, I agree,' he grunted. Though Eldred was indeed rather small, he was almost a dwarf compared to these two men. Selwyn was tall, but Riocas was enough of a giant for the mothers of Bath to use him to frighten their misbehaving children. Not only was he huge in height and girth, but his massive head and spade-like hands seemed straight from some ancient forest legend. His face was a rocky crag, with heavy eyebrow ridges, a bulbous nose and a lantern jaw like the prow of a ship.

Selwyn resumed his story after a long swig from his tankard.

'We must get him out before the morning, because that bastard of a prior is intent on finding a culprit – any culprit – so that he can appease the bishop when he returns tomorrow.'

'I suppose he's in that fleapit that the proctors use, next to the stables?' growled Riocas. 'That's no problem – a pig with the palsy could break into that – but where could we take him?'

'It will have to be out of the city. Bath is too small to hide him for long. We'll have to keep him hidden until the real thief is discovered.'

Riocas ran sausage-like fingers through the wiry black stubble that passed for his hair. 'Out in the country then! Somewhere that most folk keep clear of, but near enough for us to get food to him.'

Their commitment to a friend in need was assumed without question and Selwyn responded with a suggestion.

'What about Solsbury Hill? Not too far away for us – and all these daft tales of haunting and evil spirits will help keep folk from snooping around there.'

They discussed details for the space of two more quarts and agreed to meet at the King's House as soon as they heard the abbey bell for matins, soon after midnight. When he left the alehouse, Selwyn called on Gytha and told her what they had planned.

'I'll hide him in the King's House for the rest of the night; we could never get him out of the city until morning, when the gates are opened. They'll come here to seek him straight away as soon as they discover he's gone, but just play dumb. You know nothing, right?'

Leaving the wife worried but hopeful, the steward went back to his kitchen, thankful that his fellow servant, the bottler, was away. With the house empty and no guests expected for several weeks, he was free to find a hiding place for Eldred. The cellar, with its stores of food and wine, were obvious targets for a search and, deciding that boldness was the best solution, he went upstairs to the four bedchambers and chose the largest, the one reserved for King John himself. A thick mattress stuffed with lambswool lay on a wooden plinth and two large clothes chests stood opposite. A chair and a table were the only other furniture, set near the empty fireplace. As steward, Selwyn knew every inch of the house and decided that here was the best place for concealing his unfortunate friend.

Soon after the abbey bell rang out its midnight summons to matins, the first holy office of the day, Riocas slipped into the house, moving very quietly for a man of such bulk. After a quick consultation, he and Selwyn went out into the abbey yard and sidled along the back of the stables, taking care not to awaken any of the grooms and cleaners, young boys who slept on the hay with the horses. Rounding the far end, they went to the last door, that of the proctor's cell, where Riocas examined the securing bar in the dim starlight.

'Not even a lock on it!' he whispered, as he carefully lifted the stout piece of oak from its iron brackets. It was never contemplated that any outsider would wish to rescue the usual run of prisoners, mostly drunks and petty thieves.

Selwyn vanished inside and almost immediately reappeared with a dishevelled Eldred, who seemed quite composed, considering the tribulations of the day. The cat-catcher quietly replaced the bar and they slid back behind the row of stables and made their way back along the palace wall to the King's House.

Once in the kitchen, Selwyn sat Eldred by the fire and gave him a wooden bowl of potage, which he filled from an iron pot hanging from a trivet hanging over the glowing logs.

'Get this down you, boy, compliments of King John!' he said, as he added a hunk of coarse bread. 'He doesn't know it, but I doubt he'd begrudge you.'

He got the same for Riocas and himself, and the three conspirators sat on stools around the fire to discuss how they would manage Eldred's escape.

'They're bound to come here looking for you in the morning, but I think I can keep you safe. Then later in the day, we'll get you out of the city and up to Solsbury Hill.'

Eldred shivered, but not from the cold. 'They say it's haunted and is the lair of demons!' he muttered. 'How can I survive up there?'

'Better than you'd survive the gallows-tree with a hemp rope around your neck!' retorted Riocas bluntly.

At dawn, there was a rumpus in the abbey yard, started by William, the proctor's bailiff when he found his prisoner flown. Then a succession of abbey seniors arrived, and soon the prior himself added to the fury. His normally ingratiating manner had vanished and he was livid with anger at having his prize scapegoat spirited away only hours before he intended parading him before Bishop Savaric as the perpetrator of the dastardly theft.

Once again, all the abbey brothers and servants were mobilised to search for the sacrist's assistant. The gatekeepers on the two abbey gates into the city were interrogated and all swore that no one resembling Eldred had passed through their portals.

'He must still be within the precinct,' fumed Prior Robert. 'Seek him out, wherever he might be hiding. There are others involved in this; they must also be rooted out and punished!'

Inevitably, the King's House was included in this frantic search, though as it was royal property, not within the jurisdiction of the prior or bishop, the ecclesiastical faction had to tread carefully.

The cellarer, Brother Gilbert, was deputed to tackle this task and though he tried to browbeat Selwyn, everyone knew that the steward was a royal servant, not beholden to the Abbey in any way. However, he could hardly refuse them entry without arousing grave suspicion, but did so grudgingly, saying that he would have to send word of the intrusion to Gloucester, where the King was currently quartered. He followed Gilbert, his assistant, Maurice, and William the bailiff everywhere in the house, muttering his protests. When they went upstairs to peer into the upper chambers, Selwyn at first refused to produce the key to the royal bedroom.

'That would be too much, Brother Gilbert!' he complained. 'He is your sovereign lord as much as he is mine. Would you dare to do this if you were in Westminster or Windsor?'

The cellarer looked uneasy, but was adamant. 'What is there to hide, steward? Let us just glance within from here. That can hardly amount to treason!'

Having calculated the risks, Selwyn made a great show of reluctantly producing the key from his pouch.

'This is the only room with a lock, with good reason!' he growled, and pushed open the door, but stood with his body half in the entrance. 'See, it is as bare as a widow's pantry!'

Gilbert glared around the room. 'What's in those large chests?'

'Nothing, until the King's chamberlains arrive with his robes. Send your man here to look, if nothing less will satisfy you!'

The steward grabbed Maurice, a weedy young man with a long nose, and pushed him into the room.

'May God grant that the King never learns that you defiled his bedchamber!'

The cellarer's monk scurried across the room and with quick movements raised the lids of each chest and banged them down almost instantly. 'Empty, Brother Gilbert!' he squeaked.

'Check the bed, now that you're there,' snapped Gilbert defiantly.

As he hurried back to the door, Maurice made a couple of panic-stricken prods into the mattress. 'No one hiding there, brother!' he panted, as he pushed his way out of the room and the imagined wrath of the irascible monarch.

Gilbert scowled at Selwyn, then led his fellow searchers back down the stairs, stamping his feet to mark his irritation.

'If you see hide or hair of that damned fellow, you will let me know at once – or face the consequences!' he blustered as he went out into the abbey yard once again.

Selwyn spent a few minutes needlessly brushing the kitchen floor, to make sure that the cellarer did not make a surprise return visit. Then he went back up to the King's chamber and stood by the bed.

'Are you still alive, Eldred?' he asked in a low voice. He was answered by a muffled cry of distress and going to the back of the plinth that supported the mattress, gave it a hefty tug to pull it away from the wall. It was really an inverted wooden box, open at the end against the wall. From the gap, a dishevelled figure crawled out crabwise and lay gasping on the floor.

'Another few minutes and I would have suffocated,' he croaked. 'Thank God I'm thin, for the space was the same height as my body. I could hardly breathe!'

Selwyn helped him up and dusted the dirt and cobwebs from his habit. 'You'd not have breathed very well with a rope around your neck, either,' he said unsympathetically. 'Come down and have some food and drink. We'll have to decide what to do with you next.'

When Eldred was reminded of the plan to smuggle him out of the city to a hiding place several miles away, he refused to countenance the idea.

'I cannot leave my wife so far away,' he protested, to the exasperation of his two friends. 'How will she survive without me being nearby?'

'What good can you do here, skulking in some cellar, afraid to show your face to any man?' demanded Riocas.

'And where will you find such a cellar, eh?' snapped Selwyn, annoyed that Eldred was proving so difficult after all the effort and risks that he and the cat-catcher had taken. 'No way can you be hidden here in the King's House, for the other steward will be returning in a day or two. Also I would not put it past the prior or sheriff to make another search in their desperation to find you.'

They argued the matter for several minutes, then the lay brother came up with another suggestion, which the other two received with a marked lack of enthusiasm.

'I could seek sanctuary in one of the churches,' proposed Eldred. 'That would give me more than a month of immunity from arrest. Surely evidence of my innocence will be forthcoming long before then!'

Riocas, whose fondness for the Church and all its attributes was sadly lacking, was scathing about the idea. 'And if it doesn't, you'll be dragged out at the end and will have gained nothing.'

'I could claim "benefit of clergy",' replied Eldred, stubbornly. 'I am able to recite "the neck verse" well enough.'

This was a device whereby men, including lay brothers, could avoid being tried in the secular courts by showing that they could read and were therefore in holy orders. The ability to recite a short excerpt of the Twenty-first Psalm was accepted as a convenient test of literacy, even though it was often learned parrot-fashion by illiterates. This had saved many a man from being hanged and was therefore cynically known as 'the neck verse'.

'In the circumstances, I doubt the bishop's court would resist handing you over to the Commissioners of Assize for sentence,' retorted Riocas. 'So you'd still end up dancing on the end of a rope.'

Selwyn's brow was furrowed in thought. 'It would be a terrible gamble, for if the real villains were not found in that time, you would be doomed.'

Eldred was still obdurate about his intention, but Selwyn had not finished. 'If you are really intent about seeking sanctuary, why seek a church in the city? You are already on consecrated ground – an abbey, no less.'

Riocas was doubtful. 'Is the King's House included in that? You were quick enough to claim its immunity when they came here searching.'

'If he steps outside, then he is safe, for every inch of a church's domain constitutes sanctuary. There is no need to be within the building itself, prostrate in the chancel, clutching the altar-cloth!' Selwyn added sarcastically.

The cat-catcher refused to abandon his objections. 'If that

be so, then the proctor's cell is also included in sanctuary!'

'In strict canon law, perhaps it is!' retorted the steward. 'But I'm damned sure that the bishop and rest of his crew would take little notice of that, unless someone took a year to go to Rome to protest to the Pope!'

The agitated lay brother became impatient with this bickering.

'I will creep out tonight and seek sanctuary in one of the city churches. St Michael Within is the nearest. I have met Father Eustace, its parish priest, he seems a compassionate man. I will prevail upon him to offer me the protection of his church.'

Selwyn and Riocas tried to dissuade Eldred of this dangerous venture, but he was firmly set on the plan. A devout man, he was of the opinion that the ages-old traditions of the Church would be proof against any machinations of the abbey prior and his Chapter. Eventually, they came to a compromise.

'I also have some slight acquaintance with Father Eustace,' said Selwyn. 'Before you expose yourself in the city streets to try to reach his church, I will speak with him and make sure that he is willing to offer you sanctuary. You are in the employ of his bishop, for one thing, and he may be reluctant to cross Savaric Fitzgeldewine.'

When Eldred reluctantly agreed, the royal steward set off across the small city to St Michael's. He found the parish priest huddled in a corner of the nave, hearing a whispered confession from a fat matron, down on her knees before him. Selwyn stayed a respectful distance away, out of earshot and when the woman had struggled to her feet after receiving a trivial penance and a benediction, he approached the priest and asked if he might discuss something with him.

Eustace was a short, slightly fat man with a round red face

under his tonsured ginger hair. A glowing nose suggested a fondness for the wineskin, but he had an amiable nature that went well with his broad country accent indicating his Dorset origins.

'If you've come to confess, my son, I hope it's more interesting than that poor widow who's just left!' he said with an impish grin. 'She comes thrice each week to waste my time with trivialities, just to have someone to talk to!'

When Selwyn indicated that this was something much more serious, Eustace invited him into the sacristy, a tiny room off the chancel where vestments and service books were kept.

Pulling out a couple of stools, the priest then produced a pottery flask of red Anjou wine and two pewter cups. When they were settled over a drink each, Selwyn broached his problem.

'I trust this will enjoy the sanctity of the confessional, as much as your dealings with the widow just now,' he began. 'For I might be revealing my own complicity in aiding an alleged criminal, though it concerns an unjust accusation.'

The cheerful vicar immediately became serious, but assured the steward that his lips would be sealed. Selwyn set out all the facts and ended by asking if it would compromise Eustace with Bishop Savaric if Eldred sought sanctuary in his church.

The parish priest looked crestfallen, saying that it was an impossible request. 'But not because of the bishop's undoubted anger at my agreement – though in fact that is not required when someone seeks sanctuary, as it is an ancient and compassionate act provided by God Almighty, not within the gift of some insignificant priest, be he vicar, bishop or even Pope.'

'Why cannot it be granted in this case, then?' asked

Selwyn, secretly relieved that Eldred's scheme had been defeated before it had even begun.

'Because the Church withholds the privilege of sanctuary from those accused of sacrilege – and the theft of holy vessels would certainly be considered as such.'

'But he is innocent of that crime! We just need some time to find the true culprits.'

Eustace shook his head. 'I fear it is the nature of the *allegation* that matters, not the eventual truth.' He paused to take a mouthful of his wine. 'Even if he was granted sanctuary, he would have to confess his guilt to the coroner before his forty days' grace was up, otherwise he would not be able to abjure the realm.'

This meant leaving England, dressed in sackcloth and carrying a rough cross, by going to a port nominated by the coroner where he had to take the first available ship out of the country.

Eustace shook his head sadly. 'There are several reasons why this will not work, my son. If your friend entered here under the impression that he was safe, it would be a false hope, as because of the sacrilege issue, the sheriff would be entitled to immediately drag him out and behead him in the street outside!'

When they had finished their wine, the priest reassured Selwyn that their conversation would remain confidential, leaving him with the impression that Eustace was not too fond of the arrogant, overbearing Bishop Savaric.

Selwyn returned to the King's House and gave the priest's verdict to Eldred, who accepted it more philosophically that the steward expected.

'So be it. Then I am fated to share Solsbury Hill with outlaws, ghosts and other fiends,' he said, crossing himself as he saw the sacrist and prior do twenty times a day.

'You'll not be there long,' said Riocas heartily, trying to reassure their friend that he would be safe from the reputed demons that inhabited the hill. 'Now we need to decide how we are to go about getting you there.'

The escape had to be made in two stages, as the city gates were locked at dusk. The sheriff was obsessional about keeping out the bands of outlaws who roamed the countryside, pillaging villages and small towns. Not long before, he had hanged one of the gate-keepers who had accepted a bribe to let in a thief after midnight. So Eldred's exit from the city had to be made in daylight, but to get such a well-known face out of the abbey compound needed darkness.

An hour before midnight, when the priests and monks were still asleep before being called for matins, Selwyn and Eldred slipped out of the King's House and, keeping to the wall of the precinct, went behind the bath-house opposite and then past the back of the infirmary beyond it. The night was dark, with heavy clouds obscuring a crescent moon as they slunk along the wall. Where the lay cemetery gave way to the monks' burial ground there was no night porter to challenge anyone entering or leaving. Moments later, they were walking along the nearby High Street to reach Twichen Lane, where Riocas had his shop. Though nominally there was a curfew after dark, there were still a few people about, mostly drunks. Prompted by Selwyn, Eldred feigned a slight stagger whenever anyone came within a few yards, until they reached the doorway in the alley that housed the home and business premises of their friend.

The cat-catcher was waiting for them and soon they were in his cramped room, which smelled strongly of the animal skins that were curing out in the yard behind. Over ale and bread, they discussed the second phase of the escape to be mounted early next morning.

'I'll take my cart out of town, as I often do, looking for cony skins in the villages around. People are happy to sell them to me at four for a half-penny.'

The gaunt giant seemed to be enjoying this escapade, but come the dawn, Eldred was less than happy at being hidden under a stinking heap of part-tanned cowhides in the small cart that was pulled by Riocas' donkey. As well as trading in small furs, he had a sideline carrying hides for tanners, who often needed to send some skins to other tanneries in the area for further processing. The porter at the North Gate knew him well and waved him through without any question, other than a bawdy remark about the smell that wafted from his cart.

Once well outside the city, Eldred emerged gasping from under the pile of rank skins, which he declared was worse than being hidden for an hour under the King's bed. Looking around, he saw that they were already within sight of Solsbury Hill, which loomed up as a green cone on the north side of the road from Bath towards Chippenham.

The little cart jogged along the track, the old Roman Fosse Way, until it neared the base of the hill, the lower slopes of which were heavily wooded. Then the skinny donkey had a harder task, as Riocas pulled it off the road into a steep lane on the left, which went up the valley on the eastern side of the base of Solsbury Hill towards the hamlet of Swainswick, a collection of dismal huts.

'We'll stop here, before the village,' announced Riocas. 'They're a nosy lot, best that they don't see me dropping you.'

As Eldred clambered out, Riocas handed him down a bundle tied up in a blanket provided by Gytha, in which was a fresh loaf, a lump of hard cheese and a cooked lamb shank wrapped in a cloth.

'This will keep you alive until tomorrow morning. Be here about this time and I'll bring you some more food and hopefully news of what's happening back in the city.'

With that, he flicked the backside of the long-suffering donkey with his willow switch and clattered off, leaving a bemused Eldred to his lonely sojourn on Solsbury Hill.

The fugitive lay brother slung the bundle over his shoulder and with a quick glance up and down the lane to make sure no one was spying on him, vanished into the bushes at the side of the track. After a few hundred yards, the ground began to rise steeply and soon he was puffing as he climbed through the dense thickets of spindly ash, birch and beech that clothed the lower slopes of the hill. There were bigger oaks and elms here and there, but charcoal burners had felled many of them over the years, leaving clearings clogged with brambles, coarse grass and seedling trees.

Eldred kept wary eyes and ears open for signs of other men, as he knew that Solsbury was the haunt of outlaws and other fugitives, but at present it seemed deserted, apart from the sound of birds and the occasional rustle of unseen animals in the undergrowth. With only a blanket for protection, he needed somewhere to shelter for the night – and perhaps for many nights to follow, if his friends failed to discover who had really stolen the abbey treasures.

Though he was a city dweller rather than a countryman, Eldred had plenty of common sense and felt confident of surviving for a time on his own, as long as he was supplied with a little food. But he needed somewhere to hide, as much from other people on the hill as from the inevitable rain and cold winds, even though so far it had been a mild September. As he climbed towards the summit, he saw several fox and badger dens, but they were too small for him to creep into. Several clear springs seeped out from under overhanging banks, but again there was insufficient shelter for him under these.

Panting with the effort of hauling himself up the incline, he was almost at the end of the trees, where they gave way to the earth rampart that encircled the flat top, before he found a place to settle. Here a very steep part of the hill had crumbled, exposing a weathered rock-face a few yards long and a dozen feet high. He thought perhaps the ancient people who had occupied the top of Solsbury long ago had used this as a quarry to obtain the yellow-grey stone for their defences up above. But whatever the cause, he was happy to see a small cavity at the bottom, where rock had either fallen out or been taken way. The hole was too small to be called a cave, but was enough for him to crouch inside under a lintel formed by a band of the limestone strata. In front was a narrow weed-covered platform, with brambles loaded with ripe blackberries growing part-way across the hole.

Relieved, Eldred evicted a pair of squawking magpies from the hole and kicked away some loose stones from the bottom of the crude shelter. Dropping his bundle outside, he collected an armful of loose bracken and grass to pad the floor of his new home. Sinking down on it with a sigh of relief, he found that he could manage to sit with his head just clear of the rock above – and that if he pulled his knees up, he could lie sideways under the overhang. It was just as well, for at that moment, it started to rain.

Riocas was back in Bath by noon, having completed his business in Swainswick. Though he often went there during his tour of the surrounding villages for skins, he had made a point of visiting it today as a cover for dropping off Eldred at Solsbury. He had picked up a dozen coney and six red squirrel pelts there – and had only just missed catching a black cat on his way out of the village.

Now he was back with Selwyn at his shop, earnestly discussing how they should proceed. They were in the cat-catcher's back room, out of hearing of Riocas' young apprentice, who sat in the shop at the front, the window-shutter opened down to form a counter to display their goods to passers-by.

'Eldred can't stay up there for long,' declared Selwyn. 'The autumn is upon us, the nights are getting colder. We have to lift the suspicion hanging over the little fellow – or else smuggle him and his wife somewhere far away if we wish to save his neck.'

'Any news from the abbey today?' demanded Riocas, his coarse features glowering over the rim of a tankard.

'The prior is still smarting over the harsh words that the bishop no doubt gave him. They searched the abbey again this morning, then came once more to the King's House and virtually ransacked it, without any result. They knew that I had befriended Eldred, so probably only my status as a King's servant prevented them from arresting me.'

Riocas grunted. 'I doubt many know that he was also my friend, so we should be safe enough there. But what can we do now?'

'Discover the true culprits – and the whereabouts of that chalice and pyx. Any ideas?'

The Breton rubbed his massive jaw, now bristling with coarse stubble. 'As it stands, that treasure is worth little to any thief. It's too recognizable. They would want to sell it on for coinage, even at half its true value.'

Selwyn agreed. 'And where would they be likely to do that?'

The giant shrugged his great shoulders. 'Some jeweller or moneylender, almost certainly a Jew. Better to do it in Bristol or Winchester for safety.'

The royal steward looked dubious. 'They'd have to get there first. Easier to dispose of it in Bath, even if they got less money for it. There are several gold- and silversmiths in the city.'

After more discussion, they agreed to tour the alehouses to listen discreetly to any gossip. They both had acquaintances who had an ear to the less savoury activities that went on in the narrow streets and more squalid alleys.

After sharing a bowl of potage and more ale, Selwyn went off to see Gytha, to tell her that her husband had been safely delivered to Solsbury Hill, and to collect another blanket and some more bread and meat for delivery next morning – to which he added a small wineskin filched from the King's stores.

When the two conspirators met again in the evening, Riocas had some news from his spying around the city taverns.

'I talked with Alfred, the night-soil collector, who I know well. He told me what he heard this morning at the shop of Ranulf of Exeter.'

Selwyn was dubious, not about Ranulf the goldsmith, but about Alfred, the lowliest of the low, who scratched a living from shovelling out the ordure from privies in the town and taking it in his stinking handcart to dump in the River Avon.

'That Alfred is half-way mad!' he objected. 'Surely you don't rely on anything he tells you?'

The furrier shook his head. 'He's odd, I grant you. But Alfred usually tells the truth as he sees it, being too lacking in imagination to make things up. Anyway, he says that when he was in Ranulf's yard yesterday, emptying his privy-pit, he heard the goldsmith telling his journeyman that if they came back, not to have any dealings with the men who tried to sell him a gold-lined silver box.'

Selwyn's eyebrows went up his forehead. 'That would have to be the missing pyx! But everyone in Bath knows it's been stolen from the abbey. Are you sure that Alfred wasn't making this up?'

Riocas shook his formidable head. 'Why should he pick on that one thing? He had no reason to invent it – and he didn't mention the gold chalice, which would have been much more dramatic.'

'But what about Ranulf? He would know straight away where it came from. Why didn't he rush off and tell the prior or the sheriff?'

The cat-catcher gave a cynical grin. 'Ranulf? He's well-known for buying stolen goods, but not ones this valuable – and from our own abbey! Yet he'd keep quiet about it, for if it became known that he had a loose mouth, he'd forever lose the custom from all the thieves for miles around.'

Selwyn stirred these new facts around in his mind for a moment. 'Alfred didn't hear who those men were, did he?'

'No, I asked him that. The goldsmith only spoke to his journeyman for a moment, as they were standing at the back door. That's all Alfred heard.'

Selwyn looked out of his friend's unglazed window. The shutter was open and he could see that it was already getting dark.

'Too late tonight, but first thing in the morning, I'll be having a word with that Ranulf.'

But Fate had other plans.

Riocas could hardly visit Swainswick two days in succession, so next morning he stopped his cart on the main road at the

junction of the lane and walked up a little way, trusting to
Eldred's common sense to look out for him. Soon, the fugitive emerged from the bushes and eagerly took the bundle
from the cat-catcher. He was hungry and also grateful for
another blanket; although he had slept fitfully in his rocky
shelter, the autumn night had been chilly.

'If Selwyn is successful today, you may not need to spend
much longer here,' announced Riocas, optimistically. He
told Eldred what he had heard from the night-soil collector
and the fact that the King's steward was at that moment
trying to discover who had offered the stolen pyx for sale.

The lay brother was so overcome with relief and gratitude that he flung his arms around Riocas, the difference in
their sizes making him look like a squirrel clinging to an oak
tree.

'Have you any idea who the thieves might be?' demanded
the embarrassed giant. 'From what Alfred heard there must
have been more than one who approached the goldsmith.'

Eldred stepped back, then shrugged. 'It surely has to be
someone from the abbey,' he said pensively, but their conversation was cut short, as they heard the clopping of hoofs
coming along the main road and Eldred rapidly vanished
after a hurried farewell. Riocas ostentatiously stood emptying his bladder into the bushes as an excuse for stopping his
cart in such a lonely spot, then as soon as two merchants
had passed on their horses, he turned his donkey round and
headed back towards Bath, anxious to hear if Selwyn had
learned anything from Ranulf of Exeter.

When he had stabled his beast and walked to the King's
House, he discovered the sad fact that neither Selwyn nor
anyone else would learn anything ever again from the goldsmith, for he had suffered a violent death.

'His house was plundered late last night,' said the steward, as they sat in the kitchen over quarts of the King's best ale. 'Ranulf lived alone, and his journeyman found him when he opened up this morning. He was lying in the shop, beaten to death, his head a bloody mess.'

Riocas shook his head in disgust. 'So now we'll never know who offered him the pyx! You say the place was robbed?'

'It was in great disorder and his journeyman, after taking stock, said that some of the smaller, more valuable things were missing. Large objects, like silver plate, dishes and cruets, were left behind.'

Riocas used the back of his hand to wipe ale from the dark beard that rimmed his jutting jaw. 'And I'd given poor Eldred hope that his exile would soon be over. Now he'll have to stay on Solsbury Hill for a while longer until we find who those bastards were!'

The news of the goldsmith's murder spread all over the city within minutes, rather than hours, including to the abbey.

They knew nothing about the fact that someone had offered the dead victim one of the objects stolen from the cathedral church and Selwyn pondered whether he should tell the sheriff, or even Prior Robert, what the night-soil man had alleged. The problem was that even if the feeble-minded man was believed, could it make matters even worse for Eldred? If the men who offered the pyx to Ranulf could not be identified, then Eldred might be accused not only of a sacrilegious theft, but also a callous murder! The steward decided to hold his tongue for the moment and hope that the murdering thieves would give themselves away by some other means.

That evening, Selwyn and Riocas met at Gytha's humble dwelling in Binnebury Lane, to discuss the situation and for the furrier to pick up a clean pair of breeches and a tunic to take to Eldred. As Gytha was now virtually destitute, without even the few pence a week that lay brothers earned from the abbey, Selwyn and Riocas provided food for both Eldred and his wife.

'It's going be harder each day for me to take provisions to him,' said Riocas gravely. 'I can't find an excuse to go every day to Swainswick, or even along the Chippenham road. The gate-keepers will get suspicious, even though they know me. There are plenty of spies about reporting to both the sheriff and the Abbey – and with this murder, they'll be more vigilant that ever.'

Gytha became tearful, suggesting that it might be best for her husband to make a run for it and try to go somewhere like Gloucester or Salisbury to start a new life, where one day she could join him. Selwyn tried to calm and reassure her.

'Running away would look as if he was admitting his guilt, woman! And how would he make a living elsewhere? There are few places where he could get employment polishing the brasses in a cathedral!'

Riocas nodded his agreement. 'This murder and robbery is to his advantage, much as it inconvenienced poor Ranulf. Sooner or later, it will be learned who those villains are – and that will prove that Eldred must be innocent.'

In the Chapter meeting at the abbey that day, Eldred's innocence was not on the agenda, only his assumed guilt and the frustrating fact of his disappearance.

'He must be excommunicated, of course,' the precentor angrily declared, but the prior's response was scathing.

'What use is that, brother? Will it restore our chalice and pyx?' he snapped, his usual veneer of affability now stripped away.

Hubert, the sacrist, had a more practical observation. 'We have heard that the workshop of Ranulf was pillaged when he was killed last night. I dislike slandering the dead, but he had a poor reputation for honesty. Could it be that he had obtained our treasure from whoever was the thief and it was then stolen again by others, who had learned that it was in his possession?'

As usual, the cellarer was keen to deride the sacrist's opinion.

'Brother Hubert, you need not include "whoever was the thief" in your speeches. We all know it was Eldred, may God curse him!'

'I rather thought that the Almighty was the fount of forgiveness,' retorted Hubert in his mild voice. 'And I still need some proof before I am satisfied that my assistant is guilty of this crime.'

Brother Gilbert muttered, 'Then you are an old fool!' under his breath, but the prior brought them to order.

'It is useless for us to bicker over this matter, brothers. We have searched the abbey time and again with no result, so we have no option but to leave it to the sheriff and his men.'

The cellarer was determined to have the last word. 'I still suspect that royal steward had a hand in this, somehow. The damned man was too thick with Eldred. I've seen them together many times.' He glowered around at his colleagues. 'If I was the sheriff, I'd put him to the torture, King's man or not!'

Up on Solsbury Hill, Eldred decided to explore a little. He had spent an uncomfortable night in his rocky cleft, but now that the day had improved, he felt the need to stretch his legs. Though he was still nervous about meeting others on the hill, whether human or fiendish, he urgently needed a change from the constriction of the rock face. Leaving his blankets hidden under some fern fronds in his sleeping place, he moved sideways to regain the trees and clambered up from them onto a grassy bank. A deep groove ran beyond this, a long-overgrown ditch the height of a man, which ran almost entirely around the top of the hill, which was a flat, rounded triangle.

The inner bank of the ditch was steep and rose higher than his head, but some yards to his left there was a break in the rampart, with a gap that went through at an angle to give easier access to the enclosure, a couple of acres of weedy grass. He knew from years of listening to gossip and old men's tales, that in ancient times this had been a fortress with a stockade all around it. There were many lurid theories as to who once lived up here, varying from a race of giants to the Roman legions, but today it was deserted as Eldred ventured warily through the gap on to the small plain. The sun was shining intermittently between the scudding clouds and in the brightness of an autumn afternoon, he felt more confident about being on this hill, which had such a mystical and often threatening reputation. There was a striking view, especially to the south and west, and he could see the tower of the abbey church and the city walls alongside the silver streak of the Avon, as it ran at the foot of the many hills that surrounded Bath.

His eyes misted as he wondered if he would ever see his wife and the familiar things of his everyday life back in the city. Unless his two staunch friends could discover who had stolen the abbey's treasures, he would become a hunted outlaw, cut off from God and man for the rest of his miserable life. Overcome by grief and self-pity, he sank on to the grass and began to sob.

After a few moments, Eldred pulled himself together and

wiped his eyes with the sleeve of his tunic. He had abandoned his lay brother's brown cassock for this exile in the
countryside, and wore instead the thigh-length belted tunic
and worsted breeches that were the usual garb of the com-
moner.

Squatting there in the sunshine, he plucked a grassy stem
and chewed it ruminatively, staring unseeingly at the distant
view as he tried to make sense of the catastrophe that had so
suddenly disrupted his ordered life. He fully realised that
he'd had to take the blame for the theft merely because he
was the nearest and most convenient scapegoat, rather than
that he was the target of some foul conspiracy. But who
could possibly be the true culprits?

The abbey was a tightly knit community, full of petty
squabbles and jealousies, for all that the religious life was
supposed to be a haven of peace, tranquillity and benign
tolerance. Monks and their acolytes had the same emotions
and faults as men anywhere, saints being very few and far
between. Many were there because their families had pushed
them into the life as children, others were escaping from
problems with their personal affairs – and others merely
sought advancement in the ecclesiastical hierarchy, often
linked to secular politics, the prime example being the ambitious Bishop Savaric.

But who had stolen the chalice and the pyx, agonised
Eldred. Was it someone from outside or was it an inhabi-
tant of the abbey? And if the latter, was it a lay brother or a
monk? But what would a monk, many of whom were
ordained priests, want with gold and silver?

Eldred immediately realised that that was a stupid question, as many of the higher ranks of the clergy were amongst
the richest men in England – and rich men often coveted
even more wealth. However, he could hardly credit that the

bishop or the prior were likely to have stolen treasures from their own church.

As he sat looking over the rolling hills of Somerset, he could not help thinking of those he disliked most in the abbey. Though a mild-natured fellow, like all men Eldred had those whose company he preferred to avoid. His immediate master, the sacrist Hubert, was a miserable, carping man, but had never caused him any serious trouble, and indeed, had been the only Chapter member to express doubts about Eldred's guilt.

He thought of Prior Robert as a 'whited sepulchre', as the Bible had it, for his permanent affability and ostentatious devoutness was a sham, but he was an unlikely robber. This applied also to the mean-minded precentor, Brother Seymour, whose Spartan existence suggested that he would not know how to spend gold even if he had any. The treasurer, Thomas de Granville, was an unknown quantity to Eldred, a silent, rather sinister character who spoke rarely and then only in French or Latin, as he had never bothered to learn English since coming from an abbey in Normandy.

Time and again, Eldred's mind came back to the cellarer. Brother Gilbert was a bluff, worldly man who had been a soldier and then a cloth merchant before taking the vows of a Benedictine a dozen years ago. As with so many monks, some of whom had something to hide in their past, little was known of his previous life except that he was originally a Bristol man. He had gained the post of cellarer because of his previous experience of commerce. Certainly his efficiency in running the complex business of feeding and housing the abbey community was notable, exceeding his enthusiasm for devotional duties, which he often evaded with the excuse that he had to attend to some urgent matter in his stores. Eldred had not a shred of evidence that Gilbert might be involved in the theft, but his personal antipathy to the man's abrasive character and contemptuous manner made him a possible candidate in the lay brother's mind.

A cloud passed over the sun and a sudden cold breeze brought Eldred out of his reverie, so he rose and began walking around the inside of the ditch, eating the last of his bread and cheese, which he had saved in the pouch on his belt. He felt a sudden overwhelming loneliness and yearned for the next morning, when he would go down to the track to meet Riocas and, he hoped, learn some good news that would end his exile in this strange place.

Riocas and Selwyn were endeavouring to find that good news for their lonely friend when they met again in the fur-trader's shop late that afternoon. The steward would have preferred to have used his royal kitchen for their discussion, as the pervading smell of partly cured animal pelts was not particularly pleasant, but he realised that if Riocas was seen to be visiting him too often in the abbey enclave, it might arouse suspicion about who might have been responsible for Eldred's escape.

The cat-catcher pushed aside a basket of rabbit skins from his table and replaced it with a crock of cider and two pottery mugs.

'What do we do now, my friend?' he asked, as he poured out the murky liquid. 'If all the sheriff's men have failed to find Ranulf's thieving killers, what chance do we have?'

'That's assuming that they have any connection with the missing valuables from the abbey,' added Selwyn, rather despondently. 'We have no evidence that the murder of Ranulf is anything to do with the theft.'

Riocas disagreed, thumping his mug down on the table. 'It's too much of coincidence that the night-soil man heard about two men offering what must have been the pyx to Ranulf, on the very day of his killing.'

'You may be right,' admitted the steward. 'But what can we do about it?'

After some more discussion, the two men decided, mainly from a lack of any other ideas, to visit the scene of the crime to see if they could find anything that may have escaped the attention of the sheriff's men. When they had fortified themselves with some bread and the remains of a rabbit pie, together with what was left of the cider, they walked across the town almost to the West Gate, which led out on to the Bristol road. A lane ran around inside the town wall, in which was a row of houses and shops, the first being Ranulf's premises. The two heavily shuttered windows on each side of the door were firmly closed, but when Riocas banged on the panels, the door was opened and a timorous face appeared. They recognised the late owner's assistant, who was qualified as a craftsman by his guild, but had not yet been able to set up his own business. Being paid by the day or *journee*, he was known as a 'journeyman'.

Selwyn and Riocas commiserated with him over the loss of his master and learned that, much to the man's relief, the business had been taken over by Ranulf's cousin, so his job would be saved. They explained that they wanted to see the place where his master had been fatally assaulted. To justify this strange request, they truthfully explained that they were trying to clear their friend Eldred's name, though carefully omitting any mention of their part in his escape.

Their frankness – plus the passage of a silver penny from Riocas' purse – persuaded the smith to let them into the shop, which consisted of a front room where articles were displayed for sale, together with a workshop at the back and living quarters on the upper floor.

'I found him in this room,' explained the journeyman. 'He was lying here, in the middle of the floor, his head covered in blood!' He made a dramatic gesture with his arm. Though the floor had been washed, there were still ominous brown stains between the cracks in the flagstones.

Selwyn looked around at the trestle tables against three walls, where a few silver brooches, bracelets and earrings were on display.

'They took nothing made of gold then?' he asked.

'The master kept all that locked in a stout chest in his chamber upstairs,' explained the journeyman. 'They took some silver bracelets and necklaces from here, which were quite valuable. I suspect that when they found that they had killed him, they ran away without looking for anything more.'

Riocas looked around the shop, where a chair lay against a wall, one of its legs broken off and a large pot lay smashed on the floor.

'There was quite a struggle, by the looks of it!'

'My master was a big man, with a quick temper,' declared the smith, with some feeling. 'He would not have given in easily!'

Selwyn noticed something on the floor and bent down to retrieve it from behind one of the legs of a trestle table. He showed a small piece of leather to Riocas, then questioned the journeyman again.

'Is this room cleaned often?'

The man stared at him in surprise at such an odd query. 'Our apprentice brushes it out every morning without fail – though since the shock of discovering the master's bloody corpse, he has not been coming to work.'

Selwyn held up the object he had found. 'So this is unlikely to have been on the floor before the robbery?'

As the journeyman shook his head in mystification, Riocas took the piece of leather from his friend and stared at it with a frown on his big face.

'What's this, then? Looks like part of a strap.'

Selwyn nodded. 'And it's part of a sandal strap. Look, it's worn through where the buckle crossed it.'

Riocas, for whom leather goods were part of his trade, held it nearer to his eyes. 'Yes, torn across at the weakened part. But what use is this to us?'

'If it fell to the floor when Ranulf was killed, then it may well have been lost by one of the robbers during the fight.'

Riocas still looked dubious. 'Half the citizens of Bath wear sandals, so how does that help?' He turned to the journeyman. 'What did your master wear on his feet?' he demanded.

'Good stout shoes, for he could well afford them,' said the man, rather bitterly. 'So that didn't come from him.'

Selwyn had taken the strap back from the cat-catcher and was examining it intently. 'I know where this came from,' he said, tense with excitement. 'Look there, near the tip.' He pushed it back under Riocas' nose. 'There's a small punch mark, see?'

The short-sighted furrier peered again at the worn leather. 'A little cross, you mean?'

'Yes! The abbey cordwainer always marks his work with that. It must have come from there, so almost certainly the owner of the sandal is either a monk or a lay brother!'

Both Riocas and Selwyn knew that all the leather-work for the abbey was done in the saddlery, next to the farrier's forge on the end of the stable block furthest from the proctor's cell. The present cordwainer was Roger of Devizes, who had given up his shop there to become a lay brother. He had a cobbler and a novice to help him, as they had to look after all the abbey's harness and leather-work.

Riocas and Selwyn hurried back towards the precinct, and as they turned in through the main gate, Riocas wondered if it would be possible to match the broken sandal-strap to any particular person.

'We can but try, friend,' replied Selwyn. 'I'm sure that sandal was damaged during the scuffle – and we know it wasn't from the goldsmith's footwear.'

They reached the saddlery where, inside the open double doors, two men were at work at a pair of benches and another was sitting on a stool with an iron last sticking up between his knees, punching holes in a long strip of leather. Ox-collars, bridles, traces and other pieces of harness were hanging around the walls, and a row of shelves bore shoes, riding boots and sandals, both old and new. The man on the stool, dressed in a short brown tunic and breeches, was Roger of Devizes, a thin fellow with a face as leathery as the material he worked on.

He greeted Selwyn with a quizzical look. 'The royal steward, no less!' he quipped. 'Does the King want a new pair of shoes, then?'

Selwyn grinned. He had known Roger for a long time and they were comfortable with each other, if not close friends.

'I have a puzzle for you, Master Shoemaker! Do you recognise this?' He held out the broken strap, which the wizened cordwainer took between his fingers, then peered at it closely.

'Where did you find this, Master Steward?'

Selwyn avoided the question. 'Is it one of yours, Roger? It has the abbey mark upon it.'

The seated man nodded. 'It is indeed – and the sandal it came from is up there.' He pointed to a nearby shelf, where a collection of used footwear was awaiting repair.

This was more than Selwyn or Riocas had hoped for and

the steward seized on the opportunity. 'You mean you have it here already? Who brought it?'

Roger did not reply, but rose from his seat and picked the sandal from the shelf. With the torn strap still in his hand, he fitted the two ragged ends together, showing how they corresponded exactly, even the discoloured line matching where the bar of the buckle had chafed the leather.

'No doubt about that!' he muttered. 'But I can't mend the strap, it will need a whole new piece sewn to the sole.'

Riocas had no concern about the state of the sandal; he wanted to know only who had brought it for repair.

'But who does it belong to, for God's sake?' he barked.

Roger, now sensing that something serious was amiss, bent his head towards them, then murmured a name in a confidential manner.

They found Brother Hubert on his knees before one of the small altars in the north transept of the great church of St Peter and St Paul. Built in place of the older Saxon abbey church, it was far too large for its purpose, being a monument to the grandiose ambitions of the physician-bishop, John of Tours.

Selwyn and Riocas had decided that the sacrist was the best person to approach with their suspicions of who had stolen the Church's treasure, as he had been the only one to express his doubts about Eldred's guilt. The bare, echoing transept was empty apart from Hubert, who kneeled in front of a gilded statue of the Virgin placed on a velvet-covered table against the wall.

They padded up behind him on the flagged floor, making their own automatic obeisance to the altar. For a moment, Selwyn thought that the old sacrist was asleep, as he kneeled with his chin bowed onto his chest, his hands clasped across his belly. He was about to cough to attract his attention, when Hubert suddenly raised his head and looked around.

'Who are you? What do you want?' he snapped in alarm, perhaps mindful of the grievous theft that had so recently desecrated this place. Then he focused on Selwyn, whom he now recognised. 'You are the King's steward, are you not? Who is this with you?'

Selwyn explained who Riocas was as the old sacrist hauled himself to his feet. 'We are sorry to disturb your devotions, brother, but the matter is important.'

Hubert testily motioned them away from the altar and led them to a corner of the transept, which was curtained off as a place where spare cassocks and cleaning materials were concealed.

Pulling back the hangings, he sat on a stool and looked up at the two visitors, the squint in his eye being more pronounced as he swivelled his gaze between Selwyn and Riocas.

'So what is this about, eh?'

Selwyn explained the situation and the sacrist's impatience vanished as he saw the possibility of justifying his doubts about Eldred's guilt. He had little fraternal love for either the prior or most of the members of the abbey Chapter, so the prospect of confounding them was appealing.

'Have you got the proof of this?' he demanded.

Selwyn produced both the sandal and the broken strap and handed them to the sacrist, pointing at the obvious match between the broken ends of the leather. 'The cordwainer has no doubt at all that it came from that sandal, Brother Hubert.'

The monk rose from his stool, still clutching the footwear. 'I hope for your sake that you are telling the truth!' he warned. 'For I will seek out the prior at once to tell him of your story.'

He padded off towards the cloister door, but threw one last question over his shoulder. 'Do you know where Eldred has hidden himself?'

'I hear that he is outside the city,' replied Selwyn evasively. 'But I am sure that he could be found as soon as his innocence is accepted.'

The sacrist made no response and vanished rapidly into the gloomy nave. Riocas looked at his friend uneasily. 'Let's hope we can trust him to act honourably over this.'

Brother Hubert of Frome certainly wished to act honourably. In fact, when he made his next confession, he would have to admit to his secret satisfaction at the discomfiture of the prior and his cronies for being proved wrong about Eldred. Unfortunately, a factor unbeknown to him would prevent him getting the credit for having the real criminals arrested within the hour.

He found the prior in his parlour, conferring with the treasurer, the precentor and the cellarer about the rising cost of provisions bought for the abbey. The prior's secretary, a skinny young monk, hesitantly tapped the door and admitted Hubert. The four men who were gathered around the prior's desk examining account rolls, turned irritably at the interruption, but Prior Robert at once put on his jovial face.

'Brother Hubert, have you come to add to our worries with demands for more furniture or vestments? Or do you want a few dozen more shoes, as you are carrying one in your hand?'

Hubert ignored the weak jest and went straight to the heart of the matter.

'Prior, I have discovered who robbed us of our treasured vessels. It was not Eldred, as I declared from the outset.'

There was a sudden silence, broken then by the clamour as the three men demanded to know how he knew.

Savouring his moment of triumph, the sacrist held up the sandal and explained how it had been found at the scene of the murder of the goldsmith, who had been offered what could only have been the cathedral's gold and silver pyx.

'And our cordwainer has definitely identified it as belonging to your clerk, Maurice, Brother Gilbert!'

All eyes turned to the cellarer, who glared at the sacrist with unconcealed dislike. 'What foolishness is this, Hubert! Of course Maurice is not involved. What mischief are you plotting now?'

'It is *his* sandal strap that was found at the place of Ranulf's murder,' retorted Hubert in triumph. 'How else could it have got there?'

Red-faced with anger, Gilbert stepped threateningly close to Hubert. 'Nonsense! Have you lost your reason? If it is his sandal, then either someone else was wearing it or he went there for some legitimate purpose.'

The prior felt that he had lost his dominance in this verbal battle and he stepped into the fray to challenge Gilbert.

'Unlikely though this story seems, brother, why should anyone else wear a monk's sandal? And why should he, a penniless novitiate, visit a goldsmith?'

The cellarer, looking like a bull-baited dog, glared from one to other. 'I don't know, but by St Michael and all his angels, I'll soon find out!'

As he marched to the door, his face thunderous, the prior called after him, 'Bring Maurice back here at once, brother! Call upon the proctor's men, if needs be!'

While they waited for the cellarer's clerk to be fetched, the prior and the other Chapter members questioned Hubert closely and he again had to go through the story that Selwyn and Riocas had told him.

'So where is this Eldred?' demanded the treasurer. 'If he is innocent, as you claim, why did he run away? And who helped to escape?'

Hubert shrugged his thin shoulders. 'He had little chance to defend himself, didn't he? You were all convinced that he was the culprit, though you had no shred of evidence.'

'He may still be guilty,' pronounced the prior heavily. 'We have to hear more than your unlikely tale of a shoe to be certain that Brother Maurice is the culprit.'

'That idea is preposterous,' gabbled the precentor. 'Maurice is a monk – and a monk who has already taken his vows. This Eldred is merely a menial lay worker.'

'We shall soon clear this matter up when we hear Maurice's explanation, if this really is his sandal,' concluded Prior Robert, looking expectantly at the door where the cellarer would soon appear with his assistant.

They waited for several more minutes, then Hubert became restive. 'Where is the fellow? We need to resolve this immediately.'

After another delay, the prior also became impatient and waved an imperious hand at his own secretary. 'Go and hurry them up! Surely Brother Gilbert must have been able to find his own clerk by now!'

The nervous chaplain hurried off and the group waited with mounting impatience. It should have taken the messenger no more than five minutes to get to the cellarer's office and back again, but a quarter of an hour went by without a sign of him. Then the door burst open, and he almost fell inside in his haste.

'Prior, the cellarium is in disarray! It seems that both Brother Gilbert and Maurice have gone!'

*

Several hours later, two men in dark Benedictine habits rode their horses along the Chippenham road until they came to the foot of Solsbury Hill. Some way beyond where the lane turned up to Swainswick, they reined in and looked intently up and down the track to make sure that no one else was within sight.

'This will do!' said Gilbert harshly, sliding from his saddle and leading his brown mare into the trees at the side of the road. Maurice, on a grey pony, did the same, and in a moment they were out of sight amongst the greenery. The ground here was flat and heavily wooded, then sloped gently before the steeper gradient of the hill began. They threaded their way between the saplings and more mature trees until they found an open area where a large beech had fallen in last winter's gales. A small stream ran at one side and the cellarer decided that this would have to do for an overnight stop, as the autumn evening was closing in and it was already twilight. They roped their horses to trees near the stream, so that the beasts could crop the grass between the bushes and get water to drink. Settling themselves down with their bulky saddlebags, they prepared to spend an uncomfortable night in the open.

Gilbert seemed the least affected by their sudden change of circumstances, but the weedy Maurice whined incessantly about their plight.

'Are you sure that we needed to run away so precipitately?' he complained, in a high-pitched voice that irritated his senior companion. 'We had planned to leave our departure until next month.'

'Of course we had to run, you fool!' snarled Gilbert. 'And don't dare complain. It was your stupidity in leaving that sandal strap in the goldsmith's shop that caused all this trouble.'

Chastened, the young monk began groping in his bag, pulling out some clothing, a loaf of bread and a block of cheese that he had hastily grabbed from their storeroom before their hurried flight from the abbey.

'Shall we take off our habits now and change into these tunics and breeches?' he asked humbly.

Gilbert climbed back to his feet and grabbed some of the more anonymous garments from Maurice. 'We may as well – then use the robes to cover us during the night – it will be a lot colder than the abbey dormer!'

As he put on the dowdy garments, Maurice sadly dropped his cowled Benedictine habit to the ground, realising that he would never again wear this uniform of the religious life. He had agreed some time ago to join Gilbert in his ambition of forsaking holy office for the worldly pleasures of an affluent secular life. With this in mind, they had been systematically rifling the abbey finances to provide themselves with sufficient money and valuables to keep them in comfort for some time.

Now, while Maurice's saddlebag had contained their clothing and food, that of the cellarer was heavy with a leather sack of silver pennies and some golden besants, as well as the chalice, pyx and other smaller items of considerable value.

They did their best to make themselves comfortable on the hard ground, eating half of the loaf and some cheese, and drinking water from the stream. It was impossible to light a fire, partly because of lack of the materials to do so, but also they needed to avoid drawing attention to themselves by making smoke.

As the gloom deepened, both in the sky and in Maurice's mind, they rolled up in their discarded robes and attempted to sleep. Gilbert, a man nearing forty, was by far the most sanguine about their situation. He was not all that concerned about their premature departure, his main concern being getting clear of Bath before any pursuit caught up with them. This was obviously on Maurice's mind as well.

'Do you think we will get to your house safely, brother?' asked Maurice, as he stared up at the stars, visible between the patchy clouds.

'I see no reason why not,' grunted Gilbert, irritated at his former clerk's timidity. 'We left openly by the West Gate, so when a hunt is begun – if it ever is – they will not know that we doubled back over the hills down to this road.'

They were aiming for Southampton, as Gilbert possessed a house within the walled seaport. He had been embezzling abbey funds steadily for several years, secretly selling stores to unscrupulous merchants and creaming off some of the cash obtained from the sale of wool from the abbey farms outside the city. He had invested some of the proceeds in buying a small burgage in Southampton, anticipating the time when he would slip away from the monastic life. Unfortunately, six months earlier, his clerk had discovered his nefarious activities and the only way that Gilbert could cover it up was by taking Maurice into partnership, though he had to admit that with both of them corrupted, their criminal enterprise had been much easier and more fruitful.

He had been fortunate in that the clerk had quite readily accepted the sacriligious partnership, mainly because Maurice had never been enthusiastic about the monastic life, his parents having dumped him on the abbey when he was a child.

As the sounds of the forest increased as darkness fell, with the hooting of owls and rustling and occasional crashes as larger beasts went about their nocturnal business, the two

fugitives fell into an uneasy sleep, indifferent to the confusion
that reigned in their erstwhile home back in Bath.

The prior had called a late evening meeting in the Chapter
House to discuss the emergency caused by the disappearance of their cellarer and his clerk.

'There is no doubt that Gilbert de Lacy is deeply involved
in this heinous plot,' brayed Thomas, the abbey treasurer.
'Not only do we know that two men were involved in this
murder of the goldsmith, but a large amount of money is
missing from the cellarer's chest downstairs. This was the
fund that I regularly gave him to pay for all the provisions he
purchased for the abbey.'

'We need no convincing that Gilbert was involved,' said
the precentor sarcastically. 'He was seen by the porters riding
brazenly out of the West Gate with Brother Maurice – may
they rot in hell for this!'

The prior's usual benign expression had failed to survive
the events of the evening. 'Of course those two were the
plotters!' he snapped. 'And I have little doubt that Gilbert
was the main instigator. That clerk of his was a poor thing,
with not the brains to do other than his master commanded.'
He chewed at his lip in agitation, looking around at the ring
of senior monks huddled in the candle-lit gloom. 'What matters now is how we are to proceed. The bishop has gone to
Wells again today, but I know he will be livid with anger on
his return tomorrow, when he hears of this catastrophe.'

Hubert the sacrist ventured a comment: 'There is little
we can do as a religious house, Prior. The miscreants have
left the city, God alone knows where they have gone. We
cannot mount any search, we have no men-at-arms, no constables apart from those two louts who act for the proctors.'

One of the older brothers, one of the proctors mentioned,

protested. 'They do their best, brother, but they are not equipped in mind nor body for this sort of disaster. We need the services of the King's men, through his officers.'

Prior Robert scowled. 'That is easier said than done! Our sheriff is theoretically Hubert de Burgh, but he never sets foot in Somerset – and rarely in England, these days, as he is too busy trying to save Normandy from the French. But I suppose those knights who do his work for him in Bristol might help.'

'We have asked the city council for aid,' offered the precentor. 'The portreeve and the wardens of the guilds have agreed to organise a search party tomorrow. The guilds of the goldsmiths are particularly incensed at the murder of Ranulf, who was one of their prominent officials. And some of the men who serve the under-sheriff in Bristol say they will join in. They say they can have a score of men assembled at dawn, who will ride out and seek any trace of this evil pair.'

The prior nodded resignedly. 'I cannot imagine how they can be successful, but I suppose in time we might track them down. Certainly every religious house in England will be on the lookout – and any sanctuary they might seek will be denied them.'

Hubert took advantage of a lull in the discussion to consolidate his original contention that his lay assistant was innocent.

'I take it, Prior, that no one now contests the fact that Eldred had no part in this affair, and that he can be safely reinstated in his position. I feel he deserves an apology for our false accusations, which I might remind you, I did not believe from the outset!'

There were some grudging murmurs of assent, though no one seemed particularly interested in Eldred, being too

concerned with the loss of their funds and the valuable holy
vessels. They also disliked the fact that the sacrist had been
proved right and was doing all he could to remind them of
the fact.

As dawn broke, Eldred left his hole in the cliff and, stiff in
the limbs and empty in the stomach, made his way down
the hill to meet Riocas, hoping for both food and good news.

He reached the bottom of the steepest part of Solsbury
and began cautiously to aim for the lane up to Swainswick,
where Riocas arranged to meet him. He was too early, he
knew, as the city gates were not opened until first light and
then his friend had to trot for a few miles in his little cart.

Eldred squatted on a fallen tree to wait, still well inside
the belt of trees. The birds were still at their morning chorus
and, if it were not for his fugitive state and his absence from
wife and hearth, he could have found it a quiet and restful
interlude in his life.

However, after a few minutes he realised that a distant
noise was not part of this arboreal idyll. Into his conscious-
ness crept the sound of a horse neighing, well away to his
left. Riocas had a donkey to pull his cart, so it couldn't be his.

Curious, but fearful of strangers, Eldred rose and quietly
moved through the trees in the direction of the sounds, which
were repeated several times, becoming clearer as he
approached. Warily, moving his feet a step at a time to avoid
breaking fallen sticks, he closed on the horse until he stopped
short and dropped behind a large bramble bush, for he had
heard someone berating the animal, telling it to be quiet. But
more than that, he swore he knew the voice – and a moment
later, his suspicions were confirmed, as another person spoke,
one he knew equally well. This was Brother Maurice and the
first utterance had come from Gilbert, the cellarer!

Eldred sank to his haunches behind the bush, quivering with fright. He assumed that brother Gilbert and his weedy assistant were part of a search party sent out by the prior to seize him and drag him back to the abbey for trial and probable execution. But how did they know he was on Solsbury Hill? Perhaps Selwyn or Riocas had been interrogated, maybe even tortured by the sheriff's men – or had Riocas been followed on his journeys to bring food to the hill?

Petrified with fright, he hardly dared breathe, but his ears still functioned well. The other two were barely a score of paces away and were not guarding their voices, as the main road was far enough away at this point.

'By the Virgin, my back is breaking after a night on this ground!' growled Gilbert. 'I'll not complain about the pallets in the abbey dormer after this – not that I need to, now.'

There was some coughing and scuffling, then Maurice's familiar voice filtered through the brambles.

'Here, take the last of this bread and cheese. What are we going to do about finding something else to eat today?'

'As soon as we get well beyond Chippenham, we can stop in a tavern and fill our bellies. God knows I've got enough money now.'

This conversation puzzled Eldred. If they were part of the abbey's hunt for him, what was this about them going beyond Chippenham? And why the comment about money? The truth never occurred to him, as it was so far removed from his present concerns. His ears almost wagged as he listened for more.

'How can we keep up this pretence that we are simple merchants, travelling in pursuit of our lawful business?' whined Maurice. 'Even though we've discarded our habits, we both have shaven heads that mark us instantly as being in holy orders!'

'I have a wide pilgrim's hat, don't I?' retorted Gilbert roughly. 'And you had better tie the laces of that coif under your chin and keep it on, if you don't want your neck stretched on the gallows!'

Though now totally confused, Eldred gathered from this that he was not the target of their search and that they themselves were on the run. They were two of the people he had disliked most in the abbey, and indeed, when the chalice and pyx had gone missing, their names had passed through his mind when he was seeking culprits. Now it gradually dawned upon him that he had been right, but did the rest of the world know that?

He heard them moving around and feared that they were on the point of leaving, as Gilbert was telling his clerk to wrap the treasure in the redundant habits to protect them inside their sack. Eldred saw no way of preventing them from escaping, and all he could do was to move back to where he was to meet Riocas and tell the cat-catcher what he had learned, so that some kind of hue and cry could be mounted – though by then they would probably be far away.

Carefully, he rose to a crouch and started to move back the way he had come. Then disaster struck, as his foot caught in a loop of bramble that had sent down sucker roots to anchor itself firmly in the soil. He pitched forwards on to his hands and knees with a crash and, seconds later, cries of fury heralded the arrival of Gilbert, closely followed by his clerk.

The burly monk grabbed him and hooked a brawny arm around his neck, hoisting him to his feet in one powerful movement.

'Who the hell are you, you damned spy?' roared the former cellarer, able only to see the back of Eldred's head. Then Maurice, nervously circling around them, saw to his shock that it was the sacrist's lay brother.

'It's Eldred, Gilbert!' he shrieked. 'We are discovered!'

The older man grabbed his captive by the hair and jerked his head round to confirm his identity.

'What in hell's name are you doing here?' he bellowed. 'Is this where you've been hiding out as well?'

Half-strangled, Eldred was unable to answer, especially as Gilbert began dragging him back into the clearing where the horses were tethered.

'What do we do?' screeched the terrified Maurice. 'He will betray us!'

'I'll kill the bastard! We've murdered already, so another will make no difference, either on earth or in hell,' grated Gilbert callously. He reached with his free hand for the dagger he carried in a sheath on his belt, but as he did so, his hold on Eldred's throat slackened. Convinced that he was about to die, his prisoner let out a scream of terror and a loud plea for help, in which he was joined by the two horses, who, frightened by the noise, gave out loud whinnies and thrashed their hoofs against the undergrowth.

'Shut up, blast you!' howled Gilbert, who, regaining his grip on the struggling victim, hauled the knife clear of its scabbard.

Maurice was paralysed with horror, for it was one thing to beat a burly, outraged goldsmith on the head during a fight, but another to cold-bloodedly cut the throat of a lay brother.

'Gilbert, stay your hand, for the sake of Christ!' he blubbered, but his former master appeared to take no notice of his entreaties.

However, a stay of execution was close at hand . . .

When the sacrist had left the meeting in the Chapter House the previous evening, he found the King's steward and the cat-catcher waiting for him outside the door. As it was they who had exposed the truth about the murderous scandal that was rocking the abbey, they felt entitled to be the first to know if their friend Eldred was now officially considered to be innocent.

'The prior and chapter have lost interest in him now,' confirmed Hubert sarcastically. 'They are too concerned with pursuing our cellarer and his acolyte to be concerned with my brass-polisher! They are more interested in both retribution and recovering the abbey's gold and silver.'

'So we can get a message to Eldred that it is safe for him to return home, Brother Hubert?'

The scrawny old sacrist nodded. 'Yes, bring him back when you like. In the circumstances, I won't ask who aided his escape nor where he has been hiding himself.'

Relieved, the two men went back to Selwyn's kitchen and celebrated with some of the best ale he had there, then went around to Eldred's mean lodging, where they gave the anxious Gytha the good news.

'We'll both go first thing in the morning to Riocas' usual rendezvous and fetch the poor fellow back,' said Selwyn. 'No need for the donkey-cart now, the time for that subterfuge is past, thank God. I'll borrow a couple of rounseys from my friend who keeps the livery stable in Goat Street. Eldred can ride back behind my saddle.'

As soon as the North Gate was opened at dawn, the two friends rode out on a pair of rather short-legged mounts, the general-purpose rounseys used for a variety of purposes. They covered the couple of miles to Solsbury in half an hour and reined in on the lower part of the side road to Swainswick, where Eldred should appear from the trees. After some time, there was no sign of him and Riocas began to get concerned.

'He's usually waiting for me; let's hope nothing has befallen him.'

'We rode faster than your poor old ass can pull that cart,' soothed Selwyn. 'We're probably earlier than he expected.'

They sat in their saddles for another quarter of an hour, when the big furrier became too impatient to wait any longer.

'Let's go in a little way and see if we can find him. Knowing his luck, he may have twisted an ankle scrambling down the hill.'

They led their steeds some way into the trees and tied them to saplings where there was a patch of grass for them to browse.

Then the pair stood irresolute for a moment, unsure whether to start climbing the slope in the hope of meeting Eldred. Their minds were made up for them when a distant, but quite clear scream was heard, way off towards the main road. Without a word, they both turned and ran through the leaf-mould and sparse undergrowth in the direction of the noise, obviously made by a human voice. A couple of minutes later, they heard horses neighing and then, as they got nearer, another scream of terror and a cry for help resounded through the trees, followed immediately by more sounds of agitated horses.

'I'll swear that's Eldred!' panted Selwyn, running at the heels of his stronger companion. 'Let's shout for him. He can't be far away now.'

Riocas let out a mighty bellow that echoed through the forest, followed by similar shouts from Selwyn, as they continued to run in what they hoped was the right direction. There were no more cries from ahead, but the uneasy stamping and neighing of horses soon led them to the clearing.

As they burst past the bramble clump, they saw the two

beasts tethered to trees and a pair of saddlebags on the ground. But of human beings, there was no sign.

The moment Gilbert heard the distant shouts, he knew they must run for it. His captive, still squirming in his arms, managed to scream for help, and instantly the cellarer slapped a hand over his mouth and increased his choking grip.

'Bring that sack, then run!' he yelled at Maurice, who was standing in the clearing, paralysed with fear. Without waiting for him, Gilbert dragged Eldred bodily into the trees, still stifling his attempts at crying for help. He was a powerful man, stocky and muscular, able to trot across the gently sloping ground at a fair pace while half-carrying his wriggling victim.

Left alone, Maurice was suddenly galvanised into action and, grabbing the sack with the money and treasures, he raced after Gilbert. When they had covered a few hundred paces, Gilbert stopped and listened for any sounds of pursuit. His keen ears picked up some shouts in the distance, but none that seemed to be coming their way.

'Go forward slowly and don't make any noise!' he hissed at the panting Maurice. Still keeping a hand firmly over Eldred's mouth, he moved onward at a walking pace for a few score yards, before dropping to the ground behind a clump of hazel bushes. Pulling out his dagger again, he touched the point to Eldred's neck. 'Make a sound and you're dead, damn you!' he hissed.

He motioned Maurice to lie down nearby and they waited and listened. A few distant shouts eventually died away and there was silence, but the cautious Gilbert, knowing his neck may depend on it, waited almost motionless for many more minutes, his knife still drawing a small bead of blood from Eldred's neck.

The pause gave him time to get his breath back after his

exertions and also provided time to think out a plan of campaign. The original idea of riding to Southampton was ruined. Their horses were lost to them and no doubt search parties would soon be combing these woods. On the positive side, he still had his loot and now also a hostage, who might be of some value if they were trapped.

When the silence had lasted for what seemed to be an age, but was probably no more than half an hour, he rose cautiously and pulled Eldred up with him, his knife now being brandished in front of the terrified lay brother's face.

'Those others have gone in another direction, so there's no point in your yelling – and if you do, I'll cut your damned throat!' he snarled. With a jerk of the head at the almost equally terrified Maurice, he grabbed Eldred by the collar of his tunic and began marching him up the lower slopes of Solsbury Hill.

Selwyn and Riocas stood in the clearing and shouted repeatedly for Eldred, but silence was the only response. They made a few forays into the undergrowth and trees surrounding them, but soon returned to the clearing, as there was no indication of which direction the fugitives had taken.

'We're townsmen, not trackers,' exclaimed Selwyn in exasperation. 'We need help to find the little fellow.'

'You mean we need a damned big posse with hounds to search the area,' growled Riocas, equally frustrated by the disappearance of their friend.

Although they had not yet guessed who had spirited him away, the horses tethered at the edge of the clearing soon raised their suspicions. Selwyn went over to the two rounseys to pacify them, as they were still skittish from all the recent disturbances. As he patted the neck of the nearest to soothe it, he gave a sudden exclamation.

'Riocas, these are from the abbey stables! Their harness has the same cross stamped on the harness that Roger the saddler uses, like the one he put on that sandal.'

The bigger man came across to see for himself. 'Two abbey horses hidden in a forest! It's those two thieving, murdering swine from the cellarium! And now they've got our Eldred!'

After an agitated discussion, they had to accept that there was nothing the two of them could do alone, as they had no idea where to look for the fugitives and their captive.

'You ride back to Bath as fast as you can, Selwyn,' suggested Riocas. 'That search party was supposed to be leaving early. If you can find some of them, raise the alarm and bring them back straight away.'

'What about you?' demanded the steward. 'What are you going to do?'

'I'll follow with these two animals on head ropes. We can't just leave them here,' replied the cat-catcher, though he was lying about his intentions. When Selwyn had left to hurry back to their own horses, Riocas untied the tethers on the two abbey rounseys and hitched them up where they could crop a fresh patch of grass.

'Don't worry, I won't forget you're here,' he reassured them, and then slipped into the trees, heading for the top of the hill.

Gilbert reached it a good twenty minutes before the furrier, in spite of having to march his captive in front of him. He took a diagonal path up the incline to lessen the gradient, steering Eldred between the trees and bushes, his knife still prominent in his left hand. Maurice stumbled after him, clutching the precious bag with the valuables and mumbling a litany of anxiety and fear as he went.

The trees thinned, and almost abruptly they found themselves at the lower edge of the grassy rampart and ditch that encircled the top of Solsbury Hill. The renegade monk shoved Eldred over the rim and down into the gully beyond, a good ten feet below the level of the flat summit.

'Keep going or I'll skewer your kidneys,' he snarled, pricking the small of Eldred's back with the point of his dagger. With Maurice trailing behind, they hurried along the flat bottom of the ditch until they had reached a point almost halfway round the circuit. This was the furthest point away from the 'nose' of the hill that looked south over the Chippenham road far below and was nearest to where the forest came along the ridge from the north. Here the trees were in a small valley, their tops almost level with the crest of the hill. Gilbert used a break in the lower rampart to climb out again and pushed his captive across to the forest edge, forcing him to stand with his back to a slim birch, just inside the tree line.

'Our habits are in that bag,' he snapped at Maurice. 'Take the girdles from them and tie this fellow up.'

The plaited black cords that had belted their robes were now used to lash Eldred to the tree, one from wrist to wrist around the trunk. At Gilbert's direction, the other was passed around his neck – firmly, but not enough to strangle him unless he struggled. Satisfied that the lay brother was now immobilised, Gilbert used his knife to cut a strip of cloth from one of the habits. He gagged Eldred with it, the material cutting between his lips to produce a maniacal grin. Frightened and exhausted, the captive's head dropped on to his chest and he seemed uncaring as to what happened to him. After all the panic and exertion, there now seemed to be a sense of anticlimax, as the two criminals regained their breath and stared at each other.

'Now what do we do, brother?' demanded Maurice, with a fragile show of defiance. 'We have no horses, no food and we are stuck on top of a hill, miles from anywhere – especially Southampton!'

Gilbert had his own ideas about solving this dilemma, but he had no intention of sharing them with his former assistant.

'We get away from here as soon as possible, before they come searching for us. We'll keep to the forest and aim north towards Sodbury, then go east, giving Chippenham a wide berth.'

He dipped into the bag and retrieved a few handfuls of silver pennies, which he stuffed into the pouch on his belt.

'I'll hide the rest, we can't lug it all across England. Then we can creep back here in a few weeks to collect it, when all the hue and cry has died down.'

He lifted the leather sack and began walking back to the ditch, Maurice following him uneasily.

'What about Eldred?' he whined. 'You can't just leave him there!'

'Why not? He'll either be found by the searchers – or he'll die of starvation, I don't care which,' Gilbert grunted callously, striding along the deep cutting. He scanned the sides of the ditch as he went and stopped opposite a patch of loose earth where a rabbit had kicked the soil out while digging a burrow. It was one of many such excavations around the top of the hill, where conies, foxes and badgers had dug shelters for themselves.

Gilbert squatted in front of the hole and thrust his arm inside to check that it went deeply into the ground. Satisfied, he pushed the bag inside as far as he could reach, then kicked earth back into the burrow and tamped it firmly with his fist to hide all trace of the treasure.

As he peered into the hole to satisfy himself that the bag was completely hidden, a sudden sound behind him made him wheel around to find Maurice looming over him with a knife held high in his hand. With a yell, Gilbert threw himself sideways as his clerk lunged desperately downwards, aiming to bury the blade between the cellarer's shoulder blades.

The puny Maurice was no match for the other man, who grabbed his ankle and pulled him violently to the ground, the knife skittering away out of reach. Leaping to his feet, Gilbert gave the clerk a vicious kick in the belly to keep him down, then unsheathing his own knife, drove it deep into Maurice's chest.

'Stab me in the back, would you, you bastard!' he hissed. 'I was going to kill you anyway. Did you think I was going to share any of my hard-won spoils with you?'

His former assistant made no reply as he was already dead, the long blade having sliced through the root of his heart. Gilbert pulled it out and wiped it on the grass, then stood quivering as he regarded the corpse.

'Now I've got to hide you as well, damn you!' he muttered.

He climbed the outer bank and looked around cautiously, but the hill top was deserted, apart from the still figure of Eldred tied to his tree.

Going back down to the body, Gilbert seized one hand and unceremoniously dragged it along the bottom of the ditch, looking for a large enough hiding place. He wanted to get away as fast as he could and this further encumbrance was highly unwelcome. He staggered along for a few hundred paces without finding any suitable grave for the clerk, so went out through a gap in the outer rampart and walked until he found a gaping hole under the roots of a solitary beech tree, which grew on the edge of a depression half filled with dead leaves. It must have been an old badger sett, but was large enough for him to push Maurice's body inside. Thankfully, the former monk was small and skinny, and when Gilbert had pulled down a small avalanche of earth from the upper lip of the hole and liberally scattered armfuls of leaves, nothing was visible. As he did so, he wondered why he was bothering to hide Maurice's corpse, as one more killing would make no difference to his final penalty if he was caught. The act was an almost instinctive one, to hide all traces of his most recent felony.

Then, almost exhausted by his recent efforts, he trudged back towards the ditch in order to get his bearings, as he had become disorientated and urgently needed to set off along the ridge that led northwards through the forest. Deciding that the clearest view would be from the flat top of the hill, he clambered up the inner bank of the dyke – and came face to face with a very large and very angry man!

Some years earlier, Riocas had explored Solsbury Hill, hoping to trap animals for his trade. However, the effort of climbing up and down every few days proved not worth the few rabbits he managed to snare, but he had learned something of the layout of the hill. This proved helpful now, as he laboured straight up the steep slope, stopping every few yards to listen for any sign of Eldred or his captors. As Gilbert had gone diagonally to the left, their paths diverged and when Riocas came out of the trees below the ditch and bank, he was on the southern side, a considerable distance from the other men.

All was silent, apart from the birds and the breeze. The cat-catcher stood for a moment on the lip of the first embankment, uncertain what to do next. Deciding that the higher he could get, the better the view, he climbed down into the ditch and up the other side to gain the grassy field on top. Across on the other side of the enclosure, he could see the dense trees of the ridge, but there was no movement to be seen anywhere and no cries of help. He began walking around the edge, peering down as he went into the ditch and at the trees lower down the hill. He stayed wary and alert, his only weapons being his dagger and a heavy stick, part of a fallen branch that he had picked up in the woods.

As he neared the trees on the north side, his eye caught a distant movement, which at first he thought was due to the wind. Then, a few yards further on, he saw that something was thrashing up and down. Hurrying towards it, he saw a leg waving and kicking back against a tree. It belonged to a figure tied to the trunk and a seconds later, he saw it was Eldred, bound and gagged.

Racing towards him, Riocas tore off the crude gag and untied the bonds that held him. The frail lay brother promptly collapsed at his feet and Riocas, surprisingly gentle for such a hulking fellow, cradled him in his arms and murmured reassurance into his ear.

When Eldred had recovered a little, he managed to flap a hand towards the further trees and whisper, 'They went that way – Gilbert and Maurice, just a few minutes ago!'

After making sure that his friend had suffered no serious injury, Riocas propped him sitting up against the tree.

'Selwyn has ridden for help – there will be city men here very soon, so you're quite safe now.' He rose to his feet and grabbed his makeshift club. 'I'm going to follow those swine! When Selwyn and the posse get here, they'll need to know which way they've gone.'

Leaving a limp and very apprehensive Eldred slumped

against the beech, Riocas ran back to the ditch and climbed once again to the summit, unknowingly stepping over the rabbit hole that contained a small fortune.

On top, he reasoned that the only safe way off the hill for the fugitives was northwards through the forest, so he marched across the ancient enclosure in that direction. As he once more reached the rampart, he heard a noise and stopped to listen. Right in front of him came the sounds of scrabbling and heavy breathing, and a moment later the ruddy face of Gilbert appeared over the edge.

Shock, surprise and rage passed in succession over those belligerent features as he recognised who was glaring down at him – for everyone in Bath knew the oversized cat-catcher. Riocas had similar emotions and with a roar of anger, raised his impromptu club to strike the head of the man who was now heaving himself over the lip of the embankment. But just as he had bested Maurice, Gilbert now grabbed Riocas' leg and toppled him over. The cudgel flew from his hand.

Though not nearly as large as his opponent, Gilbert was strong and fit, and was now fighting for his very life. He crawled over the edge and grappled with the fallen Riocas, the two men rolling about, each trying to kick, punch or strangle the other, all the while shouting abuse at his adversary.

The combat was short, sharp and nasty. Riocas managed to get on top and, lifting his huge body momentarily, let it fall on to Gilbert, squeezing the breath out of him like the closing of a bellows. Then the furrier leaned back and punched the other in the face with a fist the size of a boot. Somehow, both men crawled to a crouch, but Riocas ended the fight by seizing Gilbert by the throat and an ankle and throwing him bodily over the edge into the ditch.

Panting, and with blood running into one eye from a cut, Riocas staggered to his feet to look into the ditch, prepared to go down and continue the fracas, but there was no need. Gilbert was lying motionless at the bottom, his head against a large stone, a remnant of the ancient fortifications.

Riocas waited for a few moments to get his breath back, then clambered down the bank and warily approached the inert figure, in case he was shamming. Close up, the furrier thought that Gilbert must be dead, but then saw his chest moving slightly. Prodding him with the toe of his boot produced a guttural sigh, but he was obviously deeply unconscious.

'I hope you'll live long enough to be hanged!' muttered Riocas, as he turned and began making his way back to where he had left Eldred.

The lay brother had recovered a little and was now leaning against the tree, rubbing his throat, which was sore after Gilbert's prolonged armlock.

'I heard you shouting just now,' he croaked. 'What's happened? Have they escaped?'

'I don't know where Maurice has gone, but that swine Gilbert is lying up there, his wits completely lost from a blow on the head.'

Riocas picked up the two girdles that had fallen to the ground and went back to the fallen man. As he was tying Gilbert's flaccid arms and legs together with the plaited cords, Eldred appeared, having stumbled wearily after his friend.

'What's going to happen now?' he asked anxiously. 'Am I still accused of this theft?'

The cat-catcher shook his head. 'Everyone knows that you're as innocent as a newborn lamb, Eldred! It looks as if

Maurice has made off with the chalice and pyx, but that's not our concern now.'

That evening, Selwyn and Riocas called at Eldred's dwelling, where Gytha was fussing over her man like a hen with one chick. Tearfully grateful to the two men for saving her husband, she plied them with rabbit stew and ale before being brought up to date with events.

'Gilbert is in the city gaol, as the prior has disowned him as a monk and won't have him in the abbey infirmary,' reported Selwyn. 'He has regained his senses, but won't admit to anything. That evil man blames it all on Maurice, whom he says has run away with the treasure.'

'No one believes it was all Maurice's idea, surely?' exclaimed Eldred. He looked pale and wan, but unharmed after his ordeal on Solsbury Hill.

'Of course not. The facts speak for themselves,' said Selwyn. 'He'll hang for this. The bishop has waived his right to try him before his own court and has left him to the custody of the sheriff's men.'

The King's steward had met the search party just outside the city that morning and twenty men had hastened back to Solsbury, where they found Riocas and Eldred on top of the hill, guarding Gilbert, who was trussed like a fowl.

They talked about these momentous happenings for a while, until there was a rap on the door into the lane. It was Hubert of Frome, come to enquire after his assistant.

The black-robed sacrist looked uneasy at being out of the abbey, which he rarely left, but was very solicitous about Eldred's health. 'You must rest for a few days, brother, before you return to your duties.'

This was the most welcome thing he could have said to Eldred, who had feared for his beloved job in the cathedral.

'I will miss my task of cleaning the chalice and the pyx, sir,' he said sadly. 'I am told that the posse comitatus found no sign of Maurice or the treasure he stole, even though they searched the forest almost as far as Sodbury.'

Hubert shrugged. 'It must be God's will, Eldred. The Almighty will extract vengeance one day, though it may be a long time before Maurice is found.'

The squinting sacrist was right, but he had no idea how long it would be before the cellarer's clerk was discovered.

ACT THREE

Brean, Somerset, Good Friday, 1453

Old Joan found the first corpse just before dawn or, to be more accurate, she fell over it and banged her knee hard on a sharp rock jutting out of the sand. She cursed loudly as she massaged the bruise, but she could not afford to indulge her pain for long. Distant voices, carried towards her on the salt breeze, compelled her to focus her attention on the man lying on the beach.

There was no question that he was dead. His bulging eyes were open and glassy, staring sightless up at the ghost of the moon. Strands of wet grey hair clung to his forehead and a crust of salt was already beginning to frost the stubble on his grizzled chin. Wincing, Joan crouched down on the damp sand. She slid her hand over the stranger's fish-cold face and closed his eyes.

She crossed herself, muttering a swift prayer to St Nicholas, patron saint of sailors, and Our Lady of the Sea, for them to have mercy on this stranger's soul. Then, in less time than it takes to say a '*Paternoster*', Joan ran her callused fingers over the body of the corpse and stripped it of what few items of value she could find – an enamel amulet in the form of a blue eye, a small leather bag containing a couple of silver coins and a belt with a broad brass buckle. Painfully, the old woman struggled to her feet and moved

on, searching for another corpse or, if she was lucky, a
barrel or chest she could prise open.

She knew there would be other bodies. Last night there
had been a storm. Seeing the purple clouds massing, all the
local boatmen had beached their little fishing boats high up
on the shore long before nightfall. But when the villagers
left the church of St Bridget, after the vigil for the Eve of
Good Friday, they spotted the lanterns of a ship rising and
falling in the darkness far out in the bay. They stood silently
huddled against the wind, watching the ship being driven
relentlessly towards the cliffs of Brean Down at the far end
of the sands. They saw the wind rip her sails into rags and
her back break on the rocks. Then, as one, the villagers
crossed themselves as the foaming waves surged over her
decks, dragging men and masts alike down into the thun-
dering depths.

The sailors and fishermen among the villagers – and there
were many – shook their heads. The storm was a bad one, to
be sure, but it was not so violent as to drive a well-manned
ship onto the rocks, not if the sails had been furled in time
and the captain had been doing his job. They muttered
darkly that the ship was on a doomed voyage, cursed from
the outset. Maybe an enemy had hidden a hare's foot on
board, or else a sailor's daughter had neglected to crush the
shell of her boiled egg, but whatever the cause, once the ship
was on the rocks there was no saving her, nor any man who
sailed on her.

The villagers had gone to their beds then, knowing that
neither kegs nor corpses would drift ashore until the tide
turned. The priest had remained a while on his knees before
the altar, praying for the souls of the men drowning out
there, but at the same time he could not help adding a plea
to the Blessed Virgin for the ship to be carrying a valuable

cargo that might wash ashore, for the church was badly in need of repair.

And so it was that as the rind of the sun crept above the horizon, the shoreline was already crawling with villagers, who, like Joan, were searching for anything of value they could salvage from the stricken ship and drowned men. They worked in haste, not only to beat their neighbours to the treasures that might be strewn along the sand, but also because they knew only too well the penalties of getting caught.

Anything washed up on the shoreline belonged to King Henry, a milksop of a king, they all agreed, who had once vomited so violently at the sight of a traitor's quartered body, that he gave orders that no such mutilation was to occur again. But a feeble king cannot control his own officers, and the local sheriff interpreted the law exactly as he pleased, inflicting cruel punishment on anyone who deprived him of spoils that would otherwise mysteriously disappear into his own coffers. The villagers had learned to spirit away anything they could salvage before the sheriff's men arrived to search their homes – that was the way of it and had been for generations.

Old Joan was losing ground. Years of beachcombing had lent her fingers skill in searching, but in payment those same years had taken swiftness from her feet and strength from her back. She couldn't carry off the great barrels like the men, nor run like the girls to be first at a corpse. So, like the gulls, she sidled around the other villagers, her eyes searching for any unfamiliar shape against the distant rocks she knew so well, in the hope of spotting a body lying apart from the others.

Joan was in desperate need of any scrap she could find. First her poor daughter had died in childbirth. Then, within weeks, her grieving son-in-law had been crushed by an over-turned wagon, and Joan had suddenly found herself the sole provider for her three grandchildren. And if that was not trouble enough to heap on any old woman's head, the eldest grandchild, Margaret, had of late been struck down with pains in the guts and frequent vomiting, which no amount of purges or physic could cure. If ever a woman deserved a crumb of good luck in her life, poor old Joan did.

Her attention was caught by a pair of gulls repeatedly diving at something on the water's edge. She raised her hand to shield her eyes and squinted against the sun dazzling off the sea. There was something drifting out there in the shallows, though it might be nothing more than a splintered plank from the ship. She edged cautiously along the shore, trying to look as if she was still searching the ground at her feet so as not to draw attention to the distant shape. When she was close enough not to be overtaken, even by the young men, she hurried over.

The top of a ship's mast was floating in the shallow water, rising and falling in the gentle wavelets. The wood had broken off in such a way as to form the shape of a cross. But it was not the shape of the wood that made Joan gasp and stare. The body of a man was stretched out on the mast. The corpse's feet were bound fast to the down spar with a stout rope. His arms had been stretched out on either side of him, and his wrists were bound equally firmly to the cross spar.

As the old woman stared, a larger wave lifted the wooden mast, pushing it higher up the beach, as if the sea was offering her a gift. She hitched her skirts into her belt and waded into the water. Seizing the top of the spar, where the man's head lolled, she tried to pull it higher up the sand. It was so heavy that at first she could only drag it an inch or two, but

using the force of the next wave to lift it, she finally managed
to beach it where it would not easily be pulled back into the
sea.

Joan stared down. The eyes of all the other corpses had
been opened wide as if desperate for a last glimpse of this
world before they entered purgatory. But not this one; his eyes
were closed and there was an expression that you might almost
have called triumph about those slightly parted lips. He looked
to be in his thirties. His hair and beard were long, thick and,
beneath the salt shimmer, dark as a mussel shell. With a
straight, thin nose and sharp cheekbones, he would have been
a striking figure when he lived – not handsome exactly, but
with the kind of face that would command a second look.

Her gaze travelled to his hands, bound tightly against the
dark wood. They were as soft and elegant as a highborn
lady's. This man was no sailor, that much was plain. She felt
her pulse quicken. He must have been a passenger on the ill-
fated voyage, a gentleman perhaps, even a noble. What
might such a man have concealed beneath his sodden
clothes – ingots of silver or gold, a jewel?

She ran her hands over his chest and felt the cord beneath
his shirt. She traced it down with her fingertips to the bulge
of what felt like a leather pouch. Joan slid her knife from
her belt. It would be easier to cut the cloth than to try to
drag the pouch up under his clothes.

'Spare me, I beg you!'

Joan started so violently that her legs shot from under her
and she found herself sitting in the shallow icy water.

The man on the cross ran his tongue over parched lips
and his voice, when he spoke again, was cracked and hoarse.
'Almighty God has brought me safe through the storm and
raging seas. His curse will be upon you if you harm me now,
for I am under His protection.'

Joan could scarcely take in what he was saying for the sheer amazement of his being alive. He turned his head towards her, and now that his eyes were opened she saw that they were a brilliant green, like the first flush of grass in spring.

The bell in the parish church began to toll, calling the villagers to prime. Joan suddenly remembered that this was the morning of Good Friday, the day Christ had hung on the Cross. And now, here, right in front of her, was a man who might have been the statue of Christ sprung to life. With a look of wonderment dawning in her eyes, Joan struggled to her feet. Heedless of her sodden skirts she began to run as fast as her old legs would carry her, stumbling back towards the main beach and the other villagers.

'A miracle! A miracle. It's our Lord. He has returned!'

Godfrey pressed his ear closer to the door of the royal chamber where his master, King Henry VI of England, slept, dressed and these days even ate, if you could call the meagre amount he consumed 'eating'. Godfrey was sure his master was alone, he usually was. Even the Queen seldom entered his chamber and would wait patiently in her own apartments for him to visit her, but those visits too had become less frequent of late. Godfrey, his head hard against the wood, strained to listen. On the King's orders, he had kept guard outside the door this past hour and had admitted no one. Yet now he could hear voices inside.

Henry had retired to meditate and pray, something he did several times a day, a practice that was growing more frequent, much to the mockery of the Court, but His Majesty was resigned to being interrupted. He would never send his ministers away with an angry word, but that only made them despise him the more. A gentle, meek, forgiving king was no king at all.

The voice was rising inside the chamber, shouting and raging. The words were pouring out too hysterically for Godfrey to distinguish them, but it was Henry's voice, he was sure it was, though he'd never heard it raised like this.

Godfrey hesitated, his fingers gripping the metal ring of the door handle. Should he enter, despite the King's orders?

'No, no, have mercy!' The voice was shrieking in fear.

Someone was surely threatening the King's life. An assassin must have crept into the chamber and hidden there, one of Richard of York's men, maybe even Richard himself. Henry would never offer any resistance if attacked, but even if he tried, his efforts would be as useless as an infant's, for he refused to practise any form of fighting.

Godfrey snatched his fingers from the handle and backed a few paces away into the shelter of a doorway. If this was an attempt to murder the King, he certainly wasn't going to prevent it. He shrank into the shadows and waited. But there was no sound of violence coming from the small chamber, no furniture overturning, no one came running out.

Taking a deep breath, Godfrey crept back towards the solid oak door. Someone was still talking, but the tone was low and dull now.

'Sire, are you in need of assistance?'

He called out to warn of his approach to anyone who might be with the King. He did not want a dagger intended for the royal heart to be plunged into his own.

Receiving no reply, Godfrey turned the handle and made to enter, but the door would not move more than an inch. He put his shoulder to it and shoved; slowly it grated open just far enough for him to look through the gap. The chamber appeared empty save for Henry himself, who was crouched

beside his bed, muttering under his breath as if he was praying. The bedcovers were crumpled and half tumbling off
the bed. A small wooden table had been wedged against the
door. Godfrey gave a violent shove and stepped inside, closing the door behind him.

'Sire?'

Henry was hugging his long black coat tightly across his
chest, like a beggar on a cold winter's day. He slowly raised
his head. His tight black cap, the one he always wore, made
him seem more pale and haggard than usual.

'Shall I fetch the Queen, sire?' Then seeing the look of
incomprehension on Henry's face, Godfrey added,
'Margaret, sire, your wife, shall I send for her?'

Henry adored her and when he was in one of his reclusive
moods only Margaret could coax him out of his chamber.

'I saw a face,' Henry said. He pointed across the chamber.

Godfrey crossed to the casement. On such a bitter day
the gardens below were almost deserted, save for two gar-
deners tidying up the fallen twigs and branches after the
storm.

'Not the window, in there. That!' Henry gesticulated wildly
at an object on the floor just as Godfrey stumbled over it.

He stooped and retrieved it. It was a silver mirror, perfectly circular and about the breadth of a man's hand. The
reflective surface was set in a silver frame gilded with gold
and decorated with rubies and pearls. Godfrey knew it well.
It had once been a gift from King Richard II of England to
Henry's maternal grandfather, Charles VI of France. Now it
belonged to Henry. But normally it rested on a stand.

He peered about. The stand was lying smashed in three
pieces in the corner of the room. He glanced at the King,
who was staring at the mirror with an expression of horror
in his eyes, as if Godfrey was holding up a severed head.

187

'Sire, it was just your own face you saw reflected in the mirror. Sometimes if I catch a glimpse of myself unawares, I am startled—'

'No, no!' Henry waved his hands agitatedly. 'It was not *my* face . . . it was my grandfather's face staring out at me.'

'Some say you favour your grandfather in appearance,' Godfrey replied cautiously. He could not think what else Henry meant.

'It was Charles's face, I tell you . . . the face of my grandfather, watching me. Look in the mirror. Look! Can't you see him in there?'

Godfrey struggled to think of a diplomatic answer that would not suggest that he thought his master was a raving lunatic. 'Sire, a little diversion might dispel these phantasms – some dancing, perhaps, or music. You should not spend so much time alone.'

'Dancing is a sin, don't you know that? And it is sin my grandfather is trying to warn me of. I must meditate upon the mirror. I have to pray! I have to pray!'

Godfrey looked down at the object he still held. On the reverse of the mirror was a scene engraved on gilded copper. The figures were set on a background of translucent red enamel and depicted the murder of St Thomas Becket by the knights in Canterbury Cathedral. Godfrey grimaced. Staring at that bloody murder for hours on end was enough to addle anyone's wits.

'Majesty, the stand is broken. Shall I not send it to a craftsman to be mended? Then when it's returned, if the mirror distresses you, you might bestow it as a gift on—'

He staggered backwards as the King leaped to his feet, snatching the mirror from his hands and sending him reeling.

'I must not let it out of my sight. My grandfather is

trapped in that mirror and I must release him. I have to help him, don't you see? I must help him.' He clutched the mirror to his chest, rocking back and forth like a child cradling a precious toy.

Then, as if he was awakening from an enchantment, he slowly let the mirror fall upon his bed.

He grasped Godfrey's arm, his voice now tremulous and his eyes full of fear. 'Tell me, Godfrey, speak the truth. Is this madness? Is my grandfather's madness coming upon me at last?'

William broke off a morsel of the bitter salty bread and wiped it around the bottom of the bowl, cleaning up the last juices of the fish stew. Joan's grandchildren stared bug-eyed at him as if they had never seen a man devour three great bowlfuls before. With a slight twinge of guilt, William wondered if he had just eaten their meal for tomorrow as well as today. But it was only a momentary pang, like the twitch of a wasted limb, for guilt was an emotion William seldom experienced.

He drained his beaker of ale and leaned back in the low narrow bed. The one-roomed cottage stank of fish, wood smoke and what William thought might be dried seaweed, which he suspected was a major ingredient in the strange-tasting bread. The priest had wanted to conduct him to his own house, but one glance at the little man's patched habit and pinched sallow face had convinced him that Father Jerome ate no better than his parishioners, probably worse. So when Joan had claimed him firmly as her prize and insisted on caring for him, William had graciously agreed, kissing the old woman's hand with murmurs of gratitude that had made her simper like a virgin maid.

But much to his irritation, Father Jerome had insisted on accompanying him to Joan's cottage and, having firmly shut the door on the other curious villagers, sat patiently in the only chair watching William eat. Now he cleared his throat with a dry nervous cough and leaned forward.

'I have known men lash themselves to masts to keep themselves from being washed overboard in a storm and if that mast should break, they have drifted ashore upon it, but ... both your hands were tied. A man cannot tie himself like that. For what crime had you been bound up in such a manner by your companions?'

'What are you saying, Father?' Joan asked in a scandalised tone. 'Crime indeed. It was a miracle, Father. A miracle for Holy Easter. God has sent us a saint.'

She glowered at Father Jerome. It had taken a lot of persuasion on his part to convince the old woman that William was not Christ returned, but she was determined not to be done out of a saint.

The priest gnawed anxiously at his lip. 'I did not mean to accuse ... it may be that this man was the victim of pirates who had captured him and bound him as their prisoner. If I am to bury their corpses on the morrow, I must know what manner of men they were and if they should be accorded a Christian burial.'

Father Jerome had presented William with a perfectly reasonable explanation, furthermore one that the priest was bound to accept since he himself had fashioned it. But William had never settled for merely *reasonable*. When both the priest and the old woman turned to him, the words slid as smoothly as melted butter from his tongue.

'Father, you are astute indeed. For I was a prisoner of pirates, wicked, godless men, heathens who prey on the innocent.'

Joan's granddaughter, Margaret, shook her head in disbelief. She had not said a word up to then; now she made up for it with a defiant tilt of her head. 'But some of them was good Christians, I know, 'cause Anne showed me the crucifixes and rosaries her father had taken from the bodies.'

'I'll speak to her family tomorrow,' Father Jerome said sharply. 'Such things should have been given over to the Church.'

William noticed the priest did not object to the dead being robbed. But he ignored Father Jerome's indignation and turned a beatific smile on the annoying little brat.

'Such pious objects that were found on the men were stolen from the good Christians they robbed and murdered, even . . .' and here he shook his head in grief, '. . . even from girls as young as you, and they did worse than steal from those poor girls, far worse.'

Old Joan crossed herself and spat three times on the back of her fingers to ward off such a dreadful fate ever befalling her innocent granddaughter.

'How then,' Father Jerome asked, 'were you spared?'

'It was as this good woman says, a miracle. I have a gift, a rare gift, of prophecy. I am shown many mysteries, given many warnings of things to come that are denied to other men. It is as if I walk as a seeing man in a world where all others are blind. I saw in a vision how a great storm would rise up and destroy the ship. I warned the pirate captain to put in to port, but he wouldn't believe me, for there was no hint of cloud in the sky, nor any sign of rough weather approaching. He accused me of trying to spread fear and mutiny amongst his men. When I told them I could plainly see it, he said that if I wanted to see clearly, he would oblige me. He gave orders that I be hauled up to the top of the highest mast and tied up there in the burning sun till I died of thirst. As I hung there they all mocked me, saying to be sure to tell them if I saw a cloud.

'I saw the storm flying towards me. I saw black hounds with eyes of fire streaming across the sky, howling our deaths, their slavering jaws opened wide to devour us. But I said nothing more, for I give warning but once. Even when they too could see the weather turning the captain refused to lose face and furl the sails, too proud to admit I was right. The first crack of lightning severed the mast and I was cast into the sea, thrown safely away from the rocks upon which the ship foundered, and so upon my holy cross of wood I floated ashore.'

Joan gave a sigh of satisfaction and wonder. Her old eyes gazed upon him with such adoration that William felt a sudden thrill course through him, like the fire that surges through a man's belly when he stakes all the money he possesses on the single tumble of the dice.

The burial of the sailors' corpses was a hasty affair, delayed only by the length of time it took for the sexton and his sons to dig a grave large enough to contain all the bodies. They buried them on common ground. Heathen pirates were not to be accorded a good Christian burial. All the same, Father Jerome was uneasy. He only had this stranger's word for the fact that the men were pirates, but a man who so miraculously survives the waves must be, if not exactly a saint, at least blessed by divine favour, and God would surely not save a liar while He let good Christians perish.

William asked to be shown the bodies that he might forgive the men who had so cruelly wronged him, a gesture of compassion that brought a tear to the eye of many a woman in the village. He walked along the line searching each face carefully. Finally he turned to Martin, the sexton's youngest son, leaning wearily on his spade.

'There were more men aboard the ship than this. Where are the other bodies?'

The lad pointed to a mass of gulls circling out over the bay. 'See those birds flying there where the ship was lost? Those gulls are the souls of the men who drowned and they'll not leave that spot 'cause they know their bodies are still down there beneath the waves. Not every man who's lost in these parts washes ashore. Sometimes the current carries them out instead of in, and they pitch up weeks or months later further along the coast. My father reckons if the sea wants them for her own she'll never give them back.'

William stared at the row of corpses. There was one face he had been desperate to see lying among the dead, but it was not there. He hoped with every fibre of his being that the sexton's lad was right and that Edgar was lying somewhere at the bottom of the bay. He had to be dead. He must be. No one could have survived that wreck. Yet he himself had survived, hadn't he?

That Easter Sunday the little church of St Bridget was crammed to the door with villagers celebrating the holy feast and for once they had something to celebrate. There was not a family in Brean who didn't have some of the spoils from the wreck hidden under their byre floors or concealed in the thatch of their roofs. And when, out of sight of Father Jerome, they'd swum the Easter sun in a pail of water, the reflection had been clear and strong, a good omen for the rest of the year.

Even Father Jerome, worn down by years of battling against poverty, superstition and the cruelty of the sea, felt a little of the old joy returning that he had once felt as a newly ordained priest. But his contentment was short-lived for, as he was in the very act of raising the Holy Chalice before his little flock, Joan's granddaughter, Margaret, gave a cry of pain and fell to the ground clutching her belly, her face blanched to the colour of milk.

The congregation crowded round, the Mass forgotten in their concern.

One woman prodded the child. 'Get one of the lads to carry her to my cottage, Joan. I've a good strong purge ready.'

As people bent to lift her, Margaret fought and screamed. 'I won't drink any purge. It makes it hurt more.'

Joan folded her lips grimly. 'Now you know fine rightly Martha's treated every man, woman and child in this village since afore you were born, and her mam afore that. If she's says a purge is the cure, then it is.'

But Margaret stubbornly resisted every attempt to lift her.

William pushed his way through the crowd. 'Let me examine the child.'

'Are you a physician?' Father Jerome asked.

But William ignored him and, kneeling, took Margaret's hot little hands in his, stroking them until her fists unclenched. 'Now look at me, child.'

Reluctantly she opened her eyes and looked into his startlingly green ones. He did not blink and after a few moments, neither did she. He was muttering, softly at first, in a language she did not understand, full of strange guttural noises that seemed more like the warning growl of some wild beast. As his voice grew louder and deeper, his hand pressed down upon her belly. She screamed, arching her back, trying to squirm away. Joan and the priest started forward in alarm, but William waved them back.

In that touch, he had felt all he needed to know. His former master, a physician and alchemist, had taught him well. William had paid scant attention to his books and dusty phials, finding girls and cockfighting far more to his taste; nevertheless, he learned easily, though more by absorption than conscious study, and had acquired a knowledge that sometimes even surprised him. Purges would not cure the child, nor indeed would any physic. She would recover for a while, but the pain would return and one day kill her. There was no cure.

But why tell these simple people that? She might have days, months or, with luck, even longer. Why should the child and her grandmother live in fear and dread of something they could not prevent? And at least he could stop them adding to her misery with these purges that would only hasten her death. Besides, they believed he was a saint, didn't they? They were expecting a miracle. He could not disappoint them.

He looked round at the anxious faces. 'The child is possessed. A demon dwells in her belly. It bites and torments her. I must expel it.'

Father Jerome grabbed his arm. 'I cannot allow this. Only those who are in holy orders—'

William rose and stood towering over the little priest. 'Have you forgotten the miracle of my saving, on this day of all days? Why do you think I was delivered to your shore? I told you I am the prophet. I have the gift of sight beyond the powers of mortal men and I tell you that if this poor child is not released, the demon will grow inside, tormenting her with pain beyond imagining, feeding on her and growing ever stronger, until it bursts forth to devour the souls of every man, woman and child in this village. Is that what you want, Father? Would you have me abandon her to this foul fiend?'

Margaret was sobbing, trying to crawl across the floor as if she could get away from the creature inside her. Joan was wailing and even Father Jerome was trembling.

195

'I must send word at once to the bishop for him to dispatch his exorcist to us.'

Martin, the sexton's youngest son, elbowed his way through the crowd. 'And how long will it be afore he comes, Father? Weeks, maybe – that's if he bothers to come at all. Besides, old Joan can't afford what the likes of them would charge. Let William try. I reckon that's why God sent him here.'

The sexton grabbed his son by the arm, cuffing him vigorously several times around the head. 'How dare you gainsay the priest? Think you know better than your elders and betters, do you?' He struck the cowering lad again, and would have gone on doing so, had William not caught the sexton's arm to prevent him.

Father Jerome held up his hands in a gesture of peace. 'Leave the boy. He means well.'

Joan could bear it no longer. She fell at William's feet, clutching at his knees and begging him to save her grandchild. Many in the crowd nodded eagerly, and when William turned an enquiring look upon Father Jerome, the little priest gave a resigned shrug. He'd lived long enough in this parish to know that even if he forbade it, the villagers would do it anyway behind his back, just as they stole holy water from the church for their heathen spells however often he denounced such things from the pulpit.

William helped Joan to her feet and calmly bade the crowd to close the shutters of the church. He sent Martin to fetch a lighted candle, which he placed behind the child's head. Then William commanded all to kneel. He crouched beside little Margaret and ordered her once more to look into his eyes.

The strange words poured out of him again, rising in a crescendo so that his voice reverberated from the walls of the church. He laid his hands on Margaret's belly, his eyes closed, his head thrown back and sweat bursting from his forehead as if he was wrestling with a ferocious monster. A shriek of unearthly laughter echoed through the church, like the cry of a thousand gulls. At that instant the candle blew out and the church was plunged into darkness.

Father Jerome blundered to the door and, with trembling hands, flung it wide. Most of the villagers, dragging their children, charged out after him as if the devil himself was at their heels. But once safely out in the daylight their panic subsided. They huddled together, clutching their little ones and staring back at the church.

Inside Joan was sobbing and hugging her granddaughter to her, but the child, though pale as the moon, was not crying any more.

'It's gone . . . it doesn't hurt now,' she whispered.

William strolled to the church door and, calmly surveying the little crowd, announced, 'All is well. I have expelled the demon from the child.'

He held out something in his palm. There were gasps of wonder as everyone pressed forward. The creature was tiny to be sure, but they later learned this was because it was a mere infant, a baby demon that would have grown into a monster were it not for William's skill. For there was no mistaking it was the most unearthly and satanic-looking beast they had ever seen in the flesh, and very like the demons painted on the wall of their own little church. It was grey and wizened. It had no discernible body, only a broad triangular head that tapered into a long arrow-shaped tail, two bulging black eyes and a wide curved mouth full of black needle-sharp teeth.

When the tale was later told, as it was to be many times throughout the long winters in those parts, some of the villagers swore they had seen the demon twitching, others said that it was lashing in fury. But the truth was they barely had time to glimpse anything at all for just as deftly as William revealed it, so he slid it into a small stone flask and rammed the stopper home.

'I will bury the demon in the bed of the next river I come to,' William declared. 'Evil spirits cannot escape from running water.'

The villagers were no fools. They were as sharp as scythe blades when bargaining in the market place and were not the sort to waste their precious coins on betting which cup the pea was under, or buying elixirs from passing pedlars who promised immortality. But even the oldest among them had never heard tell of a man so strangely saved from a storm, and now they had seen with their own eyes one of their own children delivered from a demon, and by this same stranger.

So William ate his fill that night, for the good people of Brean were determined to lavish whatever they had on this man from the sea. And as he ate, he talked. He was good at talking.

The following morning William was rudely torn from his sleep by a malicious cockerel, which had perched itself right outside the small window above his bed, and was announcing the coming dawn with such raucous insistence that even a deaf man would have felt the vibration of it. William peered blearily over at Joan and her grandchildren who lay, wrapped together under the same blanket, by the embers of the fire, but none of them stirred. Thoroughly awake now, William pulled on his clothes and slipped from the cottage to relieve himself outside. If he could catch that wretched bird, he'd wring its scrawny neck, or at least drive it off where a fox might take it.

Outside the tiny cottage it was as yet barely light enough

to see where he was walking. If the sun had indeed struggled over the horizon, it was well concealed beneath a thick fleece of grey clouds scudding across the sky. The wind had a raw damp edge to it, as if rain were not far off. William shivered, suddenly grateful for a warm bed and stout walls.

He hurried round to the midden heap, anxious to get back inside to the fire as quickly as he could. As he reached the back of the cottage, the cockerel, which seemed to sense William's murderous intent, hopped onto the low thatched roof. William tried to grab the bird, but it fluttered sideways, stabbing at his hand with a beak as sharp as a dagger, before swaggering up to the top of the roof. William cursed soundly and sucked at a bleeding hole in his finger, but the bird was well out of reach and no amount of threatening had the slightest effect on it.

With his bladder now empty, William was making his way back to the cottage again when he noticed something pinned to the door, flapping in the wind. He hadn't seen it as he came out, if indeed it had been there then. As he came closer he saw that it was a small square of sailcloth. He reached up and held it flat against the door. Someone had used a piece of charcoal to fashion a careful little drawing on the cloth. The picture was simple enough, just a stick with a serpent twined around the length, its mouth wide open revealing sharp fangs and a long tongue.

William stifled a cry of fear. For a moment he could do nothing except stare, his limbs frozen in shock. Then he forced himself to move. He tore the sailcloth from the door and whipped round, glancing fearfully up and down the length of the lane, but it was deserted. The shutters and doors of all the cottages were still firmly fastened. None of the villagers was yet stirring, but someone was abroad, he was certain of that.

His legs trembling, William staggered backwards, leaning on the wall of the cottage for support. He looked down again at the scrap of sail he was clutching. The snake's forked tongue seemed to vibrate in William's shaking hand as if it was scenting its prey and as he stared at it, three fat drops of scarlet blood from the wound on his finger fell onto the cloth and trickled into the serpent's open mouth.

The morning was already half done before William was finally on the track and striding out of the village. His first instinct had been to flee immediately, but once he had stopped shaking he was forced to see the sense in at least waiting to eat breakfast before he left. As Joan anxiously reminded him, he was already weak from the shipwreck; if he tried to walk for miles on an empty stomach he would more than likely faint on the road, and that was the last thing William could afford to do. The thought of lying helpless and unable to defend himself was too terrifying to contemplate.

If that serpent was a sign, a sign that Edgar was still alive, then he needed to put as much distance between himself and this village as he could. Edgar had already been injured before the storm. Surely it would take a week or two before the man was fit enough to travel any great distance, and William intended to make good use of that time to cover as much ground as possible. If he got far enough ahead, Edgar would not be able to track him. But if Edgar found him again ... William tried to fight off the icy flood of fear that engulfed him. That monster must not find him!

Naturally, William had said nothing to Joan about the piece of sailcloth. She had been only too willing to accept his explanation that he had received a vision in the night telling him to set out at once for a place he would be led to, a place where the demons and angels fought each other for the souls of men. Joan had hurried out to beg bread and dried mutton from her neighbours, for she would not have it said that she sent a holy prophet out on the road without a bite of food in his scrip. Why, God would never forgive such an uncharitable act. She was gone so long that several times William nearly gave up waiting, for he was desperate to be miles away from Brean by nightfall. But Joan had finally returned with cheese and salt fish as well as bread and mutton. In addition she'd brought a battered old leather scrip to carry them in and a good stout staff, for which William was more grateful than he dared express.

He struck out at first on the track that led around the bay to the south, as if he were making for the village of Berrow, but as soon as he thought he was not observed he turned off on a rough track heading inland towards the river Axe. The path wound its way along the edge of rough pasture and through a coppice where the villagers cut their wood.

Though the trees were not yet in bud, they still afforded too much cover for William's comfort. If Edgar had pinned the sign to the cottage door, then he had to be holed up somewhere nearby, perhaps in a seldom-used barn or byre, or even in a place like this. William took a firmer grip of the staff and glanced nervously around him, searching every shadow for signs of movement; in consequence he repeatedly stumbled over tree roots and only just managed to stop himself sprawling headlong. He paused to steady himself and catch his breath. When he was glancing once more over his shoulder, a movement caught his eye. He whirled round, the staff gripped tightly between both fists, but saw only some saplings whipping back and forth. Was it the wind that had sent them rocking, or something else?

Even as he stood there, William heard the unmistakable

crunch of boots on dried leaves. He slipped behind the trunk of a stout oak and waited as the footsteps came closer. He was gripping his upraised staff so tightly that his arms ached. The footsteps faltered, then stopped. He held his breath as he heard them start up again and come towards him. From his hiding place William glimpsed a hooded figure as it passed the oak tree.

William sprang out, swinging the staff in both hands, aiming for the back of the hooded head. At the same instant the man in front of him heard William's movement and twisted aside with a cry of shock and fear. Trying to avoid the blow, the man stumbled backwards and fell just as William brought his staff crashing down. It missed the man's head by an inch. He lay, sprawled on his back, staring up in wide-eyed fear, and William found himself looking down, not into the face of Edgar, but of the sexton's youngest son, Martin.

'What the devil are you doing following me?' William demanded, the staff still raised menacingly, for it occurred to him that this youth might yet be in the pay of Edgar.

'M-Master, I came to join you . . . on your journey. I want to be your disciple.'

'My disciple?' William said incredulously, lowering his weapon.

The youth bounced to his feet, and brushed his ginger hair out of his eyes. 'Yes, master. I saw how you cast out that demon and how you were saved from the wreck on the cross. I know you are a holy man. I believe in you. I have the faith, Master. Take me with you.'

'But why creep up on me like that?'

'I wasn't creeping,' Martin protested. 'I couldn't join you openly. Not till we were away from the village. My father would thrash me black and blue if he thought I was running off. You too, if he could, for taking me away.'

William, remembering the sexton's blows in the church, knew the lad was probably not exaggerating.

'How long before you're missed?' William asked. He had enough troubles already without some irate bull of a father lumbering after him as well.

'He thinks I've gone out with one of the boats. He'll not look for me till after he comes back from the alehouse tonight.' Martin suddenly sank to his knees, his hands clasped and his eyes closed as if in prayer. 'Bless me, Master; make me your disciple.'

He looked so solemn that William almost laughed, until he saw the lad was in earnest.

It was on the tip of his tongue to send the boy packing, but it occurred to William that a companion might be just what he needed. The lad was short but stocky, with a chest as broad as an ox and, judging by the way he'd dug those graves, he had the strength of a man twice his size. Martin would be another pair of eyes to keep watch, especially in the night, and if Edgar did attack, then it would be two against one. The lad would surely fight to the death to defend his master, if he really believed he was a prophet. Besides, disciples did all the cooking and tending to their master's needs, didn't they? It would be as good as having his own manservant again.

Solsbury Hill, August 1453

The horses' flanks were soaked with sweat by the time they finally crested the steep slopes of the hill. Even the five young women who rode them were breathless with the effort of keeping their balance in the saddles on the steep incline. Their grooms, who had been forced to climb alongside the horses, almost dragging them upwards, were more exhausted than the beasts. Their faces were flushed to the colour of ripe plums and beads of perspiration burst out on their fore-heads. The sun burned relentlessly down from a cloudless blue sky, baking the valleys below, but at least up on the flat table top of the hill there was the blessing of a breeze to ruffle the brown grass stalks and cool the air. With undisguised relief the grooms assisted their mistresses to dismount and led the palfreys away to a clump of gorse bushes where they might be safely tethered until they were wanted again.

It was several minutes before the falconer and his lad managed to reach the party. The tiny merlins were not heavy to lift on the wooden frame, but they had to be carried smoothly. Any sudden jerking and they would start to flap or even throw themselves from their perches, breaking feathers, legs or even wings. The falconer could not afford to slip or stumble.

For once, though, the merchants' daughters were not impatiently demanding to begin their sport or stamping their pretty little shoes. They too were far too grateful for the breeze to make a fuss. Arm in arm, they strolled around on the flat top of the hill, listening to the trilling of a hundred larks as they flew for sheer joy up into the hot blue sky.

Ursula, the youngest of the five friends, caught the distant glint of the river, and breathed deeply, filling her lungs with the sweet air after the foul stench of Bath. It was hard to know if the city was more unpleasant in the winter or summer. In winter the streets were ankle-deep in the mud and filth from the blocked and overflowing ditches and sewers. In summer the pigs snuffled among the rotting waste from houses and butchers' shops, thrown haphazardly into the streets where it was left to stink beneath writhing heaps of bone-white maggots.

Ursula had often begged to move out of the city at least
for the summer months. As she repeatedly told her father, no
one, by which she meant no marriageable nobleman, lived
in Bath any more. Even the Bishop of Bath had sought a
more comfortable abode in Wells. But as her doting but practical father told her, a good businessman keeps a constant
eye on his livelihood, and since the wool and cloth trade was
flourishing in Bath, he had no cause to move. And, he added,
before she started turning her nose up at the stench of a
good honest trade, she should remember that it was wool
and cloth that put the food on her plate and the jewels in her
hair.

'Ursula, come and choose your bird,' one of the girls sang
out and Ursula sauntered across to join her friends as they
clustered around the falconer.

The girls donned their leather gloves and collected their
favourite birds, laying wagers amongst themselves as to
which would be the first to bring down the quarry. Then
they released them. As the merlins took flight, the larks rose,
still singing, higher and higher into the sky. The little birds of
prey winged up after them, until they were almost invisible
in the glare of the sun. Then the tiny songbirds dropped as
if they had been pierced by an arrow, slipping sideways at the
last moment before they hit the ground, as their pursuers
swooped down after them. The merlins were forced to twist
and turn as they reversed their dive and climbed back up
after the soaring larks again. It could take as much as half an
hour for a merlin to kill a lark, and the girls gasped, laughed
and held their breath as a kill seemed inevitable only for the
lark to escape by a mere feather's breadth.

They were but an hour into their sport when Ursula, turning to follow the progress of her bird, glimpsed a man
scrambling up the last few feet of the rise and onto the flat

top of the hill. Soon more heads appeared, then still more, until a small crowd stood rather breathlessly on the top of the hill, heaving their packs off their backs and bending over their staves as they tried to regain their breath.

One by one the young women turned their attention from the battle of the birds in the sky to stare at the newcomers who had so rudely interrupted their pleasure. The twenty or so people who stood gazing around the flattened hill were of mixed ages: some had grey hair, others were barely more than children. But it was plain from their patched and dung-coloured clothes, their worn shoes and filthy coarse-spun cloaks that they were not the kind of people who could afford to own falcons, much less enjoy the leisure time to fly them.

The grooms moved swiftly in front of their mistresses, knives at the ready, in case they should be required to defend the ladies from this pack of beggars and vagabonds, but the little band made no move to approach the women.

A man stepped a little apart from the crowd and all eyes turned expectantly to him. He flung himself down on his knees and the rest of the group followed suit. A clamour of voices rose into the hot sunshine, like some great cliff-side colony of nesting gulls, and with as little meaning in sound. Their arms were flung up to heaven, their eyes closed and their heads thrown back. They seemed to be praying with as much fervour as a man condemned to death might desperately beg clemency from a judge.

Finally their leader rose and turned to face the kneeling crowd.

'Yes, yes, my chosen ones. This is the very place I saw in my vision. I know it! I can feel it! And now God has confirmed it!'

A chorus of, 'Yes, it is here. Hallelujah! This is the place!' burst out of many throats.

Ursula edged a little closer. Her groom put a warning arm out to try to stop her, but she was used to getting her own way and moved resolutely to a distance where she could hear more clearly. Her companions, with nervous giggles, followed her.

The leader of the band was a tall man, with high prominent cheekbones and a mass of thick black hair that hung in lank elflocks onto his shoulders. He was dressed simply in a grubby white robe that almost resembled that of a monk, save that his left shoulder and arm were bare and about his waist was a blue cord dyed to almost the same hue as the summer sky above him.

His voice rang out once more. 'This is the place where the legions of darkness meet the army of light. This is the very hill where demons and angels wrestle for the future of the world. Abraham and Isaac, Moses, even our Lord Himself, were all led to the hill tops and there put to the test for the very salvation of the world. We have been led here to serve a great purpose in the divine plan, a purpose that He will make known to us. Here we shall set up camp and wait for the vision to be revealed to us.'

A great cheer went up from the crowd. Their leader turned away, firmly clasping his hands behind his back, and appeared to be contemplating the great sweep of the valley that lay below him. The crowd waited for a few minutes, but no more words came from him.

Finally one of their number, a broad squat youth with arms like an ape, jumped up and gesticulated wildly at them. 'Well, you heard the prophet, make camp, quickly now.'

Everyone scrambled to their feet and, as if following a familiar routine, began their chores. Some started to dig fire pits, others gathered kindling or searched for herbs for the pot. With somewhat more reluctance, a few armed themselves with water-carriers and darted miserable glances at each other when they realised the only visible source of water was the distant river at the bottom of that very steep hill.

Seeing some of the men arming themselves with bows and arrows and with slingshots for hunting, the falconer rushed forward with his baited lure, whirling it about his head and whistling in a desperate attempt to bring the merlins down before this pack of lunatics started firing.

All the girls hurried back towards their horses, except Ursula, who did not move. She was still staring at the back of the white-robed figure who stood gazing out over the edge of the hill.

'He's calling you, is he?' a voice murmured in her ear.

She jumped at finding the little ape-armed youth by her elbow. Up close, Ursula thought, he looked even more like a monkey. His arms were covered in a thick mat of red hair and, judging by the bush escaping from the top of his coarse shirt, she rather suspected his body might be equally hairy.

She flushed, taking a few steps back. 'Calling me?'

'I was the first disciple he called and I've been with him ever since. Not everyone who wants to come with him can. He knows who's been chosen by God and only they can join him.' He lifted his head with evident pride.

'I can't imagine anyone wanting to join him. I should think those who haven't been chosen are very much relieved.' Ursula said it with every intention of wounding, but the ape-boy didn't seem to take offence.

'You might say that now, but wait till you see the miracles he performs.'

'So he can do a few tricks, can he? I've seen conjurors at the fairs bring dead toads to life and make coins disappear.'

'Ah,' the lad said, 'but have you seen them capture demons

in front of your very eyes or pull a venomous worm from a man's skull that was tormenting him with agonising pain. My master is a holy prophet. He was captured by a fierce band of murderous pirates that bound him hand and foot, and carried him off on their ship to sell as a slave. So he conjured a great storm that cracked the ship open on the rocks and every wicked man aboard perished, but though he was bound fast, he calmed the waves and floated ashore as safe as a babe in its cradle.'

Ursula snorted. 'I don't believe you.'

'I swear, on the Holy Virgin's crown, that I saw it with my own two eyes. Stood on the shore and watched it, I did. And so did the whole village, including the priest. There's not a man, woman or child in Brean who doesn't know him for a holy man and prophet. I tell you, he's been sent to save us all.'

The young man's blue eyes shone with such a radiance of belief that it seemed as if a candle was burning behind them. Ursula, for all that she was trying to sound unimpressed, felt her pulse quicken, as her eyes were drawn once more to the tall figure who had not moved so much as a muscle, despite all the bustle and noise behind him. The breeze tugged the folds of his robe and blew his long black hair out behind him so that suddenly he seemed the very image of a carving she had seen in a church, of Moses standing on top of the mountain holding the tablets of stone.

'What is his name?' she asked without taking her gaze from the figure.

The youth leaned closer to her as if he was imparting a great secret. 'His holy name is Serkan. It means leader, a leader anointed in blood.'

It was dark now. William drew his cloak tighter about his shoulders, trying not to shiver. The sun had sucked the heat from the earth as it set, taking back the warmth it had lent it, and the breeze whipping up from the valley seemed to carry all the chill of the cold river in it. Stars, like tiny shards of ice, hung in the black sky and the blades of grass turned the colour of steel in the moonlight.

Martin had come running as soon as he'd seen the pin-points of orange and yellow light winding their way up the valley towards the hill. But William had already seen them. That was why he'd chosen this place. It was like having his own castle. No walls to be sure, but no forest of trees or narrow alleys where someone could lie in wait. All these weeks he'd had no sign that Edgar had followed him from Brean, but somehow that only made him more nervous, as if Edgar were lying out there somewhere, gathering his strength, waiting until William relaxed his guard before he struck.

William felt a little safer up here, where he could see danger coming. But those lights were nothing to fear. Those torches did not belong to an angry mob. The procession was too slow and orderly. They were bringing the mad and sick with them, not sticks and swords. Those giggling girls and their servants had clearly wasted no time in spreading the word in Bath about his arrival.

He felt his blood throbbing through his body with a thrill that was almost like bedding a beautiful woman. He under-stood now what it felt like to be a great minstrel. There was the trepidation that tonight you might not be able to deliver, that this time your talents might fail you, but stronger by far was the thrill of anticipation, knowing that success would bring adulation.

It was as if at first he had been only a player in costume, an actor in one of the great Mystery Play tableaux such as they had at York. But now he was becoming that very person. He no longer had to pretend to sense the demons in the bodies of those that came to him, he could feel them. In his dreams he really saw the visions of which he spoke, and almost ... almost he was beginning to believe that all the events in his life had been leading to this. He had, after all, been saved from the raging sea; surely that meant that he had been chosen for some great task.

He had not set out to attract a following. Nothing had been further from his mind. His only intention had been to get away from Brean as quickly as possible. But with no money to buy decent lodgings, one night he and Martin had found themselves camping on the heath with a band of holy beggars who tramped from town to town begging for themselves and the poor, with their cry of, 'Bread, for God's sake.' The beggars had generously shared their food with the pair, and it was rich pickings too, for townsfolk feared the beggars' curses as much as they desired a blessing from them that would bring them luck.

Talk had naturally turned to where William was bound and, before he could prevent it, Martin had launched into an account of his master's miraculous deliverance and his exorcism of the girl, both of which lost nothing in the telling. There were, of course, jeers from the more cynical beggars; after all, these men spent their lives persuading the gullible that miracles would follow if they gave generously. But others in the band, who genuinely believed in their own holy calling, were more willing to accept that William too had seen visions. And it wasn't long therefore before William was challenged to demonstrate his powers. He obliged: plucking a stone from the head of one man who suffered headaches; convincing another that his falling sickness was caused by the menstrual blood of the Lilith, queen of demons, falling into a well from which he had drunk. And the beggar was

211

full of gratitude when William carved on a piece of wood the names of the three angels that would henceforth protect him.

By the time they parted company the next day, three of the holy beggars had become William's new disciples. One was a devout young man, who might have made a good life for himself in a monastery were it not for a restlessness that always drove him onwards. The second, an old man called Alfred, claimed to be a soldier who'd lost his right hand in battle, though since both his ears had been severed too, William rather suspected he'd been mutilated for some crime. The third was Letice, a crone so filthy and bedraggled it was hard to tell her age. Like a craggy outcrop of rock, it seemed as if she had looked that way for countless generations and would remain so for countless more to come.

Letice was something of an irritation. She would stare fixedly at you for hours at a time, but never meet your gaze. She talked constantly to herself about the people around her as if they couldn't hear her, and saw doom-laden omens in everything, from the number of birds in a flock to the way twigs burned on the fire. But even William had to admit she was useful. As soon as they entered a town or village, she would stand on the street corner and shout about the new prophet come among them, with a boldness that not even the ardent Martin could muster.

It was Letice who had revealed that William's holy name was Serkan. The voices in her head had told her this. Martin had sulked for days that he had not been the one to discover the master's hidden name, but he used it along with the others. And William couldn't deny it had a certain grandeur to it.

He gazed around at the motley group of followers he had assembled in the last few months. Most were hunched around the campfires, ravenously devouring the spit-roasted birds and rabbits they had caught, and hiding any food that remained. They'd no wish to be forced to share with those townsfolk who were making their way here. There were a few more women among them now, mostly those that other men had no use for: the maimed and disfigured; the ex-whore too old and scarred by pox to earn a living on her back now; the bruised and battered scrap of a girl on the run from her master. They were grateful for the company and protection, and threw themselves willingly into cooking and mending, glad for any kind word and gentle touch he might offer them.

But why were there no voluptuous beauties among his disciples, no fallen angels, no flame-haired Mary Magdalenes to whom he could offer intimate consolation? He groaned. It had been months since he'd bedded a woman, and he ached for it so much that sometimes he could hardly concentrate on anything else.

'Master, they are here.' Martin pointed to where the torches were appearing over the edge of the hill. Sighing, William rose and prepared for his performance.

Ursula positioned herself a little way from the crowd, who sat or kneeled on the short springy turf before the fire. She had deliberately selected a gown of white, impractical for riding, but she knew it would make her stand out in the dark, and she wanted to be noticed.

Her parents were away for the night at the house of an old friend of her father, a wealthy farmer, and would not return until midday tomorrow, after her father's business was concluded. Normally she would have welcomed any chance to get out of Bath. The farmer and his stolid daughters were as dull as her own parents, but there were usually some farmhands to flirt with when her father's back was turned. But now that she'd seen Serkan, these farmhands seemed nothing more than clumsy little boys.

So she had feigned a sick stomach and her parents had reluctantly left her at home under the care of her childhood nurse. But the old woman was now as deaf as a blacksmith's dog, and could be relied upon to fall asleep straight after supper, especially if she was helped to a more than generous measure of her favourite wine. The groom had travelled with Ursula's parents, but the stable boy, who constantly followed her around like an unweaned calf, was easily persuaded to saddle up her palfrey and lead it up the hill, if it meant he could spend the evening gazing at her. Even now she supposed he was somewhere in the shadows watching her, but she didn't look. Her gaze never left Serkan's face.

He stood behind the fire, so that it looked as if he was speaking out of it. His white robe took on a rich ruby glow in the light of the flames and the twin fires burned deep in those emerald-green eyes. His voice rang out with thunder, and his words cascaded over the lip of the hill like some great waterfall.

'... the city of sin and corruption, of squalor and filth, that city you call Bath, which now lies under the power of darkness, shall be changed, transformed into a city of light, it shall be filled with sweet perfumes and the song of angels. Great men shall flock to it.'

A few of the crowd who had come out from Bath jeered in disbelief, but his disciples fervently shouted 'Praise be' and 'Amen' to the night sky.

A woman who seemed to be one of Serkan's disciples tottered out from the crowd. She stood in front of the fire and began to turn, her arms flung out, singing some wordless ditty in a cracked voice, punctuated with sudden whoops and barks. Her dance became wilder and more abandoned. Then, as if she had been struck down, she fell onto the ground. Her body arched, shaking violently, and her heels drummed against the turf. A cry of alarm went up from the visitors, but Serkan, raising his hand for silence, stepped swiftly between her and the crowd.

'Bring me water and a scrap of leather or parchment.'

The ape-boy ran off and just as swiftly returned with a pot of water and a torn piece of parchment. Serkan pulled a stick from the fire, extinguished the burned end, then using the charred stick as a quill, he drew something upon the parchment and held it up to the crowd. Ursula vaguely recognised the two letters – alpha and omega – like the ones over the altar of the church she attended. Serkan stretched out his arms over the prone woman and began to speak fervently in a strange, guttural language. The orange glow of the fire haloed Serkan's head and the very darkness seemed to vibrate with those unearthly sounds that were pouring from his lips. The hairs on the back of Ursula's neck prickled.

As the words died away, he dropped the parchment into the jar of water. Then, dipping his fingers in the jar, he flung water at the woman's face. She stopped jerking and lay still. He kneeled and, cradling her head in the crook of his arm, helped her to drink. Then he laid the jar aside and extended his hand. 'Rise now.'

The crowd uttered soft little sighs as Serkan pulled the woman to her feet. She stood there in the firelight, swaying a little as if she was half asleep, but her face had a calmness about it that was almost beautiful.

Ursula found that she was trembling with excitement and some strange stirring in her body that she could not immediately identify. She pressed her hands together beneath her chin, her fingertips tingling as she imagined that strong firm hand clasping hers. As if he felt it too, Serkan's gaze suddenly turned in her direction and as their eyes met, he smiled at her – and only at her. She was quite certain of that.

William yawned and stretched. He stood for a moment, breathing in the cool morning air. He felt more relaxed than he had done in months. He hadn't realised how much tension there had been in his body until now. Only yesterday he had desired a beautiful girl to come to him and that very night his wish had been granted. He felt as if he only had to stretch out his hand for whatever he wanted to appear in it.

He had known from the moment he saw her standing there in her virginal white dress, like one of those martyred saints, that she had been given to him. When the visitors from Bath had begun to depart, she had lingered and when he'd beckoned her to approach she had come joyously. Her wide fawn-eyes looked up at him from under those dark lashes, with an expression of what you might call adoration, though definitely not submissiveness; he liked that, and he was captivated by that little habit she had of tossing her head like a spirited horse.

When he finally led her down the hill she ran laughing ahead of him, unafraid of the perilous slope or the darkness. In a hollow near the bottom, screened by gorse and birch, she turned to face him, her hands clasped behind her back in the semblance of a demure child. But in the moonlight he could see she was trying to suppress a grin, and her eyes were dancing under the stars. And it was under the stars they lay together, naked as Adam and Eve before the fall.

He did not force her. He did not have to; she gave herself to him. Suddenly shy and hesitant, she lay quite still on top of his robe which he had spread on the ground for her.

She made no move to touch him, but offered no resistance. Then as he gently caressed her, a passion seized her and she dug her fingers into his bare back, thrusting up at him, her head thrown back and her slender white throat arched like a bow.

Three times he had taken her, before rolling into an exhausted sleep in her arms. When he had awoken sometime before dawn she was gone. He had climbed back up the hill and lain down among his snoring disciples, and sunk once more into sleep.

William smiled to himself. Would she come again? He hoped she would. No, he *knew* she would.

He was startled by a sudden tugging on his sleeve.

'Master, Master. You must come with me.'

He turned to see Martin standing behind him, panting and sweating as if he had been running.

'Come where?' William asked. Then seeing the fearful expression on the lad's face, he added, 'What is it? What's wrong?'

Martin's gaze darted nervously around at the other disciples, but all were occupied with the morning's tasks of stoking the fires and preparing breakfast. Martin leaned in towards William, his voice low. 'You must come. She's . . . she's dead.'

William felt an icy hand gripping his insides. 'Who? Who's dead?' He made a grab for the lad, determined to shake the answer out of him, but Martin was already bounding over the lip of the hill and scrambling down the other side. William followed.

It was a miracle neither of them broke his neck in his haste to get down the hill. Martin reached the bottom first and stood aside, pointing towards a clump of bushes.

'She's behind there . . . I was going to fetch water from

the river, when ... I trod on something soft and when I looked down I saw ...'

William swallowed hard, then, bracing himself, he strode towards the bushes. The body of a woman lay on the ground. He couldn't see her face for a sack had been pulled over her head. But she lay as if she was already in a coffin, her legs neatly stretched out and her hands crossed over her chest.

William's first emotion was one of profound relief, for even though he couldn't see her face he could tell at once that this was not Ursula. The woman's robe was old and torn. Her fingernails were broken and grimed with dirt, but beneath the dirt the fingertips were blue. William lightly touched her leg, hoping that there was still life in her, but the moment he felt the skin he knew there was not. Bracing himself, he kneeled behind the woman's head and, grasping the corners of the sack, pulled it off. The jerk sent the woman's head lolling sideways. William gave a stifled cry, scrambling away from the body in horror.

There was no mistaking who it was beneath the sack. Poor Letice lay there, her face frozen in a distorted mask of pain, her mouth open wide as if she had been gasping for breath. It wasn't the sight of her face, though, that made William cry out, but what lay upon her throat. An adder was wound around her neck, with its head inside her open mouth. And the snake was as dead as the woman.

William's legs gave way and he sank onto the grass. He knew exactly who had done this. Edgar had been here last night! That fiend, that devil, had finally caught up with him and this was his warning. William stared wildly about him. Had Edgar been hiding down here in the dark, or had he been standing up there on the hill among the people from Bath? William would surely have recognised him in the crowd ... but he hadn't last time, had he, not until it was too late?

He struggled to his feet. 'Martin, did you see anyone here this morning? A man, did you see a man?'

Martin, still staring numbly at the body, slowly shook his head. 'It doesn't make sense. Was she trying to catch the viper in the sack and it bit her?'

'Snake's longer dead than she is,' William said dully.

'Then how did she die?'

William knew the moment he had uncovered her how she'd died. Letice's lips were blue and he could smell the stench of vomit on her gown. He recognised the signs only too well. He shuddered.

'Poison,' he whispered. The word slid from his mouth before he had time to think. As soon as he saw the panic and fear on Martin's face, he knew he should never have uttered it, but it was too late now.

Martin stared at him aghast. 'That drink you gave her last night—'

'No! I didn't do this.' William raised his hands as if warding off the very idea. 'I didn't harm her. I gave her nothing except water. It couldn't have killed her.'

'But everyone saw you give it to her and now she's dead, poisoned ... Master, I know you wouldn't have harmed her, but the other disciples and the people who came out here from Bath, what will they think? How will you prove you had no hand in this?' Martin suddenly pressed his fist to his mouth as an even more terrible thought occurred to him. 'What about me? I fetched the water. What if they think—'

William's fevered brain had reached the same conclusion even before the lad had finished speaking, and now it raced ahead.

'She must not be discovered. Go back up and fetch the

spade that is used to dig the fire pit and bring it back here. And fetch a fire pot and something that will burn well – tallow, pitch, anything you can find. But don't let anyone know what you are doing.'

Martin looked bewildered. 'What are you going to do with it, Master?'

'Just go! No, wait, help me to lift her over my shoulder . . . Now go, and meet me at the bottom of the west side of the hill.'

William knew his followers would be gathered round the cooking fires at the southern end of the hill, just above where he was now standing. Although the bushes would screen the body from a casual glance, any movement he made might be enough to draw attention to it. He had to move the corpse to a place where he could dispose of it without being seen.

As Martin scrambled back up the hillside, William pulled the knife from his belt and held it ready in his hand, peering at every clump of trees or hollow where his assassin might conceal himself. He staggered round the base of the hill with his burden, trying to make as much use of the cover of rocks and bushes as he could.

All the time his mind was racing feverishly. If Edgar could murder a poor mad woman just to let William know he had caught up with him, then what might he do to William when he finally moved in for the kill? This was his warning that he could strike at any time he pleased. William suspected he would not do it straight away. He would want him to suffer the torture of waiting first, but for how long – days, weeks? One thing was certain: nowhere in England was safe, not even this hill, as long as Edgar was out there.

He would have to find another ship, leave England for good, but to do that he needed money, a great deal of money, and where was he to get that? Plans formed and reformed in his mind like drifting smoke, but nothing solidified. He knew only one thing: he had to dispose of Letice's body before her corpse was seen by anyone else.

Fear of discovery and terror of attack gave William a physical strength and stamina he did not normally possess and he had almost reached the place when loose stones clattered down, giving warning of Martin's precipitous descent. Behind a clump of bushes, William found the hollow where he and Ursula had lain last night, and put Martin to work at once digging a pit. As soon as he had a spade in his hands the lad's panic seemed to subside a little; digging graves was something he knew how to do.

William set about collecting dry bracken, gorse and kindling, thanking heaven that there had not been a drop of rain these past weeks. But when he returned, Martin was sweating and almost sobbing in frustration. At every turn of the spade he'd hit rock and stones, and though he worked feverishly he'd scarcely been able to dig a trench more than a foot deep in the bottom of the depression.

William wrenched the spade from the boy's hands and threw it aside. He lined the pit with kindling and bracken. Then he stood back. 'Help me to get her in there.'

'But it's not nearly deep enough,' the lad wailed.

'Don't you think I don't know that?' he snapped. But seeing the fear on the lad's face, he added gently, 'Trust me, Martin. I am Serkan. There is nothing to fear. Now did you bring tallow?'

Martin fished in his scrip and pulled out a clay pot. 'It's the goose grease and turpentine that Alfred rubs on his chest to keep out the cold. I saw him use it once to get a stubborn fire going.'

William wiped the sack in the grease and laid it across

Letice's face, then heaped the rest of the dry gorse and bracken over the corpse.

'Give me the fire pot. Now go on back to the others. If anyone should see the smoke from the fire, tell them it is a holy rite, tell them that I am purifying myself, and must not be disturbed.'

When the lad had gone, William set the fire. As the gorse began to crackle and burn, he stood with his back to the hill, and raised his arms as if he was praying, which indeed he was and more fervently than he had done for many weeks, though his prayers were not for purification. The fire blazed fiercely but it did not burn for long. He added more dried gorse, but dared not make the fire any bigger for fear that it would arouse the curiosity of some wayfarer or shepherd who would not so easily be convinced by holy rites.

When a third blaze had died down, he kneeled and, brushing away the soft grey ash, examined the pit, trying not to gag at the stench. Letice's gown had burned away, no doubt helped by the cooking fat and grease that her grubby fingers had wiped on it over the years. The sacking had also burned, and the face beneath was charred black; the features, though clearly human, were now unrecognisable. Where the skin had cracked patches of raw red flesh showed through. But the body, though blackened, was still very much intact and unmistakably that of a woman. The fire had not been nearly hot enough to consume it. But William tried to console himself with the thought that if anyone did discover the body, not even Letice's own mother could identify her now, nor say how she had met her death.

He began to shovel the heap of soil and stones, which Martin had dug out, over the remains. The lad was right, it was nowhere near deep enough, and to make matters worse the edges of the charred pit stood out black against the ground. He scraped at them, trying to make them blend in, but there was no way he could flatten the mound. He heaved what stones he could find over it to deter animals from digging at it, but even then he could not afford to heap them up for that would only make the mound bigger and easier to see. In desperation he hacked at some nearby bushes with his knife, dragging the branches over the grave to try to disguise it from anyone glancing down from above.

Then, seeing that there was nothing more he could do, he hurried away in the direction of the river to bathe. It wasn't only the dirt and ash he needed to clean off, it was the stench of burned human flesh that clung to him like a noose round a felon's neck.

The tavern maid leaned over Godfrey deliberately, or so it seemed to him, thrusting her plump breasts under his nose as she poured more wine into his goblet. He caught her by the waist and pulled her down onto his lap, nuzzling his face in her cleavage, before she good-naturedly pushed him away and rose to answer the raucous calls of her other customers.

Godfrey chuckled. He had every intention of bedding that wench later when he'd drunk his fill. He knew her sort. Slip her a few coins and she'd do whatever he asked, and willingly too; so much easier than having to woo, coax and flatter the noble ladies at Court for weeks before they'd even open the doors of their bedchambers.

Godfrey leaned across the rough wooden table and grinned at the stranger sitting opposite him in the dark corner of the inn. 'See, now that's what I mean. Nothing wrong with a comely woman showing what gifts the Good Lord gave her, for the pleasure of others. Brings a bit of joy into this world, but if my master had seen that he'd have had her covered up like a nun. At the Christmas feast last year, three pretty virgins dressed as nymphs were brought in to dance for his pleasure. And what did he do? Put his hands over his eyes and ran out of the hall like a frightened child, just 'cause their rosy little nipples were bare. He wore a hair shirt all night to punish himself for having seen them. I know, 'cause I had to help him into it.'

The stranger grimaced. 'Riches are wasted on men like him. But then it's only the wealthy who can afford to disdain good food and girls, the rest of us are only too grateful for any crumbs of pleasure that fall our way.' He took a gulp of ale, rolling his tongue round his mouth as if even that had soured as soon as the liquid touched his lips.

If Godfrey had not been feeling so hard done by himself he might have enquired about the stranger's troubles, but a man who feels aggrieved is interested in no one's misery but his own. And Godfrey did feel sorely aggrieved. It was bad enough having to deal with the King's black mood at court, but at least there he could moan with the other servants. But now that Henry had insisted on making this fool's trip to Bath, Godfrey had no one to grumble with. For apart from himself, a groom and a couple of armed men, the King had insisted on travelling alone and in disguise. Not even the monks at the abbey knew who they were entertaining under their roof, not that entertaining was a word Godfrey would ever use to describe the misery of that squalid place.

The stranger took another gulp of ale. 'So what brings your master to Bath? Business is it, the cloth trade?'

Godfrey snorted. 'Nothing as frivolous as business. Would that it was. No, he thinks he's going mad. He's mistaken, of course, he's not *going* mad, he *is* mad. But he's come to the abbey in the hope of a cure, which just proves how insane he is.'

'Why Bath, of all places? The abbey here is falling into

ruin. Surely he'd be more comfortable at one of the wealthy ones.'

'Well, I would, that's for certain,' Godfrey said bitterly. 'The lodgings are as cold as a witch's tit, and as for the food! A starving hound wouldn't eat it. Why do you think I've escaped here for the evening? There's nothing else to do in this stinking town. I'd thought to pass a few hours at the bear-baiting they hold outside the city walls, lay a few wagers on the dogs, but it seems they had only one bear and even that escaped last week. Probably couldn't stand the stench of this place. But my master doesn't want comfort and entertainment; he wants mortification and misery.

'Apparently there's one old monk at the abbey who claims some skill at easing melancholy and phantasms of the mind with healing water he draws from a hot spring. The water smells foul, but that suits my master; the more disgusting the remedy, the more he's convinced it will cure him. If it was in any way pleasant, he'd shun it. It's not doing him any good, though. He's spending more time with his mirror than ever. Did I tell you, he thinks his mirror is talking to him? He's terrified of the thing, yet he spends hours sitting in front of it just staring at it.'

The stranger shuffled on the bench, turning his face slightly so that the yellow light from the candle fell on his weather-beaten face. 'So if it frightens him, why doesn't he just destroy it?'

'It's worth a fortune. It's decorated with rubies and pearls, not to mention some very costly enamel work.' Godfrey drained his second goblet of wine and snapped his fingers at the tavern maid, holding his goblet upside down to indicate it was empty. She refilled it, this time managing to keep the table between herself and Godfrey, much to his disappointment.

The man leaned forward, the candle flame reflecting in the pupils of his green eyes. 'You were saying that this mirror is very valuable.'

'Yeh, but that's not why my master won't destroy it. Its value means nothing to him. But he says that the image on the back is holy. It shows St Thomas Becket being slain by the knights, a cheerful subject to meditate upon for any man. Stare at that for too long and it's bound to have you jumping at your own shadow. If I have to gaze upon a saint let it be a fresh-faced virgin stripped for martyrdom. Now that is an image a man can linger on. There was one statue I saw in a church once – St Agatha just about to be put to the torture, she was. You should have seen the way the artist had moulded her bare breasts.' Godfrey's eyes glazed over as he pictured the statue; doubtless she been modelled on the local bishop's mistress, which was usually the case.

The stranger nudged him with his foot. 'So he won't part with it because of the holy icon?'

Godfrey took another swig of his wine. 'That's what he says, but it's my belief he's too afraid of it to destroy it himself. Thinks if he does, it'll call down a greater curse.'

For a while the stranger said nothing more, his brow creased in thought. Godfrey rested his chin in his hand and gazed around the inn. There were two wenches who took his fancy, the one who'd served him and a younger, prettier girl, a sister or cousin maybe. Innocence or experience – both had their attractions. He liked a well-fleshed woman, but on the other hand that young one's lips were delectable. Why shouldn't he have both? Maybe even the two together.

He had fallen into such a reverie that when the man finally spoke again, Godfrey jerked from his daydream so suddenly that the arm supporting his head shot off the table and he almost tumbled off the bench. A couple of men sitting a few benches along roared with laughter. Godfrey half rose to challenge them, but the stranger pulled him back down.

'Leave them. This is more important. I think I have a way to help your master. Have you heard of a man named Serkan?'

'I've heard vague rumours; some kind of preacher isn't he? A miracle-worker? They're always springing up. The gullible will believe anything.'

'This one's different,' the man said earnestly. 'They say he really can work miracles and exorcise the most stubborn of demons. As it happens he's set up camp not far from here, a place called Solsbury Hill. If your master were to take this mirror to him, he would be able to exorcise it and cure your master of this madness.'

Godfrey waved a dismissive hand. 'I tell you they're all charlatans. Neither that foul spring-water the monks are dipping him in nor any miracle-worker is going to restore his sanity.'

'What harm can it do to try?' the man persisted.

'It's a waste of . . .' Godfrey suddenly paused. It had taken a few moments for that little word 'harm' to penetrate the wine fumes fogging his brain, but now that it had, he fastened upon it. Harm, yes, just what harm could it do? Perhaps the harm in question could even prove to be lethal. Richard of York was a generous benefactor and would reward with wealth and position anyone who helped him to take his rightful place on the throne. Not even Richard would risk openly raising his hand against the King, but if the King's death could be blamed on some vagabond miracle-worker, that might be very fortuitous. Richard could have the man hanged, drawn and quartered, or burned alive for treason, in a suitable display of grief and outrage that would gain him only favour with the populace. Of course, it would not be so fortuitous for this Serkan, whoever he was, but then prophets loved to be martyred. It's what they dreamed of, wasn't it?

Godfrey grinned. 'Solsbury Hill, did you say? Can you tell me how to find it?'

'Rouse yourself,' William bellowed in Alfred's ear. 'Do you call this a faithful watch?'

The old man started violently and gazed bemusedly around him as if he couldn't recall where he was. 'I was only closing my eyes, Master, the better to listen.'

'But you didn't hear me coming, did you?'

Alfred shrugged sullenly. 'Anyway, it's near dawn. Them evil spirits has to return to the earth at cockcrow. They'll not work mischief now.' He shivered and held out the stump of his right arm towards the little fire, one of several fires William had ordered to be lit around the perimeter of the hill top.

'Demons are at work night and day without ceasing, Alfred. We must constantly be vigilant.'

But as William watched the first streaks of red creeping into the eastern sky, he felt the tightness in his chest ease just a little. He was almost sure the demon who was hunting him would not risk attacking in daylight. The danger was over for another night.

He patted Alfred on the shoulder. 'Go and rest awhile 'till it's time to eat.'

Alfred painfully levered himself to his feet with his staff and glanced across the hill top towards the east. The sun was rising as a ball of blood into the fiery sky.

He grunted. 'Don't like the look of that. You know what they say – "A red sun has water in his eye." I reckon we're in for a soaking afore it rises again.'

For the last two nights since Letice had been murdered, William had posted men on watch through the night. The excuse was that the devil's minions, angry that he was casting out demons, were massing, prowling around their fortress, trying to destroy them. He was vague about whether these dogs of the devil were human or spirit.

His followers had, of course, noticed the absence of Letice, not least because of her constant mutterings, but also because of her skill at catching anything that moved for her cooking pot, which was constantly bubbling away. William said only that Letice had been taken from them and that they should not try to seek her, for there were mysteries on this hill that had no earthly explanation, forces that were stronger than any power they had yet encountered. Even Martin seemed willing to be convinced now that Letice had not met her death by any human hand, and little wonder, for though as a sexton's son he had seen more corpses than most village lads, none had been so strangely adorned.

The sudden vanishing of Letice, and William's warning, had been unnerving enough to have every one of his disciples volunteering to keep watch, swearing to rouse their master at the first sign of attack. Not that William would have taken much rousing. What little sleep he'd had these past two days had been disturbed by dreams in which serpents, as huge as dragons, had erupted out of the hillside and wriggled up on all sides towards him, their long fangs dripping with green poison that burst into flames as it fell. William would wake screaming and sweating. His disciples watched him wide-eyed, whispering that his spirit had been wrestling with demons as he slept. That much was true, but the demons William fought in his sleep were not the spirits that haunted Solsbury Hill.

A rose-pink light had begun to trickle down into the valley.

Despite the sun not yet having fully risen, it was already beginning to feel close and airless, even up on the hill. William glanced down. Two horses and their riders were approaching along the track leading from Bath. He stiffened, and then tried to calm himself with the knowledge that Edgar would never approach him so openly and in company. The riders tethered their mounts to some trees at the bottom of the hill and toiled slowly up towards the camp.

Martin, as always, bustled up to greet them and soon led them over to where William stood on the rim of the hill, before respectfully withdrawing.

As soon as the lad was out of earshot, one of the two men bowed in courtly manner and cleared his throat. 'My master seeks your help. He is suffering from . . . a melancholia.'

William scarcely needed to be told that. The man's master was a thin, sallow-faced man, his skin made paler by his black clothes. He stared into the middle distance, his eyes dull and unfocused, his shoulders hunched as if he was hiding even from himself.

'And is it a lover's melancholy, a malcontent's melancholy or a melancholy of reason?' The question came out of William's lips without thought. When he had learned his trade as a physician it was the first thing he had been taught to ask.

The servant uneasily glanced at his master. 'Of reason, but more than that. My master possesses a silver mirror, the nature of which troubles him.'

'How does it trouble him?'

'He sees things in it that are not reflections of what stands before it. He sees the face of a man long dead.' Again the servant glanced at his master, but the man gave no sign he'd even heard what was said.

William frowned. 'I must see this mirror.'

It took the servant several attempts to rouse his master to respond, as if his spirit had travelled a long way from his body and had to be recalled. Finally, and with great reluctance, the master opened his black coat and revealed a leather bag hanging from his neck. With hands trembling so violently he could scarcely unfasten the buckles, he withdrew a flat, round object about the span of his own hand.

As soon as William laid eyes on it the blood began to pound in his temples. It was as if the sun itself had fallen to earth, for the gold and silver and blood-red rubies glittered so brightly in the morning light that he could scarcely look at it without being dazzled. The mirror must be worth a king's ransom.

His mind raced. These men would probably pay him something for a cure, but judging by the plainness of their clothes, he guessed it wasn't going to be a generous amount, not nearly enough to buy passage on a ship. But if he could get his hands on this mirror, he could go to any distant land he pleased and live in the lap of luxury when he got there.

But it was plain from the way this man reverently clasped the mirror, unable to tear his gaze from it, that he was not simply going to hand it over, even if William convinced him it was cursed. No, something more elaborate would be required if he was going to part this man and his mirror.

William adopted his most authoritative voice. 'There is a demon in this mirror, which takes the semblance of a dead man. It is a trick they often use.'

For the first time, the thin man spoke, but still did not lift his eyes from the mirror. 'No, you are wrong. It bears the image of a holy saint,' he said in a dull tone.

'On the reverse,' William said firmly. 'The saint faces away from the mirror, so that the demon is able to hide behind the holy image, just as on a coin the head of the King can never see what is stamped on the other side. You must return tonight, so that I may exorcise it and when I do, the melancholy and all else that troubles your mind will vanish with the demon.'

A look of desperate hope flickered across the man's face. 'But why can you not do so now?'

To William's surprise it was the servant who came to his rescue. 'Master, the mirror is silver and it's the moon that governs that element. Therefore, the chances of success will be greatly improved if the exorcism is carried out under her domain.'

His master seemed to wilt again, retreating back into himself.

The servant nodded to William. 'I will bring my master back tonight, as soon as it is dark. I assure you, he will be here.'

Godfrey purchased a beaker of tepid cider from one of the market stalls and threw it down his throat almost in a single swallow. He drew out a kerchief and waved it ineffectually at a cloud of flies buzzing round his head, before mopping the sweat from his forehead. The air was as hot and sticky as a blacksmith's armpit. Since noon thick clouds had been building in the sky, giving it a dense yellowish haze that seemed only to intensify the heat. The stench from the rubbish and offal lying around the market place was enough to sicken the stomach for life. But, he consoled himself, if all went to plan he had to endure only one more day in this stinking sewer of Bath.

This man Serkan had proved to be all he had hoped for and more. He had gambled that this prophet would take little persuasion to perform his healing at night. Such things were always more dramatic and appealing to the crowd then, and these charlatans loved to perform for a crowd. He had little doubt the unwitting Serkan would play his part beautifully; all Godfrey had to do was to arrange a little performance of his own, but for that he needed a player.

He'd been watching the actors at the far end of the market place for a couple of hours now. Five men, and a couple of lads dressed as women, had been struggling to entertain the crowd, but most people were either too occupied with the business of buying and selling, or too exhausted by the heat, to want to stand around and watch. The players had given up the struggle and were packing up their wooden wagon for the day.

Godfrey sidled up to one of them, a giant of a man, who was sitting on a barrel, pulling off a mask. He'd been playing the part of a lion or perhaps it was a wolf – the costume was so ragged it was hard to tell.

'You want to make some money?' Godfrey said, trying not to show his disgust at the overpowering stench of sweat and onions, which was oozing out of every pore.

'Make a change,' the actor grumbled. 'People in this city are so mean they'd not even share their fleas with you. So what are you offering?'

Godfrey tipped the contents of a leather purse into his own palm and thrust it out. The man whistled, as well he might for it would take him months to earn as much.

'Half now, the other half when the job's done.'

'And what's the job? You want me to kill a man for that?' He sounded as if he wouldn't have objected even to a spot of murder for that size of a purse.

Godfrey grinned. 'No, nothing like that. I just want to play a little jest on a friend of mine. Tonight he's going up to Solsbury Hill. You know it?'

The actor nodded.

'There's some new prophet camped up there. You know the type, says the world is going to end in thirty days.'

The man rolled his eyes and grimaced.

'I've been teasing my friend that this hill is haunted by the ghosts of the wild men and outlaws who've lived there. So what I thought was, you could dress as a wild man and leap out at him, give him a bit of a fright.'

'I could dress up as an outlaw, that'd be easier,' the actor said.

'No,' Godfrey said hastily. 'It must be a wild man. It's a private jest, you understand. His wife calls him her wild man.'

The player grinned. 'Gets a bit carried away in the bedchamber, does he?'

'Something like that,' Godfrey agreed. 'Here, see, I have a costume already for you.' He opened a sack and showed the actor the bundle inside. 'What do you say?'

The proffered coins disappeared into the player's scrip in less time than it takes for a hound to swallow a piece of meat. Hands were shaken and pressed to the market cross to seal the bargain, and they parted, both men grinning to themselves at their good fortune.

Godfrey watched the player amble off in the direction of the nearest inn, clutching the sack. He only hoped the actor wouldn't get too drunk and forget to turn up, but he was counting on the man's greed for the other half of the purse.

Though he said so himself, the costume had been a masterstroke: linen cloth, covered in pitch to which had been stuck frazzled hemp, so that the wearer would appear as a shaggy monster covered in long hair from head to foot. The final addition was a set of light chains that would clank whenever the wearer moved. It was identical to the now infamous costume Henry's grandfather Charles had worn at a ball, a costume that had nearly cost the French King his life.

Henry was teetering on the very brink of madness; the appearance of his grandfather would be just the little push he needed to send him over the edge of sanity, and as he fled in terror, over the edge of the hill too, with a dagger between his ribs. King Charles had miraculously survived his attempted assassination. Godfrey would make quite sure his grandson would not be so lucky.

Ursula looked somewhat less appealing in the daylight than she had three nights ago in the dark. Her swollen, red-rimmed eyes didn't help, but nevertheless there was something about the way she was frantically wringing her hands and gazing up so helplessly at William that made him long to kiss her again. But kissing was evidently the last thing on the girl's mind.

'My father has discovered I was out all night. The watch-man on the city gate told him he'd seen me go out and what time I returned. Father is furious. He says my reputation is ruined. He's going to send me to a nunnery. He means it. But I can't be walled up in one of those places for the rest of my life. I won't! I'd go mad. I'd kill myself!' She lifted her chin with a flash of her old spirit. 'That's why I've run away.'

William stared distractedly at her. 'Run away. Where will you go? Have you friends who—'

'Here. I've run away here to you. I'm going to stay with you, become one of your disciples. And . . .' she hesitated, blushing, '. . . when we are married, then—'

'Married!' William repeated aghast.

'Of course we will be married. Did you think I wouldn't consent to be your wife? You said that I was chosen to be your consort. You said our lovemaking would create the divine energy that would transform the world, like the alchemist can turn lead into gold.' She beamed at him. 'Did

235

you think I wouldn't accept you as my husband? How modest you are.'

For a moment, William was at a loss for words, then he recovered himself. 'What . . . what about your father – does he know this is where you were that night?'

'He questioned the stable boy and the snivelling little sneak told him everything.'

William groaned. The last thing he needed tonight was some irate father storming up the hill to retrieve his run-away daughter and interrupting the exorcism. That would ruin everything. If he didn't get his hands on the mirror tonight, he'd never get another chance, for the man would hardly be likely to return, not if some merchant arrived and accused him of seducing the girl.

'Ursula, you can't stay here. This is the first place your father will look when he finds you missing and you don't want him discovering you here and dragging you straight off to that nunnery.'

'But where can I go? I can't go back home.' She was strug-gling to hold back the tears.

William suddenly saw that she was no wanton seductress, only a scared little girl. A spasm of guilt flickered through him, but it passed almost before he recognised it.

'Do you have an aunt or uncle, a cousin perhaps, in some neighbouring town?'

'My grandmother lives in Saltford, but I can't go there. She's more strict than my father. She'd take me straight to the nunnery herself, probably an even worse one.'

William frowned, thinking rapidly. 'If I send Martin to your father's house with a message to say you are with your grandmother that will give you time to get away.'

And, he thought, stop the old man charging up here, at least for tonight. Tomorrow, he didn't care where the girl's father searched, he would be on his way to a port with that mirror.

Ursula's fearful expression melted away and, smiling, she held out her hand to him. 'Then I can stay here.'

'No!' The word burst out of William more forcibly than he had intended.

Ursula's eyes opened wide in alarm.

William tried to speak more calmly. 'Martin's message will buy you only a night and, perhaps a day, at the most. Sooner or later your father is bound to find out you are not with your grandmother and come searching up here. Do you have money with you?'

The abrupt question seemed to startle her. 'A . . . a little and my jewels.'

At least that was something, William thought. Best to send her to a city where she could easily lose herself among the crowd and where the arrival of a girl travelling alone would pass unremarked and unremembered.

'You must ride to Bristol, Ursula. There, take lodgings at an inn and wait for me.'

Ursula looked stricken. 'But I've been there only once with my parents. I can't travel alone. You have to come with me!'

'There are many troubled souls coming to see me tonight. I must stay to help them, but in a day or two my work here will be over and I will follow you. There is a woman in the city who sells spices in the market place near the cross. Everyone knows her. Goes by the name of Pavia. I will leave word with her when I've arrived and tell you where to meet me.'

'But why—'

He pressed his fingers gently to her soft hot lips. He had to get rid of her, and quickly.

'Listen to me, Ursula. I am Serkan the prophet and God

has chosen you to be my consort. No power on earth will be able to separate us. He will watch over you until I am at your side once more.' He took both her hands in his and lifted them to his chest. 'You believe in me, Ursula, don't you? You have faith in me? I need to know you do not doubt me or my powers. I must know that you believe!'

'I do! I swear I do.' Her eyes once more took on that shine of adoration.

He bent and kissed her chastely on the forehead, laying his hand on her head. 'Bless you, Ursula, bless you, my beloved. Now go and do as I command. Have faith and I will come to you.'

He watched as she led her horse down the steep hillside. She turned once and he held up his hand as if in benediction. He sighed. She was a beautiful creature, a man could be very happy with her for a few months at least. Though he hadn't intended to do so, now he rather thought he might go and find her once he had the mirror safely in his possession. Sea voyages could be long and exceedingly dull without a woman to while away the hours.

Having dispatched Martin on his errand to Ursula's house, William devoted his attention to the preparations for that night. He had constructed a fire pit close to the northern lip of the hill. The pit was shallow, and the kindling dry and thin. He wanted the fire to give off more flame than heat, at least to begin with. Just behind it, he carefully cut a sod from the soil, and excavated a shallow hole beneath it. Then he filled the hole with a small leafy branch cut from a bush and replaced the sod. The branch held the sod at ground level, disguising the hole beneath. As long as no one trod on it, no casual glance would reveal it and William intended he should be the only one standing behind the fire. He checked that all the things he would need lay ready beside the pit –

an earthenware jar of water, a fire pot in which charcoal burned, and the fumigant. All was ready, there was nothing more he could do now but wait.

Twilight crept in even before the sun had set. Deep purple and slate-coloured clouds had been rising all afternoon and now they towered like great battlements around the hill, plunging it into premature darkness. The wind was gathering strength; dry and hot as the blast from an oven, it dashed dust into stinging eyes and whipped limbs with fragments of broken twigs.

William stared anxiously down at the valley. There was no procession of torches winding its way towards the hill. The people of Bath had evidently decided to stay safely in their homes on a night like this. But what about the man with the mirror – was he desperate enough to make the journey? On the hillside the bushes swayed in the darkness so that it looked as if they were creeping up towards him. On such a night an assassin might easily steal up the hill and not even the sharpest lookout would see him. William found himself frantically praying for the man with the mirror to come. He could not bear another night of terror waiting for a dagger to be plunged in his back, or a blade to be drawn across his throat. He had to get away. He had to get that mirror tonight.

He was so consumed with fear that he didn't even notice the pinprick of lantern-light coming along the track from Bath, until the two riders had almost reached the base of the hill. When he finally glimpsed them, he had to stop himself running down the hill to meet them. Instead he forced himself to concentrate on the task of lighting the fire. His fear and the gusting wind made him fumble, but finally, after blowing out several times, the dried kindling took hold and the wind whipped up the blaze, sending the flames whirling around the pit like witches at the Devil's Sabbat.

As he looked up again he saw the two men advancing and his stomach gave a lurch of relief. But William could afford to waste no time in greetings. With an imperious wave of his hand he summoned his disciples who had been watching and waiting, knowing that something was afoot.

William motioned his two visitors to sit on the ground a little way from the fire and his followers sat themselves down behind them. An expectant hush fell upon the crowd as they waited to see what he would do. William could feel their mounting anticipation. They were expecting something special tonight. And he was determined they would not be disappointed.

He took a long stick and charred the end in the fire, then solemnly drew three wide concentric circles around the fire. No one moved or spoke. He could feel the gaze of every man and woman fixed intently upon him.

Charring the stick anew each time, he wrote signs and symbols in each of the circles in turn, calling out the names of what he wrote in a deep booming voice that rose above the roar of the wind. First, 'Armatus', the name of the summer moon, though there was not a glimpse of a moon to be seen tonight beneath the deep clouds. Next he wrote the names of the angels of summer – 'Gargatel', 'Tariel' and 'Gaviel'. Then he called out the names of all the angels of the air and the four names of God. Finally, in the outer circle, with a great flourish he inscribed four pentagrams, pointing towards the north, east, south and west of the hill. He had just drawn the last stroke when a long rumble of thunder echoed round the valley. William raised his stick as if he was commanding the thunder and the disciples huddled closer together, staring up in awe.

William dipped a bunch of broom fronds into the jar of water and flung drops around the circles and over the small crowd, who flinched and gasped as the water touched them as if the drops were gold coins thrown by a king.

Then he strode into the circles and stood before the fire in silence, his arms folded. His disciples held their breath in expectation.

'Bring the cursed mirror to me,' he commanded.

But the man did not move and, for a few sickening moments, William thought he was going to refuse. Finally his servant scrambled to his feet and, wrenching the mirror from his master's trembling fingers, he marched towards William and placed it in his hands, before retreating to stand in the shadows behind the group of disciples.

William almost howled in delight as he finally felt the weight of the silver mirror in his hands. He stared down into it. His face was reflected back up at him, framed by a halo of glistening pearls, and rubies that drew the very flames of the fire into their blood-red hearts.

He was close now, so close. He scooped up a handful of sulphur from the fumigant jar. With the other hand he held the mirror high aloft in the raven-black sky. There was another great rumble of thunder, louder than before. William felt the power surge through him as if he could command the whole universe.

'By the thrones of Beralans, Baldachis, Paumachia and Apologia, by their kings and proud powers and powerful princes, by the attendant spirits of Liachis, the servant of the throne of hell, I invoke you. I conjure you. I command you in the three secret names – Agla, On and Tetragrammaton – foul fiend come forth from this mirror!'

William threw the handful of sulphur onto the flames and a dense cloud of stinking yellow smoke exploded upwards, swallowing him and the mirror. All he had to do now was lift the turf off the hole he had prepared behind the fire and drop the mirror into it, but he never got the chance.

Just as he threw the sulphur there was a great roar and something huge and shaggy rose up the hill and burst out of the darkness behind him. William shrieked and stumbled backwards, stepping onto the hole; the twigs supporting the turf broke under his weight and he was pitched forward. The mirror flew out of his hand and fell into the dense smoke and flames of the fire.

With a clanking of iron chains and maniacal howls, the creature skirted around the prone figure of William and bounded towards the crowd. At the sight of the wild man cavorting towards them out of the dense yellow smoke, the disciples tried to scramble up, but they had huddled together so tightly that they were pushing each other back down in their struggle.

Godfrey had eyes for only one man. The king, sitting slightly forward of the disciples, had scrambled to his feet as soon as he caught sight of the figure. Now he was backing away to the edge of the hill, his arms held protectively across his face. He seemed to be praying or whimpering, Godfrey didn't know which, and wasn't going to wait to find out. His dagger was already in his hand as he crept around to the edge of the hill, and crouched, waiting for Henry to back just a little further away from the glow of the fire.

One swift thrust of the dagger, a hard shove over the edge, was all it would take to change the fate of England. And when the crumpled body was found tomorrow at the bottom of the hill, why, who would be blamed but the vagabond prophet who had stolen the valuable mirror?

'Come to me, my liege,' Godfrey whispered into the roaring wind. 'Just a little further, just a few more steps and it will all be over.'

242

A crack of blue lightning split the sky, and at once rain began to pour down in fat heavy drops. Godfrey was distracted for only a moment, but for Henry this new omen from the sky was more than his battered mind could cope with. He threw himself, face down, on the ground, his arms stretched out in the form of a cross, as if he was a monk doing penance before the altar.

Godfrey dashed the water from his eyes and swiftly glanced around. The disciples were fleeing in all directions. The wild man had slipped on the wet grass and was floundering around trying to regain his footing under the cumbersome costume, and Serkan seemed to have vanished. Henry lay motionless on the ground, as if waiting for the mercy of the executioner's knife that would put an end to his nightmare.

Godfrey crept forward as silently as he could, not that any stealth was needed, for the beating of the rain and crash of thunder would have masked the sound of an army. As he reached the King's feet he hesitated. It is much easier to stab a standing man in the back than one who is prone. He'd have to kneel and strike in one fluid movement before Henry could sense the presence of someone beside him and turn his head.

He braced himself, choosing the spot, raising the dagger in both fists ready to plunge it in. If he hadn't been so intent on his mark, he might have seen the wild man throw up his hands in horror. He might have heard the actor cry out a warning, but he didn't.

He had taken but a single step towards the prone body of the King when he heard the savage roar behind him; he half turned to glimpse something huge and dark rearing up behind him, the red mouth open in a snarl, the long white fangs bared. As another crack of lightning illuminated the full savagery of the great beast towering over him, Godfrey tried to strike out with the dagger he held, but he was too late, far too late. A huge paw struck him on the side of his head. The curved claws tore the flesh from his face, and with a single agonised scream, Godfrey tumbled over the side of the hill and vanished into the darkness below.

The bear flopped heavily down onto all four paws. As the rain pounded down, he sniffed at the prone body of the King, then turned away. For a long moment, the bear stood alone on the top of Solsbury Hill, its great head lifted as if it was looking out over the darkened valley, out over England, out over time itself.

As the thunder rumbled once more around the hill, more distant now, Henry finally came to and began to stir. The great bear looked down at him one last time before it turned and lumbered off down the hill, vanishing into the cavernous night.

A pale primrose light was creeping into the sky. The air had the sharp, fresh scent of wet earth and grass. It had rained all night, washing stones down the hillside in muddy torrents, but with the coming of dawn the clouds had finally rolled away. William, resting heavily on his staff, limped painfully across the sodden grass, his progress made even slower by his soaking robe, which twisted itself around his legs. His ankle had swollen to twice its size from his wrenching it in the hole. It was going to be agony getting down that hill, with the grass so slippery after the storm. But it had to be done; up here alone and injured he may as well have been staked out like a lamb for a wolf.

There was no sign of any of his disciples, not even Martin. The traitors had fled, leaving him completely alone and unprotected. He had lain all night, curled tightly in a ball against the pounding rain, his limbs numb with cold and his brain frozen with fear that the devil he had conjured would return.

He had not for one moment believed that the spell would really bring forth a demon, but when that monster had lumbered towards him, rattling the chains of hell, he had thought that Satan himself had risen out of the earth to take him. He had, he supposed, fainted, for when he came to he could see nothing in the blinding rain, hear nothing except the wind raging. He'd crawled away and hidden in a clump of bushes, reciting every prayer and charm he'd ever learned or even half learned, until it was light enough for him to dare to move.

Now the only thought in his head was to get off this accursed hill as quickly as possible. Nothing would induce him to spend another night here. But first there was something he had to retrieve. It was his only hope of getting so far away from here that he'd never have to lay eyes on England again.

He limped painfully towards the fire pit. The pots and the jar of sulphur still lay where he had left them. The pit had filled with black water on which the dust and ashes of last night's fire floated. He struggled down onto his knees, and began frantically groping around until his fingers touched the edge of a heavy disc. Almost sobbing with relief, he pulled the mirror out and carefully wiped it on the hem of his sodden robe. The silver was blackened and fragments of the red enamel on the back had cracked and fallen off.

For a moment he felt the crushing weight of disappointment, but he consoled himself. Had the rain not extinguished the fire so quickly, the damage could have been far worse. Besides, he would not have been able to sell it as a mirror, for it would be far too easily identified, and who in these parts could possibly afford to pay the kind of sum that the complete mirror was worth? No, far better to break it apart, sell a ruby here, some pearls there and melt the silver down into smaller pieces.

Hastily he drew his knife, and set about prising a single ruby from its setting. He must have something ready to barter with at the first village he came to, for he was in desperate need of food, new clothes and, most importantly, a strong horse. He wouldn't get very far on foot with his injured ankle.

Without warning he felt a sharp pain stabbing into his back. He jerked upwards, dropping the mirror for the second time into the black puddle of the fire pit.

'Throw your knife away,' a voice growled behind him, 'or I'll push this dagger so far into you it'll cut your navel out.'

Sick with fear, William did as he was bid and heard his staff being kicked out of his reach.

'Don't stand up. Just turn around, nice and slowly. I want to see your face, you bastard.'

William couldn't have stood, even if he'd tried. Wincing in pain he twisted around and looked up into the face of the one man he prayed he'd never see again.

'So, William, or should I call you Serkan? Oh, where are my manners? I should address you as "Master" now, shouldn't I?'

The man, towering over him, was smiling coldly. His dark hair was streaked with grey. His scarred face was gaunt and as tanned as old leather, and several of his teeth were missing. But his eyes were the same emerald green as William's own.

William tried to force his mouth into a smile, but failed miserably. 'Edgar. Thank God, you ... you live. I was so afraid you'd perished in the wreck.'

Edgar gave a bitter laugh. 'So afraid I'd survived, you mean. But you knew I was still alive, didn't you? You got the little message I pinned to the cottage door. I thought you'd recognise the sign – the staff of Asclepius with a serpent entwined about it – the emblem of a physician. But then the serpent has another meaning too, doesn't it, William? One you'd know all about – *treachery.*'

'And you left another of your little marks too, didn't you?' William said. 'On the body of that poor woman you murdered.'

'Only sporting to give you fair warning I was here. I've followed you every sorry step of the way from Brean, biding my time. But you'd surrounded yourself with followers, hiding behind women's skirts as usual. I suppose I could have picked them off one at a time, but that would have attracted attention. I was trying to figure out how to get you alone when, by good fortune, I met a servant in an inn who told me about his master's valuable mirror. As soon as I heard about that mirror I knew you wouldn't be able to resist the temptation to steal it. So I persuaded the servant to bring his master here, because I knew your greed would get the better of you, and it has. Why didn't you flee last night when you had the chance? You could have been well away by now. But I know you too well, William. I knew you would come back for the mirror and here you are, snouting around in the mud for it, like the swine you are.'

Despite the chill of his wet robes, William's face was flushed. 'What . . . what do you want of me?'

Edgar fingered the blade of his dagger. 'I want you, dear brother. I want your death. I want revenge.'

'But after all these years, you can't still—'

'Fifteen years and three months, to be exact, and I should know; I counted every rotten, stinking back-breaking day of it. And now you are going to pay. I'm only sorry I can't make you suffer as long as I did, but I can ensure you do suffer. The question is, how? Staking you to the ground and roasting your feet in a fire – how would that be to begin with? What a pity all your followers have deserted you. There'll be no one to hear your screams up here.'

'Except me!' a voice yelled out behind him. Martin launched himself at Edgar, knocking him to the ground and pinning his arms behind him. 'Quick, Master, give me your girdle.'

He held the struggling man until William had managed to unfasten the blue cord he wore about his waist and had crawled on his hands and knees over to bind Edgar's arms behind him. Martin used his own belt to lash Edgar's ankles. Once the prisoner was firmly secured, Martin hauled him into a sitting position.

'What should I do with him, Master?'

'Wait, boy,' Edgar said. 'Before you do anything with me, there are things you need to know. Things about this *master* of yours.'

'Ignore him,' William snapped. 'Fetch my staff and help me to my feet. We're leaving. This wretch can stay here until someone eventually comes up and stumbles upon him.'

'Don't you want to know why I was trying to kill your master?' Edgar said calmly. 'Aren't you at all curious about why I followed him here?'

'Fetch my staff now, I command you,' William said with all the authority he could muster.

Martin hesitated, looking at the two men on the ground. Then he picked up William's staff and Edgar's dagger, and sat down a little way from the two men, holding the dagger ready in his hand.

'I want to hear what he has to say. You!' He pointed with

the dagger at Edgar. 'You called my master "brother". Is he really your kin?'

Edgar arched his back, trying to ease the ache of the tight bonds. 'He is my father's son, though by God, I swear he has shown no brotherly loyalty to me.'

Martin frowned. 'I used to fight with my brothers all the time, but I never wanted to see them dead. What was the quarrel between you?'

'Will you tell him, William, or shall I?'

'Don't listen to him,' William roared.

'I'll tell it then, shall I?' Edgar said coldly. 'The *quarrel*, as you put it, happened when I was just sixteen and my brother here, a year younger. We were both apprenticed to a great physician and alchemist, a man much respected in the district. I was betrothed to Aliena, the physician's only child, whom I adored, and it seemed that my life was mapped out for me. Aliena and I would marry and raise our children. In time I would inherit my father-in-law's business and devote my life to healing the sick.

'I worked hard, eager to become as good a physician as my master. But William had no interest in studying. He didn't need to; knowledge came easily to him and somehow he managed to convince our master that he was studying diligently. He always had a gift for words, but the truth was that when the master left us alone, my brother would sneak off to lay wagers on the cockfights or seduce some tavern wench.

'One day, our master set us both to making up potions and purges for the patients he would visit later that day. He left recipes, which we were to follow to the letter. But a pretty young maid called with a message for the physician. William was supposed to be making up a sleeping draught for a woman who suffered much pain, but he was so busy flirting with the maid that he forgot he had already added the drops of hemlock to the potion and added more. Of course, the woman died. My dear brother swore that it was I, not he, who had prepared that sleeping draught and everyone believed him.

'I was terrified I would be hanged, but my master pleaded that it was an accident and my sentence was commuted to a public flogging in the market place, and then I was sold to a ship's captain to pay the heavy fine imposed on my master.

'I had lost everything, while my brother had it all. He even took my beloved Aliena, until he tired of her and left her with a child swelling her belly. For fifteen years I sweated and slaved before the mast, rowing till my hands were raw and my muscles screamed in agony, climbing the rigging as storms raged, blistering in the heat, shivering in the ice of winter, eating food rotten with maggots and drinking foul water. And if my strength failed me, there was always the encouragement of the lash to spur me on.

'Then a few months ago a passenger came aboard. I recognised him at once, but he didn't even notice me. Why should he? He scarcely glanced at the filthy, sunburned sailors toiling over the rigging. I thought time might have improved his character, but it hadn't. The captain's mistress was aboard, and it wasn't long before I saw him groping her in the castle of the ship, when the captain was occupied elsewhere.

'I confronted him and he finally realised who I was. He grabbed an iron grappling hook and swung it at my head, determined to silence me for good. But years of dodging heavy ropes and tackle on a rolling ship had taught me swiftness. The hook missed my head, but broke my arm. One of my shipmates saw what he did and when the captain questioned me about the quarrel, I told him all about William and his mistress.

'The captain flew into a rage, threatening to throw them both overboard. His mistress protested that William had forced his attentions on her. So the captain had William lashed to the topmost mast to suffer the full motion of the ship and punishment of the weather. And finally, after fifteen years, I felt a little crumb of justice had fallen my way; for once in his life my brother was going to understand what it meant to endure hunger and thirst, burning sun and biting rain.

'But in all the commotion no one had noticed how close we were to the headland. Almost at once the storm hit us. The mast was the first thing to topple into the sea. We were driven onto the rocks and fought for our lives. I struggled ashore, though how I did so with a broken arm was more than I could fathom. Rage and bitterness spurred me on. I searched for the others, but they were all drowned. I thought William had perished as well, and I was glad of it. Until I heard that a man had survived, a man tied to the mast of the ship. And I knew then that somehow that bastard had once again survived. But I was determined that this time he would not get away with it.'

The look of disgust on Martin's face had been deepening all the time Edgar had been speaking, and now the lad turned to look at his master.

'It's all lies,' William shouted, his face contorted. 'You're surely not going take his word over mine. Remember the miracles I've performed. I am Serkan, and he is . . . is nothing!'

'Like me, you mean.' The boy sprang to his feet. 'I'm nothing to you either, am I? You let me think that you were a prophet, a holy man. I left my family, my village, everything, to follow you and all this time you've lied to me. Everything you've done has been nothing but cheap swindler's tricks.'

Martin raised the dagger and ran at him, but William grabbed a handful of sulphur from the pot behind him and dashed into the lad's face. Martin squealed, and blindly staggered backward. William reached out and grabbed his ankle, bringing him crashing to the ground. The knife flew from Martin's hand.

William rolled onto his knees and crawled towards the blade. He stretched out his hand, but just as his fingertips touched it, a large leather boot came down on the dagger, pinning it to the ground.

William stared up. One of the sheriff's men was looking down at him, his sword pointed straight at William's throat. A second soldier had his sword pointed at Martin's chest, an unnecessary precaution since he could do nothing except rub his streaming eyes.

Two men came panting over the rise. The stouter of the two stood bent double for a few minutes, evidently suffering from a stitch. But the second, a bailiff, hurried across to the group.

'Which of you is the man they call Serkan?'

'He is,' Edgar jerked his head towards William.

The bailiff turned to William and said rather breathlessly, 'Master Thomas says his daughter's run away and he thinks she's come here. He claims that four nights ago you seduced his daughter, Ursula. And yesterday, when he returned home after seeing to his business affairs, his maid reported that a lad had come with a message that Ursula had gone to her grandmother's house. So Master Thomas set off to bring her home, only to discover the good lady hadn't laid eyes on her granddaughter. So, is the girl with you?'

The stout man, who by now had joined them, rounded on William, his eyes bulging in fury. 'What have you done with my little Ursula? Where is she?' He stared around the flat hilltop as if he thought to see her standing there.

'I haven't seen her.'

The bailiff hauled William to his feet by the front of his robe. He yelped at the pain in his ankle.

'Where is she?' the bailiff demanded. 'It would be wiser for you to tell me now. I've other ways of getting the information I want, far more unpleasant ways,' he added with a nasty grin.

'All right!' William groaned. 'She came here yesterday afternoon. I told her to go home, but she wouldn't, she said she was going to Bristol.'

'Bristol!' Master Thomas shouted, his face turning scarlet. 'What would my daughter want to go to Bristol for? She knows no one there. She wouldn't even know the way. What have you done with my little girl?'

William swayed in the bailiff's grip. 'I swear on the Holy Cross, I—'

But they never learned what William was going to swear, for at that moment there was a shout from another soldier struggling over the rise.

'We found her, bailiff. Leastways we found a body. It was buried in a shallow grave near the bottom of the hill. The rain must have washed some of the soil and stones off the grave. That's how we saw the corpse, else we might never have found it.' He turned to Master Thomas, gnawing his lip. 'I'm sorry, sir. Body's been burned, but there's no mistaking it's a woman. I reckon it must be your daughter.'

The merchant rocked on his heels, his mouth working convulsively. 'Not my daughter. Please, not her ... My little Ursula dead ... burned!' He flung himself at William and it took the strength of two soldiers to hold him back. 'He murdered her ... He murdered my innocent child!'

William stared aghast, his face blanched to the colour of whey. 'No, no, that's not her, that's not Ursula. I didn't kill her. I swear by all the saints in Heaven, Ursula's alive. She's in Bristol. Tell them, Martin, tell them it isn't Ursula in that grave.'

For a long moment Martin stared at him through swollen and bloodshot eyes. Then he said quite calmly, 'But who else could it be, Master. Who else could it possibly be?'

Historical Notes

After the truce was agreed between France and England in 1396, Richard II of England and Charles VI of France exchanged gifts every year at the time of the New Year feast. Some of the gifts are well documented, and were lavish and costly pieces such as drinking vessels and ornaments. The mirror in the story is not recorded, but is typical of the kind of work done at that period, decorated with *rouge cler* enamel, which was in use from the beginning of the fourteenth century.

During his reign, Charles VI suffered several bouts of 'madness', violently attacking courtiers and friends. The entrances in his castles even had to be walled up to prevent him escaping. On one occasion at a party he dressed as a wild man with several of his lords, who chained themselves together and cavorted about. The King's brother, Louis of Valois, approached the wild men with a flaming torch, allegedly to determine their identity. The pitch that covered their costumes was set alight and four of the lords perished. Charles was only saved by a quick-thinking lady-in-waiting, who smothered the flames with the train of her dress. Whether this was, as his brother claimed, an accident or a deliberate attempt at assassination we shall probably never know, but the incident became known as *Bal des Ardents*, the Ball of the Burning Men.

In the summer of 1453, following the loss of his lands in France, the gentle and saintly Henry VI suffered his first period of 'madness'. Whether it was, as he feared, a condition inherited from his grandfather Charles, or a nervous breakdown brought about by stress, is difficult to determine. Richard of York, who had an equal claim to the throne, was appointed as Protector in March 1454. When Henry regained his sanity for a short time in 1455, Richard of York was dismissed, but took up arms against the Crown in May of that year, in a conflict that was later to be called The War of the Roses.

The ritual that Serkan used to exorcise the demon from the mirror was based upon the detailed instructions for conjuring of spirits recorded by authors such as Pietro d'Abano, 1250–1316, in his treatise *Heptameron seu elementa magica*. Pietro d'Abano was an Italian physician, who is said to have 'accidentally died' while being interrogated by the Inquisition.

ACT FOUR

I

I'd been dead for about five minutes now and it was a comfortable experience. I had taken care to fall on my back and lay there quite at ease, arms outstretched, gazing up at the darkening sky. The moon, almost at the full, was poised on the gable of one of the buildings overlooking the yard. If I squinted slightly I could make out a white face peering from a window in the gable. Some child, probably, or a penny-pinching adult who was reluctant to pay up to see me dead.

From a few yards away came the sound of several voices raised in argument. I was aware that I was being referred to, and not in a complimentary way. No one seemed to regret my death. Indeed, there was talk of vengeance and justice. Then the argument turned to scuffling, accompanied by blows and gasps, and the thud of another body hitting the ground. The dead man had the good manners and the skill to fall a little distance away, leaving me to contemplate the moon and the face at the window. Now, after more scuffles and groans, the bodies began to fall as fast as rotten fruit from the tree. I counted three more thuds followed by silence apart from the odd satisfied groan or murmur of approval from the dark pit beyond where we lay scattered, all five of us.

Then it was time for the summing-up. One of the few

survivors of this violent action – his name was
Malcontento – spoke up to explain how these five sudden
killings had been necessary on account of other and earlier
murders. Naturally, being dead, I didn't turn my head but
kept my eyes fixed on the moon, which was inching its way
above the rooftops. In my mind's eye, though, I saw
Malcontento pointing an accusatory finger at me and my
fellow corpses. I heard him as he ran through a list of poi-
sonings, stranglings and stabbings before wrapping things
up with a couple of little rhymes.

> 'An honest life, however low, outweighs
> The deeds of these. Each one his debt now pays.
> So Heaven's law trumps false device and reason,
> May their guilty blood wash off all sin and treason.'

There was a pause to allow this harmless moral to sink in,
before we corpses rose from the dead and joined our fellows
at the front of the makeshift stage to acknowledge the plau-
dits of the audience. To judge by their clapping and their
calls, they seemed pleased with our depiction of the lechery
and violence that everyone expects to find at the court of
an Italian duke, especially one who's planning to marry his
half-sister after disposing of her husband. We – or rather
our author – had even included a scene in a madhouse,
something that audiences of every type and class always
appreciate.

Finally we players did a little jig in gratitude and as a way
of bringing our performance of *A House Divided* to a merry
close. In truth, we were already well disposed towards the
audience. They had been more respectful than a London
crowd – but then any crowd is more respectful than a
London one – and although we didn't have an exact tally on

the amount of money brought in by the 'gathering' taken before the performance the word was that the citizens of the city of Bath had been open-handed. And this sum would be supplemented by a grant from the town corporation, since they wanted to keep in good odour with our royal patron.

We finished our jig with a flourish and filed behind the curtained screens that provided the off-stage area. We were playing in the yard of the Bear Inn, which lies off Cock Lane in the central part of Bath. The Bear didn't have the amenities of our own Globe Theatre or fashionable London venues such as Blackfriars. In fact, it didn't have any amenities at all apart from the hastily erected stage, some moth-eaten drapes and, for furniture, a table, a few stools and an imposing chair (the duke's throne) provided by the landlord, Harry Cuff. Everything else – props, costumes, masks, face-paints – had to be laboriously transported from town to town across the kingdom by wagon. But there's a special quality to being out on the road when the weather is fair and the audience is made up not of jaded Londoners but honest provincials eager for entertainment provided by the cream of the capital's players.

We of the King's Men certainly regarded ourselves as that cream, pouring out our riches as we progressed across the West Country to our last destination of Bristol. This was home territory for me, Nicholas Revill, a member of the King's Men for more than six years by now. In the latter days of Queen Elizabeth's reign I had arrived in London from the village of Miching, which lies to the south-west of Bristol. If you climb the hills above this village there is a fine view of the channel that separates England from Wales. My father was the parson of the village and my mother the parson's wife. They and many other folk in Miching died in an outbreak of the plague. I was in Bristol at the time, vainly seeking employment as a player, and although I returned home disappointed I soon realised there were greater blessings than finding a job: I was still alive.

With my good parents no longer in this world and no other family to keep me behind, I escaped to the metropolis where I once again had a piece of good fortune when I fell among the Chamberlain's Men, as they were called at the time. Even then, as the Chamberlain's, they had a high reputation, with the Burbage brothers as the principal shareholders and William Shakespeare as their principal author. Now King James was our patron, and the Burbages and Shakespeare enjoyed the royal link with a quiet pride. Perhaps it made them reluctant to leave London, for neither the brothers nor WS were with us on this trip to the west.

'A good audience, this Bath one,' I said to my friend Abel Glaze. It was he who had tumbled down dead on stage right after my demise, landing a careful distance away.

'Yes,' chipped in Michael Donegrace, one of our boy players. A dozen of us were taking turns to shuck off our costumes in the cramped and dimly illuminated area to one side of the stage, before folding our garments and storing them away in one of the tiring-chests. Being on tour meant we had no tire-master to nag us about the tears and lost buttons and stains on our outfits, but equally it meant that each individual was responsible for stowing his garb and keeping it fit for the next performance.

'You come from this part of the world, don't you, Nick?' said Laurence Savage.

'I believe I have heard Nicholas mention the fact from time to time,' said Abel.

'A world separates Bath from my old village of Miching,' I said.

'What surprised me,' said Laurence, 'was how quick the audience was here, how ready to lap up all the wickedness on stage. I'd heard they were a bit strait-laced in these parts. You know, afflicted with a touch of the . . .' He pulled his mouth down and mimed the conical hat that was worn by the Puritans and, as he did so, unintentionally jabbed with his elbow a boy pushing his way through the drapes that fronted the tire-room.

Once he'd recovered from the blow in the stomach, the lad gazed around in wonderment and perhaps alarm. He saw a dozen grown men and a couple of boys of about his own age with their faces still painted and their costumes half off, in the light of a single lantern and a spill of moon from overhead. The boy's eyes then darted about as if he were searching for someone.

'Hello, Leonard,' said Laurence Savage to him. And then to the rest of us: 'This is Leonard Cuff, son to our host at the Bear. I was chatting to his father this afternoon and had the honour of being introduced to the members of that gentleman's family.'

Laurence possessed the knack of remembering names and faces even after the most fleeting meeting. For his part, the boy was relieved to recognise a friendly face. He held up a letter.

'This is for the duke,' he said in an uncertain voice. 'Is – is the duke here?'

There was a moment's silence, then the sharper of my fellows looked at me, realising before I did what the lad was on about. The duke – Duke Peccato, to give him his name – was the Italian part that I had so recently enacted in *A House Divided*. It was I who had schemed to marry my half-sister, played by Michael Donegrace, and in the process found it expedient to kill off my brother-in-law. My machinations

led inevitably to my own violent death and those of my asso-
ciates, chiefly at the hands of Malcontento, played by
Laurence. I was pleased to have been Duke Peccato. It was
quite a big part and, more important, it was a very bad part.
There's nothing players like more than a true villain to sink
their teeth into. The audience like it too.

'I am the duke,' I said. 'Duke Peccato.'

'You are?' said Leonard.

'Not really,' I said. 'That is my part, I mean. My name is
Nicholas Revill.'

'Well, sir, whoever you may be, this is for you.'

The boy handed me the letter rather gingerly as if he
thought some of the duke's evil might have rubbed off on
the person playing him.

He added, 'It's from a lady.'

'What lady?'

'Don't know. She was wearing a hat pulled low and I
couldn't see her face clear.'

There was an outburst of ooh-ing and ah-ing from my
fellows at the mention of 'a lady'. I knew what they were
thinking. It was more or less what I was thinking too.

'I'm not acquainted with any ladies in Bath,' I said, half
apologetic but a bit smug as well. I might have asked more
questions of the landlord's son – could he guess at the mystery woman's age? what about the style of her voice? – but
the lad had already slipped away through the drapes.

'Your lucky night,' said Laurence.

'You dog,' said Abel.

'I am jealous, I confess it, Duke Peccato,' said Michael
Donegrace, who had so recently glided across the boards as
my half-sister and would-be bride, and on whose behalf I
had already killed extensively that night.

I ignored their ribaldry and held the folded paper close to

the lantern so as to read the superscription. 'To him who plays the Duke', it said in a large but elegant hand. Well, of course, whoever wrote this could not have known my name, only the part I played in *A House Divided*. There was another line of writing under the address, slightly smaller but in the same hand. No more than three words: 'A privy message'. I felt my cheeks grow warm and was glad I hadn't completely wiped off my face-paint because I was being looked at very intently by Laurence Savage and the others. My fingers were itching to tear open this private message – which was sealed with a red blob of wax – but I was not going to give my fellows the satisfaction of reading my expression while I examined its contents.

'If you'll excuse me,' I said, folding up the last bit of my ducal costume with exaggerated care and putting it in one of the tire-chests.

'Will we be seeing you later at Mother Treadwell's?' said Laurence.

Most of us King's Men were lodging at a couple of rooms in a house near the North Gate of the town, where all of us were crammed into too few beds. The place was run by a good-natured, twinkle-eyed widow woman who welcomed travelling players, and more particularly their gossip.

'Oh, no, we won't be seeing *him* later,' said Abel Glaze, answering for me. 'Nicholas will be *treading well* elsewhere tonight, won't he?'

'More room in the bed for the rest of us then,' said Michael Donegrace.

I left them to their envious jokes and made my way out of the changing room and slowly through the inn yard. Most of the audience had watched *A House Divided* on their feet, like the groundlings at the Globe, although there was a cluster of benches near the front for those who preferred to sit and were willing to pay a bit more. It was a close, warm evening with a little light remaining in the west as well as that provided by the rising moon. There were a few stragglers remaining after the performance, drinking and smoking in corners, the embers of their pipes glowing softly in the near dark. Murmurs of male conversation. No women that I could see, no enticing female strangers with hats pulled low over their brows.

It was not unknown for players to receive messages from, ah, the better class of women who had been present at our performances on stage. Messages that offered favours. Sadly, it had never happened to me or my immediate fellows, but there were tales about a few of the older men in the company, including an amusing one about William Shakespeare and Dick Burbage having planned an assignation at the same time with the same man's wife. Mind you, they were much younger then, and playing has become more respectable in these latter days.

So it was with hope in my heart, and the enticing words 'A privy message' tapping in my brain like a drumbeat, that I exited the yard into Cock Lane and turned down towards a thoroughfare that I think is called Cheap Street. The bulk of the great city church of Bath loomed to my left.

From the first-floor window of a house at the corner of Cheap Street came a gleam of light where the curtain was not completely drawn. That, combined with the beams from the moon, should, I decided, enable me to read the letter. As I stopped under the window, all eager to tear the thing open, I spied a figure carrying a staff and lantern and emerging from the shadows of the great church. A little dog trotted at his heels. It was the bellman on the first leg of his nightly round of the city of Bath. He rang his bell and called out the time – ten o'clock – and gave me a wary look as he passed on down Cheap Street. The dog growled softly before slinking after its master. If the bellman was here, the watch would probably be close at his heels. I did not want to get taken up on suspicion of attempting a house robbery. Being a foreigner in town, and a player as well, would make that all too likely.

I turned back towards the Bear Inn and waited until a pair of watchmen had gone by in the same direction as the bellman. My fingers fumbled impatiently with the wax seal of the 'privy message'. I returned to the corner house and the window with its crack of light, and raised the unfolded sheet closer to my eyes. Only to understand that I had been played for a fool for the sheet was completely blank. Even by the uncertain light I could see nothing, nothing at all. There was not a single word on the sheet, let alone a place of assignation, or any fond endearments and promises.

My first reaction was irritation, more with myself than the unknown 'lady' who had given the letter to the landlord's boy. I wondered whether one of my friends was playing a joke on me but swiftly discounted the idea. Then I thought that I would have to spend an hour or two drinking ale in a town inn, before slinking back to Mother Treadwell's and pretending to Laurence Savage and the rest that I had indeed enjoyed the favours of some high-born Bath lady. It would be too humiliating to do anything else. Then it further occurred to me – being primed for the event, as it were – that I should go in search of a house of ill repute and purchase what I was not going to be given tonight for free. Which direction to go, though? In London I'd have known, but in a strange town I was at a loss for a bordello.

There must surely be one or two such places in Bath, which, although not a very large or populous city, is much visited on account of its curative waters. But since our arrival the previous day, all our time had been spent preparing the stage in the yard of the Bear Inn and then rehearsing for this evening's performance and the other plays that were to follow. Consequently, I had little notion of the city's more disreputable quarters although I supposed they'd be away from the shadow of the great church and the centre of the town. Most probably close to one of the old gates. The North Gate wasn't a good prospect. Nearby was both the city lock-up and a proper gaol, as the twinkle-eyed Mrs Treadwell had informed us, 'very conveniently placed for naughty players'. And the East Gate in the wall, which we had glimpsed on our approach to the city, was not much more than a postern onto the river bank.

I was still standing underneath the lighted window on the corner of Cheap Street, clutching the blank sheet of paper. By now indecisive as well as irritated, I mused on whether I'd be more likely to find what I was looking for down by the South Gate or the West one. Then I wondered how sensible it was to go wandering around unfamiliar streets in a darkened city, no doubt encountering the bellman and the members of his watch. In the process I found my appetite, my itch, subsiding.

It was a surprise when I felt a gentle tap on my shoulder. I hadn't heard anyone come up behind me. I spun round and there she was! A woman, quite tall and slender from her outline, and wearing a large hat.

'You were the duke, sir? In the recent play?' Her voice was low, well bred. Doubtless a lady.

'You are responsible for this, madam?' I said, flourishing the blank 'privy message' and not hiding my anger.

'I must apologise, sir. I was in a great hurry and although a thousand phrases were whirling through my head, I could think of nothing to write that would guarantee your attention. But I believed you would be intrigued enough by what I wrote on the cover not to want to break the seal in front of your friends in the company. I thought you'd want to open it in private, by yourself. I have been watching you since you left the inn yard.'

All this was said in a rush with hardly a pause for breath. It was irritating that she had been able to predict my response to the letter so exactly. Hardly reassured, I said: 'So you watched our play sitting in the yard of the Bear Inn? I didn't notice you.'

'I wasn't in the yard but in a house, standing at a window high above the stage. I could see and hear quite well from up there.'

I remembered the face glimpsed while I was lying down dead, the white countenance peering from the gable window. For some reason, I shivered at the memory, and to cover the moment I laughed and said, 'Well, madam, not only do you draw me away from my company and my bed-rest with a silly note – a blank sheet of paper – but now you inform me that you didn't even pay good money to watch our play. I hope you enjoyed it.'

'I did. I was much struck by your duke.'

'That was a part that I played. I am not Duke Peccato,' I said wearily.

'I was frightened by the scene in the madhouse,' she said.

'We meant to frighten,' I said, wondering where these compliments were leading. Still, it was good to know that the devilish masks and the white smocks worn by the players acting as lunatics were effective.

To put an end to our conversation, I said: 'Sorry to disappoint you but I'm not a duke or lunatic after all, merely a member of the King's Men, and one who is tired after an evening's work and now intends to return—'

I stopped as she stretched out a hand and clasped my arm tight.

'Help me.'

That was the point where I should have shaken off her hand, turned on my heel and gone back to Mother Treadwell's to face the jokes and the prying questions of my fellows. But I didn't. Foolishly, I stayed and said: 'At least give me the courtesy of your name since you did not include it in this – this privy message.'

'Katherine Hawkins. I live there, in a house overlooking the yard of the Bear.'

Still holding my arm, as if afraid I might break away, she gestured behind her with her other hand.

'Well, I'm Nick Revill. I live in London.'

'You can do me a great service, sir.'

'How?'

'By visiting a dying man.'

'You need a priest, not a player,' I said. Gently I prised her fingers from my arm.

'The priest will come soon enough. I need you now.'

It's hard to resist when a young woman appeals to you directly. At least, I found it so. It had occurred to me that this might be a trap but she was speaking very earnestly and I believed her honest – or wanted to believe it.

'Who is dying? What can I do? I'm a player, I say again, not a priest or a doctor of physic.'

We were disturbed by the scrape of a window opening overhead, from where the gleam of light shone. A head thrust out. A male voice said: 'Do your business elsewhere. Be off or I'll call the watch.'

We both looked up. She quickly averted her head from the man above, perhaps fearful of being recognised, but I had a glimpse of her face, pale, drawn, beautiful. The window was shut, firmly. We were speaking quietly after my initial burst of anger but we'd been there for a few minutes. Anybody looking down on a man and woman in a public street late at night, talking low, negotiating, would have come to the obvious conclusion.

'Please. Come with me, Mr Revill – Nicholas,' said Katherine Hawkins. 'I promise you . . . promise you on . . . on my mother's grave . . . that there is nothing to be wary of. I will explain as we go.'

We walked round the corner and along Cheap Street, keeping clear of the kennel that ran down the middle of the street and which, in this dry midsummer, smelled of the muck and waste deposited there.

In the same soft tones, the woman said that she lived with her uncle, Christopher Hawkins, a respectable and well-to-do cloth merchant and a member of the town corporation. It was he who was dying. He had no more than a day or two of life left in him. The crisis might come at any moment, according to Dr Price. Although Christopher Hawkins was rambling in his wits he had clear moments. He was half deaf and almost blind too. His wife was dead and he had a single surviving son called William, a young man whom he had not seen for several years. William Hawkins was of about my age and build.

'Where is your cousin, this William?'

'I do not know. He is restless. The last I heard he was in London. He was searching for his course in life. He once said he wanted to be a player, like you,' she said, folding her arm under mine and pressing close. 'Then he said in a letter to me that he might try his fortunes in the New World, in the Americas.'

'If he did, then he is thousands of miles away. He may as well be dead.'

'I know. But my uncle has been calling out for his son, mumbling his name, asking for him. He has taken it into his head that William is quite close, that he may arrive at any minute.'

'Perhaps he will.'

'No, no, he will not. Or if he did it would be a miracle. I cannot depend on miracles. I do not need a miracle now that you are here, Mr Revill. Nicholas.'

She made to turn up a lane between houses but I stopped, forcing her to a standstill. The only light was that shed by the moon and, from down the lane, a couple of lanterns outside the houses.

'I see what you're proposing, madam. You want me to go and see your dying uncle and impersonate his son and clasp his hand and speak some words of greeting and comfort to him.'

'Yes.'

'I will not do it.'

'But you are a player.'

'This isn't a play. It's real.'

'So much the more important, sir. My uncle is all in all to me. He and his wife took me in when my parents died in the plague in the old Queen's time. I have no one else in the world except my absent cousin. I would be glad for Uncle to die happy.'

The mention of her parents' death in the plague may have caused me to lean more attentively towards her. At any rate she sensed a slight softening in my attitude, for she went on: 'You see, there was an estrangement between William and Uncle Christopher, a quarrel over nothing, but the last of many quarrels for he quit this house soon afterwards and went off to make his way in the world. I know that my uncle blames himself for what occurred. He would die happy knowing that you – he, I mean – had come back again. You have the manner of Cousin William, the height, something of the look, the voice even.'

'As to the voice, I come from this part of the world,' I said.

'I knew it! I could almost believe this was fated.'

'It is an imposture, madam, a lie.'

'A white one. No guilt or blame attaches or, if it does, it is mine alone. It will only take an instant.'

'What if he recognises me?' I said. 'I mean, what if he recognises that I am *not* his son, William. That would be worse than doing nothing.'

'Uncle Christopher can hardly see, he can hardly hear,' she said. 'It is enough if he knows you are in the same room. I promise that if my uncle is not in a fit state to receive you, if he is wandering too much in his mind, I will not ask you again. It is now or never.'

'Let it be now then,' I said.

II

Had I stopped to think the matter through, I would have refused her request. A great deal of trouble would have been avoided. Some danger too. But I was persuaded to do this merciful deed by her manner, by her pleading – by her attractions too, of course. If I hoped anything at all it was that the old uncle might be so deep asleep or far gone that no pretence on my part would be necessary. As I followed Katherine Hawkins down the narrow road, which I later learned was called Vicarage Lane, I reflected that this errand was very different from what I'd been imagining when I was handed the 'privy message'.

We halted outside a doorway over which hung a lantern.

As far as I was able to see, the houses in the lane were newer than some others in the city, rising to three or four storeys rather than two, and constructed of stone instead of timber. I remembered that Katherine said her uncle was a cloth merchant, a well-to-do one. She produced a key and unlocked the door. Inside the lobby, which was illuminated by a couple of wax candles, a woman of uncertain age started up from a chair. She'd been dozing.

'Why, Mistress Katherine, where have you been?'

'It's all right, Hannah. It's a close night. I needed a little air.'

The woman, who was wearing a grey overdress, looked curiously at me. I would have done the same in her position. I waited for whatever explanation Katherine Hawkins would give. I wasn't going to help her out. She hung the door key on a hook by the entrance and then removed her hat, doing each action slowly as if to give herself time to think. I saw that, although strained, she had an enticing face, a wide mobile mouth, a delicate chin, large eyes.

'Oh, here is an extraordinary coincidence, Hannah. This is Mr Revill. He is a member of the King's Men who have been playing in the yard of the Bear. He and the others have come all the way from London. Mr Revill knew William.'

'William?' said the woman, who I supposed was some long-time retainer. She struggled to catch up with Katherine Hawkins, who now said with deliberate slowness: 'Yes, our cousin William. Mr Revill knew him in London.'

The older woman's face lit up even as I felt myself growing more and more uncomfortable with the deception.

'You are friends with William, sir! How is he? Where is he?'

I shrugged, to hide my unease, and said, 'I've no idea where your William is. I met him only once – or perhaps it was twice – many years ago. I . . . I was told he had gone to the Americas.'

'I thought it might be a comfort for Uncle Christopher to see Mr Revill,' said Katherine smoothly. She was very adept at spinning a tale. I wondered what else she had said that was half true or outright false.

'Of course, of course,' said Hannah.

'I will take him up to my uncle. Go to bed now, Hannah.'

Hastily, to avoid further comment or question, she snatched up one of the wax candles and we left the lobby. I followed her up the stairs.

Half-way up, when we were out of earshot of the woman, I stopped and whispered urgently to her, 'Already you have involved me in a complete falsehood and I have not even seen your uncle. Whatever you may say to the woman in the lobby, I've never met your cousin.'

'You *could* have encountered him in London,' she whispered back. 'I told you Cousin William wanted to be a player. And I had to explain your presence to Hannah somehow.'

She was very close to me and standing on the stair above so we were at the same height. She bent forward a degree and kissed me on the lips, holding the candle delicately poised to one side. I felt her breasts against me. She stayed for just long enough before pulling back and saying, 'I beg you to do this one thing that we have already discussed, Mr Revill. I shall ask no more of you, while you . . . you may ask of me what you please.'

She turned down a passage at the top of the first flight of stairs, without looking back to see whether I was behind her. She came to a door, tapped on it once, softly, and almost straight away twisted the handle and entered the chamber. I halted in the entrance, peering through the gloom, wondering what I had been foolish enough to let myself in for and wishing with (almost) all my heart that I was back with my fellows at Mother Treadwell's.

What followed was painful but not entirely painful. I'll tell it in brief. The room belonging to the dying uncle Christopher – at least that part was true, he really was very near death – was stiflingly hot, not only on account of the general airlessness of the night but because a fire smouldered in the chimneypiece while a half-dozen candles consumed themselves in different corners. There were grand tapestries on the wall, depicting knights in the lists or knights out hunting or knights conversing with ladies in pointed hats.

Katherine went forward to a large four-poster bed, its curtains drawn back. A sharp-nosed man was lying there. His head was almost sunk into a pile of pillows, his body buried under thick blankets, his reed-thin arms stretched out flat on the covers. Resting under his right hand was a small black-bound book. Perhaps nothing confirmed how close he was to dying as the presence of the Bible.

When Katherine beckoned me forward to stand beside her, I could scarcely make out anything but the nose, the glimmer of white in the almost closed eyes, the threads of hair sticking out from under his nightcap.

She shook her uncle gently by the shoulder to ensure that he was awake or at least not completely asleep. She said several times, 'William is here. Your Will is here, Uncle.' And to vary it, 'He has returned, your son has returned.'

Eventually his right hand fluttered and a kind of twitch affected the dying man's lips. His head moved towards me a fraction and I sat on the edge of the bed, took his dry, cold hand in mine and said, 'Yes, I am here.' I could not bring myself to say the name of William. I said, 'I am here,' again, but more loudly, and his fingers tightened slightly on my wrist while his mouth seemed to widen into a smile or a grimace.

He struggled to say something even as his feeble grip slackened and his fingers scrabbled at the cover of the Bible. He was making a vain attempt to pick it up. I had to lean very close to hear him but, striving with every word, he was saying, 'Take – it – take – it – William.'

At first I was not sure what he meant, then understood he must be referring to the black-bound testament. I looked towards Katherine, standing beside and above me. She gestured, yes, yes, take it, so I took up the Bible from the dying man's hand and, without thinking, slipped it into a pocket in my doublet. While all this was going on, the old uncle appeared almost animated. Then the expression vanished altogether and his head subsided even further into the white pillows. I had the image of a man drowning in foam. And I do not know whether that man was Uncle Christopher or me, for I had never felt more uneasy or uncertain in my life.

The less painful part came afterwards. Indeed, there was some pleasure in it. After a few more minutes by the bedside of Uncle Christopher – who might now have been truly dead apart from the odd tremor in his chest and a sound from his gaping mouth like fallen leaves being blown along – Katherine took me by the hand and ushered me from the room. There was another staircase leading to the next floor where two or three rooms were clustered together under the roof. Guided by the single candle she held in her other hand, up we crept and she opened the door to a low-ceilinged chamber, equipped with a simple bedstead and a chest.

Without saying anything, Katherine gestured towards the window. I went to look. The window was still half open. I leaned out. Down below was the yard of the Bear Inn and the stage where the King's Men had presented our production of *A House Divided*. To one side was a portion of the garden that must belong to the house, separated from the inn yard by a stone wall. In the moonlight I could see the whole scene quite clearly. There was no one left in the yard now, no murmuring idlers, no pipe embers.

Katherine came to stand beside me. She closed and latched the window.

'I was in a hurry when I left,' she said, turning aside and putting the candle on top of the chest. 'I saw you on stage and straightaway I thought you looked and sounded very like Cousin William. My . . . scheme . . . was brewing in my head all the while I watched but I did not pluck up the courage to write you a note until the performance was over and you were all doing your little dance. There was so little time then, if I was to catch you before you left.'

'So you wrote the note but had nothing to say,' I said. My mood was an odd mixture of anger and sadness, and a return of the itch that had driven me through the yard of the Bear.

'All I could think of was that way of addressing you on the cover of the letter, putting three words.'

'"A privy message",' I said. 'It certainly got my attention.'

'I ran down and round, and handed it to some lad in the inn. I gave him a coin to pass it to "To him who plays the Duke". Then I waited until you emerged, as I knew you would.'

'Well, madam, I think my business here is done.'

But I did not move. I did not even wonder why she had led me upstairs rather than back to the ground floor. I knew why.

'You have brought comfort to a dying man, Nicholas,' she said. 'Your deed will surely be noted in heaven.'

Maybe it was her words that made me think of the dying
man's Bible in my doublet pocket. I made to retrieve it but
was distracted by Katherine's next move. She licked her fingers and with a decisive motion snuffed the candle she'd
placed on the chest. Then she started forward and kissed
me full on the lips and pressed herself against me. We
descended, almost tumbled, onto the narrow bedstead, and
she fumbled with my hose even as I struggled to undo my
doublet with one hand and raise her skirts with the other.
The smell of the snuffed candle lingered in the room.

In the beginning of what followed, with one tiny corner of
my mind, I wondered whether this deed that we were about
to perform was also one to be noted in heaven. Yet she was
eager and grateful, and now I was more than glad to be
here, in the house of a dying man, with his niece. Then all
my discomfort and scruples disappeared. Everything vanished in the moonlit delights of the summer night.

When I woke, the sky was turning pale. I didn't know where
I was. Soon the details of last night began to return, slow at
first and then all at once. My part as the wicked Duke
Peccato in *A House Divided*, the note with its teasing superscription, the nocturnal meeting with Katherine, the mission
of mercy to the dying man, the pretence that I was his
returned son, William. Then Katherine Hawkins and I afterwards, up here in this little chamber with the gable window,
and the bed, which now seemed small and hard. Katherine
had gone. I was a little disappointed but couldn't blame her.
Whether it was remorse or second thoughts or the straight-
forward desire for her own bed, she'd left me.

I must have fallen asleep once more for I came to with a
start, woken by some noise outside. Almost dashing my head
against a ceiling beam, I went to the window. Down below

in the inn yard were a couple of travellers taking charge of their horses from the ostler. These early leavers mounted up and clattered out of the yard where we'd played the previous evening. It seemed like a signal that I should leave too. There was no noise from the rest of the house. I wanted to sneak out even if no one was up yet. *Especially* if no one was up yet. I recalled that the key to the door was hanging on a hook beside it. I wouldn't have minded seeing Katherine again – indeed, had it been later in the day, and had my stomach been full and my senses sharper, I would definitely have wanted to see her again – but I was reluctant to encounter the old retainer Hannah or, God forbid, to come anywhere near the dying Uncle Christopher once more. I laced and fastened my garments and put on my doublet. An unfamiliar weight to one side made me remember old Christopher's Bible, the volume which I'd stuffed in a pocket. 'Take – it – William', he'd gasped to me, and I had obeyed his words.

I took it out of my pocket and straight away saw what hadn't been apparent to me in the heat and confusion of the previous evening: namely, that it wasn't a Bible at all. Rather, it was a notebook or a commonplace book, handsomely bound in black leather, and full of scribblings and comments, together with some longer stretches of writing and even the odd sketch, each labelled with letters and arrows. I puzzled over the mechanisms depicted in the sketches before realising, from their general shape and the rollers and pedals, that they were weavers' looms. Perhaps Christopher Hawkins was designing a more efficient machinery for his trade. Elsewhere in the book were remarks and quotations that he liked sufficiently to note down. 'Age and wedlock tames man and beast' and 'Neither a borrower, nor a lender be' – that sort of thing, cautious sayings as befitted a merchant.

There were several pages of verse, which I guessed had been written by Hawkins himself rather than copied from another's work, since the lines were blotted with crossings-out and at first glance appeared somewhat feeble.

Their fame and renown these knights so far did spread
By deeds and valour that scarce may be uttered.
Their names will live for ever scribed in stone
Long after we mortals are nothing more than bone.

et cetera.

I was about to put the book down on the chest, where it might be found later by a servant, or perhaps by Katherine herself, when it came to me that this was a careless, disrespectful way to treat a dying man's property. After all, he had urged me to take the thing even if he was under the misapprehension that I was his son. It must be important to him since he was clutching it with his cold, dry hand. I should not abandon it in this upstairs chamber. But nor did I want to look for a member of the household to whom I could hand back the book since I planned to slip away unseen.

So I tucked the commonplace book inside my doublet, took one last look around the little bedchamber, unlatched the door, listened for sounds from below, heard nothing, trod silently downstairs to the first floor where the dying man's room was located, together with the other larger bedrooms, heard nothing here either, stole down to ground level and out into the lobby, listened to the clack of pans from the kitchen quarter of the house, plucked the key from the hook by the front door – turned key in lock – opened door – replaced key on hook – stepped out into Vicarage Lane – closed door behind me – all as quiet as could be.

I was still carrying Christopher Hawkins' notebook. I had no intention of taking it away for good. Rather, I thought it would give me an excuse for returning to the house and seeing Katherine again. The King's Men had two more days and nights in Bath before we travelled on to Bristol. I should be able to squeeze out a spare hour or two for Katherine.

It was a bright summer morning. I emerged into Cheap Street and was straight away reminded that this city, for all its health-giving waters and handsome new buildings, is a market town. A herd of brindled cows was trotting unwillingly along, urged by a drover to their rear, and churning up the muck in the street still further. I approached the town centre to see pigs at liberty and rootling around the stocks and pillory, which were set between the Guild Hall and the great church. It had never occurred to me before that the rubbish flung at the malefactors in the pillory – rotten apples, dead cats and the like – would make natural picking for pigs.

Hungry in my stomach and tired in my limbs, but with the bounce that comes from a good night well spent, I walked up the slight incline towards the North Gate and Mother Treadwell's. In the lodging house I found my fellows still half asleep round the breakfast table but suddenly all alert and talkative when they realised I'd come back. I parried their questions and salacious remarks with casual understatement. Naturally, I said nothing at all of the way I'd impersonated a dying man's son. Yes, I had passed a very pleasant night. No, she is a lady, well bred, not one of the women of the streets you usually consort with. Her name? Is she married? None of your business, Laurence Savage.

There was cold meat, bread and ale for breakfast. Mother Treadwell prided herself on her table. One of the others – I suspected it was Abel Glaze – must have informed on me to the landlady, for she paid me particular attention as she fussed over the breakfast items, winking and tapping the side of her nose and enquiring whether the beds of Bath were soft enough for me and telling me to eat plenty of cold meats so as to regain my vigour.

We had no rehearsal for later that day but were still required to report to the senior player in our company, John Sincklo, to ensure that there were no tasks to be done before the play itself. This was particularly necessary on tour where the stage and other gear were not kept in such an ordered state as at home in the Globe Theatre. Sincklo was staying in comfort at the Bear Inn as a favoured guest of the land-lord, Harry Cuff, since we were bringing plenty of business to his establishment. Those of us at Mother Treadwell's duly reported to John Sincklo only to be told, rather brusquely, that we weren't needed. He was a somewhat reserved fellow, our senior, not much used to drink, and I suspect he'd enjoyed more than a few glasses with Landlord Cuff after last night's successful production.

So we were free for the larger part of the day. I thought about returning to the Hawkins' house in Vicarage Lane although it seemed a little too soon. In any case there was a diversion planned by my companions, which they had obvi-ously been concocting the night before. They wouldn't tell me what it was but dragged me with them down Cheap Street and then to the west of the great church, which I was surprised to see in the clear light of day was not yet finished. Perhaps the money had run out. The church was not our destination, however.

Beyond the church precincts was a cluster of stone build-ings with steam rising from among them. Led by Laurence Savage, who promised us it would be worth it, half a dozen of us paid a penny each to a doorkeeper to be allowed into a viewing area. We climbed a flight of stone steps and found ourselves in a gallery overlooking a very large four-sided pool of water, which was open to the air and from which rose a slightly sulphurous smell as well as steam and a perceptible wave of heat. In the middle of the pool was a structure like a monstrous salt cellar, with pinnacles and jutting eaves.

Even though it was still quite early in the morning, the bath was full of folk. Some clung to the side as though afraid to venture far in, but the majority were standing in the water talking together or half swimming, half wading through it or else simply lying on their backs, buoyed up by the air trapped in their smocks and drawers. A few sat on stone recesses at the base of the great salt cellar.

Men and women mixed together without distinction. When one of the bathers made to get out, their garments clung close as an onion skin and showed most or all of what lay beneath. We gawped, of course, but it was, in truth, not much of a spectacle. Or at least it was not a stirring spectacle. The majority of the bathers were far from young and it was generally apparent why they had come to try the healing waters of Bath. Some were as rotund as the inflated bladders carried by jesters, others were so thin they looked as though they were being consumed from within. And I have never seen so many misshapen limbs, so large a quantity of bent backs, as I saw gathered together in this steamy pool. Why, if you half closed your eyes, and added a little bit of screaming and groaning to the picture, you might have imagined you were present at one of the infernal pits. The smell of the brimstone and the white, ghost-like garments of the bathers added to this impression.

Just occasionally, however, our watch was made worthwhile when a woman younger and more comely than the mass climbed from the water or sank herself slowly into it

and so revealed much more under her clinging garments
than would normally be considered decent. The odd thing
was that these women seemed to know the effect they were
having and to be prolonging their actions by a few instants.
This, no doubt, was why we'd paid our pennies to the doorkeeper.

A wizened-looking individual emerged from a corner of
the gallery and took it upon himself to act as our guide. He
told us this was the King's Bath, which we knew, and that the
area round the pinnacled construction in the middle was
called the Kitchen on account of its being situated directly
over the source of the hot spring. Then he said that there
were other interesting sights to be seen elsewhere at the
Queen's Bath and the Lepers' Bath. Sights of a fleshly
nature, he said, both more enticing and more grotesque than
anything likely to be seen here at the King's. If we good gentlemen would like to accompany him . . .

The others were ready enough but I was not in a the
mood. Partly it was because I was thinking of Katherine
Hawkins – one of the few younger women in the pool below
had hair of a similar colour to hers, although this bather
was handsome rather than pretty. I considered that now
might be time to return the commonplace book belonging to
her uncle. Then I might invite Katherine to attend a performance in the yard of the Bear that evening, and
afterwards we could . . .

Lost in my warm imagination, I hardly realised that I'd
been left alone in the gallery, so eager were my fellows to
see the sights of the Lepers' and the Queen's Baths. I took
one final look at the pool with its ghostly bathers and started
towards the entrance.

At the top of the stairs my way was blocked by a burly
individual.

'Are you Nicholas?' he said.

'What business is it of yours?'

'Nicholas of the ...' he fumbled in his mind to get the right words in the right order, '... of the King's Men presently playing in this town?'

I nodded. He stuck out his doubleted chest and pushed forward into the gallery. Instinctively I stepped back towards the stone parapet, which prevented spectators from tumbling into the steam bath. I thought, I'm growing weary of being sought out by strangers with an interest in plays and players. This one did not have the advantage of being young, attractive and female.

'You have got something that doesn't belong to you,' he said presently.

'I have?'

'A book,' said this gentleman. He uttered the word 'book' as though it didn't pass his lips very often.

I understood straight away that he must be referring to Uncle Christopher's commonplace book. I only just prevented myself from feeling for the pocket where it was stowed.

'I don't know what you're talking about.'

'Give it me now.'

He lumbered forward and I stepped back in equal measure with him until I felt the parapet against my buttocks. He was a big man with beetling brows and a seamed forehead. With one push he could have shoved me over into the steamy pool.

'I haven't got the book with me,' I said.

'So you do have it,' he said. He wasn't as slow and stupid as he looked.

He came to within a couple of inches, face to face, close enough that I smelled his meaty breath. He gripped me by the upper arms. I'm not sure what would have happened next, whether he would have manhandled me or shoved me out and over into the bath. Fortunately, we were interrupted by a shout from the entrance to the gallery. Over my new friend's shoulder I saw an individual who was dressed in some sort of blue livery and carrying a mace.

'We'll have none of that filthy behaviour here,' said this person. 'Bringing disrepute on the royal baths. Be off with you.'

The bulky man had taken a pace back from me. I slipped out of his shadow and walked briskly to the stairs, nodding to the individual with the mace on the way. I did not stop to ask what he thought we were up to. I could guess. (Later I learned that he was the sergeant-at-arms for the King's Bath, employed to ensure decorous conduct among the bathers and the watchers.) I clattered down the stone stairs and out into fresh air and the precincts of the great church.

I walked fast up Cheap Street towards Vicarage Lane, looking behind me occasionally to see if the lumbering man was on my tail. I was going to return the commonplace book to Katherine Hawkins and I was going to do it now. My thoughts of inviting her to a play performance, and then to something rather more personal after the play, had faded. Instead I felt aggrieved, angry. No one else in Bath knew that I was Nicholas of the King's Men. No one else was aware I possessed the wretched notebook apart from Katherine, since she had seen me take it from her sick uncle. She had encouraged me to take it! Therefore it must have been she who had set that blockish individual on me. Why hadn't she simply asked me to return the notebook? I was meaning to do that anyway. Why were threats necessary? Yes, I felt angry and aggrieved.

The one question I did not ask myself was why a book

containing second-hand quotations and bits of bad verse should be so important.

I strode up Vicarage Lane, reached the merchant's house and knocked loudly on the door. It was Katherine herself who opened it. Her eyes were red, her hair was disordered, her dress careless. I was glad to see she was in a state of distress. So distressed, it seemed, that she didn't even recognise me at first. When she did realise who it was, she said only three words.

'He is dead.'

No need to ask the identity of the dead man.

'I'm sorry to hear it,' I said, almost without thought.

'You had better come in, Nicholas.'

'No, you had better come outside first.'

I took her by the shoulders and gently but firmly drew her through the front door. Before she could object, I explained that I had just been accosted by a man in the baths who'd roughly demanded the return of the black-bound book that Uncle Christopher had given me the previous evening, and that it could only have been she – Katherine – who put him on my tail.

I had scarcely got to the end of my speech when I registered growing confusion on her face.

'My uncle's black notebook?' she said. 'Oh, what does that matter? I don't know of any man in the baths, Nicholas.'

The figure of Hannah passed through the lobby. Katherine glanced over her shoulder through the still open door of the house while the old retainer peered curiously in our direction. I realised two things at once: that Katherine Hawkins had nothing to do with the stranger in the King's Bath and that it must be Hannah who had described me to him. The servant was the only other person to know my name and the acting company I belonged to, as well as the fact that I'd visited this house last night. How she deduced that I had the book, I don't know.

Now it was my turn to feel confused. And guilty for having spoken bluntly to Katherine while her grief for her uncle was so raw. I took her more tenderly by the shoulders and ushered her back into the lobby of her own home. Hannah had vanished. If she appeared again, and if I had the chance, I'd have a word with her.

'I am very sorry to hear of your uncle's death,' I said, this time with feeling.

'It was early this morning,' she said. 'So long expected yet so surprising when it happens. Thank God the parson got here in time.'

Uncle Christopher's demise must have occurred after I crept out of the house, otherwise I would have been alerted by the fuss and alarm of a death, the summoning of the parson and so on. Selfishly, I was glad to have made my exit in time.

We'd been slowly pacing towards the back of the house and by now we were standing outside the door to what was the dining room. A window gave a view of some apple trees, sun-lit. Inside the panelled chamber it was stuffy and gloomy. A long table stood in the centre of the room, with chairs at each end and benches set on either side. Huddled towards one end were three men, two sitting next to each other, the other on the bench opposite. Wooden boxes and sheafs of paper and documents were arrayed on the table between them, together with a clutch of lighted candles. The men were so absorbed in leafing through the papers that our presence went unnoticed.

Eventually one of them looked up. He was a very plump individual with a large face. He seemed to start and coughed to draw the attention of the one beside him. This second man was wearing spectacles. He must have been long-sighted for he now removed them in order to scrutinise us – more precisely, to scrutinise me – as we stood in the doorway. This gentleman did not start in surprise but his brow furrowed as if was I presenting him with a puzzle, and not a very welcome one either. By now the third man, who'd been sitting with his back to us, was aware of us too. He twisted his head round. His eyes narrowed.

'This is Nicholas Revill,' said Katherine Hawkins, as the four of us gave the smallest dip of the head in acknowledgement. 'He is a friend of my cousin William. They knew each other in London. He is here as a member of the King's Men. They are playing in the yard of the Bear.'

I wasn't very happy that the fiction about my knowing her cousin was being maintained but it was becoming such a frequent story that it might shortly turn out to be true. It transpired that the three men were notable Bath citizens. The one with the spectacles was Edward Downey, a lawyer. Uncle Christopher was both client and friend to him. The plump one was John Maltravers and, like the late Christopher Hawkins, he was a cloth merchant and a member of the city corporation. The third was Dr Price. I remembered that Katherine had mentioned him by name when we first met. On hearing of their friend's death they had immediately come round to the Vicarage Lane house. I was surprised that the doctor of physic was not upstairs with the body. I thought that if this trio were here to offer comfort and condolence, they were going about it in an odd way, fencing themselves in behind a mass of documents on the dining table.

I sensed hostility emanating from them, slight but unmistakable. Particularly from Mr Maltravers. Perhaps it was because I was a player, for he had grunted and humphed when Katherine described what I did. I tried to be civil, remembering that Bath corporation was supplementing our takings in the city – even if these important people were doing so not out of love for the drama but because they didn't want to offend our royal sponsor, King James.

'I hope that you gentlemen will attend a performance,' I said. 'We have two nights remaining at the Bear.'

'Two too many,' said Maltravers.

'Now, now, John,' said Downey the lawyer. 'It may not be to your taste but the players provide a diversion for our citizenry. And remember that they are not your run-of-the-mill fellows but the King's Men.'

'A little diversion does no great harm,' said Dr Price with a judicious air as though he were measuring out a dose of medicine.

'Plays are not a diversion but a corruption,' said Maltravers. He rose from the table and waddled towards where we were standing in the doorway. He stuck out a stubby, accusatory forefinger. 'The days of plays and players in this city would be numbered if I had my way. We should go back to the times when players were treated as vagrants, when they were stripped naked from the middle upward and whipped when found anywhere they were not wanted.'

He seemed to grow excited as he said this. This sort of hostile talk is familiar enough if you're a player, at least from those who incline towards the puritan view. It was disturbing to be talked of as a vagrant but I tried to maintain the civil tone.

'If you had heard and seen our audience last night, sir, you would have known that we were very much wanted.'

'John, John,' said Downey, making downward motions with his hand in a placating way, 'this Mr ... Mr ... er ...?'

'Revill.'

'This Mr Revill is right. I have heard that their efforts were well received last night. Remember they are the King's Men.'

'And guests in our city,' added Dr Price.

Maltravers might have said more but he merely humphed again, waddled back to the dining table and returned his attention to the documents. The others soon followed. I wondered why Katherine had wanted to introduce me to them.

She motioned me back into the passageway and said, 'Did you notice how they stared at you? For a moment they thought you were William Hawkins, returned at long last to the house of his father. I told you that you look like him – a little like, anyway.'

My affairs in this place were done. I did not want any further involvement with the Hawkinses. I certainly had no intention of urging Katherine to come to this evening's performance, let alone to any renewal of last night's post-play activities. She was thinking only of her uncle. I would intrude no longer on a house of grief.

There was one more thing to do: to return Uncle Christopher's commonplace book. If I was accosted again by the burly man from the baths I could genuinely claim not to have it. Even better, to avoid such a disagreeable situation in the first place, I'd make sure I was not out of the protective company of my fellow players for as long as we remained in the city of Bath.

I was about to get the wretched black book out of my doublet when there came a great commotion from the lobby. The sound of women's voices raised, crying out, interrupting each other. Underneath was a male voice, trying to make itself heard. Was this grief for the dead Christopher? It did not sound like grief.

Then Hannah came running down the passageway and

almost collided with Katherine. The young woman put her hands on the shoulders of the older one. She gave the white-faced servant a few moments to recover her breath before asking, 'What *is* it? What's happened?'

'Oh, it is only William come back,' panted Hannah. 'Only William, your cousin and Mr Christopher's long-lost son!'

I didn't wait to hear any more. It was as if I was the guilty party in all this. I almost ran through the lobby, past a gaggle of female servants, and a young man who was standing there, looking about him like a stranger. I thought, I played the part of you last night. In passing, I did not note any very strong resemblance between us.

III

The play we were performing that evening in the yard of the Bear Inn was called *A City Pleasure*. It was written by Edgar Boscombe, a playwright who may not be familiar to you. He was never very prolific and now he can write no more for he is dead. *A City Pleasure* is a satirical comedy about a young man from the provinces who comes to London with his sister, looking for pleasure and edification. There are other things in the story but this is the main one. The city of London takes its pleasure with this young couple, duping them and trying to assail their virtue, but throughout the action the two retain a curious integrity and when they return home – sadder, wiser and poorer – they discover that they never were brother and sister. Instead, they are cousins. And so they may marry. Which they do at the end of Act Five under the eye of a kindly, bumbling country parson. This is a play well suited to a provincial audience, for it shows how dreadful and corrupt London is, how honest and honourable are those who dwell outside the capital, and how virtue always triumphs in the end.

A City Pleasure was also a contrast to the blood-letting of the previous night, *A House Divided*. Contrast and variety make for happy audiences.

I didn't have such a big part in this satire as in the revenge tragedy, and I confess I spent some of my time off-stage mulling over the strange events of that morning, and the way in which William Hawkins had turned up at the house in Vicarage Lane mere hours after his father's death. Was this a piece of very unfortunate timing? Or very neat timing? Was it even William Hawkins? Maybe it was another imposter. I had not waited around to see Katherine greet her (presumed) cousin. I would have been uncomfortable in the presence of a man I'd impersonated, even if the act had been done with the best of intentions.

And still I had in my possession the commonplace book belonging to the late Uncle Christopher. At one point I'd flicked through its pages again to see why the burly fellow in the King's Bath should – under orders, no doubt – have been wanting to take it from me by force. But I saw nothing different from my first examination of it: pages of home-made verses and a few drawings, interspersed with copied-out comments. The subject of Christopher's poetry, if one could call it that, seemed to be some great battle involving knights of old, the kind of subject that was popular years ago and that has now fallen from favour.

We of the King's Men finished our second play for the second evening in the Bear Inn yard. *A City Pleasure* was well received by the Bath audience. They enjoyed our depiction of innocent country cousins who are able to withstand the lures of the big city. As we disrobed in the makeshift tire-room after the performance, there was some suggestive speculation from my friends about my plans for the dregs of the evening. Where was the next letter from my sweetheart? Would I be joining the lady from the town that night? I retaliated by asking whether they'd enjoyed their tour of the Queen's Bath and the Lepers' Bath. I was pleased to hear that it had been disappointing.

I had not thought to see Katherine Hawkins again so as I left the Bear, in company with Laurence Savage and Abel Glaze, I was surprised to find her in the inn yard.

'Nicholas,' she called softly, nearly cooing my name. The evening was still light since our play tonight had not been as lengthy as the previous one. My heart beat slightly faster to see her standing there, tall and elegant, in the dusk of the inn yard.

'Oh-ho,' murmured the others, straining to catch a glimpse of her. 'Oh-ho.' I waved them on and went over to join her.

She was not alone. A young man was standing a little behind her. It was William Hawkins, I recognised him before she introduced us. She was not so foolish as to maintain that we'd met before. I might have almost run from their house that morning but now curiosity got the better of me. Why were they here in the inn yard? Shouldn't they be closeted in mourning for a dead father and uncle? And another equally pressing question: did this young man really look like me?

From some remark he made it was apparent that she'd already described to her cousin how the two of us had become acquainted at the play the previous evening – which was true enough. I don't suppose she said anything of the further services I did for her, either the one at his dying father's bedside or the other up in the little gable room.

'We must talk, Nicholas,' Katherine said to me. 'But not

here or in the house in Vicarage Lane either. Too many eyes there.'

'Cousin Kate tells me she trusts you,' said William Hawkins.

They were a trusting pair of cousins, these Hawkinses. What secrets was I going to find out now?

The three of us went to a nearby tavern called the Raven. The interior was dim and smoky, ripe for a consultation. We found a quiet corner with a table, bench and stool. I sat opposite the cousins.

I took a better look at William Hawkins. He was about my height and build, although his voice did not – to my ears – sound very much like mine. I suppose he would be accounted handsome, which I took as a kind of compliment (to myself, of course). Mr Hawkins did not seem to have changed since his arrival home that morning, for his clothes were creased and travel-stained. I guessed he was normally clean-shaven like me, but now he was stubbly, as if he'd had no time to attend to himself. The only mark of mourning worn by either cousin was a black armband.

When we were seated and provisioned with drink – beer for William and me, canary wine for Katherine – I asked him where he had been all these years and how it happened that he returned to his father's house just too late. He was not a boastful fellow and did not pretend to great adventures.

He said that, after many arguments with his father, he left Bath and went to seek his fortune in London. It even crossed his mind to become a player, like me. Failing in that, and making little progress in anything else, he wrote to Cousin Kate that he was planning to try his luck in the Americas. Somehow he ended up in Edinburgh instead and become secretary to a wealthy cloth maker. Memories of his father's much smaller business, together with a clear head and a neat

293

hand, enabled him to get the post and even to prosper in it, but it was hardly the daring voyage of discovery he'd proposed to himself on quitting home. A mixture of pride and shame had prevented him communicating again with his father or his cousin, but lately he'd been contemplating a return south. The decision was made for him when the old manufacturer died. That happened a month ago. It had taken William that time to travel back to Bath. His arrival on the day of his father's death was good fortune – or bad fortune – depending on which way you looked at it.

'I will not say I had any great love for my father, Nick,' he said. 'But I would have been glad to have seen him for one last time and to have him see me.'

Katherine and I exchanged looks. For certain, she had not told him of my pretence on the previous night. She squeezed her cousin's hand – they were sitting side by side – and said, 'I believe Uncle Christopher died content, William. Even if he could not see you, I know for a fact that you were in his mind's eye.'

William looked fondly at her. Considering what had passed between us the previous night, I might have felt jealous but I did not. Instead I thought of the play we had just staged, *A City Pleasure*, about the kissing cousins from the country. Then I ordered another round of drinks from the potboy.

This – the life story of William Hawkins, the obvious affection between him and Katherine – was all beside the point. Why did the Hawkinses want to talk with me? Before we could get to that point I handed over the commonplace book to Katherine, happy to get rid of it. She was happy to receive it too, saying it was the very item that she wanted to speak to me about and that she had, in her confusion and grief that morning, brushed aside when I intended to return it.

'I recognise this,' said William. 'It was father's.'

'I entrusted it to Nick,' said Katherine. 'And I am glad I did, for I fear that Uncle Christopher's friends would have taken it otherwise.'

'The gentlemen who were in the house?' I said.

'Yes. They came to condole with me but they seemed more interested in going through Uncle's papers and documents.'

'Looking for his will?'

'Mr Downey the lawyer already has a copy of that. They were in search of something else.'

I waited for her to explain. They seemed reluctant to say more. Katherine looked at her cousin.

Eventually, as if confessing to something slightly shameful, William Hawkins said, 'My father was much occupied with stories of olden times, the days of knights and damsels and chivalry. He read fables and poetry. He even wrote verses himself. For years he attempted a great romance about one of King Arthur's battles.'

That explained the scrawled pages of poetry, the tapestries depicting knights jousting and hunting in Uncle Christopher's bedchamber.

William said, 'There is a tale that Arthur himself fought a final battle close to Bath, a battle in which he slew many of the Saxon foe single-handed.'

'It was on a hill outside the town,' said Katherine. 'Solsbury Hill, it is called now, but then it was known as Badon.'

'There are other stories about the place,' pursued William. 'I suppose there are bound to be stories in a very old region like this. They say that treasures are buried on Solsbury Hill. There is talk of a magical mirror, for instance. Even of items that date from Arthur's time. My father went searching on the hill, although I do not know whether it was for inspiration or for relics.'

'And found them?' I said.

William shrugged.

Katherine said, 'He carried this book with him wherever he went. He made notes, he took down sayings that he approved of. He had ideas about how the manufacture of cloth might be improved and tried to design better looms.'

She flicked through the book and held it open at one of the mechanical sketches. I nodded, then noticed something different on the opposite page. It wasn't a weaver's loom but a drawing of a hillside, dotted with trees. There was an arrow indicating north. There were a couple of crosses and other arrows and question marks. There was even an image of a bear a couple of inches tall, delicately drawn. I indicated the page.

Katherine examined it and said: 'This is most likely Solsbury Hill. The bear was the emblem of King Arthur. My uncle believed he had found the place where Arthur slew more than nine hundred of the enemy.'

'Nine hundred!'

'It was an age of heroes,' said William Hawkins with a straight face.

'He did sometimes talk of treasure on Solsbury Hill and of spirits who still linger about the place but I think this is what he meant,' continued Katherine, thumbing through more pages until she came to some of old Christopher's verses. She recited:

'Of gold and silver they interr'd many a pound
When these knightes' corses were laid i'th'ground
And Britain's foes no footing found perdee
After Arthur won full soverayntee.'

'He used to read his verses to me when I was young,' said Cousin William. 'I am afraid that I did not always show a proper reverence for his words, and he struck me more than once when I yawned.'

We were interrupted by the potboy returning with our drinks. I took a draught of mine.

'The gold and silver aren't real,' I said after a moment, feeling on familiar ground since we talked of gold and silver all the time on stage and it was nothing more than words. 'This is the language of poetry. Your uncle merely means the fallen bodies of Arthur's knights, and so on. Just as the bear stands for Arthur, the knights' bodies represent the treasure that is buried there.'

'I know that,' said Katherine. 'But I do not think that Mr Maltravers or Mr Downey or Dr Price know it. They believe my uncle left some ... some guide ... to finding hidden treasures on Solsbury Hill or elsewhere. Mr Maltravers asked me before he left the house today whether there were any other papers, anything hidden away.'

'What did you say?'

'I said the only papers my uncle valued were his poetry. Said they were welcome to look at Uncle Christopher's work if they wished. He would be pleased to have readers. What is in this book is only scribbled bits and pieces. Uncle paid to have his Arthur poem copied out properly in the new italic style.'

'And what did they say to that?'

'They aren't interested in his poetry, Nicholas. Mr Maltravers laughed when I mentioned it. He did enquire about his black book, though, and I remembered you said that someone had asked you for it at the baths.'

'"Asked" is one way of putting it.'

Now William Hawkins spoke up: 'Then I stepped in to protect my dear cousin from these intrusive questions so soon after my father's death. I said that they could direct their questions to me.'

'They must have been surprised to see you again after so many years.'

'They were, but their real concern was whether I'd get in the way of their search through my father's effects.'

'Are you sure there is nothing in that book?' I said. 'Other people certainly seem to think so.'

'See for yourself,' said Katherine, passing the volume back across the table. The very casualness of the gesture told me she thought the book held no secrets and I did not even bother to pick it up again. I was glad to see the back of it, to be honest. Let others attend to the tangled affairs of the Hawkins family.

From outside the Raven tavern I heard the bellman pass, ringing his bell, telling us all that it was ten o'clock. Time for honest citizens and players to be in bed. I drained the last of my drink.

'I wish you well,' I said. 'I am returning to Mother Treadwell's.'

We said goodbye rather formally. Perhaps Katherine would have embraced me had it not been for the presence of William as well as of a dozen other individuals in the tavern. Before leaving the Raven I stopped to relieve myself – being a modern place it had its own house of office in the back yard – and then I went out into the street via an alley. The moon was up and near the full, as last night, but it was veiled by thin clouds and cast only a faint light.

Perhaps a couple of minutes had elapsed since I'd parted from the Hawkinses. I could just about make out two individuals walking close together ahead of me. The cousins, presumably. Were they arm in arm? Hard to tell in the gloom. Anyway, what business was it of mine?

Even as I looked the two figures increased to three. For a

moment I thought they had been joined by a friend, but no friend would be moving so fast or raising his arms in such a threatening way. The sounds that came from up the street, grunts and cries, then a woman's scream, sent me running towards them. But the cobbles were slippery with muck and I slid in something and fell with a thump. By the time I'd got to my feet again, the noise had stopped and I could see no one at all up the street.

Although moving less rapidly now, I almost stumbled over the figure of William Hawkins. He was crouching above Katherine, who lay stretched on the ground. Hawkins stood up, panting hard, expecting a fresh attack and ready to lash out.

I said, 'It's all right, it's me, Nick Revill. What happened?'

'I don't know. Some man . . . Kate . . . oh, Kate . . .'

He sank to his knees next to her. For an instant, I feared the worst, but she groaned and tried to sit up. William sighed in relief and supported her as she rose shakily to her feet. I stepped back. In the distance I saw a dancing speck of light, a firefly, then two of them. I thought the attacker was returning with reinforcements before realising that they would hardly be carrying lanterns. The fireflies converged, then drew nearer. There were footsteps on the cobbles, the bark of a dog, the ting of a bell.

Too late, of course. This was typical of the bellman and the watch in any town. Where were they when you really needed them?

William Hawkins and I were sitting in the dining room of the Vicarage Lane house. It was nearing midnight. The cousins had returned home after giving what little information they had to the watch – an unidentified man springing out of the dark from the porch where he'd been lying in wait, followed by a quick theft. The theft of the black book, which Katherine had been still holding as she walked along. Naturally, I recalled the rogue who'd accosted me in the King's Bath. The same man? It seemed likely.

Since the real malefactor had escaped, the bellman and his watch did their duty and detained me instead, imagining that I had a hand in the attack. This, despite the assurances of the Hawkinses as they limped off to dress their wounds that the opposite was true: I had actually come to their rescue.

It took me a quarter of an hour before my protestations of innocence were accepted. In the end, I was allowed to go only after stressing my elevated position in the company of the *King*'s Men and insinuating that *King* James himself would be displeased if he heard that one of his principal players had been thrown into the local lock-up. Quite casually I said that I had an appointment in Whitehall to see him – *King* James, that is – when I returned to London, and that I would assure His Majesty of the loyal and intelligent servants he possessed among the Bath watch. If they detained me for a moment longer, however, I would have a very different tale to tell.

They believed me. I might have said they were men of limited understanding but I nearly believed myself by the time I was done speaking. In fact, we parted on such good terms that I urged them to attend our performance on the next evening. They could easily do this before they went on duty at ten o'clock.

I could have returned to Mother Treadwell's but my blood was up after all this activity and I decided to call on the Hawkins household and see how things stood there. I would almost have welcomed an attacker in the few hundred yards it took to reach the house, so ready was I for a fight, but I arrived unassailed.

William Hawkins welcomed me in and now we sat in the

dining room. The house was hushed. It was late. The body of his father was laid out upstairs. The funeral would take place in a couple of days. We were recovering with a dose of his father's aqua vitae. I did not find the fiery liquid soothing.

Cousin Kate was in bed recovering from her ordeal in the street. She was not badly hurt but she was bruised and shaken. William was angry, not so much for himself but on her behalf. He was angry too with Hannah, the old servant, who had been – unwittingly, perhaps – the indirect cause of what had happened. I had described to William my morning encounter with the rogue in the King's Bath, and how he tried to take the black notebook from me. I said the only person who could have deduced it was in my possession was Hannah. She must have spoken to one of the men in the house that morning. Hawkins strode from the room and went upstairs to where the old retainer was attending on Katherine. He was back within minutes, looking a whit less angry, and confirming what I'd thought. Hannah had referred to my presence in the house the previous night as well as to my position in the King's Men. She said I'd been taken to see the dying man. She couldn't remember whether she'd said all this to John Maltravers or to the lawyer Downey. Or was it Dr Price? She was very distressed at the state of her mistress. She hoped she had not done any wrong.

Anyway, one or more of the trio must have deduced I had the book and set the rogue on my trail – this was the conclusion William and I came to. The same rogue must have been watching us in the smoky, dim interior of the Raven tavern or else he had an accomplice there; had seen the book being passed back to Kate Hawkins; had lurked to waylay her and William on the way home.

'He shall not get away with this,' said William. 'Whoever's responsible will not get away with it either.'

'Who is behind it?'

'I do not know. One of the three men here this morning, surely. The doctor, the lawyer or the merchant. They are all respectable citizens but one of them is evidently prepared to resort to force . . . to attack my cousin . . .'

'So there is something valuable in your father's personal book after all?'

'My father was an odd mixture of businessman and dreamer, Nick. What he wrote down in his little volume showed both sides. His plans for better machinery were the practical part, while the dreams were the verses about King Arthur.'

'And drawings of Solsbury Hill with signs and markings . . .'

'Yes, with markings that could cause someone to believe there was buried treasure there,' conceded William.

'But there is no treasure?'

'I am not about to go off and dig up a hillside in pursuit of my father's dreams.'

'Others may be.'

'Yes,' said William.

'If they're going to search on this Solsbury Hill of yours they're going to do it soon. To strike while the iron is hot.'

'Yes, they are,' said William.

'I have an idea,' I said.

IV

'Are you sure this is such a good idea?' said Laurence Savage.

'Nick knows what he's doing,' said Abel Glaze, 'even if the rest of us haven't the faintest notion.'

I looked towards William Hawkins for support but he

stayed silent. The scheme that the two of us contrived the previous night in the Vicarage Lane house, while fortified with generous doses of his father's aqua vitae, did not seem so plausible in the cold light of day. The literal cold light, since we were sheltering behind some low bushes near the top of Solsbury Hill. Away from the fuggy air of the city, the breeze blew sharp and clear, and the morning sun was scarcely beginning to warm the slope we sat on. Bath is ringed with hills – they say there are seven of them, just as in Rome – and this Solsbury one is located to the north-east of the city. It is a hill much like any other, distinguished only by an unnatural flatness on top and the even slant of its sides. William Hawkins said that it might have been used in the old times as some kind of fort.

We had struck out from the town that morning, the four of us, Laurence having established that we weren't required at the Bear Inn to prepare for our final night's performance. I'd explained to my friends that we were set to catch some villains who had attacked my new friend, William, and his cousin, Kate. Laurence and Abel might have taken this as a tall story but they'd seen with their own eyes the young woman in the inn yard, together with a male companion. Furthermore they knew I'd been engaged on nocturnal adventures, since I returned to Mother Treadwell's very late the previous night, or rather in the small hours of the morning. They thought I'd been up to you-know-what again and I didn't bother to disabuse them of the notion.

I outlined the situation: the attack in the street, the reason for it; the fact that the villains had stolen a map – or plan, or guide – call it what you will – which they hoped would reveal the whereabouts of some hidden items; relics buried not far from the city of Bath. Hawkins said that he thought his father's sketch, the one we'd looked at in the Raven tavern,

303

showed the south-western flank of the hill, the one facing the city. Like his cousin, he was of the opinion that Christopher's crosses and arrows most likely indicated the place where King Arthur had personally vanquished his Saxon enemies, all nine hundred of them. But to a more greedy eye the markings might appear to show the burial places of treasure. We were assuming that whoever was in quest of treasure would waste no time. After stealing Christopher's book, they would want to make use of it straight away.

Abel and Laurence were happy enough to join in the adventure. To be honest, I think they were growing a little tired of our stay in Bath. I've noticed this before on our summer tours. You spend a couple of days in a place and then you get restless, looking towards the next destination, wondering what pastimes and delights will be offered by the town over the horizon. Abel and Laurence hadn't experienced the excitements of the city of Bath as I had, and the prospect of smoking out a malefactor or two – with the very remote possibility that buried treasure and King Arthur could be involved – was sufficient to bring them along.

We left by the North Gate, and passed through an area of wooden houses and hovels that grew more ragged the further we shifted from the walls of the city. We went from lanes to paths to rough tracks, passing orchards and small farmsteads and neat fields, some with sheep grazing. We moved at a slight upward incline until we reached the flank of the hill after the better part of an hour.

There were few people about and no one at all that we could see on the hillside. By now, Laurence and Abel were openly sceptical about the entire enterprise. Faced with a steepish hillside they talked openly about turning round and going back to Bath. To get them to go on, I had to promise that all the drinks would be put on my slate when we reached Bristol.

'Every day, mind, Nick,' said Laurence. I nodded.

So we clambered up the slope and were rewarded at the top with a fine view of the country in every direction. Down below in a loop of the river was the city of Bath, neatly girdled by its walls and lapped by pastures and woods. From here you could hardly recall the odour of its close, stinky air, nor see the mean habitations clinging to its skirts. I breathed deep and looked about with pleasure. I wondered whether this was truly the place where a mighty battle had been fought by King Arthur, whether it was the field where the Saxon enemy had been vanquished. I thought of the little image of the bear in Christopher's book. Had bears wandered across this place during those far-off days? Who knew?

Now it was as quiet and peaceful as the day of creation. The only living creatures were small and unassuming. Larks sang high in the air. Rabbits scuttered across the grass. I thought how these rolling hills meant more to me than the others, with the exception of William, since they were not so far from the Somerset village of my birth. William spent some time looking about, like me, pleased to be home again.

We'd brought some ale and bread and cheese with us. We established ourselves behind a line of bushes that gave some protection from the breeze and through which we could see the west-facing approaches to the hill. We chatted and drank and ate. William talked about Edinburgh, another city of hills, as he described it. He talked about his work as secretary to a cloth manufacturer. He had been present when King James set out from Edinburgh on his long, meandering progress to London to claim the throne. James had promised to return to the Scots capital every three years but he had not done so yet. I told the others the story I'd spun to the Bath watchmen about my familiarity with the King.

We talked about plays and players in the way – half proud, half mocking – that you talk with your fellows about your own work. Then we fell silent and thought about the wisdom of sitting hundreds of feet up a hillside waiting for the arrival of treasure-hunters, and wondered who was really engaged on a wild-goose chase here. The sun was high in the sky by now and the ale was making me sleepy. Pretty soon we'd have to give this up for the fruitless enterprise it was and return to the town to prepare for our final evening's performance.

It was Abel who spotted them first. He jabbed me as I lay at a slant on the grass, squinting at the sun. I sat up and peered through the leaves. In the distance, beginning their ascent, were two figures. Out for a stroll? But who strolls anywhere except a gentleman in a city street or a lady in her garden? These two were about some business. One of them, wearing a labourer's clothes, was carrying a mattock and spade over his shoulder. The other, better dressed, carried no implements and walked some way to the rear, either because he found the slope of the hill very effortful or to disassociate himself from his companion. In the further distance was a carriage, with a driver left behind to mind it and the two horses. He had been able to steer part of the way along one of the tracks leading towards Solsbury Hill but it was pleasing that the occupants of the carriage were compelled to get out to complete their journey and tire themselves out in the process.

I was glad that we were right, William and I. Glad as well to recognise two people I knew, enemies not friends. The fat man in the rear was John Maltravers, the merchant and corporation member, and hater of plays and players. The one who wanted us whipped as vagrants. The fellow in front, stocky rather than fat, was the wretch who accosted me in the King's Bath and most likely attacked the Hawkins cousins in the street. William was peering through the shrubbery beside me. He knew Maltravers, of course. He was able to identify the other man, the one with the spade and mattock.

'That is Rowley. George Rowley. I remember him. He has been Maltravers' creature these many years. He collects the merchant's debts, for example.'

'I reckon it was he who attacked you last night.'

'Very likely.'

Speaking hardly above a whisper I indicated to Laurence and Abel who these gents were. The whispering was instinctive – and not really necessary since the wind was blowing in our direction. We could hear them, though, the wheezing and groans of Maltravers as he strove to climb the slope and the more regular panting of Rowley.

Then they stopped at a point between a spur of rock and a clump of stunted oak trees. Maltravers waited for a long time for his breath to come back. From a pocket he drew what looked very like Uncle Christopher's black book, together with a larger sheet of paper, which he proceeded to unfold. I guessed he'd made a more detailed plan of the area. He consulted book and plan, nodded at his man, strode backwards and forwards a few times before finally settling on a spot where there appeared to be a slight hollow in the grass. Pointing at the place with his stubby forefinger, he marked it with his heel, nodded again at Rowley, then settled himself down on the spur of rock and watched while the excavation began.

Rowley started to break up the soil with the mattock. We heard the sound of the implement striking the ground, we heard his involuntary grunts when he struck a stony patch. Eventually he'd loosened enough topsoil to start digging properly. The next question was when we should reveal ourselves. William and I had not planned in much detail for this moment.

In the end we gave them a half-hour or so. I suppose the thought was in all our minds that this was not a wild-goose chase, that George Rowley the digger might actually turn up something. At several points the servant paused and looked in the direction of his master who, with a shake of that peremptory forefinger and a barked command, indicated that he should continue digging. Eventually – quite soon, in fact – the interest of watching a man dig a hole starts to fade. I looked at William Hawkins, who nodded his agreement. Abel and Laurence were already gazing elsewhere, up at the sky, around at the countryside.

'Let's do it,' I said.

From the pouch that I was carrying I extracted four items that Laurence had filched, temporarily, from the tire-chest at the Bear Inn. These were the masks or vizards that had been worn for the lunatic scene in the first play we'd done in Bath, *A House Divided*. The masks were half animal, half devil. A couple had birdlike beaks, one a snout, the other the suggestion of horns. When they were combined with white smocks and wild gestures and gibbering speech, they proved most effective on stage, as Kate Hawkins told me when we first met. Now we were about to find out whether they'd put the fear of God – or the devil – into a couple of treasure-hunters. It was Kate's reference to 'spirits' lingering on the hill that had made me think of using the masks. We looked at each other through the eye-holes. William Hawkins laughed nervously. Laurence and Abel grinned. This was meat and drink to them.

We were about to rise up from our hiding place behind the shrubbery when we were halted by a call from below. Rowley must have found something, for he beckoned to Maltravers and then pointed to the bottom of the little pit he'd made. Maltravers levered himself up from his rock and crossed the few yards to the place. He leaned forward, supporting himself by resting his fat hands on his bent knees. One hand still clasped the black notebook and sheet of paper. With his spade, Rowley gestured at some object in the hole. The servant moved back slightly. Maltravers bent forward a bit more. Any further and he might topple over.

Maybe the same idea occurred to Rowley for he raised the spade in a hesitant manner as if he might give his master a thwack on his rump. Or perhaps he was considering a more final stroke, for he now lifted the spade a little higher. From this position he might strike the merchant round the head. How many years of bad-tempered words and shouted orders and resentment lurked behind that moment? I was almost disappointed when Rowley lowered the spade just before Maltravers looked back over his shoulder. Evidently the merchant was not very impressed with the discovery, whatever it was. Time to move.

'Ready?' I said to the others.

We adjusted our masks with their beaks, horns and snouts. We bared our wolfish teeth.

'Now!' I said.

The four of us jumped up from where we had been concealing ourselves. With windmilling arms and ear-piercing shrieks, we raced around the bushes and launched ourselves at a downhill pelt. It took Maltravers and Rowley several seconds even to locate the source of all this hullabaloo. It took them several more to respond. Rowley dropped the spade. Maltravers let go of the black book. The sheet of paper fluttered to the ground. They turned and took to their heels, running, if anything, even faster than we were. Maltravers stumbled and fell. He rolled several yards like a barrel before scrambling to his feet once more. Unfortunately for them, the path of their flight nearer the base of the hill led through a patch of boggy ground. Maltravers and Rowley squelched and floundered into this. Neither man showed any concern for the other. They reached the far side of the boggy stretch and staggered towards the waiting carriage. The coachman was staring apprehensively. At least I assume he was, since all I could see was the white dot of his face.

Meanwhile Laurence, Abel, William and I had halted our pursuit in the region of the little excavation made by Rowley. There was no point in going any further. We had accomplished our task of scaring off these ne'er-do-wells and, into the bargain, we had regained Uncle Christopher's black book. We would not have wanted to go on with the chase anyway because we were curious to see whether there really was any buried treasure. Also because we were out of breath ourselves, what with the running and our shrieks and laughter.

I picked up the black notebook and waved it in the air in triumph. We tore off our masks and made gleeful whooping noises at the runaways, who stopped and gazed at the spectacle for a moment before clambering aboard the carriage. The driver turned it as fast as he could – I had hopes it might overturn but it did not – and within little more than a minute they were bumping and rocking down the track in the direction of Bath.

We turned our attention to the hole in the ground. Rowley's digging had indeed turned up something. I bent down and picked up what appeared to be part of a helmet.

Was I holding a relic of Arthur's time? Perhaps. But it was made of leather and a strip of rusted metal, which was probably a nose-piece, not an artefact of gold or silver or precious stones. I threw it back into the hole. William Hawkins retrieved the sheet of paper that John Maltravers had dropped in his panic. It was a larger drawing of this aspect of the hillside, with the oaks and the stone outcrop crudely depicted and a cross roughly at the point where we stood.

'Do you think there's anything further down there?' said Laurence.

'We could dig,' said Abel, eyeing the mattock and spade abandoned on the ground.

'It is all a story, a fable,' said William. 'There's nothing there.'

'And we must return to town,' I said. 'We have a play to do.'

A slight sense of disappointment came over us. Into the distance jolted the coach belonging to Mr Maltravers, citizen of Bath. After a brief time we strolled down the lower slopes of Solsbury Hill, taking care to avoid the marshy patch near the bottom. We threaded our way back, past the fields and orchards, through the lanes of tumble-down houses outside the city wall and so on through the North Gate.

But that wasn't the end of it, of course. Did you think it would be?

The play we were performing on our last night at the Bear Inn was *A Fair Day*. This is a comedy about a summer fair, as the title suggests. Set on the outskirts of London – although I don't think the city is ever named – it shows a world populated by good-hearted or venal stall-holders, cutpurses, gamesters, fortune-tellers and the like. There are confidence tricksters too, of course, the ones who sell little bottles containing the elixir of life or the infallible prescription for turning base metal into gold, once you have parted with your money. And then there are the visitors to the fair. All these characters are thrown together and left to simmer like the ingredients of a stew until the flavour is rich and rare.

I was playing the part of a justice of the peace, Mr Justice Righthead, who stalks the fairground looking for breaches of the law in between announcing his determination to close the whole thing down. The idea had already occurred to me that I could slip one or two touches into my performance that hinted at a certain Bath gentleman. I padded myself out around the middle and practised wagging my forefinger and emphasising my Somerset burr. It was a joke that would only be appreciated by Abel and Laurence, and perhaps one or two of the audience who might be reminded of Mr John Maltravers. It was also a way of exacting a further little revenge on the merchant. There could be no adverse consequences, surely, since we were quitting the town the next day.

Shortly before we were due to go on, Abel said to me, 'They're here.'

'Who's here?'

'The men on the hill today. Mr Maltravers and whatsisname, Rowley. They're sitting in the audience.'

'You're certain?'

'See for yourself.'

I peered through a gap in the tattered hangings that concealed the tiring-room to the side of the stage. On a bench only a few yards away squatted the portly merchant and his servant. They looked disgruntled and battered after the day's experiences. Furthermore, sitting near to them were two other gents I knew: Edward Downey, the lawyer, and Dr

Price. These two wore expressions that indicated they might actually be looking forward to the evening's entertainment. Also on the benches were the cousins, Kate and William Hawkins. Then, casting my eyes further back towards the individuals standing behind the benches, I noticed the two members of the night watch. I remembered that I'd urged them to attend this evening. But it also came to me that they might be here in some official capacity, perhaps to do the bidding of John Maltravers. I had to remind myself that it was Maltravers and Rowley who had done wrong, who stole Christopher's notebook and assaulted the Hawkinses.

'Why is he here?' said Abel.

By now Laurence Savage was also taking a peek through the hangings. He said to me, 'I thought you said this Maltravers hates plays.'

'So he does.'

'Do you think they recognised us this morning? Do you think they knew us for players?' said Abel.

I shrugged. 'So what if they did? We are here under licence. They can do no harm.'

'Who can do no harm?'

This was John Sincklo speaking, the senior member of the King's Men on our tour. He had caught the last words of our anxious conversation. A serious individual, John Sincklo would not approve of anything that I and the others had been doing that day away from the stage. So we made light of our comments and readied ourselves for the final performance in Bath.

All was going well with *A Fair Day*, or so it seemed. The audience enjoyed our antics as stall-holders, con men, customers. There is not much of a plot to the play but there is a lot of coming and going and confusion of identities and a good measure of bawdiness mixed with finely crafted insults.

Among all this, I strode as Mr Justice Righthead, denounc-
ing the pleasures of ordinary folk and trying to put a stop to
them. I quickly forgot about the presence of John Maltravers
and George Rowley in the audience, carried away with my
windy proclamations and buoyed up by the laughter in the
inn yard.

Trouble did not start until quite near the end of the action.
In my part as Justice Righthead, I had just received my
comeuppance. Among the visitors to our fictional fair were
an innocent young man and a comely young woman. I had
taken both under my wing, especially the woman, upon
whom I had designs. Now this pair were exposed as a notorious cutpurse and his wench. So Mr Justice Righthead was
in his turn exposed as both a fool and a hypocrite, when the
woman gleefully described his clumsy attempts to seduce
her. Instead of hanging my head in shame, I launched on a
fresh tirade. Attack is the best defence. I was in full flow
when I became aware of a disturbance among the audience.
The weighty figure of John Maltravers lumbered to his feet
and, wagging his finger in the style that I'd been imitating on
stage, started his own rant.

I won't bore you with the details of what he said. Plays
were a disgrace, players were a blot upon the common-
wealth, authority was being undermined, we should be
whipped for our pains, et cetera. This was so much an echo
of the lines that I was delivering that at first people might
have believed Maltravers' words were all part of the action.
But some among the audience recognised him and, pretty
soon, everyone was able to distinguish between play-acting
and the real thing. Curiously, he did not sound as convincing
as an actor would have done. Edward Downey and Dr Price
made ineffectual attempts to hold him back but he waddled
to the edge of the raised stage and continued his harangue.

Now we of the King's Men are used to dealing with interruptions. Usually they come from drunks, occasionally from mischief-makers. They tend to be short-lived. This Maltravers man went on and on. He was genuinely angry, working himself up further with every spluttered sentence. His round face turned a dark red and his finger waggled ever more furiously. The audience were reduced to mutters, interspersed with a bit of booing and some laughter. They might not have been entertained as we'd been entertaining them, but they could not take their eyes off the merchant. I'd stopped speaking some time ago since there was no point in continuing with my own rant. My fellows were all on stage, for it was the climax of the action. We formed a ragged semi-circle staring at our attacker, waiting for him to exhaust himself. John Sincklo looked outraged, since there is nothing to rouse the ire of a player like an attack on his profession.

Then I noticed that George Rowley was nowhere to be seen. The stocky servant was not sitting on the bench, nor could I spot him in the gathering gloom of the inn yard. Some instinct caused me to glance sideways at the little curtained-off tire-room where our costume baskets and other effects were stored. I broke away from the group and within a few strides had reached the side of the stage.

Inside the tire-room everything was in a state of disorder. Costumes, props were tumbled out of the baskets. Among the pile was a frantically rummaging Rowley. I could guess what he was looking for. Instantly I realised that John Maltravers' intervention in our play was planned. Oh, he meant every one of the words he was still booming out in condemnation of the players. He'd love to see us whipped, run out of town and the rest of it. But he was acting too. It was a diversion to keep all eyes in the audience fixed on him and to give his man a chance to sneak into the tire-room and ransack our property. Undoubtedly, Maltravers had realised the identity of his ambushers on Solsbury Hill this morning, had seen us retrieve the black book, and, driven by fury, was determined to get it back. It was a desperate scheme, guaranteed to make an exhibition in front of his fellow citizens. But perhaps he did not care.

All this passed through my mind in a flash. About as long as it took Rowley to look up from his mad search and observe that there was someone else in the tire-room with him. This was when things turned serious. He grunted and produced from somewhere in his garments a wicked little knife. Humiliated this morning on Solsbury Hill, discovered now in the middle of his wrongdoing, he was driven by the same rage as his master. He slashed out at me and, more by luck than design, I staggered back out of range. But I tumbled over a heap of clothing and lay there sprawled on my back, helpless. Time seemed to slow down. From outside I could hear the continued ranting of Maltravers, from within this curtained-off space the heavy breathing of my assailant. Above me was the darkening summer sky and the same old moon and a corner of the gable and the little window from which Katherine Hawkins had spied on me at the beginning of this business.

Rowley paused for a second to position his dagger so that he might make a more effective strike. My hand closed round a dagger, one of our props, but it was a paltry wooden thing. Rowley stamped on my hand, then fell forward, intending to stab me in the guts. If he'd known he would be hanged for the deed, it would have made no difference. I cried out but the sound was feeble to my own ears. There was murder in his eyes, the real thing and not the simulated rage you see on stage. From playing dead two nights ago I was about to become genuinely so.

Yet I was saved by the part I played as Mr Justice Righthead. I'd wound padding about my stomach in imitation of Maltravers' fatness, and Rowley's knife became buried and deflected among all the stuffing, the fustian cloth and rags bulking out my midriff. Rowley looked confused and I twisted away from him. He extricated the knife and was lifting it to strike once more when the front curtains to the tire-house were not so much opened as torn away. Rowley paused, then faltered.

We must have presented a dramatic tableau, the player lying on the ground and the knifeman with his arm raised uncertainly. Crowded in the entrance to the tire-room were the Hawkinses and the two members of the night watch. I'll think twice before saying again that they're never there when you need them.

We finished the play, by the way. It would have been unprofessional not to.

We had to wait until the watch took charge of George Rowley, whose guilt couldn't be doubted since he was caught knife-in-hand. Like his master, Maltravers, he had some hectic words to say before he was dragged off. It was an accusation against John Maltravers – that *he* had put him up to this, that *he* was the one responsible. I remembered that moment on the hillside when Rowley appeared willing to strike his master about the pate with his spade. Maltravers, crestfallen after all his shouting, looked increasingly uncomfortable. His face went from pure red to mottled red and white. Eventually he strode out of the yard, but I noticed Downey the lawyer and Price the physician gazing after him, and I would have bet they had a few questions of their own to put to him.

The assumption was that Rowley was rummaging through

the tire-room gear in search of some valuables. It was merely bad luck that I had stumbled across him. And good luck that I was unharmed. No one mentioned the black-bound commonplace book belonging to Uncle Christopher. It was no longer in my possession anyway, since I had already returned it to William Hawkins while we were on Solsbury Hill.

After a half-hour or so we resumed *A Fair Day*. I took up my part as Mr Justice Righthead, although my costume was somewhat torn and shredded about the middle, with the stuffing coming out. It was only when we were all done that I started to shiver and shake at having so nearly escaped a severe wounding or even death. It took the company of my fellows and a few drinks in the Raven afterwards to steady my nerves.

For their part, the Bath citizens sitting or standing in the yard of the Bear appreciated our resilience and our dedication to the craft of the stage play. They cheered us loudly at the end, so much so that we were encouraged enough to take up an extra collection of money. John Sincklo looked doubtfully at me and Laurence and Abel after it was all over, as if we knew more about the incident than we were letting on, but he did not ask any questions. In fact, he was gratified at the way the crowd showed themselves to be on the side of the players, and pleased by the additional money that came in. We did better than that when we received an extra subvention from Bath corporation as if in tacit apology for the misbehaviour of one of their own at our final performance.

Later, when we reached Bristol, I gave Sincklo an outline of the story. I felt that I owed him that much.

We left Bath the next day. As we passed through on our way to the West Gate and the fresher air of the Bristol road, we paused to observe that some preliminary justice had been meted out to George Rowley. He was standing in the pillory by the Guild Hall, smeared with rotten fruit and draped with vegetable peelings. The pigs were still waddling about at liberty on the city cobbles, in expectation of what they might scavenge. I was glad to see Rowley in the pillory, although it does not usually give me much pleasure to watch the public punishment of malefactors.

Much later, when we had returned to London, Kate Hawkins wrote to me, a genuine 'privy message' this time. She thanked me for the service I had performed for her dying uncle (but made no mention of our later connection). She said that an indictment was being laid against John Maltravers largely on the testimony of George Rowley. But the evidence was thin and, Maltravers being a respectable citizen and his accuser a mere servant, he would probably wriggle his way out of punishment. His standing in the town had been irredeemably harmed, however, by his ranting in the yard of the Bear Inn. Edward Downey and Dr Price had turned against their old friend and even apologised to her for their unseemly behaviour on the morning of Christopher's death. She and William were still grieving for Uncle Christopher but she wrote that, when a suitable period of mourning was passed, they intended to marry. I thought it was a happy ending and very similar to the plot of the second play we'd done in Bath, the one entitled *A City Pleasure*.

As for the black notebook, which might have revealed the whereabouts of precious items buried on Solsbury Hill, that had been locked away as a family keepsake. Neither she nor William had any interest in scrabbling about on a bare hill in search of Arthur's gold or any other relics. They had enough treasures to look forward to in their domestic lives, which was a nice comment, although one that for a moment made me feel envious. If there were any relics to be found on Solsbury Hill, Kate added in a postscript, let's leave them to the future. That's what the future's for, after all.

ACT FIVE

A Deadly Dig

Having removed the outer layers of bindings that covered the body, Joe Malinferno delicately cut away the lower garment from the corpse's torso. It resembled a bag that had been doubled and seamed on two sides. A fringe decorated the bottom hem. Under the garment he found little ornaments decorated with figures of ancient gods. He laid these aside on the surface of the polished oak table he was using as a makeshift mortuary slab. He stood up for a moment, easing the ache in his lower back caused by his bent posture. He heard a church clock chiming somewhere nearby, and he estimated he had been working on the body for almost an hour. He would have to hurry. Wiping the beads of sweat from his brow with the back of his hand, he continued the process of discovery.

His next step was to reveal the corpse's face. The lips were pulled back in what resembled a grimace of horror. It seemed as if the man had died a violent death, but Malinferno as yet had no idea if that were true. In fact he had not yet even figured out the identity of the man who lay under his steady hands. He continued his examination in absolute silence, noting that the hair of the head, eyebrows and beard were all shaved off. The skin was a livid grey colour, and when he touched it, it felt greasy. There was a

321

layer of something perfumed over the skin, the odour redolent of cinnamon. The facial features were shrivelled, and the eyes were still in their orbits. He looked at the hands, which were crossed over the body's chest. Their well-manicured fingernails reflected the person's privileged lifestyle. What he didn't know and was endeavouring to find out was the cause of his death.

For the first time, Malinferno broke the silence that hung like a pall over the assembled throng.

'I estimate this body is ...'

There was a communal intake of breath as those gathered to hear the professor's deductions awaited his opinion. Malinferno did not disappoint them.

'... three thousand years old.'

There was a gasp from the crowd, followed by a ripple of noise as gloved hands were slapped together in the most refined of ways to applaud his skill, and their hostess's generously proffered entertainment.

Rosamund, Duchess of Avon, was a widow with too much money, and too much time on her hands since the death of her elderly husband, the fifth duke. Her cold and echoing mausoleum of an ancestral home had for all too long induced in her a stultifying boredom that she ached to assuage. Her childless life was tedious and unfulfilled. The idea of purchasing an Egyptian mummy had suddenly come to her over a dull breakfast one day.

She had been reading the *Bathhampton Packet*, to which her husband had subscribed, and which, by an oversight, she had failed to cancel after his death. In fact she had never previously read the slender sheet, it being her husband's predilection to monopolise the rag. A week after his death, she had had occasion to pick it up idly from the breakfast table where the duke's old butler had continued to reverently lay it in lieu of other orders. She had been going to tell Goring to dispose of it, but an article caught her eye. It appeared that one of her neighbours had set up shotguns attached to tripwires to dispose of unwanted trespassers on his land. A court case had ensued on the death of a gypsy, and the wrangling of the lawyers and judge, as reported in the *Packet*, was all about whether in such circumstances human life was as forfeit as an errant dog. Lady Rosamund was clear as to her own opinion on the matter, and snorted with satisfaction that the editor of the *Bathhampton Packet* seemed to concur. Since that date, she had read the newssheet assiduously.

On one particular rather dull and drizzly morning, next to a piece about the scandalous goings-on of the Prince Regent, she saw an item concerning Countess Shrewsbury and an Egyptian mummy. It seemed the latest craze was to unroll these beastly things at a soiree, and offer your neighbours the chance of some grisly voyeurism. She instinctively realised this would provide the ideal opportunity to demonstrate her new-found intention to be the centre of social, if not exactly intellectual, life in her corner of the county. She had undertaken enquiries, and soon made the necessary purchase from a man at the British Museum, who was willing illicitly to supply her needs. Along with a man who could effect the unrolling.

For his part Il Professore Giuseppe Malinferno had been delighted when he had been contacted by his old friend from the BM, Thomas Elder, with a request to examine a mummy. He had been both eager to lay his hands on such a rare object, and fearful that his limited knowledge might be exposed. He realised he need not have worried. The unrolling was not going to take place in the presence of expert Egyptologists – of which there were a small but growing number – but at some remote and exotic site before a bunch of provincial socialites, leavened with the odd vicar and bibulous Member of Parliament. Malinferno soon saw that he could bamboozle them with any old nonsense he cared to utter. This he had proceeded to do, along with a subtle touch of showmanship.

When he had stepped out in front of his audience, a magnificent, white-robed figure, a gasp had come from the gentry present in the marquee. He seemed preternaturally tall as his head was topped with a cruel, staring jackal's mask, its ears abnormally pricked. It was the very embodiment of Anubis – God of the Dead, Guide through the Underworld, and Hearer of Prayers. Several ladies recoiled in terror, and had to fan themselves for fear of fainting. The unbearable heat in the tent and the anticipation was literally breathtaking. Malinferno as Anubis threw his arms high into the air, and cried out, causing another *frisson* to run through the crowd.

> 'O Great One who became Sky,
> You are strong, you are mighty,
> You fill every place with your beauty,
> The whole earth is beneath you, you possess it!
> As you enfold earth and all things in your arms,
> So have you taken this great lady to you,
> An indestructible star within you!'

The audience was enraptured. But beneath the mask, beads of sweat were pouring down Malinferno's forehead, and stinging his eyes. However, he was in no position to wipe them away, and blinked, shaking his head slightly. The mask of Anubis wobbled, and settled at a more uncertain, rather jaunty angle on his brow. He invoked the gods once more.

'Oh Imsety, Hapy, Duamutef, Kebehsenuef,
Who live by *maat*,
Who lean on their staffs,
Who watch over Upper Egypt,

O Boatman of the boatless just,
Ferryman of the Field of Rushes!

Ferry Ankh-Wadjet to us.'

This had been Doll's cue, but nothing happened. He had cursed under his breath, and called out again, louder this time, 'Ferry Ankh-Wadjet to us.'

At the last moment, a form appeared as if by magic at the head of the mummy. It was a tall, voluptuous figure wearing the horned mask of Hathor. The diaphanous robe did little to hide the curvaceous attractions of his mysterious companion, whom he had named as Madam Nefre. She was scandalously nude underneath her robe, and the audience loved the fact.

'Couldn't 'ear you because of this stupid mask,' whispered Doll Pocket into Malinferno's jackal ear, her dulcet tones melting with the heat. 'And I'm sweating like a pig under it.'

'I've told you before, Hathor is a cow god not a pig, hence the horns. Now let's get on with this farrago.'

The unravelling of the bandaged mummy had then proceeded well, if a little drily. Malinferno had done his best to perform like a fairground barker, while still slaking his own genuine curiosity about the strange means of burial as practised by the ancient Egyptians. In fact, he had even managed, as he often did, to sneak several funerary souvenirs into the pocket of his jacket as he was exposing the leathery visage of the long-dead Egyptian to the general

325

gaze. He did it not for their intrinsic value, of course – though he had no doubt he could shift them for a tidy sum on the burgeoning antiquities market – but to further his own understanding of ancient Egypt.

He hoped to leave the tedious soiree as soon as his part in it was effected, and carry on with the real reason for his presence on the hill. But he knew his employer expected more. As those she had invited craned eagerly over the large dining table that held the dusty and rather smelly remains of her investment, she reflected on the success of the evening. All in all it had gone well, though she wished that the man she had engaged – this Italian professor with an unpronounceable name – had conducted the event with a little less scholarly sobriety, and a little more élan. His naked assistant had promised well, but the unrolling had been accompanied with too much talk.

'Professor Ma . . . Malapropos . . .' screeched the duchess, taking Malinferno's arm in a vicelike grip. She obviously could not even remember his name, but was determined to get full value from his celebrated, albeit bogus, erudition. 'You must talk to my dear friend the Honourable Sir Ralph St Germans about the Pyramids and suchlike. He's the Member of Parliament for . . . err . . .' She flapped her hand to denote some remote rotten borough that was represented by this august Member. 'He is fearfully keen on this Egyptian thing, and is acquiring all sorts of impedimenta from . . . well, from Egyptia, I suppose.'

She steered him towards an egregiously overweight, and obviously inebriated gentleman, who was using the edge of Malinferno's erstwhile mortuary slab to steady his wavering bulk. The small items from the mummy that were the professor's illicit bonus were burning a hole in Malinferno's pocket. But there was nothing to be done but whisk a bumper of red wine from a passing tray, and sing for his supper. He toasted the noble Member of Parliament, and enquired after his collection of artefacts, hoping the man wasn't expert enough on Egyptology to unmask him as a charlatan. Fortunately, St Germans chose that moment to pass out from an excess of alcohol, slumping heavily across the table and landing on Doll's generous bosom.

It had only been a week earlier that Malinferno had lifted his head reluctantly from that very bosom and sighed.

'I have to get out of London, Doll. What if I am found out? I will be hanged along with the others.'

The reason for his fears had to do with Malinferno's soft spot for the plight of the masses, coming as he did himself from humble beginnings. After old King George had died in January of that year – 1820 – the rumblings of the radicals got louder as the situation of the working poor got worse. Joe – he hated his proper name of Giuseppe – often took himself off to the Marylebone Union Reading Society, and filled his head with radical idealism. Doll was more down to earth, and didn't think much could be done other than looking after number one. They rowed about it off and on.

'We, who are able to look after ourselves, must help the poor.'

Joe's pronouncement astonished Doll, bearing in mind they were themselves down to their last few coppers. And the meal on the table in Joe's shabby lodgings in Creechurch Lane, London, was no more than an umble pie of offal, washed down with beer. She opened her arms to encompass their meagre feast.

'Joe, we *are* the poor, as things stand. I shall have to troll the streets if we are to pay your landlady the rent for even last month.'

Malinferno's face was set in a mask of defiance. He had
first met Doll Pocket in Madam de Trou's bawdy house in
Petticoat Lane. He had been astonished by both her quick
mind, and her obviously pulchritudinous assets. Instead of
exploiting those assets as intended, he had spent the night
teaching her all he knew about Egyptology. She had
absorbed it like a sponge. They had forgotten all about the
reason why he had paid the madam in good gold coin. And
now that they were good friends, he didn't want Doll to
return to her former trade.

'No. If the worst comes to the worst, you can become an
actress. I know Mr Saunders, the manager of the New
Theatre in Tottenham Street. He will find you a position.'

Doll pulled a face. 'An actress? Why should I want to do
that? They have the same reputation as a whore, and earn
less than half the money.'

'At least that is the lesser of two evils.' Malinferno hesitated
a moment. He was trying somehow to get round to telling
her the truth about the rent. Finally, he decided he had better
just come out and say it. 'And it's not one month we owe
but three.'

Doll pushed her rickety chair away from the table, and
put her hands on her hips in a pose of outrage.

'But I gave you the money for the other month. It was the
last of my savings.'

'I know. But Arthur wanted some funds and I—'

'You gave it all to Arthur Thistlewood?'

By now, Doll was stomping up and down their tiny room,
causing the chipped crockery on the table to rattle.
Malinferno steadied the table and grinned.

'You know, you would make a wonderful actress. They
are putting on *The Taming of the Shrew* at the Theatre Royal.'

Doll growled, and grabbed one of the plates from off the

table. She only stopped herself from throwing it at Joe, when he yelled a warning.

'Careful, Doll, we've got only two plates left. If that one goes, we will have to share our repasts like two dogs fighting over the same bowl.'

She contented herself with another growl, and sat back on her chair abruptly. It creaked ominously under her. She waved her hand at Malinferno dismissively.

'Go and plot treason with Thistlewood. That's all you are good for, you and the Spendthrift Philanderers.'

'Spencean Philanthropists,' Malinferno corrected her. 'We follow the ideas of Thomas Spence. Anyway, it's no good me going to the meeting house today. They are meeting up somewhere else, but I am not in on the secret of what's afoot.'

Doll snorted with derision. 'You are not all that important to them, then. Now they have your money. Where are they meeting, anyway?'

Malinferno tossed his head, as though his not being in on the secret meeting mattered not at all to him.

'Somewhere near Grosvenor Square. Cato Street, I think he said.'

Later, when the news came out of the murderous conspiracy led by Thistlewood, Malinferno was glad he had been excluded. After the conspirators were arrested in a pitched battle in the Cato Street hayloft, it emerged that the Spencean Philanthropists had plotted to kill every single cabinet minister at a dinner hosted by Lord Harrowby. Malinferno, pale and shaken, had refused to leave his lodgings in Creechurch Lane for days. He spent his time peering cautiously out of the dusty window on the first floor, imagining every passer-by was a Bow Street runner come to arrest him for treason. Doll scoffed at his worries, but Joe would not be reassured.

'George Edwards was an *agent provocateur* acting for the government, and I spoke to him at a meeting once. He might remember me.'

'Joe, it's been weeks since the others were arrested. Has anyone mentioned your name? No.'

Malinferno fingered his damp linen collar nervously. 'Even so, they say Thistlewood and the others will be hanged.'

He shrank back from the window, where he had been standing, and slumped down on the lumpy bed he shared with Doll. She sighed, and went off to the chop house to fetch in some food, as she had done since the Cato Street Conspiracy had been exposed.

When in April the verdict was reached on those who had refused to turn king's evidence, Brunt, Davidson, Ings, Thistlewood and Tidd – all known to Malinferno – were sentenced to be hanged, drawn and quartered. And though their sentences were later commuted to merely hanging, a deed that took place in May, Malinferno decided it was time to sneak away from London for a while. He wondered if his friend Bromhead had anything for him to do that would remove him from the febrile atmosphere of the capital.

'Actually, Giuseppe, I do, as it happens.'

Augustus Bromhead was a strange cove to look at. He was very short of stature, standing at less than five feet tall, but his head was that of a much bigger man. It topped his tiny body like the bulbous head of a tadpole, an effect that was emphasised by the unruly thatch of grey hair and goatee beard he favoured. But he was a giant of a man when it came to intellect and knowledge in his chosen field. Bromhead was an antiquarian of repute, and what he didn't know about King Arthur and all things pertaining to the glorious history of the British Isles was not worth knowing.

He swivelled on the high stool where he perched at his study table, and penetrated his friend Malinferno with a firm gaze. The young man had rushed into his study, hidden high under the eaves of Bromhead's rickety house in Bermondsey, with a look about him that suggested the devil was on his tail. Which did not surprise him, as Malinferno was often getting into scrapes. He had been surprised, however, by the young man's earnest request for a commission that might take him out of London. He knew Malinferno was obsessed with this new craze for all things Egyptian, set in motion by old Nappy Bonaparte. Why all that Egyptian stuff should matter to an Englishman, Bromhead could not fathom. But then, Malinferno was half Italian, so there was no understanding his mind. He addressed his visitor again, taking care to use his proper name, which he knew irritated Joe Malinferno beyond measure.

'But first tell me, Giuseppe, why you want to assist me, when you have nothing but scorn for my researches.'

The pale-faced Malinferno shook his head vigorously, wide-eyed with denial.

'No, no, Augustus, old friend. I have nothing but respect for your studies of English history. Did I not help you with your examination of King Arthur's bones?'

Bromhead snorted. 'Indeed you did, and nearly lost them to body-snatchers and anatomists in the process. I will not trust you with such precious items in the future. However, there is an excavation I want carried out, which I am unable to supervise myself.'

Malinferno groaned. 'Not more old bones? Arthur's bones only got me into trouble, and I am trying to avoid trouble at the moment.'

Bromhead squinted at Malinferno over his little, gold-rimmed spectacles, the light from the fire turning his gaze red. But the young man would not supply any further information about the fix he was obviously in. Bromhead smiled secretively.

'No, it is not bones this time.' He paused dramatically. 'It is treasure.'

Malinferno's eyes lit up. This was more like it – he liked the idea of digging up treasure.

'Where is this treasure?'

'In a moment. First, take a look at this. It is a map drawn up many years ago by Christopher Hawkins of Bath. I found it with the text of a poem he had written about Arthur. An awful poem, by the way.'

Bromhead reached across his desk, and pushed over to Malinferno an old crackly parchment. When he looked at it, he saw an outline of what looked like an island with a series of crosses and arrows marked on it. Malinferno's eyes lit up. This had all the hallmarks of a treasure map. He looked enquiringly at Bromhead.

'Where is this island?'

'Island? It is Solsbury Hill, near Bath.'

Malinferno had fretted for days about how to get to Bath in order to launch his treasure hunt on nearby Solsbury Hill. With no money to get him down there, he was stuck in London despite Augustus' offer. Then a chance meeting with Thomas Elder as he wandered disconsolately around the British Museum had given him part of the solution. A commission in Bath to unroll an Egyptian mummy turned up, something he had done before for the fashionable élite. And it gave him the chance to take Doll with him too. They already had a good act with which to impress their wealthy clients. The trip to Bath was assured, and the dangers of London could be left behind.

Unfortunately, when they got to Bath, he found his reward – their reward – had proved niggardly. The three guineas paid by the duchess would still not be enough to bankroll Bromhead's project.

'I don't know how we are going to get to the site with all the tools we need. The duchess is very sparing with her advance remuneration.'

He jangled the gold coins in his pocket, and looked at Doll. She was draped – dressed was too generous a word to use – in the light muslin shift that she was to wear as Hathor. It did little to hide her charms, which was all to the point. She had been promenading in Bath before returning to the tiny attic room she shared with Malinferno in Cheap Street. He could not help but wonder what the experience had done for the popinjays who frequented the resort. He could imagine the effect of the light from the flaming torchères that lit the Roman baths as they played on her body. Lit from behind, Doll would have appeared naked. An effect she meant to cultivate, as they needed a gullible sponsor for the enterprise that had really brought them to Bath. Apparently, despite a night of debauchery, no more money had been forthcoming.

He looked at the ravishing form of Doll Pocket again, and sighed. But then a thought occurred to him, and he reached over to the bed. Eagerly, he extracted from the deep pocket of his greatcoat two of his most treasured possessions and laid them on the baize-covered card table they were using as both dining and occasional table. He had purloined both items when doing some cleaning work for Thomas Elder at the BM. They had to be worth something.

The scarab beetle glimmered blood red in the evening light that filtered through the dusty windowpanes. But despite its beauty, Malinferno's gaze was drawn instead to the papyrus scroll. Cautiously, he unrolled it, praying that it would not crack into fragments. He was in luck. The ancient fragment opened up to reveal a glorious, multi-coloured spectacle of hieroglyphs. As yet, no scholar had been able to decipher these antique symbols, but Malinferno was determined he would be the one to do so. He had heard of a Frenchman called Champollion who had made some headway. But he had been engulfed in the troubles in France, and no one had heard of him for a while. In England, Thomas Young had toiled for years only to decipher one word. The name – Ptolemy. Malinferno was scornful of his efforts, and knew a golden prize could be in the grasp of the first man to unravel the mystery of the Egyptian writing. He would be that man, and would make a fortune lecturing to the wealthy. Who would then pay far more to hear him than the few paltry guineas he was getting from the duchess.

He reverently touched the surface of the scroll with his fingertips, marvelling at the finely wrought images. But was each symbol a word or a letter? That was the problem.

'Gawd. I'nt it gorgeous.'

Malinferno started from his reverie, and looked over his shoulder. Doll was tired and her accent was slipping again. She was peering over his shoulder, and her ample bosom, artfully lifted, protruded just at his eye level. It was a beautiful sight to behold.

'Oh, yes it is, Doll.'

Doll Pocket's bolstered charms often made a lustful satyr of Joe Malinferno. He licked his lips, as he surveyed Doll's figure. She barely came to his shoulder, but then he was over six feet tall himself. And her blonde curls were fixed in the latest fashion, with a golden bandeau round them holding in place a frothy feather. A severe band of the same colour drew in her thin muslin dress just below her rounded bosom, emphasising its shape. The dress draped seductively over her well-formed hips, falling to her tiny, slippered feet. Despite the rather rumpled nature of her dress, and her bleary, red-rimmed eyes, which spoke of an unsettled night for Doll, the whole effect was of half-concealed voluptuousness. Malinferno dragged his eyes from her with reluctance, looking once again at the papyrus.

'Yes. It is a beautiful thing, is it not.'

Doll snorted contemptuously, and yawned, affording Malinferno a good view of her tonsils.

'Nah. Not that bit of gaudy paper. This.' She leaned forward, pressing her bosom carelessly against him, and scooped up the little ruby scarab. 'Can I have it?'

'No, you can't.' Malinferno smiled wryly. 'Though it would match the colour of your eyes perfectly today.'

Doll pulled a face, and hissed at him cattily. But she did retreat to the oval ormolu mirror that hung over the unlit fireplace.

'Lor', I do look bad, don't I?' She pulled one bleary eyelid down, and examined the mottled orb thus revealed. She decided it was not a pretty sight, and turned away from the unpleasant reflection. 'Only it's not my fault. I was up till all hours with Lord Bywater ... or was it Lord Byworth?'

'Could it have been Lord Byron?' Malinferno offered, not a modicum pleased with his ready wit so late at night. The thought of Doll cavorting with the mad, bad poet was a delectable picture.

'Yeah, that's it. Lord Byron.'

Malinferno hooted with laughter.

'I think not, Doll. The audacious poet of that name has been abroad for a good few years. I believe he is now in Ravenna, not Bath, and good luck to him.'

Doll's features flushed, giving her pale cheeks a more rosy hue.

'The bastard. He said he was Lord Byron, and even dashed off a poem for me. I have it in my reticule.'

She dug around in her little bag for a while, finally giving up the hunt when the piece of paper refused to be found.

'Sod it, I must have lost it. Well, if he wasn't Byron, then the ode wasn't worth the paper it was written on anyway.'

She hawked and coughed in a most unladylike manner, wiping her lips with the back of her hand.

'Come to think of it, the wine he gave me was like sheep's piss too. But the point of the story is that whoever he was, he skipped without paying while I was kipping. Result was, me getting back home with no money, and only your lovely self for company.'

She drew one slender finger seductively down the front of Malinferno's partially undone, soiled linen shirt as she uttered these final words. The professor was unimpressed, and stopped her hand before it reached a region where his brain would cease to function.

'Nice try, Doll. But I will have the scarab back.'

'Damn you, Joe Malinferno.'

Doll stamped her pretty slippered foot, and dropped the ruby scarab she had purloined into Malinferno's upturned palm. He closed his fist over it, and winked at Doll.

'Anyway, I need to sell it, or you and I will not have any means of getting to Solsbury Hill after we do the unrolling for the duchess.'

Doll Pocket gave out a whoop. 'Then we are off on the treasure hunt, after all?'

Malinferno grimaced. 'Yes, if I can sell the scarab.'

As if deliberately trying to annoy him, Doll suddenly cackled like a demented hen, and grabbed Malinferno by the waist. She swung him round in a madcap dance that had the aged floorboards creaking under them.

'Oh, we'll have a real good time, won't we, Joe?'

Her celebration was suddenly drowned out by the most hideous noise Malinferno had ever heard. It resembled the sound of a pedestrianist running the race of his life, gasping for each breath. It would have to be a giant of a man, though, for the breaths were ear-splitting hisses and snorts that rent the air with their exhalations. These frenetic gasps were accompanied by a veritable thrumming, like the parts of a weaving loom, or water pump in a flooded mine, with overtones of howling dogs. Doll pulled up the sash window, and thrust her head out.

'Oh lawks, it's the very devil come to carry us away.'

Malinferno peered over her shoulder, aware of the softness of her skin and the alluring scent that perfumed it. He realised her expostulation was not far from the truth. Slowly rolling to a halt in front of their lodgings was a shiny black four-wheeled coach. But the unnerving thing was that there were no horses attached to the front of it. Smoke and steam roiled around the rear of the coach, giving it the very appearance of some demon's conveyance. The whole contraption vibrated like a living creature. On the driver's seat perched a dwarfish figure wreathed in a dirty green coat, his face obscured by a heavy black mask. Malinferno realised that the sound that resembled howling dogs had in truth been howling dogs. Wherever this hellish coach had come from, it had been chased by a gathering pack of street curs, which yelped and barked at its passage, baring their teeth in fear and loathing. The pack now stood at a safe distance from the steaming rear of the coach, growling and circling. The dwarf rose from his seat, skipped down nimbly to the ground, and threw a stone at the dogs. They slinked away,

apparently more scared of the little demon than his conveyance. He then turned towards Malinferno's lodgings, and
toiled one at a time up the steep steps to the front door. Doll
squealed in a mixture of horror and delight.

'Blimey, Joe, have you made a pact with the devil or something? Because I think he's come to collect.'

It turned out that there was nothing demonic about the
steam-shrouded carriage and its dwarfish driver. In fact, its
appearance heralded another stroke of good fortune for
Malinferno. For, when Joe descended to the front door to
admit the little man, he discovered the conveyance had
indeed come for him. But it was not sent by Satan. The
owner of the new-fangled, steam-powered horseless carriage was none other than the niggardly Duchess of Avon.
The dwarf, John Smallbone by name, pulled the leather
mask with round glass portholes for each eye from his face,
revealing a quite cherubic expression. He explained that
his mistress had sent him to collect 'the professor' as the
venue for the unrolling had been changed. Malinferno
was intrigued, but pulled a face, jingling the coins in his
pocket.

'I am not sure I can afford to work for your mistress, John
Smallbone.'

The dwarf cackled, his chubby face turning bright red
with the effort.

'The mistress is careful with her money, isn't she?' He
tapped the side of his bulbous nose. 'But I think you will
find her more generous due to these changes in circum-
stance.'

'What does the new commission entail?'

'I cannot say, but I am told you are to come with your
actress friend . . .'

Doll, who by now had come down to stand behind Joe, and was listening to the exchange, gave a cry of annoyance.

'Watch it, titch. I ain't no whore of an actress, but a lady.'

The dwarf refrained from adding the epithet 'of the night' to Doll's self-description, contenting himself with a deep bow of insincere contrition.

'My apologies, lady. I meant no offence.' He turned back to Malinferno to continue his explanation. 'As the journey is some distance, I have come in the Trevithick Flyer.' He indicated the infernal conveyance. 'It will easily carry yourselves and your Egyptian mummy to the rites and festivities the duchess has laid on for her special guests.'

Malinferno was not sure about venturing into the unknown. But the lure of further funds was sufficient to cause him to agree to the change in plans. He ushered Doll upstairs to begin packing their meagre belongings, before turning back to John Smallbone.

'You said we had a journey ahead of us. Where are these festivities to be held?'

'Oh, did I not say? The duchess plans a solemn ritual on an ancient and mysterious site some three miles outside Bath. They do say ghosts roam there at night.' His little body shuddered. 'I should not like to be there after dark. It is called Solsbury Hill.'

The journey to Solsbury Hill took longer than anticipated, so Malinferno and Doll Pocket's arrival was closer to dusk than John Smallbone fancied, bearing in mind the ghostly associations he had mentioned. The problem was the Trevithick Flyer, which, it turned out, could not cope with the gradient up from the outskirts of Bath to the hill in question. The horseless carriage huffed and puffed merrily through Bath, drawing attention to its maniacal progress every yard it moved. Fingers pointed at this strange carriage that rolled along without horses, but with a great bubbling canister of steam lashed to its rear portion. And the sight of Smallbone, with his infernal mask once again on his face, was enough to cause many a sign against the devil to be cast his way. But as the ground began to change from level to a steady incline, the carriage rolled along more and more slowly. Malinferno's scientific mind saw that this increased lack of propulsion was in inverse proportion to a growth in alarming sounds emanating from the boiler behind them. The wheezes and sighs that had marked their initial progress forward became louder and more stertorous. The engine was gasping like a labouring runner whose heart and lungs were about to burst. Doll clutched Malinferno's arm in alarm.

'Lawks, what if the boiler explodes, Joe?'

Malinferno pasted a confident smile on his face. A smile that was more optimistic than he felt at heart.

'Trust in science, Doll. Mr Trevithick is a great engineer ...'

Before he could finish his speech lauding the skills of the masterful Cornishman, however, the boiler gave a great, despairing groan. Doll rose from her seat.

'Bugger Mr Trevithick. I'm getting off before we are blown sky high.'

She jumped out of the carriage, and onto the side of the roadway. Malinferno was much pleased that the lightening of the load seemed to assist the labouring engine. The Flyer began to gain speed once more. He leaned out the window to express his sense of triumph. But he was exasperated to see that Doll, even hampered with her long skirts, was walking faster than the engine could propel the carriage. She was rapidly forging ahead, and Malinferno was too embarrassed to call out to her to wait. Finally, a steep hill was reached, and the not-so-winged Flyer gave up the ghost. With a piercing hiss, the steam pressure gave up and groaned out of the emergency release valve. The conveyance was no more, and Malinferno was left red-faced, staring out the carriage window. Doll sat down on a convenient milestone, her legs akimbo, and roared with laughter.

It took John Smallbone an hour to find a farmer who could bring a pair of heavy horses used for ploughing in order to pull the Flyer to its destination. The coach was exceptionally heavy with Trevithick's engine stuck on the back, so eventually the passengers had to descend and walk beside their cumbersome conveyance. In fact, Malinferno was reduced to carrying both his and Doll's baggage. So it was a sweating and purple-faced professor who arrived in the duchess's encampment on Solsbury Hill, along with his prettily perspiring companion and a more conventionally powered carriage, pulled by horses. Doll's muslin dress stuck to her curves, and several of the males in the crowd who had assembled at their arrival had eyes for her barely concealed bosom. Servants in knee-breeches and white powdered wigs scurried across the site, which, with its tents and men on horseback, resembled a grand hiring fair. Or maybe Mr Astley's Amphitheatre of Performing Arts, which usually stood close by Westminster Bridge, for Doll heard a terrible animalistic roar, then spotted, not far away, the brown furry outline of a performing bear tethered to a post in the ground. She almost expected to see tumblers, and a girl standing by a board having knives thrown at her.

John Smallbone leaped from the driver's box, and his dwarfish stature only added to the carnival atmosphere as he bustled across the site to find his mistress, the duchess.

Malinferno muttered in Doll's ear, 'See how the noble

lords are looking at us. I think we are the freak show at this grand spectacle.'

Doll laughed, and passed her handkerchief over her brow.

'I think they are looking at me, Joe. Not you. Though I think someone else has just distracted them.'

She pointed at another carriage, which had just arrived atop Solsbury Hill and debouched a woman dressed in what Doll could only have described as *en Venus*. That is, she was not dressed much further up than the waist, save for an outlandish peasant headdress ornamented with spangles and fluttering ribbons. Malinferno glanced over at her.

'What a trollop. She has no doubt been brought in to entertain the gentlemen after we have played our part in this . . . ridiculous melodrama. Look how they crowd around her, simply because her bosoms are on show.'

Doll poked him in the ribs. 'If her bosom troubles you, then take your eyes off it for a minute. We need to work out how we are going to set up the mummy so we can unroll him for the delectation of this crowd. And did you bring the spades? We have some digging to do when we have finished with the demonstration.'

Malinferno was irritated by Doll's suggestion that he was leering over the middle-aged tart who seemed to have attracted everyone else's attention. But he couldn't help watching until she disappeared in the crowds making their way towards the duchess's tent.

'Yes, yes, of course I have them here. And the scarab and the papyrus, so we can salt the mummy with extra finds. What is more important is how on earth we are going to sneak away in order to dig where Bromhead's map says the treasure is located.'

He fumbled in his greatcoat pocket for the precious piece of paper entrusted to him by his friend Augustus. He unfolded it and pressed the ancient map flat on top of the box that held the remains of the Egyptian mummy. He pointed a finger at the sketchy drawing. It was of the roughly triangular-shaped earthworks with one point of the equal-sided triangle at the bottom. This point was rounded, and to Doll's eyes looked more like a naughty child's sketch of a mound of Venus than anything geographical. She giggled, and Malinferno gave her a funny look before he carried on.

'Look, we came up to the hill on this track running from the south-east, and Augustus's notes suggest we should dig where he has put this cross. This means our site is . . .' He looked up in order to orientate himself, and groaned. '. . . Exactly where the duchess has pitched her tent.'

Doll looked to where Malinferno was pointing. It was one of the more extravagant tents erected on the site, and was obviously the duchess's. They could see her speaking to John Smallbone through the opening facing them. The interior was laid out with carpets and a bed, as if it were an Eastern harem. Or at least Malinferno's image of such a location, though his idea was based only on his intimate knowledge of the rooms in Madame de Trou's brothel in Petticoat Lane. The duchess peered out into the darkening sky, and waved a dismissive hand at Smallbone. The little dwarf bustled back over to Malinferno and Doll Pocket.

'The duchess is annoyed that you are late. She says the banquet has finished, and the guests are awaiting the entertainment.' He pulled a face. 'I am sorry. It is my fault you missed all the food. Let me guide you to the tent where you can prepare for your show. You are on after the dancing bear. I will try to rustle up some cold meat and potatoes.'

He hurried off before Malinferno could explain he did not put on a 'show' like some circus entertainer. He gave his audience an educational experience. He turned to Doll to express his outrage to her, but she was already following Smallbone. She waved a hand at him.

'Come on, Joe, or the show will be late.'

The whole of the southern end of the hill was littered with tents. It was as if an invading army led by Napoleon Bonaparte had landed close to Bath and was about to strike at the very heart of England. But of course rumours of the Emperor's escape from St Helena had long been scotched. England's firmest enemy seemed to be declining into comfortable old age on his tiny island empire.

After clambering over several guy ropes and almost pitching face down over a tent-peg, Malinferno grudgingly entered a small and stiflingly hot tent where Doll was already disrobing. His demeanour improved as he admired her curves, and the pinkness of her flesh. She flashed him a steely look, and threw the long white robe he wore as Anubis over his face.

'Get dressed, you overgrown satyr.'

Doll's vocabulary was improving in leaps and bounds in his company, as was her general education. Her voracious mind swallowed up every piece of history Malinferno could throw at her. She was an amazing autodidact, though often he teased her by describing her more as an idiot savant. She wasn't in any way a fool, however, but rather a very able mind that had been in its raw state when Malinferno had met her. Soon she would be more knowledgeable than he was, if indeed she wasn't already.

'Stop wool-gathering, Joe. We will solve the problem of digging the treasure up soon enough. When everyone is too drunk to stay awake, we can get to work.' She thrust the Anubis jackal-head at him. 'If you can stay sober tonight yourself.'

He nodded his agreement to her resolve. But just then

Smallbone reappeared bearing provender on a tray almost as large as he was. In the middle was a large bottle of red wine. Malinferno licked his lips.

'Just one glass, Doll. To lubricate my vocal cords.'

Doll sighed. 'Very well, but pour one for me too, if you please.'

The bottle was well nigh empty before Malinferno and Doll were led by Smallbone to the large marquee where dinner had taken place. Some of the debris from the repast was still scattered over the white tablecloth. Dramatically, Malinferno swept it all away by yanking the cloth off, and imperiously he commanded the bewigged servants carrying the linen-bound mummy to lay it straight on to the polished surface of the oak table. The guests crowded into the marquee, and his anatomical exhibition began.

Now it was over, he was occupied with levering the intoxicated body of the honourable representative of some rotten borough off Doll's bosom. The phantasmagoria laid on by the duchess had finished, and the box containing the unwrapped mummy was borne away by the servants. Most of the guests had staggered away to their carriages and Bath, or to tents set up on Solsbury Hill. One small group still hovered around the table that bore the remains of the wines and port that had been served over the meal Doll and Joe had missed. At the centre of the little clique stood the old trollop Malinferno had seen arriving soon after they had. Her turban was askew, and her face flushed from drink. Someone whispered in her ear, and she laughed coarsely. Her drooping, veiny dugs wobbled, and she absent-mindedly tweaked one exposed nipple. As though tiring of her entourage she waved them away, and slumped on a balloon-back chair that looked quite out of place on the scuffed grass

of the hill. Malinferno grimaced at the sight of her gargantuan thighs.

'Let's get the spades, and see what we can do about digging for this treasure.'

Doll ignored his whispered command, and pointed at the
old girl. 'I'll be with you in a while. I just want to make sure
she gets to her bed, poor thing.'

Malinferno gave her a curious look, but guessed her intentions were all mixed up with a fellow feeling for the old tart.
There but for the grace of God, and all that. Or for the
grace of Malinferno. He had never thought until now that
he had saved a fallen woman, but he had. It was not something he would say to Doll, though, if he valued his life. He
took one last look at the old woman, who now seemed to
have dozed off, and shrugged his shoulders.

'Very well, but don't be too long tucking her up into bed.
We have work to do tonight.'

He went off to the tent they had used to change into their
Egyptian clothes, and where he had secreted two spades
brought up in the crate containing the mummy. He would
have liked to have retained the crate but it and the mummy
had been whisked away. Doll watched Joe leave the marquee, then rose and sauntered tiredly over to the half-naked
trollop sitting snoring beside the table of scattered bottles.
She rummaged around the debris until she found a bottle
with some dregs of red wine in the bottom. Holding it to
her lips, she tipped it back and drank deep, quenching a
sudden thirst. When she lowered the empty bottle again,
she saw the old woman was scrutinising her with one bleary
eye. Doll smiled.

'Hard work, pleasing them, isn't it?'

The woman laughed with that guttural sound that Doll
had heard earlier across the tent. When she spoke her voice

sounded as though she came from one of the Germanic states, though there was a pleasing melody to it nevertheless. Doll could see there had once been an attractiveness to her, though now her coarsened features gave her more of a homely, careworn appearance. Doll was glad she had kept her vow of getting out of the bawdyhouse as quickly as possible. She wouldn't admit it to Joe, but she was grateful he had not objected when she had latched on to his coat-tails. That night they had met in Madame de Trou's she had first thought of him as an easy touch. But it was not long before she saw how unsure he was of himself, despite all his bluster. She decided he could help her, but she could also help him. They were a good team, even though they often bickered about who was in charge. She tried to concentrate on what the woman was saying.

'. . . my dear, you do not know how hard it is to please everyone. God knows, I have tried, and look where it has left me.'

Doll patted the old girl's well-padded thigh, looking over at the tired remains of the gargantuan meal consumed by the rich and famous. One or two weary-looking servants were beginning to drift into the tent in order to clear up the mess. She imagined that was what the old lady meant – that she was used to being left out with the dregs.

'Well, we can at least find a bed tonight. Some are not so lucky. My name's Doll Pocket, by the way. What's yours?'

For a moment, Doll was aware of a strange look in the other woman's eyes. Then she laughed again, more coarsely with her mouth wide open, exposing her tonsils to Doll's view. When she had managed to control her outburst, she spoke in those melodious tones again.

'You can call me Hat . . . Hattie Vaughan, dear. Now off you go. I shall be fine. They will look after me.'

She waved vaguely at two well-dressed men who were hovering at the entrance to the tent. One had a head of black curly hair and thick mustachios to match, his puffed-out chest and military uniform making Doll think he was a continental – French or Italian, maybe. The other's naval jib and dress sword, together with a languid look, was a clear sign to Doll that he was an upper-class Englishman of the sort she most disliked. He was probably of no great ancestry himself, but put on airs and looked down on anyone not of the highest rank.

Her new friend, Hattie, waddled over to them and, much to Doll's surprise, they fawned over her as if she was of high estate and not some ageing trollop. Maybe she had connections with the Prince Regent – or King, as he now was by some months. He was a rake of the greatest degree. Doll even wondered if Mrs Vaughan could be another in a long line of mistresses that included Mrs Fitzherbert, the Countess of Jersey and the Marchioness of Hertford – to name but a few whom the one-time Prince Regent had rogered. Hattie took each of her beaux by the arm and walked out of the tent and into the night. Doll, remembering her assignation with Joe and a spade, hurried after them.

As she picked her way over the obstacle course of guy-ropes and tent-pegs, she passed the Trevithick Flyer. Its boiler was now cold, and the device gave the appearance of somnolence. Or death. Unlike the carriage standing next to it. It was a small Tilbury gig, inside which someone was burning the midnight oils. She could make out, by the light of one of the side lamps, the silhouette of a man bent over a writing slope. The folding top of the Tilbury was pulled up, and as she passed the gig, she saw the man was scribbling in a notebook. He was bowed low, however, and his nether limbs were wrapped in a horse-blanket against the chill of the night.

She could not make out more than his dark greatcoat, and thinning brown hair straggling down below his beaver. His hunched shoulders suggested someone on a very secretive task, and Doll's interest was piqued. She was about to sneak up on him to assuage her curiosity, when she heard a hissing sound from behind her. She looked back at a gap between two areas of canvas, and saw the shape of a man hidden in a heavy greatcoat holding two spades. She stepped back cautiously from the Tilbury gig.

'Joe Malinferno, you nearly made me jump out of my skin.'

Malinferno dragged her further away from the man in the gig before he spoke.

'What were you doing, poking your nose in where it is not wanted? We have a job to do. I have been waiting ages for you to meet me behind the duchess's tent. I had to come looking for you.'

He thrust a spade at her, and she stared at it in horror.

'You don't think I'm going to use that, do you? I will ruin my dress, and my gloves.'

Malinferno refrained from suggesting she take both off in that case. He knew when Doll was not in the mood for his innuendo. He simply growled in frustration, and stalked off through the encampment. His noble anger was spoiled by the fact that he tripped over a guy-rope and nearly fell headlong into someone's tent. Whoever it was, their snores suggested Joe had failed to wake him with his clumsiness.

Doll stifled a giggle and followed him to the edge of the ring of tents where the duchess's gilded bivouac stood. They huddled together round the back like two schoolboys bunking off school to attend a hiring fair. Malinferno produced the much-folded sheet of paper that Augustus Bromhead had given to him.

'I've been looking at Hawkins' map again, and I think at least one of the crosses marked is here.' He scuffed the toe of his boot on a bare patch of earth a few yards away from the tent wall. Doll peered over his shoulder at the bewildering scratchings on the old piece of paper. She had looked at it before, but the blotchy arrows and crosses still meant nothing to her. She would leave it up to Joe, who seemed confident of his topographic skills. She shrugged, and offered to take his greatcoat.

'The least I can do is hold it while you dig.'

Malinferno grunted and, shrugging off the heavy coat, he handed it to her. He spat on his hands, and picked up one of the spades. His first thrust in the unyielding turf convinced him this treasure hunt was going to be harder work than he had anticipated. After half an hour of toil, he removed his jacket and loosened his cravat. Much to his indignation, Doll spread his greatcoat on the ground, and lay down on it. She yawned, staring up at the almost full moon that illuminated the scene. Grimly, Malinferno dug on. After an hour, all he had to show for his efforts was a very deep hole, some rusty nails and two rather worn old coins. As well as some blisters on his palms. He rubbed the coins vigorously, but could not figure out whose head was on them.

'I shall have to take them back to Augustus to see if they are worth anything. Maybe I should dig elsewhere.'

His comment as to the appropriateness of the site he had chosen was lost on Doll. She was fast asleep with his coat wrapped snugly around her. Just as he was about to call out to her and wake her up, there was a wail from within the duchess's tent.

Doll started into wakefulness. 'What on earth was that?'

'Some noise from the duchess's tent.'

By this time Doll was sitting up, clutching Malinferno's greatcoat around her bare shoulders.

'A noise? It was more like a banshee scream.' She shivered. 'Go and see what it was, Joe.'

'Send the poor bloody infantry in, as usual.'

Doll huffed, and waved her hands at Joe, encouraging him to his feat of bravery.

'Please, Joe.'

Malinferno was unsure what he might find in the tent, and gripped his spade all the tighter. He stalked round the tent's perimeter, advanced towards the tent flap, and nervously lifted it. In the darkness, he could just make out the shape of the crate that held what was left of the duchess's mummy. Beyond it was one of the largest beds he had ever seen. In fact he had never seen a larger one, especially one marooned on a hillside in the middle of nowhere. A woman sat on the edge of the bed staring fixedly at the wooden crate, the lid of which was askew. Malinferno breathed a sigh of relief. The duchess must have woken in the night, accidentally dislodged the lid of the crate, and been frightened by the rictus grin of the mummy's embalmed head. But as he lifted the flap of the tent higher to gain access, the moonlight spilled inside, and he saw the woman was not the Duchess of Avon. It was the old trollop. She was breathing heavily, her bare bosom heaving, and pointing to the makeshift coffin. Malinferno took a step towards her, and tried to calm her nerves.

'Don't be afraid, madam. It is only the remains of a long-dead pharaoh. He can do you no harm.'

The woman took a deep breath, and with her Germanic accent, roughly put Malinferno right. 'What is in the box is not long dead. And it can most assuredly do me great harm, young man.'

She waved a finger at the crate imperiously, and a puzzled Malinferno went to take a look. Inside the coffin was not the dried corpse of an Egyptian pharaoh, but the still-warm body of a once vigorous-looking, soldierly man with thick black hair and full moustachios. He looked back at the old woman, whose face appeared to go grey before his eyes. She looked as if she might expire in front of him, and he realised he was standing there with a weapon of violence in his hand. He laid the spade on the ground and, uneasily, called quietly to Doll.

'Doll, I need your help in here.'

Hardly daring to tear his eyes off the old woman, he heard the rustle of Doll's dress behind him. She hissed in his ear.

'What's up now? Lawks!'

Either she had peered over his shoulder and seen the body, or observed the state of her erstwhile companion of an hour ago. Whichever it was, Malinferno prayed that Doll would take control of the situation. Because it was going all to hell in front of his eyes. The old woman slumped on the bed, her fat rump presented to his view. Her swoon caused the bed to tilt alarmingly.

Doll slid past Joe, and pulled the bedsheet over Hattie Vaughan, feeling her wrist for a pulse. Hattie groaned and sat up, causing the bed once again to tip like a ship in a stormy sea.

'I'm fine, dearie. I just had a funny turn, is all. My stomach feels queer, but then, that's no surprise after seeing my dear Sacchi in that box there.'

Doll looked for the first time into the box that should have contained the mummy they had worked on that evening. She gasped.

'Joe, there's a body in the crate. And I don't mean Ozzy, the old pharaoh.'

Doll had a penchant for naming all the mummies that passed through their hands as Ozymandias, after the great carved head that had been brought back to England from Egypt four years earlier. And when two years later, Shelley had written his poem of the same name, she was confirmed in her prejudice that all dead Egyptians were called by that wonderful name. Malinferno chose not to correct her, as he was none the wiser either concerning the name of the mummy they had recently unrolled. Besides, they had more urgent matters to resolve.

'Yes, I know. The old girl called him Sacchi.'

Doll glared at Malinferno for calling Hattie so before her face. But then she began to look more closely at the body.

'Look here. He's got a big gash in his neck.'

Malinferno watched in amazement as Doll's head and shoulders disappeared into the crate, leaving her hips and legs wriggling around as she squirmed further inside. Personally, he could not get so close to a fresh corpse, much preferring the musty odour of someone long dead. Hattie was looking on surprise too, and Doll's antics must have tickled her. She broke out into a coarse peal of laughter.

'Poor Sacchi, he would have loved a romp with you, dearie. But alas all that is over for him now.'

Doll wriggled back out of the box, rather red-faced from her exertions.

'There is little blood in the box, so he must have been shoved into it some time after he was killed. And there are slashes on the fingers of his left hand. He must have got his hand on the blade, trying to save himself. But he was too late.'

Hattie gaped at Doll. 'I had you for a whore, young lady. It seems you are something else altogether.'

Doll laughed out loud. 'I had you for a trollop, Hattie Vaughan. Now I am not so sure.'

353

At that moment, another man burst through the tent flap. It was the naval officer Doll had seen accompanying Hattie along with the now deceased Italian gentleman by the name of Sacchi. The navy man seemed hot and rather unnerved, speaking hurriedly and with somewhat slurred words.

'Are you safe, Your Majesty? I came to relieve Sacchi, but he is nowhere to be seen.' He stared at Doll Pocket and Joe Malinferno. 'Who are these people?'

'Lieutenant Houghton!'

The old woman gave him a stern look, but it was too late to hide the truth now. Doll and Malinferno had heard what the man had called Hattie. It suddenly dawned on them who the old trollop was. She was no less than the errant Queen of England, Caroline of Brunswick.

Caroline, after a failed marriage to the Prince of Wales, as he was then, had retired abroad to a life bent on embarrassing England and the royal household. Openly taking a string of lovers, she had travelled Europe causing scandal. In retaliation, the Prince – no mean philanderer himself – initiated secret commissions and open smears to discredit her. The Princess of Wales, using a string of villas in Italy, finally settled down to the extent that she fixed on one of her lovers – Pergami by name – and was most often seen in his company. She was congenitally unable to moderate her behaviour, however. Servants were known to report to the Prince's spies that 'the princess is very fond of fucking', having seen her in public with her hand inside Pergami's trousers. Or having observed him emerging from the Queen's chamber dressed only in his shirt.

Close to accepting a divorce, everything changed for Caroline, when her father-in-law died. She was now Queen, and horrified the government of the day by suggesting she should return to England to take up her place on the throne alongside her husband. Malinferno was familiar with a few Radicals whose sympathy lay with the Queen. And at a time when the common mob was agitating for better conditions, the government was afraid that Caroline could be a rallying point. To many, she was an injured queen and a weak woman, who needed the mob's help to fight against a tyrant king. When she had finally arrived in London the cry was 'The Queen for ever, the King in the river.'

Malinferno was sure he had read in *The Times* that she had escaped the incessant pressure of the mob by hiding in a mansion on the Thames. He was surprised to have found her at an exotic soiree on Solsbury Hill. He bowed his head to the tired woman sitting on the edge of the grand bed, that was tilted at an alarming angle.

'Your Majesty, forgive me for not recognising you. *The Times* reported that you were at Brandenburg House in Hammersmith, on the edge of London.'

Caroline sighed. 'Indeed I was, and the countryside suited me. But those infernal watermen of the Thames made a trade of offering trips to get sightings of me walking in the gardens. When the Duchess of Avon mentioned her little soiree on Solsbury Hill, I determined to escape in secret, and have a few days unobserved. It seems I failed, however, and that there is a spy and *agent provocateur* in the camp right now.'

As the Queen spoke to Malinferno, Houghton had drifted over towards the crate. He placed a hand on the edge and leaned on it in a nonchalant pose. Caroline noticed this, and turned to him.

'I would not get too close, if I were you, Nicholas.'

The unenlightened Houghton looked down at his hand, expecting that he was being warned the wood was dirty or wet. He began to brush his hands together, and looked down at the crate. His eyes widened at the contents of the box, and he slumped against Doll Pocket in a faint.

'Oh, not again.'

She groaned as another man's head landed on her bosom, and in a not too gentle way, dumped his prostrate form on the grassy floor of the tent.

Caroline smiled sadly. 'I would hazard a guess that he is a naval man who has not been much under fire, then.'

Doll laughed. 'Nor will he be much help in present circumstances, it appears. I suppose Your Majesty is innocent of the crime concerning the body in our crate, then?'

Malinferno felt his face burning at Doll's boldness, and began to apologise for his companion's social gaffe. 'Majesty, I am afraid Miss Pocket is unused to—'

Caroline interrupted him before he could go any further. 'Stuff and nonsense, sir. Miss Pocket has asked the most necessary of questions in the circumstances. And I think you should both still call me Hattie, while I am incognito. Hat Vaughan was a name Sir William Gell gave me when we . . . we needed to be discreet, if you get my drift. It will suit the situation well for now.'

Houghton groaned and began to revive, sitting up with his head in his hands. Making a valiant effort to repair his reputation, he tried again to take control.

'Majesty, let me deal with this. I . . . oooh.'

Having made the mistake of taking one more look at the crate, he almost swooned away again, collapsing this time on the edge of the great bed. The Queen poked at him and, getting no response, slid past him to examine the contents of the crate. Though she gave a sharp intake of breath, she managed to control her reactions this time. Malinferno could see she was made of sterner stuff than the naval officer, who sat with his head between his knees.

'Perhaps then you could answer Miss Pocket's question, Your— Mrs Vaughan. Are we to eliminate you from the list of potential murderers?'

The old woman looked grim. 'I can only give you my word that I am innocent. I believe Miss Pocket saw me leave the marquee in the company of both the deceased, and ...' she poked Houghton with her finger again. '... the lieutenant here. We came back to the tent that the duchess had so kindly vacated for me, and I retired, leaving Signor Sacchi on guard outside the entrance.'

'And the box was there all the time?'

'Yes. I was led to understand that the duchess had it brought to her tent after your ... enlightening lecture. Neither she nor I had any qualms about being next to a corpse. In fact, there was something quite thrilling about sleeping with a pharaoh.'

Malinferno was about to advise her that the mummy was probably not that of a pharaoh, but of a priest or rich trader. But he could see she was keen to talk, and he let her continue.

'I fell into a deep sleep that was broken only by some noise that intruded into my dreams.'

'What sort of noise, Hattie? Can you describe it?'

It was Doll's turn to carry on the interrogation, and Malinferno marvelled at her ability to act quite normally in the presence of such a notorious figure as Queen Caroline. In only a few days, this woman standing before them was effectively to go on trial in Parliament. A Bill was to be presented in the House that accused the Queen of conducting herself with 'indecent and offensive familiarity' with Bartolomeo Pergami, and of carrying on a 'licentious, and adulterous intercourse' with him. The end result of a vote in the House in favour of the Bill would be to strip the Queen of her title and prerogatives, and dissolve her marriage with the King. Now, she seemed more concerned with establishing her innocence as concerns the murder of one of her paramours. Pergami had been left behind on the continent, but it appeared there were others in her entourage who kept her amused. Sacchi had obviously been one of them, and it would have suited her to have him silenced.

The Queen's description of what had woken her was inconclusive. Was it a scraping sound or a groan? Was it someone murdering Sacchi, or heaving his body into the crate? Caroline fiddled with the pink turban that lay on the bed, and plonked it on her head. It sat at an odd angle amidst her tangled, thinning hair.

'All I can say is that I woke up, and thought I heard a person in the tent. When I looked over towards the entrance, I could see the lid of the box had been moved. I thought at first someone had tried to steal from the box, but when I looked in, I saw Sacchi looking out at me.' She sighed. 'Only he wasn't. Looking out, I mean. His eyes were devoid of life. Poor bugger.'

Malinferno was quite taken with the Queen's strange mixture of demure English and coarse Germanic expressions. He could see how people could fall in love with her common touch. Doll, meanwhile was all business.

'Why do you think he was killed? Did he disturb a thief, who was out to rifle the treasures of the pharaoh? He would have been sorely disappointed, if he was. There was not much to take.'

She cast a meaningful glance at Malinferno, knowing that he had already stripped the body of trinkets, removing them as he unbound the wrappings in front of the crowd earlier. His hands were as nimble as any pickpocket from the lowest rookery or flash-house in the East End. Malinferno blushed, and the little hoard of jewels and keepsakes suddenly burned a hole in his pocket. Before he could say anything though, the Queen spoke up firmly.

'No. I believe this was done to further discredit me. The Government is unsure whether they can win a majority in the House to condemn me. If I were to be associated with the grisly murder of one of my equerries, it would be the end. They wouldn't have to prove anything. It would be enough for the possibility to exist, and for the rumours to fly.'

She took Doll's hand in hers, pleading in her eyes. 'You must help me find out who did this. Find the government spy in the party, and you will have the murderer. And at the same time save me from a fate worse than death. I mean the loss of all that is mine by rights.'

Strangely, it was Malinferno, not Doll, who then came up with the most practical decision. Moving over to the crate, he decisively pulled the lid closed over the corpse, and pushed one of the protruding nails down into its former hole.

'We shall say no more to anyone about the death of Sacchi, only that he is missing, and we wish to know what might have happened to him.' He turned to Queen Caroline. 'If a body will jeopardise your standing and chances of defeating this Bill in Parliament, then there will be no body. If the murder was done to embarrass you, then how to materialise the lost body will vex the killer in the extreme. He might give himself away.'

Caroline clapped her hands in delight, while Houghton at last looked relieved that the corpse was consigned out of sight, if not out of mind.

'Professor, you are a genius.'

Malinferno took the compliment with a gracious smile, only noticing over the Queen's shoulder a wry smile on Doll's face. He could tell she was not much impressed by his plan, which had been blindingly obvious. He pulled a face back at her, as much as to say, 'Well, I said it first.' What he did say was that he and Doll would undertake to make enquiries as the lords and ladies of the encampment rose from their beds.

'If the person who perpetrated the deed is still here on Solsbury Hill, we will find him out. If the murderer has already decamped in the night, then by doing that he will have revealed himself, and will just need apprehending.'

When Doll and Malinferno left the Queen to her ablutions, Lieutenant Houghton followed them out of the tent. He called for them to wait a moment, but made sure they were all three far enough away from the incognito Queen to speak without being overheard. He was nervous, poking the ground with the end of the gilded scabbard housing his ceremonial sword.

'You need to know that the Queen did not go straight to bed last night. After I had left the tent with Sacchi on guard, I was restless and took a little walk to that oak grove over there.'

He pointed to the stunted woods on the north-western edge of the encampment. Malinferno guessed that Houghton had not walked there for exercise. He had observed many male guests sneaking in that direction to piss away the drink that had been consumed in vast quantities during the festivities. Doll winked at Joe, implying she knew the purpose of Houghton's stroll also. The naval lieutenant coughed, and continued his narrative.

'When I came back past the tent, I saw Sacchi in conversation with a man. A very large gentleman with the distinctive braying voice of a politician.'

Doll and Malinferno exchanged glances. He must be

referring to the Honourable Member of Parliament who had last night nestled in Doll's bosom.

'He appeared to want to speak to the Queen, knowing her true identity. He had to pass Sacchi some coins before he could enter the tent, however. I would not have allowed it, nor have lowered myself to bribery, but Sacchi is an Italian . . .'

He waved a hand as though that was enough explanation for the misconduct of his fellow equerry. He was quite unaware of Malinferno's antecedents on his father's side, and Joe held his temper. He thanked the lieutenant tersely, and they parted company.

Doll giggled. 'Never mind, Joe. You might be a low Eye-talian on the one side, but you are all stiff, starchy Englishman on the other.'

Malinferno made a face, and poked Doll in the ribs. As they were returning to their tent, the camp began to rouse around them. It was mostly servants they saw, who were up and about lighting fires, and scurrying back and forth from the main marquee to a large tent on the periphery of the encampment. It was altogether a more functional-looking affair than the highly decorated marquee. Made of thick canvas, it bore the stains of long and heavy use. Large tin funnels stuck up above the apex of the canvas, and smoke was already rising from them. The aroma of cooking meats emerged from the tent flaps. Doll licked her lips.

'The well-to-do don't stint themselves, do they? Even when they are picnicking, so to speak.'

'Some picnic that is,' commented Malinferno, as a liver-ied servant hurried over the grassy embankment with a large silver dish in his hands. He sniffed as the man passed them.

'Boiled beef.'

Doll and Joe exchanged looks, and nodded in tacit agreement. The investigation could wait until their stomachs were fed. They followed the servant into the marquee, Malinferno providing the necessary justification.

'After all, it is most likely we will encounter those we wish to interview there. And it is not as though we have fresh linen to change into in our tent.' He brushed down his soiled coat. 'We shall have to make do as we are.'

Inside the marquee, the semi-shade might have obscured a clear view of who had already risen. But a forest of candles burned around the tables, their light gleaming off the silver cutlery set on the not so pristine white linen from the night before. When Doll and Joe cast around to see who was there, they were gratified to see the vast corpulence of the Honourable Member for the rotten borough of Plympton Erle, Sir Ralph St Germans. He was already gorging himself on a plateful of boiled beef and potatoes. With a polite murmur of apology, Malinferno sat himself and Doll opposite.

As though by magic, plates of food appeared at their elbows. Malinferno recognised the pattern of red dragons encircling the plate. It was the highest quality Meissen porcelain – a far cry from the two chipped plates they had been dining on before escaping London. He had a passing thought of slipping the plates under his coat after he had cleaned them of the beef. But when he looked guiltily up at Doll, he saw that she had read his thoughts. She was nodding towards St Germans, who had merely grunted at their intrusion and continued to eat his way through the full plate of food.

Malinferno coughed. 'Sir Ralph, my name is Malinferno. I believe we have a mutual acquaintance by the name of Mrs Hattie Vaughan.'

The corpulent Member of Parliament paused in his trencherman efforts, and gave Joe a startled look. It took in his shabby coat, and grubby linen, and caused Malinferno to blush. St Germans chortled, revealing a mouthful of half-chewed food.

'I hardly think she is an acquaintance of yours, sir. You would not presume to claim a propinquity, if you knew who she really was.'

Malinferno grinned wolfishly. 'And you, sir, make a terrible mistake, if you think, on such a short acquaintance with me, that I do not know the lady is one who will soon be the subject of an enquiry involving yourself and your parliamentary colleagues.'

St Germans' face turned bright purple, and he began to choke on the half-chewed beef he had just begun to swallow. As he coughed uproariously, Doll rose and politely patted him on the back to relieve his discomfort. Recovering, the fat man waved away the bewigged servants, who had rushed over to his side. They retreated to a more discreet distance, probably regretting being unable to listen in on a conversation that had caused such a reaction. St Germans wiped his mouth with his napkin.

'You know it is she, by God. Then you can imagine why I was in her tent last night. Though I must say there was no impropriety involved.' He glanced nervously at Doll. 'Despite the rumours of her licentiousness, I am prepared to believe the best of her. My hope in speaking to her was to convince her that her best course of action was to give up her quest to be crowned alongside the King. He will not allow it, and neither will the Government. Needless to say, I was not successful in my campaign.'

'And when you left, did you see the gentleman outside the tent? Mr Sacchi?'

St Germans looked puzzled by Malinferno's enquiry, his beady eyes almost disappearing into his puffy face.

'What of him?'

'He was there when you entered, and when you left?'

'Why, yes. When I arrived at the tent, I had to give him a guinea, or he would not have granted me access to the Quee— to Mrs Vaughan. Damned scoundrel is an Italian, you know. I should have kicked him up the backside, but I needed to speak with the lady. I cut him when I left, naturally.'

For a moment, Malinferno thought the MP meant he had been responsible for the murder. Then breathed a sigh as he realised St Germans was only employing the vernacular to point out his deliberate ignoring of the venal Italian. Swallowing yet another slight about his half-fellow country-man, he thanked the man for the information, and was about to get up, when St Germans leaned across the table. He peered at Malinferno, as if trying to gauge the man.

'What is all this about Sacchi? Why are you so interested in him?'

Malinferno waved a hand in dismissal of the enquiry. 'He has not been seen this morning, and Mrs Vaughan expressed some concern, that is all.'

St Germans pushed away from the table, causing a minor earthquake amongst the crockery on it, and rose ponderously.

'I wouldn't be surprised, if he has decamped with the duchess's silver.'

He laughed and turned to leave. Then he paused, and looked back at Malinferno and Doll Pocket.

'If you truly want to know his whereabouts, you would do no worse than ask Mr Powell. His carriage is still here, I believe. The Tilbury next to that infernal machine of the duchess's.'

With no more explanation, the august Member for

Plympton Erle waddled out of the marquee. Malinferno shot a look at Doll, who had remained silent during the whole interrogation of St Germans.

'What do you think, Doll? Was he angry enough at Sacchi to have slit his throat?'

Doll shook her head, and slipped the last piece of beef from her plate into her mouth. She stared longingly at the Meissen plate, and then sighed.

'We can't steal them, can we?'

Malinferno cast a quick, frightened look around. The servants closest to them appeared not to have heard. He hissed at Doll, 'Don't even think it.'

She laughed. 'Why not? You did, when you saw them. But in answer to your question, no, I don't think he would have killed Sacchi for the man having extorted a guinea out of him.'

'I agree. But who is this Powell he referred to? And why should he know about Sacchi's movements?'

Doll tapped the side of her nose. 'I think I have an idea about that. Eat up, and I'll be back in a minute.'

She disappeared out of the marquee, and Malinferno continued to fill his belly. When he had finished, and Doll hadn't returned, he shrugged and called for another glass of red wine. As he drank that down, she reappeared, wearing her demure poke bonnet that she only put on if she wished to play the part of his virginal sister, a role that was required normally only to win over suspicious landladies. She sat down beside Malinferno, and took off the bonnet, placing it on the table. She grinned.

'He is coming to breakfast, so we must act quickly.'

Malinferno frowned. 'Who is coming?'

Doll twirled the ribbons of her bonnet flirtatiously. 'Why, Mr Powell, of course. Look, here he is.'

She nodded her head in the direction of a slim-built man, who at that moment had just entered the marquee. His clothes looked as rumpled as Malinferno's, though being better cut, they had borne the night's depredations more sturdily. His cravat was retied and elegantly chivvied into shape, unlike Malinferno's, which hung limply under his chin and was now stained with gravy. He watched as the man chose an area of the tent well away from them, and the glare of the numerous candles. When he sat, Doll nudged Joe, and they rose from their place at the table.

'Come on. We can search his gig now.'

Malinferno was still at a loss, but followed Doll, who clutched her bonnet to her bosom. He pointed at it.

'Aren't you going to put your bonnet back on, seeing as you went out of your way to fetch it?'

Doll grinned. 'My bonnet is already well filled, Joe.'

She shook it slightly, and he heard the rattle of fine porcelain. He stopped her and peered in the bonnet. A red dragon lay curled in its straw and lace folds.

'You stole them, after all. Two Meissen plates?'

'Three. I took St Germans' plate too. I wanted to allow for breakages.'

He stopped in his tracks, shaking his head in disbelief.

Hurrying ahead, Doll motioned for him to follow. 'Come on. We don't have a lot of time.' She skipped across the grassy sward and past the Trevithick Flyer to an undistinguished-looking little gig with its hood pulled up.

'Here, hold my bonnet.'

She thrust the headgear with its stolen goods into Malinferno's hands, and clambered up the step of the Tilbury, and on to the bench seat. It was a small open gig, so there would be few places to hide what she was looking for safely. She poked around unsuccessfully at first. Malinferno, aware of the incriminating contents of Doll's bonnet, and eager not to be seen with purloined goods, poked his head inside the gig.

'What are you looking for? How do you know this is Powell's carriage? And who is he?'

She ignored him, and finally, fumbling under the seat, she found a little compartment hidden away. She felt inside, and pulled out the writing slope she had seen the man using in the early hours of the morning. Opening it, she saw the notebook he had been writing in. She waved it in Malinferno's face.

'This proves it. When St Germans hinted that Powell would know Sacchi's movements, he was telling us that Powell is the spy that Hattie feared had been dogging her footsteps. This carriage is drawn up behind ours, and must have arrived late. And after Hattie's coach. When I walked past it in the early hours, there was a man in it, wrapped in a blanket as though he had nowhere to lay his head other than the gig. So I deduced he had not planned to be here. Until he found himself following his quarry from Bath.'

She opened the notebook and looked inside. 'And who but a spy would write in code.'

Malinferno laid the bonnet on the ground and grabbed the book off her. 'You could not have known he was writing in code until you just looked at the book.'

Doll pouted. 'Well, no. But it was a good guess, wasn't it?' She hopped down and stood beside him, reading over his shoulder. 'Can you make out what it says?'

Malinferno read from the opening entry in the book: '"August, 1818. The whole affair is much canvassed by number eight and number six, though the proper authority is not forthcoming."'

Doll was perplexed, and a little disappointed.

'Who is number eight and number six? The Prince
Regent? The Prime Minister? How do we decipher it?'

Malinferno was flicking through the pages, scanning for
clues. He pointed a trembling finger at a later entry.

'"1819. Number eight has no proof of an intimate connection between number one and number ten." Number
one is surely Caroline – Hattie, I mean – as she is the purpose of Powell's investigation. That would then imply the
King – the Prince Regent then – should be number two. So
number eight or number six would be the instigator of all
this dirty work – the Prime Minister, Lord Liverpool, or the
House of Commons generally.'

'And number ten has to be Baron Pergami, who Hattie
left behind on her return to England. Are there any more
references to number ten after she came back?'

Malinferno turned page after page until he came close to
the end.

'No, there isn't. But look here. The entry for the 29th of
January this year reads merely, "Number one is now
Queen." The later entries get quite rambling after that, with
references to numbers from sixteen to twenty-three. We will
never know who they are.'

But Doll was undaunted. 'And the last entry? What was he
writing about when I saw him in the dark?'

Malinferno looked closely at the cramped hand in the
notebook. It was increasingly difficult to decipher, as though
Powell was getting more and more disturbed about his task
and its ramifications. Was number twenty-three Sacchi? Or
Houghton? He read the last entry, and gasped.

Doll looked at him. 'What is it, Joe? What have you seen?'

Just as Malinferno was about to tell Doll what he had read,
the gig gave a lurch. Someone was climbing in from the
other side, and it had to be Powell. Malinferno grabbed

Doll's arm, and they edged round the back of the Tilbury. Once out of sight of the man climbing back into his conveyance, they made for the rocky outcrop nearby. After they had sat down behind the biggest rock, Malinferno realised two things. He was still clutching the pocket book, and he had left Doll's bonnet with the stolen plates on the ground beside the gig. He opened the book where he had placed his finger.

'Listen to this. The last entry reads "I need to deal with number twenty-three."'

Doll looked questioningly at Malinferno. 'Twenty-three? Could that be Sacchi?'

'Only Powell knows that, and we can hardly ask him directly if he is the one who did for Sacchi.'

'We could ask Sir Ralph.'

'Doll, you are a genius. He was the one put us on to Powell. He may know more. But where can we find him?'

The site was still a mass of tents, and St Germans could be in any of them. They rose cautiously from behind the rock, and sauntered nonchalantly past the Tilbury gig. Powell glared suspiciously out of the interior, his empty writing slope in his hands. But Malinferno knew that all he saw was a man and a woman who looked as though they had been occupied in some indiscreet activity behind the rocks. Doll smiled sweetly at him and hugged Malinferno's arm, as if in confirmation of the spy's guess. Malinferno did notice that Doll's bonnet was no longer on the ground. As it could not have blown away with its purloined contents inside, he presumed Powell must have it. It was evidence of who had taken his notebook. They hurried on, hoping to find the duchess, who might know where Ralph St Germans was to be found. Powell got down from his gig and stared after them.

It did not take them long to find their employer. She was standing at the entrance to the marquee, talking to a tall, angular man in practical clothes and muddy shoes. She spotted Doll and Malinferno, and beckoned them over.

'I am glad to have found you, Professor. This is my managing agent, Orford. He wants to know whether you have any further need of the crate in my tent.'

Malinferno cast a wary look at the manager of the duchess's estates. Had he tried to move the crate containing Sacchi's body already? It was much heavier than would have been the case if it still contained the mummy, and may have given the game away. Orford looked a little careworn, but otherwise normal. Malinferno assumed his look was because of having to manage the whole entourage surrounding them. He shuffled as if anxious to be on the move, and thrust out his hand.

'Daniel Orford, sir. I was only desirous of arranging the movement of the crate in order to begin the dismantling of the tent. Everything must come down today, and so I have a lot to do.'

Malinferno took his hand, which was cold and dry, and felt the calluses of a working man on it. Evidently Orford did not limit his activities to the estate office. The duchess, ever full of irrelevant babble, intervened before Malinferno could say anything about the crate.

'You should talk to Orford, Professor Mal . . .' She waved her hand in a vague way to fill in her inability to remember his name. 'Daniel is a student of antiquities, and is terrifically keen on King Arthur. Is that not the case, Daniel?'

Orford blushed at the revelation, looking at the ground. 'In a very amateur way, madam.'

The duchess turned to Doll, assuming that, as a fellow female, she would be as ignorant and uncaring about such matters as she was.

'Of course, it is all beyond us, dear, this delving in the past. Digging holes in the ground to find worm-eaten skeletons and . . . other such stuff. Though I am sure the professor loves his ancient pharaohs quite as much as Bonaparte did.'

Doll remembered the abandoned trench behind the duchess's tent that Joe had dug. The discovery of the body in the crate had quite put it out of both their minds. She wondered if anyone had noticed it yet.

She smiled at the duchess. 'Oh, I am sure these men know what they are doing, standing up to their knees in mud with a spade in their hands. Myself, I would much prefer to walk down the streets of London or Bath and find a new bonnet shop.'

He saw Malinferno's face fall, as he took her hint about the trench he had dug. They would have to fill it in as quickly as they could before Daniel Orford began clearing the tents. It also made her wonder for the first time where the mummy had gone that had occupied the box before it had been used to conceal Sacchi. She nudged Malinferno as the duchess prattled on about dresses and bonnets. Roused to action, he took Orford's arm and they walked away from the women. He took savage pleasure in seeing the pleading look in Doll's eyes as the duchess compared the merits of a poke bonnet to a stove-pipe straw bonnet in full sunshine.

He and Orford walked towards the tent where the crate stood.

'I will gladly remove the crate and its contents, if I can have use of a carriage to return it to Bath, Mr Orford.'

The managing agent hesitated, breaking stride for a moment. He took Malinferno's arm.

'I had not intended to bother you with the shipping of the crate. The Egyptian mummy is the property of the duchess, is it not? I can easily arrange for it to be removed to the duchess's country house. She will not want it in Bath. No, I only wanted to ensure that there was nothing of yours in the crate first.'

Malinferno was almost inclined to say there was nothing of his there, but that there was plenty belonging to the Queen. They had stopped outside the duchess's tent. He hesitated about going inside, wondering if Orford knew of Queen Caroline's presence. And his mind was whirling, thinking how he could remove Sacchi's body before Orford loaded it on a cart, and it ended up in the duchess's stately home. There, the growing smell might cause a servant to realise it was not a three-thousand-year-old body, but one of much more recent origins.

How to divert Orford was solved by the timely arrival of Doll Pocket. Swirling the folds of her muslin dress around her curves, she took Orford's arm, and manoeuvred him away from the tent and the crated body of Sacchi.

'Mr Orford, the duchess tells me you know a lot about the history of the very hill on which we are standing. That it might have been the site of a battle involving King Arthur. Do tell me all about it. I have an interest myself in the location of Arthur's bones.'

Reluctantly, Orford allowed himself to be drawn away from the matter of the crate, and he began to relate the story of the Battle of Mount Badon. Though he did still manage to call out some advice to Malinferno: 'Don't concern yourself about the crate, sir. I will deal with it.'

Malinferno waved a hand at the retreating couple, and ducked his head through the tent flap. Inside, he was surprised to see the Queen, in the guise of Hattie Vaughan, entertaining none less than the mighty person of Sir Ralph St Germans. A jug of claret sat on a small table between them and, judging by the hilarity evinced by the two of them, it was far from full. They were clinking crystal goblets together as Malinferno entered. The Queen tilted her head in his direction, her black wig and pink turban with its long ostrich feather fully restored to their rightful place. Sir Ralph chortled, and drank down the claret in one gulp.

'Madam, though I am a Whig, and would soundly whip any Radical who called for the downfall of the King, I have to say you have convinced me that the Queen ...' here he winked knowingly at Mrs Vaughan, '... should have my support. She has been hard done by, and deserves to be crowned alongside His Majesty. And if she were present, I would tell her that.'

The Queen giggled, and drank from her own goblet.

'When I see her next, I will be sure to inform her of your support, Sir Ralph. Though as the trial is to take place in the Upper House, I fear it is in the Lords' chamber where she needs help most.'

Realising her unintentional innuendo, she put her hand to her mouth and guffawed. Sir Ralph chortled all the more merrily, sounding like a babbling stream running over pebbles. He banged the flat of his hand down on the top of the crate housing the mortal remains of Guido Sacchi.

'Now, Mrs Vaughan ...' once again he gave a grotesque wink, '... tell me again of the time in Italy that the Queen watched Mahomet the Turk perform that obscene dance.'

Malinferno retreated, seeing that he would get no sense from Sir Ralph concerning the meaning of the numbers in the spy's notebook, now nestled in his coat pocket. But he need not have concerned himself with interpreting the code, for as he backed out of the tent, he felt the end of something poking in his back. He started, and a voice hissed in his ear.

'Now, sir, return to me my notebook, or it will go ill for you.'

Thinking of the scene inside the tent, and how Powell would love to record it, Malinferno moved decisively away from the tent flap.

'Of course you may have it back. I would have had no intention of keeping it, if you hadn't startled us earlier.' He took out the notebook. 'May I have the lady's bonnet back in exchange?'

Powell sneered, and turning, Malinferno noticed that the object stuck into his back was not a pistol as he had imagined but a small twig. He sighed at his cowardice, and defeated, handed over the book. Powell laughed.

'The bonnet containing the three stolen plates? Perhaps I will keep it as evidence of your wrongdoing, should I need to ensure your silence on this matter.'

Malinferno cursed Doll's light-fingeredness, conveniently forgetting his own when it came to unravelling the bindings of the mummy. Powell dropped the twig on the ground, and flicked through his notebook, ensuring no pages had been removed. Malinferno indicated the secret document.

'Very full, and informative, your notes. May I just ask if number twenty-three is Signor Sacchi?'

'The Queen's latest Italian paramour?' The spy's disgust of the Queen's activities was evident. 'Yes, you are correct in your assumption. And the other one – Houghton – is number twenty-two. I have my eye on both of them. And anyone else who entered the duchess's tent in the night.'

'Sir Ralph St Germans, for example?

Powell coughed in embarrassment.

'I cannot say. My commission is from Parliament, so there is a conflict of interest there. Though I am sure Sir Ralph would have tried to persuade the Queen to accept a divorce. I will tell you one thing for free. That man who I saw just now hanging on to the arm of your lady-friend was hovering round the tent in the night too. I saw him sneak inside much later than Sir Ralph when I went to use the bushes for ... some relief. Sacchi must have deserted his post by then for I could not see him. He didn't come out for a while, and I returned to my carriage. It had been a tiring day, and I fell asleep almost immediately.'

Malinferno felt his gorge rise. Powell meant Orford. Could he have been the murderer? If so, Doll was even now in his clutches. He looked nervously around the tented encampment. He could see neither Doll nor Daniel Orford, but spotted Lieutenant Houghton in the distance. He thanked Powell for his information, and rushed after the naval officer.

'Lieutenant Houghton, wait a moment.'

Houghton turned around to see Malinferno running across the sward towards him, and for a moment looked as though he was going to flee. But he then stood his ground, and waited for Malinferno to catch his breath.

'Have you seen Doll? She is with the duchess's estates manager, Daniel Orford. A tall man, dark hair, rough clothes.'

Houghton's eyes clouded over, and he kicked at the tufts of grass at his feet.

'The ... lady you were with? No, I haven't seen her. I was looking for the fat man who Sacchi allowed into the Queen ... Mrs Vaughan's tent last night. I saw him there again this morning. He is a Member of Parliament, St Germans by name.'

Malinferno could have got annoyed at such people as Houghton casting doubts on the virtue of Doll Pocket by the innuendo in their voice when they mentioned her. Doll had fought hard to become who she was, using the best means at her disposal. Men like the naval lieutenant had

had their way paved with family gold. He knew who he preferred to associate with. But he contained his anger.

'Yes. Sir Ralph St Germans, and I think you will find that
he and Mrs Vaughan are bosom friends by now.'

Malinferno spoke the words without thinking and then
hoped they were not too literal a description of the friendship blossoming in the duchess's tent. Houghton, though,
was livid, his face turning a deep shade of purple.

'What are you suggesting, sir? The Queen is of a trusting
and friendly nature, on which some place a sinister interpretation.'

He had clearly forgotten the discreet incognito of the lady
concerned, and practically foamed at the mouth as he
berated Malinferno.

'I am sure Sir Ralph's intentions are honourable, and that
he merely wishes to persuade the Queen to retire from public
life. Sacchi, of course, could not see that. All he wanted to do
was make money out of his association with the Queen. He
took Sir Ralph's coin, and then later I saw him talking to
that man in the Tilbury gig. You should be chasing after
him, if you ask me, not your lady-friend.'

Malinferno was getting more confused by the hour. The
sun had risen over Solsbury Hill, and the camp was stirring.
Even the hardiest sybarites had risen from their bucolic beds.
And no doubt with thoughts of more comfortable conditions
at home, were preparing to leave the encampment. Living
alfresco had been an alluring proposition for the duchess's
guests. The reality was proving less attractive. If Malinferno
didn't resolve the murder of Guido Sacchi soon, all his suspects would be dispersed across most of the estates of the
West Country, rendering his task hopeless. And there still
remained the problem of disposing of the body in such a
way that the Queen would not be implicated by association.

Houghton was proving useless to his investigations, and he curtly bade him good day. What mattered now was finding Doll, and the possible murderer, Daniel Orford.

Malinferno hurried hither and thither, amongst collapsing tents, as Orford's men did the agent's bidding. Passing one flapping structure, he sensed rather than saw something flying down towards him. He leaped to one side over a small mound on the edge of the embankment, and fell face down, momentarily dazed. He felt a hot breath on his cheek, and opening his eyes found himself staring into the dull and rather sad brown eyes of the dancing bear. Scrambling away from the tethered creature over which he had tripped, he almost fell again over a large, wooden tent pole. It was this that had crashed down just where he had been standing a moment earlier. A roughly dressed labourer emerged from the folds of the tent, his old-fashioned wig askew and his face red. He muttered an unconvincing apology, and retrieved the pole that had very nearly done for Malinferno. He, for his part, wondered if what had just happened had been other than an unfortunate accident. Was the labourer a cohort of Orford, tasked with doing his bidding, and getting rid of Malinferno? Or at least scaring him off his hunt? If so, what he was proposing to do with Doll right now?

Malinferno quickened his pace, and moved away from where other tents were being lowered, and towards the south-west corner of Solsbury Hill. He had recalled the duchess saying that Orford was an amateur antiquarian of some skill. Perhaps he had drawn Doll to where Malinferno knew, from Hawkins' map in his pocket, the ground was peppered with treasure. His own excavation had been behind the duchess's tent, but there were other crosses marked on the map on this part of the hill. With the oak grove to his right hand, he began to scour the flat top of the hill. But he still had no luck. So he pulled the old map from his pocket, and examined it again. There were a couple of crosses marked on the down-slope of the embankment. He ran to the edge and peered down. Just below the ridge, he saw two figures, one a woman in a cloak mighty like Doll's. She was peering at a hole in the ground. The man was tall, and standing behind the woman. He was lifting a spade over his head. Malinferno called out as loud as he could, and scampered down the bank.

'Orford! What are you doing?'

As he tumbled down the slope towards them, Daniel Orford and Doll Pocket looked at him bemused. Malinferno managed to stop his descent by bumping into Doll, and clutching her arm.

'I saw ... he was ...'

Catching his breath, he realised that Orford had the spade slung casually over one shoulder now. Had it been like that before? He simply wasn't sure. He took a deep breath, and forced a smile on to his face.

'What are you doing down here, Doll?'

Doll's eyes sparkled in that special way that told Malinferno that she had learned some new facts.

'Daniel was showing me where he has been excavating the remains of an ancient battle. One that may have involved King Arthur.'

Orford exercised a word of caution. 'There is no proof that the Battle of Mount Badon was fought here, or that Arthur was more than a mere legend ...'

Doll nudged Malinferno, silently reminding him of the time they had held the bones of King Arthur in their hands.

'We know a bit about old Arthur. Don't we Joe?'

Malinferno quietened her with a glare. The bones – if

they had been Arthur's at all – were safely hidden away, and were causing no more trouble.

'Miss Pocket exaggerates, Mr Orford. My speciality ...' Doll nudged him again. '... our speciality is ancient Egypt. A far cry from old England. But tell me, what have you found here?'

He peered into the hole in the ground, being sure to keep Orford and his spade visible in the corner of his eye. He did not want another 'accident' like the tent pole to occur.

'A few things of curiosity. The frame of what might have been a mirror, and some hobnails.'

'Hobnails?'

Malinferno wondered why old nails, which he had also found in his trench, should be of the slightest interest. Orford smiled, warming to his task.

'Yes, hobnails. You see, the leather would have rotted away by now, but the nails used would have remained. It would indicate that Britons, influenced in their style of footwear by Romans, were indeed on this site.'

'What about signs of battle? Broken bones and swords?' Doll was all eagerness again with her enquiries.

In return, Malinferno thought Orford gave her a shifty look.

'Ah, yes, well, perhaps elsewhere ...'

'And treasure? Have you come across any treasure?'

This was Malinferno's question, and one that drew a sneer from Orford.

'I am not interested in treasure hunting. Now, if you will excuse me, I have work to do.'

He nodded curtly at Malinferno, then bowed more deeply towards Doll, who returned his courtesy. They watched him stride off up the hill, his spade still over his shoulder. Malinferno looked at Doll.

'I thought he was going to murder you and tip you in the hole, Doll.'

'Why would he do that? He has been the perfect gentleman.'

Malinferno did not like the way she emphasised the first word of her final sentence. Was he not a gentleman in his behaviour towards her? He pouted, and began to walk back up the hill too.

Doll laughed, and poked him in the ribs. 'Did you manage to shift the crate?'

He shook his head, and sighed. 'No, I got interrupted. By Powell, amongst others.'

She took his arm and pressed her body against his. 'So, what have you found out while I was entertaining the good agent?'

Malinferno, always quick to recover from a sulk when his opinion was being sought by Doll, gave her a quick résumé of what he had learned. How Sir Ralph might have resented Sacchi's request for money, but that the Member for Plympton Erle was now an intimate with Mrs Vaughan. If he had wished to kill Sacchi, it would have been in the open like a gentleman. He also summed up his encounter with Powell, the government spy.

'He spoke of keeping an eye on both Sacchi and Houghton. But here is the curious thing. He was keen to implicate Orford, telling me that he saw him going into the duchess's tent in the night. And he was at pains to say Sacchi was nowhere to be seen at the time. Yet Houghton, who I also spoke to, said he saw Powell talking to Sacchi. So we come back to his notebook and his statement that he must deal with Sacchi.' He looked at Doll. 'Do you think the murderer is Powell, after all?'

She pulled a face. 'You thought it was Orford not so long ago. Now do you suspect Powell?'

'I don't know. The whole thing is so messy, with everyone claiming to have seen the other entering the tent. How are we going to sort this out, Doll?'

Doll shrugged.

'I don't now, Joe. But we better do it soon, because Orford just pulled a cart up next to the duchess's tent.'

Malinferno yelped, and turned to look where Doll's gaze was aimed. A cart had indeed been positioned close to the opening of the tent where the queen had spent the night. They ran across the encampment, and into the tent, Malinferno in the lead.

Orford was crouched over the crate.

'What are you doing? Leave that crate alone.'

He went to grab Orford's shoulder, but suddenly the ground collapsed beneath his feet, and he fell into a pit. He scrabbled at the sides of the hole, but the soil was loose and poured in over him. He fell back, and felt something hard hit his cheek. He turned his head, and gazed into a leathery face with staring blank orbs in the sockets and a gaping mouth of rotten teeth. He screamed.

'Doll, help me.'

His saviour's face appeared overhead, her full lips pulled back in a wide grin.

'Ozymandias! There you are.'

Malinferno realised she was talking about his partner in the grave. It was the mummy that had previously occupied the crate where Sacchi now lay. But how had it got in the ground? A red-faced Orford appeared, holding out his hand to help Malinferno free of the pit.

'I think I had better explain.'

He heaved Malinferno back to terra firma, and pointed out the gaping hole into which the heavy bed belonging to the duchess was already slipping.

'I was excavating the land right here on the basis of an old map I had drawn up by someone obsessed with King Arthur.'

Malinferno thought of the parchment he had in his pocket, guessing that Orford also had a copy of the Hawkins map. He said nothing though at this stage. He looked at Doll, who winked at him.

'Go on.'

Orford rubbed his soil-covered hands together. 'It had several crosses on it. I had tried some of the others over several months and found nothing. Then I started digging here. From the beginning, this trench looked promising – hobnails, and rusty blades. I was sure I would find bones, and maybe even gold ornaments. And I was right. Then the duchess said she had plans for a grand event on the hill to which the gentry would be invited. It would be the social event of the year. I tried to dissuade her, but she was adamant. I had to erect a virtual military encampment on the hill top, as you saw when you arrived.'

'But what was your problem? You could leave your trench covered and wait until afterwards. Then begin again.'

Orford grimaced. 'Partly it was impatience. I felt I was so close to a great find, and to have it trampled over by lords and ladies was intolerable. And I had been observing the barometer as part of my management of the estate. The weather was due to change, and storms were forecast. Heavy rain would have been disastrous for my excavation. The only thing I could think to do was to site the duchess's tent right over the trench, which I had covered with planks.' He looked at the hole. 'Rotten planks, it would appear.'

Doll wanted to ask a question. 'But that would still not allow you access until after the site had been cleared. And the rain had started.'

As if on cue, they heard the first pitter-patter of light rain on the roof of the tent.

Orford groaned. 'It is too late already. But if my plan had worked, I could have removed much of what I had already found during the night. You see, the duchess is devoted to the delights of laudanum. She sleeps like a log, and even my exertions beneath her bed would not have disturbed her.'

Doll immediately understood his dilemma. 'But then one of the special guests – Mrs Vaughan – took over the tent.'

'Yes.' Orford frowned. 'I would never have imagined the duchess giving up her comforts for anyone but royalty. So I was surprised by this old trollop taking her bed. Who is she?'

He looked quizzically at Doll, but it was Malinferno who answered.

'Shall we say, someone very close to the King.'

Orford nodded, thinking he understood the implications of Malinferno's comment. The whole of England knew of the former Prince Regent's fondness for women.

'I see. Well, I tried to sneak in the tent several times. But that Italian was posted outside like a sentry. And there were such comings and goings, I can tell you. I debated bribing the fellow like some others seemed to do to gain access, but it was essential that I was not seen. I took a turn round the camp, thinking of what I could do. But when I came back, I saw my chance.'

Malinferno tensed, ready to spring at the tall man. If this was to be a confession, then who knows what the outcome would be for Doll and himself?

'You resolved to kill the sentry in order to carry out your plans.'

Orford's face went a delicate shade of green, as above their heads the rain got heavier.

'Good Lord, no! You can't think that of me, can you?'

Malinferno thought only of the murderous stance of Orford behind Doll as she peered into the other excavation. And the conveniently falling tent pole close to his head. But Orford did now look truly shocked, holding his hand over his mouth as though he could hardly prevent himself from being sick. He looked at Malinferno with a tear in his eye.

'I am in a hole. I see that now.'

Malinferno grabbed his arm, and shook the man. 'Tell me.'

Orford took a deep breath, steadying himself.

'I have done a very foolish thing . . .'

Doll and Malinferno were standing in front of Queen Caroline, who was now dressed in the most modest of silk gowns. Her own fair hair was just visible underneath a dark red turban that complemented her dress. This most becoming of decorous ensembles was only slightly spoiled by the surroundings. She was sitting not on a throne, but the edge of the duchess's bed, which was tilted at the precarious angle it had adopted when sliding into Daniel Orford's excavation. The central area of the tent was occupied by the crate that had transported the mummy to Solsbury Hill the previous evening. Most of the site had now been cleared, though persistent drizzle had hampered affairs. Inside the duchess's tent, those present heard another gust of rain sweep across hill, giving the place a gloomy, depressing atmosphere. With the tents gone and the clouds low, Solsbury Hill was bare and open to the worst of the elements.

The Queen, however, was happy, and her short, plump legs swung free of the grassy sward below them. She scanned the others in the tent.

'I am glad I could persuade you all to remain a little while longer. There is a matter needs settling, and each of you can help. Professor Malinferno, will you proceed?'

'Thank you, Mrs Vaughan. We are here, as you know, to plumb the depths of the disappearance of your equerry, Signor Sacchi.'

Though everyone present knew exactly who the portly German woman was who occupied the duchess's bed, the secrecy of her identity was to be preserved. As was the fact that Sacchi was dead – a fact known only to Mrs Vaughan, Malinferno, Doll Pocket, Lieutenant Houghton. And the murderer. Malinferno turned to scan the faces of those present. He prayed he had got the interpretation of the previous night's events correct. Orford's confession had provided him with the final clue to the identity of Sacchi's murderer. Now, he just had to extract the truth from the murderer's own lips. He looked first at the sweating, red face of the Honourable Member for Plympton Erle – with an electorate of thirty.

'Sir Ralph, you spoke to Sacchi when you came to the ... shall we call it the duchess's tent.'

'I did indeed, sir. And he taxed me for money in order to see the ... lady over there.' He indicated the smiling Queen, and returned her smile obsequiously. 'I told you that the Italian was still at his post when I left last night. He was not present when I came back this morning. I can tell you no more.'

Malinferno nodded sagaciously, though he did not feel all that confident of his next step.

'Yes. Mr Houghton ...' He indicated the pasty-faced naval lieutenant hovering near the tent flap. '... confirms he saw you arrive. As I believe did Mr Powell, who also saw you leave. Did you not, sir?'

Powell, true to his role as government spy, was skulking in the shadows, apparently uncomfortable at being in the same place as his quarry, the Queen. He cleared his throat, and made a considered speech.

'All I can say is that Sir Ralph can have nothing to do with the disappearance of Sacchi. The man was still at his post when Sir Ralph left the tent.'

Malinferno knew that getting information out of Powell was going to be like extracting teeth. He would be volunteering nothing. And so he threw a speculative card on to the table.

'Mr Powell, may I ask what you meant, when you wrote in your notebook that you had to "deal with" Sacchi?'

Powell's face turned bright red, and he spoke through gritted teeth. 'That is a private document, sir. And I will not comment on what I may or may not have written in it.'

'You were seen talking to Sacchi. Mr Houghton saw you. Did you *deal with* him afterwards?'

There was a sudden commotion, and Houghton leaped across the tent towards Powell, his dress sword clanking on the wooden crate.

'It was you who killed him. You wanted to get to the Queen, and he wanted money from you, as he did from St Germans.'

Houghton grabbed Powell's collar. But before he could do the man any damage, Malinferno wrapped his arms around the naval officer, and wrestled him away. Houghton slumped on a campaign chair beside the bed, his head in his hands. It was St Germans who realised first what Houghton had said.

'Sacchi is murdered?'

Doll glanced at Malinferno, and whispered, 'Well done, Joe. Now they all know.'

He shrugged. The cat was out of the bag, and there was nothing he could do about it. St Germans was livid, his jowls wobbling as he berated Malinferno.

'You were trying to get us to implicate ourselves in a murder, sir? That is ... that is ... unconstitutional.'

Malinferno was convinced that the Member of Parliament had no idea of the meaning of the word, only that it sounded good. But he stood his ground.

'Only one man is guilty of the murder. The rest cannot be implicated in a murder as they are innocent. Mr Powell, in the circumstances as they now present themselves, are you prepared to explain yourself?'

Powell sulkily straightened his collar, but then sighed. 'I had intended to deal with Sacchi, in the sense that I was prepared to offer him money for information about ... well, you know what about. He was alive when I left him. I will swear to that in a court of law, if forced. But I did see that man enter the tent later, with no Sacchi in sight.' He pointed a long, slender finger at Daniel Orford. 'Ask him where Sacchi was when he entered the tent.'

All eyes turned on the tall figure of the duchess's managing agent. Malinferno smiled, knowing where Orford's confession, which he had heard earlier, would lead.

'Tell them where Sacchi was, Mr Orford.'

Orford straightened his shoulders. 'When I entered the tent on private business, I saw Sacchi lying in a trench in the ground, his throat cut. The soil was soaked in blood.'

There was a gasp from all those assembled, except for Doll and Malinferno, who had heard this tale already.

Orford continued, 'I panicked, as I did not wish it known that I had been in the tent. I should have just left, but there were ... items I needed to recover.'

He had told Malinferno of the objects he had found in the trench below their feet, and how he wanted to recover them before someone else did.

'I transferred the body into this crate ...' he tapped the

box, '. . . having first removed the contents. I then gathered the items I was intent on recovering, and left. It was foolish of me. I should have alerted the authorities, but I panicked.'

He pressed his hands down on the crate, and lowered his head in shame at his actions.

Doll patted his shoulder. 'I understand the difficulty of your position, Mr Orford. I might have done the same thing, in order to avoid being embroiled in a murder investigation by the magistrate.'

Houghton looked up at Doll from where he sat. 'You do not believe the man, do you? Whatever these "items" were he was removing from the duchess's tent, they did not belong to him. He was a thief, and Sacchi caught him at it. He killed him, and tried to conceal the body. He must be arrested. I will go and call for the magistrate.' He rose to his feet, but Malinferno swiftly took his arm.

'You are going nowhere, Lieutenant Houghton. Isn't it strange how you wish to cast the blame for Sacchi's murder on everyone and anyone you can? You see, I have to remind myself how shocked you were when you saw the body in this crate. You fainted.'

Houghton spluttered with indignation. 'I opened the lid and saw the body of my friend Sacchi. Who wouldn't feel faint?'

'But to actually swoon like a lady? A navy man, who in battle must have seen dead comrades before? No, sir, you fainted because you weren't expecting to see the body in the crate. You expected to see it on the ground, where you had left it when you killed him. May I see your sword? I am sure you have not yet managed to clean the blood off it.'

Houghton roared, startling everyone, and sprang for the exit to the tent. He was outside before Malinferno could react. When he did manage to scramble out of the tent, he saw Hougton running across Solsbury Hill towards one of the few carriages left behind. One was Powell's Tilbury gig, but the horse was not in the shafts rendering it useless as a means of escape. The only other conveyance close by was the Trevithick Flyer.

John Smallbone had laboured long and hard to make the steam engine work and, despite the rain, had stoked the boiler with coal. Steam burst from every seam of the Flyer, and the carriage shuddered as though it were alive. Clad in a heavy and rain-soaked felt overcoat, Smallbone resembled a large toad. He was perched on the driver's seat bent on releasing the power of the steam engine. He didn't see Houghton leap up on to the seat, and was pitched unceremoniously by him to the ground. His assailant then released the brake, and the carriage began to trundle down the hill, the piston at the rear clanking faster and faster. Malinferno ran over, and helped the dwarf up, brushing his muddied coat. Smallbone seemed unconcerned by his tumble, though he was more worried by the Flyer's madcap departure.

He began to run after it, calling out wildly, 'Turn the pressure down. Turn the pressure down.'

Houghton could not or would not hear him, and the Flyer gathered speed. The engine on the rear of the carriage gave a mighty groan like some ancient beast risen from the depths of Solsbury Hill. Smallbone cried out, and threw himself to the ground. Malinferno and the other pursuers instinctively did the same. With a second great shudder, and an infernal hissing, the Trevithick steam engine blew up, tossing Houghton forwards into the air like a rag doll. The carriage, still rolling under its own momentum, crushed him under its wheels, before tipping sideways on the steep slope and coming to an abrupt and noisy halt. With the shattered engine still hissing gently, Malinferno and Doll cautiously approached the wreck. There was nothing to be done about Lieutenant Houghton. His neck was broken and he gazed sightlessly into the grey and louring sky.

It was a subdued party that gathered in the Duchess of Avon's house in Bath later that day. Queen Caroline, still in her guise of Hattie Vaughan, sat beside the fire, clutching her stomach. The pain she was suffering may have been only a symptom of her fears over the impending confrontation with the House of Lords, but it was intense nevertheless, and she thought she might die from it. But even that was a better fate than being divorced, or worse, still being excluded from her husband's coronation, as had been threatened.

Joe Malinferno and Doll Pocket had hoped for at least a share in any great treasure they may have found on Solsbury Hill. Instead, they were left with the three guineas' fee from the duchess, and two hobnails to give to Augustus Bromhead when they returned to London. They were the only visible return from the Hawkins map the antiquarian had possessed. The Queen would have liked to reward them for preventing the death of her equerry Guido Sacchi from tainting her already sullied reputation, but, as would be revealed not too much later, the Queen was bankrupt. A pall of silence hung over the three of them.

Finally, Daniel Orford entered the room, bowing courteously at Mrs Vaughan.

'It is done. The body has been discreetly moved to the duchess's country estate, where it will appear that some roving gypsy band cut Sacchi's throat for his money. His death will not reflect on ... Mrs Vaughan, and he will receive a decent Christian burial.'

Malinferno ground his teeth. 'As will Houghton, which is more than he deserves, being Sacchi's murderer. And all because he felt the man was betraying his mistress's reputation. To slit a man's throat over such a matter – he must have been insane.'

Doll might have agreed with him normally. But, deluded as he may have been, Houghton had been concerned for the reputation of a queen. She glanced over at the shrunken figure by the fire. Hattie was ignoring the conversation, deep in her own thoughts. Doll touched Joe's arm.

'Yes, but as there was no murder on Solsbury Hill, then there cannot have been a murderer. The lieutenant will be remembered as the unfortunate victim of a horseless carriage accident – perhaps its first victim – and there's an end to it.'

She looked across again at the figure by the fire. It was dark, and for a moment she thought she saw the veil of death hanging over poor Caroline. She shivered and pulled Joe into an embrace.

Queen Caroline survived the Bill of Pains and Penalties, for though it got a majority in the House of Lords, the vote was so slender that Lord Liverpool abandoned the Bill. However, her attempts to attend her husband's coronation were thwarted. She was turned away from Westminster Abbey on the pretext that she didn't have a ticket. She went home and succumbed to an intense stomach upset. Not long afterwards, she died, removing one more embarrassing burden from those of an unpopular King.

epilogue

Summer 2010

'This is getting bloody ridiculous!' muttered John Bolitho.

The detective superintendent looked around the top of Solsbury Hill and saw a scene that resembled a military operation.

However, instead of the holes in the ground being gun emplacements, they were meticulously organised excavations, replete with banded measuring sticks and yards of coloured tape marking off grids in the soil. A dozen sweating constables from the Avon and Somerset Constabulary were scraping and sieving, alongside a few press-ganged archeology students. Instead of army officers directing the operations, a couple of straw-hatted and baseball-capped academics were strutting around, clutching clipboards and peering down the holes.

Bolitho's colleague DCI Bob Bryant mopped his sweating forehead with a handkerchief, for so far this was the hottest day this year.

'I reckon that nutter has been leading us up the garden path!' he grumbled. He was not referring to the senior archeologist, even though he thought Roger Humbolt was a pain in the arse. The nutter in question was a serial killer currently banged up on remand in Bristol's Horfield Prison. While awaiting trial for the murder three years earlier of two women whose bodies had been discovered buried elsewhere in the West Country, he had recently confessed to the killing of another girl, known to have gone missing at the same period, and claimed to have buried her on Solsbury Hill.

'Bloody Albanians!' growled the superintendent. 'You're probably right, he's been leading us up the garden path, just to cause us trouble.'

'And expense!' replied Bryant, waving a hand at the scene around them. 'I'll bet this circus has cost at least a few hundred grand. Think of all the police overtime, the forensic lab fees, the equipment hire, the pathologist and the dentist – and those archeologists are no doubt charging us a bomb!'

John Bolitho agreed gloomily. 'Three weeks' work and all they've turned up is a collection of junk, none of it remotely connected to Bierta Reka.' This was the name of the third illegal immigrant who had vanished from the Bristol brothel within a week of the other two.

They walked slowly across the flat area to the top of the grassy bank and ditch, from where, through the heat haze, Bath was visible in the distance. Below them, a burly police sergeant and a constable were scraping soil out of the bank. Bolitho called down to them from above.

'Anything else in there, Edwards? That was where they found that old knife, wasn't it?'

The sergeant, stripped to the waist in the heat, straightened up and then shook his head. 'Damn all, sir! We've gone a couple of feet deeper to where those boffins were scratching around, but there's nothing more in there.'

The two senior officers wandered around several more of the scattered excavations, speaking to the people working there, but nothing new had been discovered.

'I reckon we've got all there is to find now,' grunted Bolitho.

'I hope to hell the Chief will call this off now before we make even bigger fools of ourselves. The press is starting to get sarcastic and is muttering about the cost to the rate-payers or whatever they are called these days.'

The DCI shrugged. 'What else could we do when that bastard claimed he'd buried her up here one night? He knew her name and had the right date, when she vanished from that knocking-shop in St Paul's.'

Bolitho nodded gloomily. 'Then said he couldn't remember exactly where he'd dug the hole, because it was dark! Lying swine, I'll bet he's never set foot here.'

They made their way, slowly and reluctantly, towards a large fabric shelter made of white plastic stretched on a metal frame, which stood on the north side of the enclosure. As they approached, the two scientists with the clipboards vanished inside.

'At least they've found three skeletons and a lot of spare bones, even if they have damn all to do with our case,' observed Bob Bryant. 'It beats me what's been going on up here over the years. One skeleton had the bones of a whacking great dog lying alongside it.'

'Yes, it's a cross between a cemetery and a bloody junk shop up here!' replied Bolitho, derisively. 'Those two fellows in there are at each other's throat over what it all might mean.' He waved a hand at the white tent, which was the size of a double garage.

'Thank God that butch woman is there to keep the peace, as best she can,' said Bryant. 'Otherwise we might have another murder up here!'

As they neared the exhibits tent, the entrance guarded by a uniformed PC, they heard voices from inside raised in querulous argument. Bolitho stopped with a sigh.

'I'm not getting involved in another shouting match now,'

he groaned. 'Let's go over to the refreshment trailer and get a drink. It's too bloody hot to listen to a pair of academics screaming abuse at each other.'

Inside the tent, two rows of Formica-topped trestle tables ran down its length to hold the bizarre collection of finds from Solsbury Hill. Another pair of tables were cluttered with papers, a couple of laptops, a microscope and a collection of surgical and scientific implements.

A tall, thin man strode agitatedly up and down between the tables, his straw boater now removed to reveal a shock of frizzy ginger hair. Prominent pale blue eyes bulged behind his rimless spectacles as he peered erratically at various objects lying on the white Formica.

'I tell you again, Fortescue, until we get a radio-carbon dating on these, we can't be sure. Why are you being so damned stubborn?'

The other man was sitting in a plastic picnic chair alongside the microscope. Peter Fortescue was middle-aged, short and stocky, still wearing his peaked baseball cap on his totally bald head. He had a pugnacious face, like a bad-tempered bull terrier, and was scowling at Roger Humbolt as he paraded past the exhibits.

One row of tables was devoted to a ragged collection of bones, some being roughly assembled into three human skeletons, though many of the brown or blackened parts were fragmentary, with some sections missing altogether. The trestles opposite had a motley assortment of objects, dominated by a dirty, but obviously valuable golden cup. Nearby was a large collection of tarnished silver coins, arranged carefully into piles of equal height. A small knife with an intricate handle, a part of an ancient mirror, several badly rusted buckles and part of a metal helmet sat amongst random coins, bits of iron, a few brass shot-gun cartridge bases and other detritus accumulated over more than a millennium.

Fortescue scowled at the other expert. 'The police are not going to pay for your carbon dating, are they? Now that they know that none of this stuff is relevant to their investigation, they're going to pull the plug on us.'

He was Director of Field Studies for the Southern Counties Archeology Trust, based in Dorchester, and had been retained as one of the boffins needed to evaluate what had been found during the police investigation. The carrot-haired man was a Senior Lecturer in Archeology at Wessex University, specialising in Dark Age Studies.

Apart from these two, there was also Dr Shirley Wagstaff, an assistant County Archeologist, whose main function had become acting as peacemaker between the other two, whose professional and personal animosity had increased with every day that passed.

Distinctive with her cropped grey hair and rugged, scrubbed face, as well as her man's shirt and trousers, she stood now with a hand on the aluminium door, ready to go out for a respite from her tiresome colleagues.

'Give it a rest, chaps!' she snapped impatiently. 'The police don't give a damn about dating anything, now that the Home Office people have confirmed that nothing we've found is recent!'

Peter Fortescue agreed with her, as he glared at Humbolt with evil satisfaction.

'If you want dating done, you'll have to find the money yourself, Roger. Even the coroner says he's not interested in any human remains more than a century old. He's only concerned with holding a treasure-trove inquest on that gold and silver.'

Before they could embroil her again in their disputes, Shirley stepped smartly outside and with a nod to the constable, made her way over towards the police trailer, which had a tea and coffee machine, together with a supply of cold drinks and sandwiches. Inside the spartan vehicle, furnished with a few folding chairs and a spindly table, she found the two senior CID officers, one with a cardboard cup of what the machine claimed was coffee, the other with a can of Fanta. The archeologist had got on well with both men during their frequent visits to the site over past weeks and preferred their company to the two prima donnas she had left back in the tent.

Getting a Diet Coke for herself, she dropped into a spare chair alongside the table at which they were sitting.

'Too damned hot for digging holes in the ground!' she declared.

Bolitho nodded his agreement. 'With a bit of luck, you won't be doing much more. I suspect that we'll call it off tomorrow.'

Bob Bryant asked her what would happen to all the excavations that had been made.

'The county will have to fill them in and restore the whole place, or English Heritage will play hell with us, as it's a Scheduled Site,' she replied. 'The hill has been explored several times before, going right back to Victorian times. There are records about what's been found, mainly to do with this Iron Age camp.'

'A wonder they didn't turn up some of the stuff you've managed to unearth this time,' said the superintendent.

Shirley Wagstaff shrugged. 'A few trenches can miss most of the stuff. They didn't have the fancy equipment we've got now – metal detectors, ground-penetrating radar and magnetometry gadgets.'

'I reckon those two police dogs were better than the electronic gizmos,' observed Bolitho, with a grin. 'They found all the bones, which I suppose is what you'd expect a dog to do!'

Shirley agreed, but still defended her own technology. 'Sure, but they were specially trained to sniff out human remains. The gadgets, as you call them, found the places where the soil had been disturbed or where there was metal under the ground.'

The DI was more interested in personalities than objects. 'What's the problem with your two colleagues?' he asked. 'They always seem to be slagging each other off!'

The woman rolled her eyes upwards in exasperation. 'They're like two kids fighting over a football! It all started a couple of years ago when Pete Fortescue wrote a review of a book Roger Humbolt had published about the Saxon invasions. He criticised parts of it and since then, they've been sworn enemies.'

'What was the dispute about?' asked John Bolitho.

'Roger claims to be a leading expert on the Dark Ages, especially the Arthurian campaigns. He maintains that the great battle of Mount Badon, about 500 AD, was fought here on Solsbury. In fact, that's why he was so keen to come on this dig: to a get a chance to find some confirmation. But Peter rubbished that, saying it must have been up near Swindon.'

'God help us! To think that intelligent people can get so steamed up about things like that!' said the DI, in disgust.

'Having your professional reputation challenged is a fate worse than death to some academics,' explained Shirley. 'It can mean the loss of research grants and even affect their chances of promotion.'

The superintendent took the opportunity to ask the more

sensible scientist some questions about what had been discovered during the past weeks.

'I suppose you feel that all these items are just random
finds, Doctor? There can be no connection between any of
them?'

The archeologist considered this for a moment. 'Always
dangerous to be too dogmatic, so I suppose the best answer
is that we'll never know. We've got three skeletons and a lot
of old bones, so who can say that one of those folk didn't
hide the gold cup there or bury that strange knife?'

'Except that you can exclude the remains of that
mummy!' said Bryant. 'The guy must have died centuries
before he was brought to Britain, so he couldn't have buried
anything, including himself.'

'What about that treasure?' asked Bolitho. 'It was all
together in the side of the rampart wall. Any ideas about
that?'

'From the compact mass in which it was found, I suspect
it was originally in some kind of bag, which has long rotted
away. It's odd, because the chalice is typically Saxon, the
pyx is probably late eleventh century, yet the silver coins are
Henry the Second, Richard the Lionheart and a couple of
King John. So they must have been hidden in the early thir-
teenth century.'

'Any idea where they may have come from?'

Shirley took a swig from her tin, then shrugged. 'That
communion cup is really valuable. Together with the pyx, it
must have come from a rich ecclesiastical establishment. Of
course, the nearest is Bath Abbey down there, but there's no
way of proving it.'

'Are there no records that would help?' asked Bolitho. 'It
must have been stolen, to end up in the ground here.'

'The problem is that the abbey went downhill in a big

blLL of bONES

way after those dates. It fell into ruin and most of the records were lost. I'm afraid the present abbey doesn't have much hope of claiming them back.'

'What about the mummy? How long do you reckon that's been up here?'

'That's bizarre, isn't it? An Egyptian mummy on top of a Somerset hill!' Shirley put her empty tin on the table. 'About two hundred years ago, possessing a mummy was a fad amongst the idle rich, so perhaps it was hidden around that time. That forensic anthropology lady did a good job in spotting what it was – the embalming had allowed some bits of skin to survive on the bones.'

She stood up and took her tin over to a waste bin. 'I'd better get back, I suppose. There's nothing new to examine, but maybe I can stop Tweedledum and Tweedledee from coming to blows.'

The two detectives rose as well.

'We were going over there anyway, so we'll come with you,' said Bolitho. 'I'd better tell them that I'm recommending to Headquarters that we wrap up this operation tomorrow.'

They ambled across the enclosure towards the tent, sensing that a lethargy had descended on the remaining scrapers and sievers, who had slowed down their efforts in the knowledge that the search was virtually at an end. Inside the stifling warmth of the exhibits store, they found Peter Fortescue glaring into his laptop on the desk table, baseball cap still firmly on his head. His more eccentric colleague was in the aisle between the tables, his lips moving silently as he checked the identifying labels tied to the items on display. For once, there was peace and quiet, as the two men appeared to be ignoring each other.

Bob Bryant walked over to Humbolt, who had picked up

401

a blackened object. 'Any more ideas on what that might be, Doctor?' he asked. He was not that interested, but felt he should be civil to the man.

'It's part of a hand mirror, of course,' grunted the expert. 'Badly damaged and seems to have been in a fire as well. Not surprising, as it was recovered from a pile of ashes.'

'Are those some kind of jewels on the back?'

'Yes, but I doubt they have much value now. Most are missing and the couple that are left are cracked and scorched. The mirror itself is silver and what remains of the enamel on the back suggests it was a costly piece. It needs a real specialist to evaluate it, but I suspect it must be very old.'

'Perhaps it belonged to Queen Guinevere!' called Fortescue from his place at the desk. The provocative remark triggered a furious response from Roger Humbolt.

'Mock as much you want, you moron!' he shouted. 'When I'm proved right about Badon, you'll have to eat your words.'

He snatched up another object from a table, a dented piece of rusted metal with no obvious shape, as far as the police officers could tell.

'This is part of a helmet; it could have been Saxon or Celtic. It all adds to the burden of proof that there was a battle on this hill!'

Fortescue rose from his chair and sauntered over to where the others were standing.

'With so little left, it could be from any period! Probably late medieval, could even be Tudor.'

Humbolt thrust his face towards his antagonist, his features now almost as red as his hair. 'Nonsense, it's much earlier than that!' Then he swung round to the other row of tables and jabbed a finger at the pile of darkened, crumbling bones. 'Look at this lot! Obvious battle casualties! On that skeleton over there, the pathologist pointed out a clear knife-cut on a rib and the edge of the breastbone.'

Fortescue's reply was scathing. 'One swallow doesn't make a summer and one stab wound doesn't make a battle! Where are all the victims from your Badon, eh? Arthur is supposed to have slain nine hundred himself!'

The other man was now almost purple with rage. 'You know damned well that wasn't meant literally! And if we could dig up the whole hill, there'd be hundreds more like this, even after fifteen centuries!'

Shirley Wagstaff tried to cool the argument, but Humbolt was now in full flow. He snatched up another find from the first table and held it up in a shaking hand. 'And what about this! A knife that I'd stake my life came from the Dark Ages.'

Bolitho felt he should say something to cool their passions. 'Wouldn't that blade have more rust on it after all that time?'

The older archeologist glared at the detective with his bulging eyes. 'You obviously know little about it, Officer. There were smiths in those days who could make rustless iron, like the Pillars of Delhi and Dhar!'

'Come off it, Roger, they were in India, not Celtic Britain!' countered Fortescue, derisively.

In angry response, Humbolt jabbed his other forefinger at the handle. 'Look at that carving, will you? Do you deny that is a bear carved in ivory, the symbol of Arthur the Great Bear?'

'Plenty of performing bears around until well past Shakespeare's time, chum!' sneered Fortescue. 'And where the hell would they get ivory from in the fifth century?'

'You ignoramus!' shrieked the red-headed disciple of the Once and Future King. 'I know this knife must have belonged to Arthur himself. I feel it in my very soul!'

Before the astounded policemen could stop him, Roger

Humbolt had plunged the blade into the chest of the man who had been baiting him.

Bolitho and Bryant watched while the helicopter took off and whirred its way towards Frenchay Hospital, Shirley Wagstaff being on board to comfort Peter Fortescue.

'The paramedic seemed happy enough about him,' observed the superintendent. 'He said that little knife didn't damage any organs, but caused a pneumothorax, whatever that it is.'

'He's not going to snuff it, thank God, ' said Bryant. 'Are we going to charge the mad fellow with attempted murder or just GBH? I suppose the CPS will choose the easiest option, as usual.'

Bolitho shrugged as they started to walk back to the tent, which was now a crime scene, though the miscreant was still sitting crying in the picnic chair, guarded by the PC from the door.

'Ironic, really!' said the superintendent. 'We come up trying to sort out a murder and almost end up with a totally different one. That bloody Arthur has a lot to answer for; he's been causing trouble for the past fifteen hundred years!'

His assistant agreed. 'Solsbury Hill, indeed! Damned place must be cursed!'